Praise for Sharon Baker's first novel,
Quarreling, They Met The Dragon

"In its insistence that one cannot know a society without knowing its sexual life and its economic life, its palaces and gutters, its myths and its reality, this... novel shows the...influence of the superb SF author Samuel R. Delany."
Publishers Weekly

"Real science-fictional thinking"
Isaac Asimov's Science Fiction Magazine

"Take the seamier side of urban Arrakis and add water. Toss in the wildlife of Pern and mix in the cultural life outlined in Poul Anderson's 'The Sharing of Flesh.' Into this decadent, exotic, revolting stew, throw a boy with the sensual attractiveness of Donatello's *David*....Label the whole thing with a title Philip K. Dick would have been proud of. Now don't get the idea that the book is a derivative hash. It's not. It's a fresh compote, not canned fruit cocktail."
Fantasy Review

"A considered originality"
Brian Aldiss (in *The Trillion Year Spree*)

Other Avon Books by
Sharon Baker

QUARRELING, THEY MET THE DRAGON

Coming Soon

BURNING TEARS OF SASSURUM

JOURNEY TO MEMBLIAR

SHARON BAKER

AVON
PUBLISHERS OF BARD, CAMELOT, DISCUS AND FLARE BOOKS

JOURNEY TO MEMBLIAR is an original publication of Avon Books. This work has never before appeared in book form. This work is a novel. Any similarity to actual persons or events is purely coincidental.

AVON BOOKS
A division of
The Hearst Corporation
105 Madison Avenue
New York, New York 10016

First Avon Printing: July 1987

AVON TRADEMARK REG. U.S. PAT. OFF. AND IN OTHER COUNTRIES, MARCA REGISTRADA, HECHO EN U.S.A.

Printed in the U.S.A.

K-R 10 9 8 7 6 5 4 3 2 1

Acknowledgments

I'm indebted to all who patiently answered my questions, especially Gordon Baker, M.D.; Cyrus Gordon, Director, Center for Ebla Studies, New York University; Charles Hafey, Director of Starlab Planetarium at Pacific Science Center, Seattle, WA; hustler, King County Jail, Seattle, WA; Tom McDonough, Division of Engineering and Applied Science, Caltech; Rudy Nikitins, ex-acrobat in European circuses and clubs; Eric Peterson, Department of Astronomy, University of Washington, and Diane Sklensky, botanist. The accuracies in this book are theirs, the unlikelihoods are my own.

For help with editing and occasional facts, I'm grateful to Brian Aldiss, Jean Bryant and The Class, and Gene Wolfe.

JOURNEY TO MEMBLIAR

Winter: Qaqqaδum

Oprekka Enna knelt with eleven other priestess-candidates on the temple's inner ramp. The women's pale robes glimmered as they bowed toward their knees and shut their eyes to show respect. Oprekka, however, only crouched and squinted. She edged closer to the strong room door beside her. Her sniff was almost audible as she watched her superior and classmate, High Priestess Phikola En, Co-Ruler of Qaqqadum and Northern Naphar, glide toward her. Oprekka's belly clenched in resentment.

How that woman can mimic stateliness, Oprekka thought, *when she's no better than a whore, really!* It was insufferable that Oprekka's future should depend on Phikola, and on the Mind-stone too—a plain little river rock that fitted any hand! Nose twitching with indignation, Oprekka shifted—her unbleached Robe of Humility had bunched under her knees and they hurt. Phikola glanced at her. Making a moue denoting patience, Oprekka looked soulfully out a windslit.

Through the tower's half circle of windslits she could see the dawn and dusk moons, transparent in the morning light. The moons stood still on either horizon, changing from dark to full daily as they had for sennights, horrifying the populace. Oprekka sniffed again. Simpletons! The moons acted like that each century. Had the people thought that this time they would forget? Of course, the white and dark orbs' odd behavior also brought quakes, but she wouldn't complain! Properly guided, the people's fear multiplied temple attendance, not to mention contributions.

Incense and prayers to the goddess rose from behind Phikola's ascending silhouette. Pointedly ignoring her high priestess, Oprekka gazed through an opening to the east where, above the Fire Mountains, the dawn moon slid from dark to crescent. As Phikola drew nearer still, Oprekka turned to the windslit overlooking the Western Sea and studied the dusk moon's perfect round as it grew lopsided.

Hisses interrupted the silent creep of shadow across the

moons' faces as flying lizards like jewels swooped down the thick blue sky. Sunlight flashed on their wings as it did on the sills of hammered gold.

Oprekka blinked. Phikola had paused in front of those sills. Her bright hair and blue-green robe glowed with light.

The silken folds of the robe whispered as Phikola started toward Oprekka and the strong room. Behind the ironwork of the door gleamed a second portal of blue. The doors guarded the Room of the Mindstone.

Phikola asked the priestesses the ritual question: "Is each province represented for the Choosing?"

Chorusing assent with the rest, Oprekka felt her heart thump against her surplice. She lowered her crown of brindled braids to hide the avarice in her pale blue eyes. Today she, Oprekka, *must* be the one Chosen to run Qaqqadum's Temple Space Academy.

As administrator she would join the councils of nobles and off-worlders, could overhear their plans for rebuilding and for rationing food and fuel, now the moons' wanderings had begun . . . Not that she wanted such a lucrative place for herself! Oh, dear, no. Complacently, she touched her surplice stiff with gold. Her needs were few, so unassuming, really; only what was expected from one in her position. All was for her darling son, Ibby. Until he partnered well—and she had hopes—she must support him on a simple head priestess's earnings (another racing chariot smashed, the second this season, and where she would find the coin to replace it . . .). She eyed the gems flashing in Phikola's amber braids and curls streaked with auburn.

Inclining her head, Phikola began: "I speak for Sassurum's three: the song of the stars, the wisdom of the Stone, the strength of the tree . . ."

Oprekka sighed and returned to her thoughts. So tiring and unfair, really, to work against snobbery and sneers and the ideals that could be indulged in only by those safe from poverty! Oprekka would never, never have had to scheme and plan this way if she had been born to fortune as *some* were.

". . . Sassurum knows the lightnings, the call of the deeps to the stars . . ."

Rattling off her responses with the others, Oprekka thought for the thousandth time how *she* should have had Phikola's position. Why, Phikola was not even a true member of Qaqqadum's tall ruling race! Her daughter had stayed small and had to be abandoned. Even now, with a little effort, Oprekka could find the girl, embarrass her old classmate . . . But Oprekka was merciful. The child would stay hidden. Odd; Oprekka had not thought of the chit for many springs.

In front of her, Phikola raised the great blue key. The shaft seemed to quiver as the mantle of the goddess's presence settled about her. She pushed the key into the keyhole.

Silently the iron door swung outward. Behind it stood the inner portal made of heavenstone the hazy blue of a summer sky.

The key's pulsing rose to a throaty hum. Phikola slid it into the second lock. That too snicked undone.

She touched the door. All the head priestesses but Oprekka sighed as the door reverberated with the sound of bells. Phikola pushed it open. Through the temple rang the heavenstone's deep chime.

Oprekka strained forward, wanting to run in, be first.

Across her cheeks breathed a coolness smelling of disuse and dust. Opposite her on the tower's shadowed side where the dusk moon slid from gibbous to crescent, light drifted through a pair of windslits to cushions and a double pallet. The light thinned and failed to reach the room's only other furnishing: a pedestal of translucent black firecrystal. Its severe lines were carved by the ancients to hold Naphar's most sacred relic, the Mindstone. Around the pedestal's base was an inscription.

Again the other priestesses sighed. The Stone, the safety of Naphar, lay on top. Its two ends of pinkish tan were knobbed. White crusted the central spindle that joined them. Mentally possessing it, Oprekka tensed.

The High Priestess signaled for one to rise and enter.

Oprekka started up. Not moving from the door, Phikola lifted her slim brows and shook her head. She gestured toward the plain woman with dark glowing eyes at Oprekka's side.

Oprekka breathed out with impatience and tried not to tap her foot. *Fool of a woman!* she thought, watching the other's unhurried passage across the whitestone floor. To relinquish headship of the Academy in order to start a home for the widows and orphans of Naphar's tall ruling class, of the slave race half their size, and of their half-breed mistakes, without regard for height—it was treason, blasphemy. And profitless!

The dark-eyed priestess set her hand on one end of the porous Stone. Joining her, Phikola held the other knob. Pink light glimmered, then fanned between their fingers, warming the shadows and the white plaster walls.

"Star, stone, and tree are yours to command, what would you ask Sassurum through me?" Phikola's voice took on the resonance of a Mouth of the Goddess. Behind her the air seemed to darken, the shadows to cluster around her.

"The goddess," the priestesses around Oprekka whispered. They bowed like grain in the wind as Phikola's hair became the dark flying tresses of Sassurum; the goddess's black eyes seemed to stare into Oprekka's from the place where Sassurum lived between the stars, between time, and being.

"*I* would be the goddess's new servant!" Ignoring ceremony, Oprekka cried out her need and strode across inlaid ribbons of gold and the goddess's blue-green. She pushed away the dark-eyed priestess; she set her hand on the Stone.

It burned; its radiance turned to lightning.

Biting back a scream, Oprekka held on. "You see!" she panted, trying to stare down Phikola's cool, turquoise gaze. Sweat ran off Oprekka's forehead into her eyes. She scorned to wipe it away. "The Stone chooses *me!*" The fires raging in her hand turned to a shriek, and she fainted.

When she woke she lay ignored on cushions. As the curve of the dusk moon narrowed in the windslit above her, she glanced from the moon to the back of the priestess holding the Stone while swearing to uphold the standards of the goddess, off-world knowledge, and the Academy.

Oprekka refused to look at the priestess or at Phikola En, the other usurper of Oprekka's rightful place. Muttering to herself about temple trickery, hating the cheating goddess and all she stood for, Oprekka glared instead at the script of the Old Language on the pillar's base:

The god who is not a god steals from afar.
Cursed with the Mark of Sassurum, his doom:
The slave who is not a slave whose Choices save
Them both from life with death. Stone-changed he'll trace
A place in the stars for himself, the Stone, and Naphar.

Oprekka began to smile.

When the ceremony was over she met the others' pitying glances with a cloudless gaze, scarcely conscious of the sting and ache of her burned palm; for the moons' activity and the inscription had given her an idea.

Chapter One

The names of novas differ according to the type of civilization observing them. For instance, Galactic Central's numerical codes describe each expanding star's luminosity, radiation, and location. While Naphar—a limited-access planet well into our galaxy's spiral arm which has bypassed its Industrial Age—has named the remains of its visible nova Sassurum's Veil. Thus, instead of accounting for their nova phenomenologically, the Napharese explain it with psychological and pseudo-historical legends. This is not to say the beings of Naphar are less or more sophisticated than those of Galactic Central, but their mental set is different. Similar conclusions may be drawn about reactions to the nova that Naphar's Veil so strongly resembles, and which brightened the skies of Sol III's antique Egypt and Babylon. Though contemporary names for the nova are lost...

THE SIGNIFICANCE OF NAMES: A PSYCHOHISTORY OF VOCABULARY.
VOLUME IV, ASTRONOMICAL AND GLOBAL TERMS.
ALLEN ALLENSON, ED. STUDIES IN PSYCHOHISTORY SERIES,
CAMBRIDGE-BOMBAY UNIVERSITY PRESS,
INDEPENDENT HABITAT L-1, SOL III.

Careful of the living burden on her shoulders, a tall young slave woman scanned the hillside, listening. Starlight gleamed in the dark and pale strands wound around her head; her eyes shone like silver coins.

The barkhiders had stopped in midsong. The shock of their silence was broken only by the volcanoes' distant rumble, the rush of the river glowing behind the bluff, and the wind. But before—hadn't that been the deep, free laugh of an undrugged beast, and the crackle of a fire where no fire, and no beast or master either, should be?

"Come on, Cassia!" A little boy half as long as the slave woman's arm jigged against her sweating neck. Still she hesitated.

As Ailessu the Wind God cracked his whip in the white peaks

above her, and an off-worlder scoutcraft streaked across the dome of the world, she glanced down the meadow to the track's black line.

Nothing moved on the hillside or on the road leading back to the farm but the tossing ferns that showed their pale undersides to the stars, and the flutter of her robe, molded to her by the Wind God's hand.

"I must obey you, master," the slave woman whispered as much to herself as to the boy, "but I also must keep you safe. It's so late. If your father comes back and finds us gone . . ." She drew a testing breath.

The thin high air smelled normal, safe; the tang of pines and the bitter scent of ploughed loam belonged to any highlands spring. But this was not any spring: it was the beginning of the Spring of the Twin Moons. After a winter of standing paralyzed in the skies, then sennights of hiding from the Dark One behind the earth, the dawn and dusk moons would once more travel across the stars, but this time in tandem as they did only once each century. It was a time of danger, now doubly so. For a moment ago—hadn't that been a whiff of smoke? And from where had come that trace of sweetness when as yet there were no flowers? Cassia's skin crept.

"Go on, Cassia!" the child on her shoulder urged again. "The smoke's probably from a torchpine; sometimes they flame early. Everybody's at First Rising, like we would be if Pa wasn't so mean. If you don't get on that bluff, we'll miss the best view of the moons!"

"But something's wrong, I know it. Night Demons could be flying. The Veil's almost up, the night's half over; you can watch from the road."

"But you promised!" He drummed on her arm with his heels; he wrenched at her steering braids.

Eyes smarting, she clapped her hands to her scalp. "Don't, Tadge, that hurts! I can't, I'm sworn to guard you. The smoke could be lowlands slavers. That priest today—your father sent me for a log to weight the harrow, but wasn't he talking about a raiding party? It could be close."

In the forest that enclosed the meadow, a barkhider chirped. Another answered, then another. The priest had shaken his head over so many dangers—the changes heralded by the rising of the moons together: rebellion, avalanches, floods, slave raids . . . Yet the priests' and farmers' grip on the highlands was like iron; dams stopped spring flooding from devastating riverside farms, and slavers from beyond the Fire Mountains never penetrated these remote forests. She waited for Tadge to laugh at the nursery threat.

Instead he threw his arms around her head. "The priest said nothing! Just a lot of worrying about dam repair crews in the mountains falling in the holding ponds and dying of cold. Anyhow, the worst slavers could do is take me out of here to the coast where they say the big Rabu rule. As if they could; everybody knows you Rabu need us small masters to tell you how to use all that muscle. But I'd get to the lowlands, see the ocean, have adventures, and whenever I wanted, I could escape, easy! Besides, I've got to see a good First Rising. You keep saying how you love Naphar and wish you could see more of it. You're not young like me, but don't you want to see this?"

"I'm young." Cassia's voice was low as the wanting built in her, urging her toward the black bulk of the trees above her and a view of the impossible rising of the dawn and dusk moons together. And she *was* young, she thought. She was not yet through her third Thitamanit, her third set of eight springs. But to Tadge, her fosterling, who had only finished his first Thitamanit, and with it earned the right to command her, she must seem ancient. As she agonized, the barkhiders' high silver singing rose to full choir and she shut her eyes.

They are shy, she thought. *Surely if danger lay beyond that bluff, the ears in their forelegs would tell them and they would be silent. Or is this the demon whisper of my own desires? Oh, help me, Goddess! Beasts should not have to hoose.*

She heard no anser, she saw none, but beneath her feet the hillside felt like a road. *Goddess-led,* Cassia thought, and found she had taken a step upward. She opened her eyes. The grass drenching her sandals shimmered with pink-tinted starlight. The Veil. Already.

"Oh, gods, you're a good old beast!" Tadge bounced and gave her a quick hard hug. "We've got lots of time and the Veil isn't up yet, you'll be in your straw before Pa ever stops praying, let alone leaves the Gathering."

"But the Veil is up." Cassia looked around at him. This was not the first time he had made that odd mistake.

Her nursling glanced over his shoulder at the pink wisps glowing among the stars, all that remained of a neighboring sun exploded by the goddess for her winter warmth. He stiffened. "Cassia, look!"

"Yes, the Veil's pretty, but—"

"No! Under it. The moons. And—the Dark One."

She stared. Beneath her feet the meadow seemed to drop. Her heart gave a great thump as Tadge's grip on her hair tightened convulsively; the barkhiders' chorus halted.

Though Cassia's breath shortened she had little difficulty pushing back the fear that the priests said betrayed the goddess and encouraged the Dark One. For she could not pull her gaze from the dark blue cleft between the pinnacles where two moons crept upward, thin as the goddess's fingernail parings—and, a handsbreadth from them, a coin-shaped darkness that blotted out the stars.

"I didn't know. I didn't really believe," Cassia whispered. Under her sandals the quivering grew; the great trees around her sighed across the barkhiders' silence.

"I—I almost see why Pa wants to pray." After a single glance, Tadge did not look down at the heaving meadow and the ferns shaking spores into the moonlight. His voice trembled only a little as he whispered, "Look. Two shadows."

Deep in the earth, rock grated. Continuing to deny her fright, Cassia sighted along the child's arm.

Below the icy peaks, doubled shadows crossed and recrossed a silver forest tarnished, then burnished, by shade and starlight; as the earth moved and the wind blew harder, the trees' shaggy heads tossed like an airborne river.

Cassia looked from the forest's shadows to her own. Doubled, it stretched across the waving fronds like two spread fingers pointing at either side of the hill. Into the hush grumbled a faroff avalanche.

"Cassia?" her nursling breathed. "There isn't any place we can go to be safe, is there?"

Dumb, she shook her head.

The earth's shuddering continued. The river sloshed; beyond the hill, the crash of a falling branch was followed by a bellow, then a falsetto screech.

"There *are* people there!" Yanking her robe free of her sandals, Cassia took one running step down the hill—and halted. Should she dive for the thrashing ferns and crawl? Minutely their rocking seemed to ease.

"No! I won't go!" On her shoulder, Tadge yanked a foot under him.

She grabbed it; he kicked out. Gasping apology, she let go.

He tightened his cold little fingers against her scalp. "Maybe . . . maybe they need help."

The thunder of walking mountains dimmed to a feeling of subterranean disquiet. Ferns wet with dew slapped Cassia's feet as she raced toward the track.

In her ear Tadge added clearly, "'A beast's first duty is to preserve a master's life.'"

She stopped. In her memory a white-bearded preacher screamed, "Abomination! A self-saving beast merges not with the goddess but with the teeth of ten thousand demons!"

Shaking her head to clear her vision, Cassia found another; a Beast Trainer astride her shoulder, turning her where she did not wish to go, enforcing his will with reins attached to a whitemetal rod that cut her mouth.

Now, rigid, she managed, "But my duty is to you." A final tremor rippled the ferns.

"Not if I order you to go. And I do, Cassia! They could be only a late hunting party. Or even if they are slavers, they'll never see us in all those trees. Get up there!"

Beneath them the earth lay placid. Cassia's speeding heartbeat slowed as the cries from beyond the bluff grew less urgent.

"I must not endanger you. But the Law says I can't disobey— it forbids deserting a master in need of help. I have no choice." She took a step upward, her voiceless cry of *Danger!* covering both her anger at Tadge and a hot glow of fear—or excitement. Refusing to examine her feelings more closely, Cassia climbed the hill.

Chapter Two

Thitamanit: (1) Eighth. (2) Divisions of Northern Napharese maturity. *First Thitamanit* (ages one to eight years): a child is considered sexless and heightless, and in farming areas is kept with its mother, or with the slaves. *Second Thitamanit* (ages nine to sixteen years): a child is provisionally male or female, half-breed or full-blood; may move into the appropriate quarters; starts school if it hasn't already, may order slaves and take limited responsibility for them, and may agree to sale into provisional bondage. *Third Thitamanit* (sixteen to twenty-four years): conditional adulthood. Sex and height are determined, may bear children, own slaves, enter full bondage, take a religious vocation, and partner. All decisions, however, are subject to review at the third thitamanit's end. There are abuses of this system, of course . . .

NAPHARESE VOCABULARY LISTS:
GRINELDA MAO-VANSCHUYLER, ACTING ANTHROPOLOGIST,
GALACTIC CENTRAL REST AND RESEARCH STATION,
QAQQADUM, NORTHERN NAPHAR.

Cassia flattened herself on the lip of the bluff. She lay behind Tadge, her heart thumping against the pine needles. They prickled through her robe as she peered down at the River Lathon twenty manlengths away. The phosphorescent river bisected the highlands, then dropped to the lowlands, where it emptied into the Western Sea.

Between the river's sparking shoals and the bluffs where Cassia and Tadge lay, a camp fire reached bright fingers across a crescent of beach strewn with boulders and driftwood. On the bluff the shifting light spread a nimbus around Tadge's coppery curls.

"Tadge, over here! It's safer under the trees."

The boy glanced back. In his wide pupils Cassia glimpsed her reflection—amber light danced across her metallic eyes and slipping yellow plaits streaked with red.

"But I want to see!" He wriggled closer to the edge.

The motherless boy was as tense as he had been when he woke her earlier, saying he had sassed his father again and now he couldn't go to First Rising. Swallowing her own disappointment, Cassia had refused to take him into the forest to see it. Until, back stiff with desperate anger, her fosterling had started up the track alone and she had had no choice but to join him.

Now she moved up beside Tadge, scanning the beach for danger.

The party around the fire looked normal enough. Ten tall male and female beasts leaned against drift logs and uprooted trees from last spring's floods. Most were young to middle-aged, but farthest from the fire an old man's bristle of gray hair and his black priest's robe merged with the night, his only color the flames mirrored in his eyes and the scarlet rimming his shoulder-wide collar. Beyond him a deeper darkness stirred; a few more beasts settled into hollows scooped from the sand and gravel.

She watched small Kakano masters move among their beasts,

readying them, she presumed, for their nightly tying to the captives' stake, a notched log driven into the sand at the far end of the bluff.

Tadge rolled close. "I wish it was lighter. None of those beasts is drooling. I don't think they're drugged any more than you are. And they should be if they're really beasts, or they won't do as they're told."

"But it's Festival of First Rising," Cassia objected. "Beasts aren't supposed to get Obedience Drugs on holy days. Or maybe other masters don't drug their beasts either, so they'll work better. And if they're not beasts, what are they?"

"Well, but— I wish I could *know*." Tadge wormed forward until he almost overhung the edge of the steep bank. Keeping to the trees' shadow, Cassia followed.

"Ho, prime!" he murmured. "Look at that beast by the fire. He's *big*. If Pa bught that one, the upper field would be ploughed and harrowed in a morning. He'd cost the moons, though. Full-blood, almost for sure. Have you ever seen one that size, Cassia?"

She stared downward, remembered anguish dimming her eyes till she seemed to see another tall figure beside the fire, one she had loved, but too late.

She blinked, and the form turned to the pale blue flicker of a shadowy robe and waist pouch, the outline of yellow shoulder-length curls, and the glimmer of pale skin and eyes. "No, not recently," she said, but Tadge no longer listened for her reply.

"Gods. Those hands." He nodded downward.

Light cascaded from the silver and gold border of the blond beast's sleeve; he withdrew his hand from it. Cassia jerked in a breath. His hand was gray and knotted; his chipped and blackened nails curved like lizard's talons around a whip. The beast opened the whip's jeweled base; golden pincers caught the light. Bells rang as he clinked the metal open, then shut.

A whip, the robe's richness, Tadge's doubt . . .

"That's no beast," Cassia breathed, "he's a lowlands slaver!" She pictured the true prisoners of the captives' stake—little masters, captured by the huge slavers, and taken to the river to be watered for the night. She scrambled away from the edge of the bank and started sliding backward into the trees.

Tadge grabbed her wrist; his fingers were icy.

"You knew!" she accused. "You planned this."

"I had to find them. I—I want to see what they're really like."

"But it's you they'll take." *And I'll be Sacrificed for losing you.* "Come on!"

"It's so dark, they'll never see us. And look, that one's going to play a—whatever it is."

Tadge spoke too fast. A burst of sparks showed every freckle on his pale face. He slanted her a wide, false grin.

Her fear and suspicion increased; she reached for his robe.

"I'll yell, Cassia. I will."

She wanted passionately to slap him, grab him, and run. Hands clenching, she glared from her beloved nursling to the fire. A coruscation of light caught her eye.

In the shadows behind the blond beast sat a man. Dark hair, dark eyes set in a glimmer of planes . . . His face was like the one Tadge had made her remember; both reminded her of a feeling, a kindness, a dream from her lost childhood. The elusive recognition slipped away.

Less than half the blond beast's size, the man stared at the beast's whip and pouch, and shivered. Again the ropes of gold and pendants and jewels on the smaller man's chest shook with sparks and rainbows and flame. He squared his shoulders; he drew a stringed instrument into the light. Cassia squinted, her vision helped by something like memory.

Black, shining, its neck was long. Moonlight flashed from the pale inlays on its round, deep base. An ember flared. Light glanced off yellow wires running the instrument's length; it glowed on plates the color of a windy sky.

"A golden-stringed zanglier," Cassia breathed. "And with heavenstone keys. But that's a court instrument!"

Tadge swung toward her. "How did you know, Cassia? I didn't."

"I . . . read it? The potmenders told me?" The boy's face looked pinched. "You're tired. We must go back. Now."

"No! Just till he finishes playing. Then—then you can leave. I swear it. By the goddess."

"The danger!"

He hunched his shoulders. "Listen."

"But—" Helplessly Cassia watched as, below them, the small man bent over the zanglier.

Like an ink stroke, his hair slipped forward. He flung it back. A flaming drift log broke; sparks climbed the sky and masked his face with gold.

His mouth was emphasized by shadow; it stressed the humorous quirks at the corners, and wedged darkness beneath his high cheekbones and under his tilted brows. Beneath his brows his dark eyes glinted; they glanced along the bluff. And locked with hers.

She pushed her fist against her heart. *He can't see me!* she thought. *Though he sits by the fire, I can hardly make out his features, and up here there is no fire.* She wanted to move back, she wanted . . . She could not look away.

He struck a chord. His long fingers wandered across the strings, tapping cool bell tones from the translucent keys beneath.

He sang: "Black and blind as loss, the rain glints with the falling daggers of memories . . ."

His light, clear voice and the zanglier's tones blended with the rush of the rapids and the soughing of the wind in the pines.

Feeling at one with them and the great world turning beneath her, joining her to the stars' vast dance, Cassia drew in the flat river smell and smoke, and listened. She felt as if a long thirst had ended; she forgot danger, even her own slavery and fear. She abandoned herself to the music.

"Once these bright strings struck notes of fire and our song together was more than song . . ."

The zanglier throbbed in Jarell's hands, sensitive to his wishes as a lover. Not that lovers were particularly sensitive, in his experience, but it was a nice comparison. And he knew he played well.

Annoying though to have embarked on this selection. It was very sentimental, a relic of his student days at the Royal Temple Space Academy in the capital, Qaqqadum. His student days that had ended when the Academy's administrator, the ambitious priestess Phikola En, had sold him into his present life. Phikola En whom he would destroy if he could, as she had destroyed him.

The sharp strings and cool blue keys slipped into discord. With a shower of notes he segued into the final phrases of the verse.

> "The yiann we shared (blue, blue sparks in the cup of
> night) was more than yiann.
> Heedless, I fled your tenderness, boundless and unchang-
> ing as the sky.
> Down the seasons I trod the pathless earth alone,
> lost, aching, wanting you."

He looked up from the zanglier's case with its sliding reflections of flame and stars and crimson light. Around the fire, each tall man and woman sat silent, even the scarred mercenaries who grumbled at Jarell's persuading Salimar, his owner who had bought their leadership for a season, to bring them to the highlands and this hostile wilderness. A hush fell also on their little creatures, sprawling on great laps or huddling, uncalled and unwanted, far from the fire. One miniature finger even wiped away a tear.

Gods, he should try sentiment more often, if he could stomach it. At least no one seemed to have noticed his slip.

Beside Jarell his owner twitched his massive arm; he caressed his embroidered waist pouch. The pouch in which, in these modern times, other nobles kept perfumed unguents or sweets, but that Salimar, high priest and self-proclaimed incarnation of the Dark God, filled with the traditional contact poison for which only he had the antidote. He dipped his talon into the sack. Jarell's loins grew chill.

He met the baleful gaze of an old man in the black robe and red-edged collar of the priests of the Dark God—the god whose once-a-century challenge of Sassurum must culminate this spring with the Dark One's closest approach to Naphar. Jealous of Jarell's influence with Salimar, the priest would have Jarell flayed if he could. Jarell inclined his head, vitalized by this brush with the death he skirted and coquetted with, the importunate lover to whom he must one day yield in breathless embrace. But not yet.

With the care he would show before the dual thrones, Jarell plucked the opening notes of the interlude, and breathed in the scent of his owner's costly oils. Their fragrance blew past him to the woods.

"... the flaming petals, their scalding dew, swirl to ash on an old man's sleeve ..."

Salimar withdrew his nail from the pouch.

Pulse returning to normal, Jarell glanced up at the blaze of stars shouldering across the sky, and the Veil's crimson, coiling and sparking at the edge of the heavens.

"Very pretty," he could imagine another lowlander saying. But the stars were not pretty. They were places, each with its own mass, luminosity, and periods. He should be scouting them, finding in them the possibility denied him by this tumbling rock of a world. And he would—once he had a sufficiently docile Rabu to escort him. Pity that the boy and girl watching him from the bank ten manlengths away were too young and too short for his purpose.

As he lifted his voice in the halftones and heartbreak of the refrain, he looked from the freckled child to the girl on her stomach beside him. In the clash of tinted and white light and shadow, Jarell could see only that she was fair, and that her tarnished, luminous eyes watched him as if he were music itself.

He ticked the heavenstone keys and swallowed. That absorption must mask the legendary stupidity of the highlands Rabu who had brought him here—otherwise, why did not she and her companion pull back from the light?

Still, in recent times no one had called him overfastidious, Jarell thought, and of late his conceit had been methodically razed. The creature's wonder salved it. Deliberately, he sang to the girl.

> ". . . and the black rain is cindered blossoms falling, falling, its drops tapping the counterpoint to my refrain . . ."

Recognition twinged through him. Had not, long ago, another child's opaque gray eyes seemed to absorb him and his song? The rock and sand between him and the girl felt like a road. He had to fight his wish to walk it.

Goddess-led whispered through his mind. Savagely, Jarell denied it. There was no goddess, no care, no love here! Only priests and priestesses who promised them for coin to the lonely and the credulous.

He crashed three chords across the golden strings and began the first variation's changed stresses and internal rhymes.

His glance wandered from the female's delicate features and rounded stubborn chin to the deep swell of her breasts.

So. She was older than he had thought. And taller. Excitement flicked him. Was this the one? The night?

His blood thrummed as it had not since his boyhood, but with a darker heat. And if he failed? His mouth quirked. If he failed, at least he would win the final freedom.

And whatever occurred, for almost the length of a song she had kept his mind from his owner. His owner, who had not yet touched him. Heavy, sickened desire lurched through him. He began the refrain.

Beside him, his owner lifted his gray hand. Cold, his skin trembling, Jarell looked down, sang his song and waited.

* * *

Cassia's throat tightened as she listened to the clear sadness and control of the small man singing in the camp fire's gleaming shadows. An ember burst; the racing flames illuminated his dark eyes fixed on hers. She felt his triumph, his fear, and the twisting thrust of his desire. His gaze wavered; like black fans, his lashes dropped.

She sighed. And saw nicked talons glisten in the starlight; the blond beast slid his gray palms under the singer's arms and lifted. The Kakano's feet dangled, showing an immodest length of fine, strong ankle, even a glimpse of leg.

Cassia's cheeks burned as the beast dragged the smaller man—a master—across his thighs, and set the jewels on the singer's chest swinging and shouting with light. *For the great to touch the small—abomination!* The song hesitated, then its pure melody soared on, unchanged.

In front of Cassia, stones rattled; pine needles pushed into her sleeves as Tadge wiggled backward and hissed, "They're not what I thought, I can't— I've got to think of something else." He clambered onto her shoulder. "Get going, Cassia. And—and don't look."

She staggered up. As Tadge lunged for her braids, light flared and she glanced down.

By a brief tower of flame a gray hand slid beneath the small man's hem. Appalled, she glanced away. Her gaze met the singer's—his was urgent, demanding. She started.

On her back, Tadge missed her plaits.

She bent to catch him.

The boy shot over her shoulder, arms flailing. "Ow, Cassia!" Ferns and twigs crackled; he thumped to the ground.

"What's that?" deep voices and harsh altos called from around the fire. Studded war sandals thudded, chain mail clinked.

As Cassia reached into the ferns for her nursling, the blond beast below surged upward; she glimpsed the singer spilling from his lap. Then the child's hand touched hers. Not once considering the Law or that she broke it, she grabbed his wrist and pulled.

Below, jewels flashed in the firelight. The singer was pointing. At her. "There!" His trained voice was clear. "On the bluff. Spies. Or an army to retake your captives."

With Tadge sprawled on her shoulder, Cassia sprinted along the bluff. A few manlengths away, her pursuers flowed up the bank, grunting and cursing, their shaggy heads unimaginably tall against the faint stars and a pallid shred of the Veil.

And behind them a shimmer—of jewels?

She skidded down a gully, clutching at leaves and ferns. Wet clay slid into her sandals; her feet slipped in it.

The forest was younger here; white ghost trees glimmered between the pines. Beneath their clouds of twirling leaves, moonlight splashed the ground.

"Turn, Cassia!" Tadge yanked one of her steering braids.

She swerved away from the bright stand to the evergreens' concealing double shadows.

"Over there!" sounded behind her.

"No, that way!"

"Shut your teeth, I can't hear them with you hollering like that!"

Their hunters spread out.

"Gods, Cassia, I never knew you could run so fast!" Tadge bounced by her neck. His little belly tightened; she felt him pull in a breath to shout.

"Hush!" she snapped.

But at the same moment, Tadge sang out, "Ohai, Cassia!" and dug his fingers into her scalp. "I'm sorry, I'm sorry," he repeated into the back of her head.

"There they are!" The bellows and shrill cries converged.

"Tadge! How could you?" She sped faster; twigs raked her face and hair.

By her cheek, the boy stiffened. "Look out, Cassia!"

She glanced up. A pine as high as a star and wide as a house seemed to rush at her, its thick roots coiling from the ground. The toe of her sandal caught on one, her foot slipped in the clay inside her sandal, and she catapulted forward.

Her temple hit unmoving bark. Pain arrowed through her head and the singing in her ears became a screech. The air seemed to darken; movement paused.

As Cassia began a slow fall toward the earth, she grasped the tiny body on her shoulder and pulled it free. With all her strength she threw it beyond the pine and the encircling beasts.

"Ow, Cassiaaaa!"

Tadge's surprised yell was the last thing she heard as the forest floor rose, and the dark enveloped her.

Chapter Three

Kateeb: (1) Northern Napharese term for the scroll describing the fates of children taken in their first thitamanits to bazaar fortune-tellers. (2) Used in a general sense to cover everything from "It's the will of the gods" to "Well..."

NAPHARESE VOCABULARY LISTS:
GRINELDA MAO-VANSCHUYLER, ACTING ANTHROPOLOGIST,
GALACTIC CENTRAL REST AND RESEARCH STATION,
QAQQADUM, NORTHERN NAPHAR.

A melody in a plaintive key wove through Cassia's dreams. She woke trying to grasp it.

Along her aching back and thighs she felt ridged stone. A pulse in her temple thumped—she rolled her head on the rock and winced. Her scalp felt as though a thousand fiends had ridden her, each pulling hard on her steering braids. She squinted upward.

From a rocky ceiling hung lumpy brown cones. Sunbeams threw strong shadows behind them. At the end of one was a claw.

Cassia stiffened, looked up to see leathery wings wrapped around shaggy barrel chests; pointed noseless faces masked with fur and topped by round ears; thin lips that would not close over mouthfuls of sharp teeth; closed sunken eyes... The cave was full of hibernating Night Demons!

Cassia shivered, though the day was unseasonably warm. As spring advanced and Shamash the Sun God heated this chamber, the Night Demons would wake and stream into the night skies to hunt. She had hauled away too many potmenders' white, bloodless bodies ever to shelter in a Night Demon cave. So how had she gotten here?

From beside her came the whisper of cloth and the soft sound of breathing. She froze, superstition skittering down her spine like a house lizard after a spider. Could one of the Misbegotten—

18

half human, half Night Demon—be at her side, fleshy wings spread to engulf her, toothy mouth open to tear off her head, then drink her fountaining blood? It was said that if a Night Demon's venom did not kill, in a single waxing and waning of the moons it could turn its victim into such a monster. It took all her will to look around.

Instead of the shaggy face of a fiend, she stared into an angular human one. Behind it a zanglier leaned against the cave wall. Black, shining, strung with gold, it was keyed with misty blue. The small man by the camp fire! She felt a surge of uncomplicated joy. Her glance dropped to his plain blue robe. Shouldn't it be hung with jewels?

The singer, Night Demons, her sleeping on a workday . . . Of course! She was dreaming. *Kateeb,* she would enjoy it. "Singer!" She smiled with pleasure.

He looked startled. "Just so. Awake, are you? Sit up and we'll check you for damage. I intend to be a conscientious master."

Each word sounded as distinctly as struck crystal. No highlander spoke that way—not the beasts with their tongues blurred by Obedience Drugs, nor the masters they raised and taught to speak. Yet Cassia had heard those accents before, and not in the potmenders' singsong. Now, where . . .

Groping among her few memories, she sat up and lost all interest in the small man's diction. She dropped her thudding head in her hands; her middle seemed to loop into her throat.

She smelled resin tinged with herbs. The small man parted her hair; he touched her temple and the center of her pain.

"That bad, after your long sleep? Try this. And don't spit it out. I brought only a few of the spacers' remedies."

Cassia's mouth puckered from the brown, seedlike oblong. Its fumes were blasting through her nose and head, clearing them, when she realized that twice, without thinking, she had done as she was told. In her dreams she never obeyed. With a dropping sensation in her middle, she thought, *I'm not asleep!* A small master who found she took no Obedience Drugs could have her Sacrificed. Heart bumping against her ribs, she dropped her jaw, unfocused her eyes, and dribbled saliva artistically from a corner of her mouth.

The singer looked at her as though she were a moldy husk left too long in the root cache. "Gods. Just another mindless beast. It's going to be a long journey."

She sat, dumb, as he pulled twigs and leaves from her hair. While checking her eyes and reflexes he spoke of taking her to the coastal lowlands where she would pose as his Rabu owner so he could travel unquestioned to the capital, Qaqqadum, and to Naphar's only spaceport just beyond it. Cassia stared at him: greenish rays filtered through the cave mouth, rimming his hair and robe with light.

That small rest and research station had no slavery, he said; there he could win freedom and get a ship off-planet. With increasing intensity, as if long-held restraints had snapped, he spoke of his life with his owner, and how he needed to escape. Cassia's cheeks burned. A master should not expose himself so to a beast; she should not listen. Unable to look at him, she glanced around the cave—and realized, *Tadge is missing!*

The small man pulled one of her locks into a ray of light. "Straight golden hair mixed with copper. I once knew a priestess with such coloring; her curly-headed baby girl shared it. Are there many like you here? Never mind. I expect that's too complex a question."

She did not answer. She was wondering how to ask about Tadge and still sound witless.

"Boy?" she hazarded, stiffening her tongue. When the singer did not reply, she explained, mimicking the drooling beasts she had seen. "My . . . master. Where?"

"So you do talk a little. I suppose you're asking about the child beside you last night. You're safe—they took him, at least, so it sounded. I was too busy hiding you, then dragging you up here—and making a second trip for my zanglier and the food—to go and see."

She glanced with respect at the lean lines beneath his robe. She was no lightweight and considerably the taller. Then she realized what he had said. "Tadge!" She jumped up. Tadge, her Tadge, cuffed, hurt, tied! Dizzy, she hurried to the mouth of the cave.

And stopped. Before her, blocking her path, stood the small man, his back to the sunbeams streaming through the dancing leaves, his head by her breast. He glared up at her. "Where are you going? That child has been in my owner's hands for a night and a day. He won't part with him easily. Even if he did, and you take the boy home, are you so eager for your master to Sacrifice you, since you're the slave who lost him?"

"A day!" Cassia glanced between the leaves to the western ramparts of the Fire Mountains. Long shadows darkened their purple cones. Above them, Shamash the Sun God's red eye peered through the smoky blue sky.

The singer folded his arms. "No one cares for a master. Except . . . I do recall some similarity about the chin and eyes. Is he yours?"

"No!" Shock, then anguish for her own dead child, chased the singer's warning from her head.

"In that case, the boy can be nothing to you. Sit down."

He is all I have! she wanted to shout, her mind filled with the blackness and silence that had invaded her cubicle until her master brought his infant son to her, told her the child's mother was dead, the babe was Cassia's now to live or let die, and stumped out. Again she felt her wonder at the mewling bundle in her cupped palms; at the tiny hot mouth and minute tongue that had licked, then clamped to her aching swollen breasts, suckled, and relieved their pain. Now, she could force no sound from her throat.

The priests' wild eyes and the cold ones of the beast trainer filled her memory, and their harangues, and the crack of whips.

She sat. The dry sweetish smell of the Night Demons above enclosed her. The sun drew a flickering nimbus around the singer's head. She opened her mouth—her tongue would not move. So used was she to obeying an order, any order, she could not even beg.

He touched her cheek. "Tears! Been with the child since birth, I expect, and you'd do anything for him? Anything," he said thoughtfully when she nodded. Taking a turn in front of the cave mouth, he muttered, "The gods defend me from fools and loyal slaves." A muscle in his jaw twitched. "Look here. I need you willing. I left one or two things undone in that camp by the river. If I return, do them, and free the boy, do you swear by your goddess—or whatever you believe in—to accompany me to the lowlands, and give me the devotion you do him?"

Hope jolted her. Of course she would not leave Tadge and her privileged life with its absence of Obedience Drugs for a small master whom she did not trust. But, asking the goddess's forgiveness, she crossed her eyes and drooled a little. "If you—we—succeed; yes!"

The small man looked at her through his lashes. "Idiot beast," he muttered under his breath. "So in love with your slavery, you've no existence of your own. You'll not know the difference if I get us killed." But aloud he said, "All right. We'll get him."

She jumped up.

"Not now. Tomorrow, after they've had another sleepless

night. The quakes come during the day too, but they fear them more in the dark. Until then, we stay here where we're safe."

Safe? Cassia eyed him, then looked along the rays of the lowering sun to the cave roof and its Night Demons. He must not know the danger. If he did, he could not choose to stay here. She opened her lips.

But little masters could be unpredictable. Surely the Demons' sleep would last another night. Time enough to speak when Tadge was safe. She bowed her head. Uneasily, she agreed.

Chapter Four

Cassia sat by the cave wall, hugging her pulled-up knees, and tried to keep her expression stolid as she watched her captor fidget about the chamber. At least, she hoped she concealed her amusement.

He picked up the zanglier, plucked a string, tuned it, and tapped a key beneath it. He glanced down at what he did, and with a look of disgust set the instrument against the rock with such force that it hummed and sang to itself for some time. Next the Kakano prowled the cave's perimeter, skirting the piles of Night Demon droppings. He did not glance up at what had produced them.

Looking from him to the nearest jumble of claws and wings, Cassia cleared her throat to speak. But the singer flung toward the cavern's mouth, squinted into horizontal light as thick and gold as spilled honey, and started talking. She buried her warning in a cough.

"Time to fetch our lastmeal," he announced. "I wish I'd hidden more food yesterday against an escape. I did, our first stops up here. Well, it will have to be enough. Stay! Or at least, don't go far," he added over his shoulder as he pushed into the branches that choked the opening. They swished, sunlight danced on the rock, speckling it with yellow and brown, and he was gone.

Cassia inhaled the musty smell of the sleepers overhead. Heart thumping, his command locking her to the site, she followed.

Outside, tall old pines and an occasional lacy ghost tree cast sepia shadows over a mat of green and brown needles. Pollen glittered in the air. To the west the Fire Mountains grumbled, hazy lavender with distance. Only a trace of their sulfur mingled with the forest scents. She glanced behind her, the many palms of Shamash the Sun God warm on her back.

Under the hump of the hill, the entrance to the cave looked like a fall of rocks. Young trees crowded before it; tough green ropevines laced them. On either side of the hill stood twin plantings of furbushes. At Cassia's approach their green spearlike leaves rustled and drew together. Fat buds peeked between them. The edges of their closed petals were fringed with wisps of the fur within. Most of the green air sacs beneath the buds looked too immature to sound an alarm at their presence. However, to be safe, she hummed reassurance. The hairs lining the slits in the globes beneath the buds rippled as the larger ones piped answers.

Still droning, accompanied by the click of beetles and scurry of lizards, Cassia wandered through dusty columns of light. As she walked, she snapped off boughs and gathered springy arm-loads of leaves and ghost tree bark against the night's chill and the cave's hard floor. She even tickled the throats of the furbush buds that had answered her. When they obligingly opened their petals, she drew out the fluff that, uncollected, eventually would choke them, and added it to her load.

At the cave's mouth she dropped her branches and fur. The pile was large enough now; she would drag it into the cave and separate it into two pallets.

She knelt and pulled a ropevine around the heap. The vine was too short.

Looking for another to splice to it, she brushed her hair out of her eyes with fingers pungent with sap. She sniffed them appreciatively, stretched, and smiled. Her headache and nausea were gone. The spacers' brown seed had done its work.

Behind her, leaves scraped. She heard a sharp indrawn breath. Still kneeling, she twisted around.

The small man stood in a shaft of sunlight, cradling sausage ends, crunchroots, and bread. He was staring at her pile.

"You dare!" He took one smooth step toward her and cracked his palm across her cheek. A furbush squalled.

The skin below her eye burned; she pressed it with her finger-tips. "Wh-why?"

"Whatever you may think you saw by that fire, beast, I share no one's pallet! Certainly not that of a dribbling, mind-dead Rabu."

"Share a pallet? With you?" *Mind-dead* echoing in her head, thrusting her back into her role of drugged beast, Cassia stopped the rest of the words crowding to her tongue. But as outrage clenched a hot fist in her chest, she cried, "Forbidden!" and swung her arm high to strike.

Below her the singer's face turned to amber planes and glowing shadow. He did not flinch; he did not forbid her.

She paused. He had worn that blank look by the camp fire when the blond beast had smiled, touched his waist pouch, and set between them a whip with golden tongs.

Another memory flickered behind the first: of a lizard in the road, its hind legs and stump of a tail bleeding. When she bent to carry it to safety, it had snapped and clawed her.

Cassia scanned the small man's set face, thinking, *I wish I could have given that lizard a salve.* She knelt and lowered her forehead to her knees. Watching the singer through the bright curtain of her hair, she began, "I beg pardon, master..."

He moved back, scuffling the needles by her nose; When she was half through the apology, he sighed. "Get up. Pardon granted. Possibly I misunderstood." He swallowed. "That was most uncivilized of me. I . . . I had not realized I felt so strongly. It will not happen again." Looking everywhere but at her, he set down the objects he held and filled his arms with greenery. "But we'll make two piles."

An apology, and a master doing beasts' work! So the marketplace storytellers spoke truly: lowlanders were different. Cassia picked up a fragrant armful and followed him into the cave.

When two pallets lay on opposite sides of the chamber, the lowlander brought in his provisions. He tossed them onto his heap of boughs, climbed up, and motioned for Cassia to join him.

Instead, eyes downcast, she crossed the rock floor, sat on it, and leaned against the branches, beast separate from master as the Law required.

He raised an eyebrow but said nothing as he rummaged in his robe's wide chest pocket. He produced a ridged handle, touched it, and a blade sprang out. Ignoring Cassia's start, he picked up a red waxed end of sausage and sliced into it. The scent of grease, hotspice, and tearweed cut through the cave. He speared a chunk and shoved it in front of her.

She gulped and shook her head.

He looked at her a moment, then softly repeated the Doctrine of Highest Use: "'From the scholar, insight; from the herb woman, cures; from the rebellious, the sick, the mad, the old, and the dull for whom no one will speak, their flesh.' Was someone you knew in that sausage? Never mind, I don't insist on an answer," he said as she winced.

A moment later he dropped crunchroots into Cassia's lap. Suddenly aware of her hunger, she rolled the long white feeder roots into balls and hurried them to her mouth. As their sweetness trickled down her throat and she nibbled on the sour purple main root, she realized she had not waited for her captor to finish his meal, or for his permission to begin. Stiff with resentment—beasts should not have to remember, that was masters' work—she waited for a clout.

It did not come. Instead, crumbs sifted onto her hair. She brushed them off.

"Sorry," the small man said indistinctly, and chewed hard. "Dry." He patted his nonexistent belly, then waved a torn round of bread at her. "That feels better. Been too busy to eat. Want some?" Crumbs blew out of his mouth. "Oh, I nearly forgot!" Tossing the battered hunk in her direction, he sprang down from the branches and left the cave.

The bushes thrashed. He reappeared with a jug held carefully upright, and climbed to the top of his pallet. "Fermented songfruit! Real yiann, not some farmer's belly-rotting substitute. I left it in the sun to start the phosphors working. Out there I realized: this is the end of my first day as a free man, and as a slave owner. Doubly worth celebrating. For you too, if you only knew." He flourished the jar, misquoting, "'Fixes fish, flesh, and lizard.' Washes down stale bread too."

Cassia eyed it—beasts were forbidden to drink yiann—and bit down. She forgot the jug, wanting only to spit out her unexpected mouthful of corrosive sourness. When she could, she licked her pursed lips, and glanced up.

He tilted the jug toward her.

"No!"

He laughed and pulled out his folding knife. "You look as scandalized as a Purity Priestess on her first tour of Qaqqadum's lower bazaar."

Black chips of wax rained though the dying light. With the sound of a released breath, the last of the packing came free. From the mouth of the jar, blue lights spiraled upward on curls of pablue vapor. A yeasty aroma edged through the smell of droppings and stone. As more of the songfruit squeezings came in contact with the air, galaxies of stars rose from the mouth of the jug.

Cassia swallowed. The blue sparks were very pretty. And her tongue felt thick. And dry.

He sloshed the jug. More purple-blue explosions drifted toward the ceiling; the tantalizing scent tickled her nostrils.

"Sure you won't share with me?"

She shook her head and put her hands behind her.

He raised the jar and poured a flashing blue stream down his throat. Wiping his mouth on his sleeve, he held out his hand for inspection. "I see you've heard of yiann's quality of turning man into demon. You're welcome to look—no gnarling, no talons; are horns forming here?" He lifted his hair from his forehead; a last sunbeam glittered on the black handful. "No? How about the three rows of fangs?" He bared his single set of white teeth in a hideous smile, and looked at her inquiringly.

"It's good, it went for a fabulous price. The bushes are guaranteed flooded by the Lathon each spring, well drained all the rest of the cycle. I've never corrupted a Rabu before. Give us both a new experience. No, there's no water," he said as she glanced toward the back of the cave. "I looked. Nor is it possible to sneak down to the river for a drink. We must wait until the slavers are snoring, and that won't happen until the moons set, if last night is any guide. After that blow on the head and your long fast, you must be thirsty."

He lifted the jar again, tipped back his head, paused, and said, "Last chance. You won't find the likes of this in your owner's root cache. Ever." Lowering it, he passed it under Cassia's nose.

Her mouth watered and she choked on a laugh that was half sob. "Cruel!" she exclaimed, thinking, *Curse him, goddess!*

She stretched out her hand.

Chapter Five

Yiann: (Related philologically, according to some Neo-Classical archaeologists, to Sol III's Minoan ya-ne, other Ancient Near Eastern civilizations' yayn or yen, and to Ugarit's yan.) The Napharese blue, sparking, luminous wine. Its sparks are chemiluminescent organisms drawn from Northern Naphar's phosphorescent river Lathon through the roots of the songfruit plants and stored in their fruit. When the fruit is squeezed, the organisms remain in the juice with the yeast during fermentation. These organisms are a legacy of Naphar's first days when the atmosphere had no oxygen. Since oxygen hurt them, they burned it away with chemiluminescence, helped by an enzyme, luciferase. Thus, when a jar of yiann is broached, the pressure of fermentation shoots out vapors, some of which contain the organisms. They react with the oxygen now in the air, give off a cool light, and look like sparks. When yiann is poured or stirred, oxygen reaches the organisms still in the wine; the yiann seems to swarm with drowned stars. An advantage of Napharese yiann over earth's champagne: drunk in an oxygen atmosphere, yiann will take a long, long time to go flat.

SYBARITE'S ENCYCLOPEDIA, NEW EARTH EDITION, L-4, BARNARD'S II.

Twilight darkened into night. As the shadows overhead thickened and occasionally seemed to flutter, the jug of yiann was passed back and forth, and soon was supplanted by another. The singer's teasing laughter became more personal, sometimes more lachrymose, and once, more painful.

After a diatribe against the selfishness, destructive tendencies, and treachery of lowlands Rabu, the singer moved on to the highlands variety, their lack of wit, and their habits of cleanliness, honesty, and pallet practices. He was not as outspoken as Cassia's master, but he was specific.

She jumped up, songfruit effervescing in her veins, its jug swinging forgotten in her hand, and stalked toward her own pile of branches.

Behind her the singer hiccuped, asked pardon, confessed with a dark weight of misery in his voice that he was no better, and begged her to return and incidentally bring the yiann.

Cassia's eyes stung with tears of exaggerated pity. Returning to sit beside his pallet, she handed up the jug.

After a long swig the singer brightened and bounded to his feet. They would leave the cave, he cried. He would swing through the trees, proving that at least he was a good acrobat.

Telling herself she did not care about the mad lowlander, only for his help in rescuing Tadge, Cassia drooled a little, crossed her eyes, pointed to the glow of the river below them where the slavers camped, and mimed the need for silence.

The cave seemed to revolve. Hoping it was not a true seeing, Cassia glanced up into unnervingly sober dark eyes.

The singer closed his eyes and lay back. The boughs breathed their pungence onto Cassia's face. "Quite right. I'm no performer, never was—wouldn't be now but for that priestess, Phikola En. Did I tell you about her?"

She nodded, suppressing a sigh. He had. Several times.

". . . see how she gets through the Festival of the Full Moons and the dark moon's closest passing without the Mindstone . . ."

"Mindstone?" she asked. At least this was something new.

"Surely even an ignorant beast has heard of Naphar's most sacred relic!"

She shook her head. She was *not* ignorant. She could read!

He annoyed her further by clicking his tongue and explaining: given by the goddess millennia ago to bind her people in an uneasy unity, the Mindstone was held by the corulers of northern Naphar's capital, Qaqqadum.

His voice grew smooth and fluid. Lulled by its sound and the yiann warming her veins, she found her irritation fading. Whoever touched the Mindstone, the singer chanted, tapped its power, saw into other's thoughts. One forcing another to use the stone shared evil addictive dreams, was marked by the goddess, Sassurum.

". . . sold or ransomed, the Stone would bring enough coin to outfit an army—or finance a new life, away from Naphar . . ."

His words fuzzed; the cave spun faster; its rocky floor looked unutterably inviting. Cassia sank into uneasy sleep while beneath her the earth rumbled and the shadows above her squeaked and flapped fleshy wings in the dark.

She dreamed of a tower in a city overlooking the midnight sea, and of a tiny figure climbing its outside. She looked closer: it was the singer! And in the manner of dreams, she became him, clinging to the tower's cold blocks with resined fingers and toes. Above him a scarlet flying lizard whooshed from a windslit faced with gold. It carried a stone; dropped it into a pouch slung around the man's neck. Red scaled wings flapped, and the lizard returned, a misty ring glowing in its jaws. The ring coalesced into a circle of white metal to hold the stone; it was inscribed with the Old Language's flowing script: a prophecy, a foretelling. Cassia could not read it. The ring too dropped into the pouch. The lizard vanished upward; the singer began the long trip down.

In a white sunlit room floored with black and rippling with

reflections of the sea, Cassia looked up, and up, through the singer's eyes to his owner who tore the singer's freedom papers across and across again, denying him his promised pay for stealing the stone. Then the blond giant made his newest slave hold the stone with him, and use it.

With the singer, Cassia woke in the violet dusk, terrifying visions clamoring in his head, to find his owner Changed—and mad.

Like a great spider, the blond Rabu scrabbled across the floor. He lit a lamp and thrust his hands into its golden radiance. His hands that had been white and shapely—his hands that now were lizards' claws.

Cassia dreamed the giant husked, "The goddess can't—she doesn't exist! There can be no Mark of Sassurum!" He lowered his head. As the sea below rushed at the cliff and fell away, he wept into his ruined palms like a lost and terrified child.

The images shifted.

It was day. In the temple by the sea, its high priestess stared at the Mindstone's empty pedestal. The high priestess turned her head to the glittering windslit; her dark gold hair was streaked with coppery red. The jewels netting it shot colors across the whitestone floor. "Fools!" the high priestess raged to her goddess. "Thieves, who believe the Mindstone is only a symbol of your power; a thing to be bartered and passed from hand to hand like a sword. They do not know that it *is* your power, that it forces its holders to meet each failed Choice and Choose again until all dross, all self-deceit are burned away; they do not know that no one may touch the Mindstone and remain unchanged."

For an instant Cassia understood them all: the priestess, the circlet's foretelling, Cassia's past and the singer's, and their futures. In that long tranquil moment she contemplated their symmetry.

Then her ribs felt cold as she watched the priestess's white room darken and a smoky shadow thicken on the walls. The shadow grew, became Sassurum. Cassia gave a cry of recognition.

The goddess expanded. Amber skin glowing, dark hair a drifting cloud about her shoulders, she filled the chamber. Her brilliant black eyes looked straight into Cassia's. She raised her cupped hands—and revealed the Mindstone.

Pink tinged its ends, white sparkled on its narrower center. It looked ordinary: rough, porous, comfortable to cradle in the palm.

Fearful, wondering, Cassia reached out.

An unreadable expression flashed in Sassurum's dark eyes. And the dream faded.

Cassia woke to an aching head and a tilting floor. She waited tensely while a hot wind smelling of sulfur jostled her robe, the foundation of the cavern settled beneath her breast and thighs and the dirt hailing onto her head from the roof spattered to a halt.

She ran her tongue over her lips and teeth. Bitter. Memory swam back of a sparking jug and a tenor voice that laughed and tempted. Her head throbbed.

Surreptitiously she fingered the skin over her eyebrows. Smooth. No horns. Something else must be causing her headache. Kateeb; of course! Face hot, she scolded herself for believing, even for a moment, the superstition scoffed at by her smuggled book scrolls.

The branches beside her creaked in brief disharmony with the barkhiders' high song, as she turned to look out the cave door.

The leaves that screened it flickered with pink and silver light. Followed by the Dark One, the moons lit the waving treetops, throwing double shadows onto the hillside, while above the Fire Mountains the stars sputtered alone in a volcanic haze. So the Veil was still high. She could not have slept long.

Once again the cave floor shuddered. Booms and grindings sounded deep in the earth.

Heart pounding, she sat up. More soil and gravel sifted onto her hair. Through the rustling of the leaves she heard a squeak, a flapping, and the dry scrape of wings.

Night Demons, Cassia thought. *The heat woke them early.* She pulled her legs under her and grabbed for the branches as the cave rocked again. Cries almost too high to hear shot her to her feet— too late.

The air throbbed with leathery scalloped wings. Moonlight gleamed on the claws that ended each scallop's point, and on muscular chests encased in rough fur below neckless heads set with black eyes. Grit and musty droppings swirled into Cassia's face. She hunched. One puncture from those sharp teeth and she would lie on the cave floor, paralyzed, while flapping demons drained her of her blood. She would die. Or Change into one of the Misbegotten—but that was superstition, her smuggled book scrolls said.

She burrowed into the stacked branches beside her, arms protecting her face and throat—and remembered the lowlander. Small, unknowing, he lay just above her.

She owed him nothing, certainly not her life. But he was almost half her size, clearly a master. More musty bodies whirred by.

The singer called her names, accused her of abominations! But she was pledged to preserve life, especially a master's. A claw snagged her braids. She flinched away.

The small man associated in shameful ways with the tall, and for all to see, like a beast in the breeding pens. But his singing and his beauty could twist the heart.

Her mind dinning protests, she rose to her knees and groped through the hurtling bodies to the pallet's top.

She found his arm and yanked on it. Like a half-full grain sack, the singer followed. Only he was warm, with very human contours; he fell, hard, against her.

Her cheeks burned. Shamed, terrified, and furious with a man fool enough to drink himself into a stupor in a cave filled with Night Demons, she eased his tumble to the floor and pulled a bough over him. On hands and knees she started toward the cavern's mouth.

She heard a moan behind her, and froze.

In the volcanoes' ruddy glow, the singer rolled his head. The branch slid off him. He flung his hand, palm up, across his eyes. In his exposed throat, a vein pulsed. Beneath the sound of beating wings, she heard a scraping.

Ignore it! He'll be all right, she thought. She did not move.

From the darkness at the back of the chamber, a large Night Demon hopped into the inconstant light, black fleshy wings spread, its liquid gaze fixed on the singer. Flopping to his shoulder, it squatted, thin lips wrinkling away from a mouthful of teeth. The creature folded its dull wings high, snuffled, and lowered its head to feed.

Cassia sucked in a breath, scuttled toward the pair, shut her eyes, and swiped. Her palm hit harsh fur. The Night Demon yipped. Warm, bony wings trailed across her hand. She shuddered. When she opened her eyes, the Demon was gone. She yanked on the man's sleeve. "Singer."

She jerked again. "Singer, get up! Walk!"

His sweep of black lashes stayed firmly on his cheek.

Few Night Demons blundered overhead now. The scarlet light faded, then deepened. Again the cave floor tilted, elongating the gray shadows with rosy centers. A ponderous stone bounced past the opening and crashed into the furbushes, which screamed.

Consigning her training to the fiery gods in Naphar's womb, Cassia grabbed the man, draped his body over her hip, and fled.

Just short of the entrance, the earth dropped again. She fell against the wall; her burden grunted. Between her shoulder and the rock something squirmed, and gave a thin cry; teeth like needles sank into her back. A Night Demon!

Cassia's belly contracted. As she reached behind her the singer jerked to life. With a gasped "Forgive!" she clamped him to her ribs. With her free arm she reached over her shoulder. She closed her fingers on a small furred body.

"What?" The singer twisted upward until his head was by her breast. His hair smelled of rare woods and spices.

Ignoring him, Cassia reached over her shoulder to pull on the Night Demon. Its wings beat like manskin fans against her palm; her fingertips dug into a naked belly. In her back, its teeth met.

Under her arm the singer yelled and whipped sideways.

Cassia staggered the last steps to the cave mouth. With a prayer to Sassurum, she jerked the Night Demon with all her strength. Under her feet the earth rippled; rocks pelted onto her head. The creature in her hand squealed, the muscles in its sides relaxed as it took a breath and dug in its talons. In that instant, Cassia yanked. The demon clicked its jaws open.

Cassia threw. The Demon rattled through the leaves. She burst after it into silver light.

Splatting to the ground, the Demon cried and shook itself, wings clapping. She stumbled after it.

By her feet the shadows wobbled. She skipped aside as a blot of darkness limped by her, softly keening, both wing tips trailing. *Why, it was a baby,* Cassia thought, and wanted to vomit.

The singer undulated to life, shouting to be put down. His breath was powerful.

She turned her face away. "You're endangered, Master, and not well. I must get you to safer ground, I cannot chance your stumbling—" She broke off.

In the mountain, thunder pealed. The mat of pine needles broke; dust smoked into the moons' rays while behind Cassia, boulders thudded. Pebbles cascaded over the cave's entrance; the cascade became a flood. She ran.

Chapter Six

Like telepathy, empathy has its dark practitioners. But also like telepathy, empathy's healing knowledge and acceptance are desired by the goddess. Thus, when winnowing the populace for the psychically talented to bring to her service, look for relatives of those in her temple, for sensitivity is inherited. Look too for those brutalized or ignored by authority, whose ties are to children, siblings, slaves, creatures, and plants. For empathy cannot pass through the fear and anger engendered by harshness and power, nor can it defend itself against them. Instead, the empathy we look for is a gift of wordless love crossing the gulf between equals on the bridge of compassion.

> SACRED INSTRUCTIONS FOR RECRUITERS FOR THE GODDESS,
> A SCROLL MEMORIZED BY
> THE ITINERANT SEARCHER PRIESTS OF SASSURUM.

Some distance from the cave, Cassia set down her cursing burden; she stepped back in alarm from the menace in the singer's eyes. Whip cracks in the ground pulled her gaze from him to the cave.

"Look." She pointed.

Larger rocks bounded through the avalanche pouring over the entrance. The dirt and stones swept downhill, ricocheting off trees, their knocks and clacks accompanied by the whine of wind in the branches. Above the torrent, dust rose into the moonlight like a mist off a lake. From the slavers' camp below, Cassia heard cries. *Tadge!* She started downhill.

"Oh, gods, the cave is going. My zanglier!"

She paused; the man took a step and halted.

Together they stared at the crest of the hill above the cavern, alive with the silhouettes of flailing trees. The noise in the earth became a grumbling roar; on the hilltop the pines and ghost trees seemed to sigh and lie down.

Soil and rubble poured across them. Through the clatter of

stones came the furbushes' faint laments. Cassia hummed to them
but they would not be comforted.

With a rumbling detonation, the hill collapsed. Where trees
and a bulk of rock and earth had been, stars blinked through
wreaths of dust, the Dark One a blot in their midst, and the slitted
eyes of two crescent moons glared down.

The singer cleared his throat. "Why didn't you leave me in
there? If you had, now you'd be free."

"But—but you'd be under all that!"

"Exactly." Behind him a ghost tree swayed; curls of its loose
white bark blew across the shafting moonlight. He rubbed his
face. "Gods. What do you put in the songfruit up here? Explo-
sives?" He dug in his chest pocket, threw something in his mouth,
and stretched out his palm to Cassia.

Wanting to hurry to her nursling, her mind busy with the
singer's first remark, she looked at the brown seed with suspicion
—it could hold Obedience Drugs. Most masters carried them.
She shook her thumping head that still swam with yiann. "You
have only a few. A mere beast should not—"

He shrugged and put the thing away.

Her polite refusal finished, the words she had held back rushed
out on a fizzing, sparkling blue tide. "I had to save you! Any
beast worth the keeping sets a master's life above its own. As for
freedom, 'A beast's only freedom lies in service.' But my master,
my Tadge—he's down there, hurt, tied, buried— I can't wait for
tomorrow, I have to go get him!"

"What?" The small man stared up at her.

"He's just a child. You promised; it means going sooner,
but— Oh! Goddess help me." She clapped her hand over her
mouth. "I'd heard yiann loosens the tongue."

"So you're not drugged. You never have been."

Cassia's skin chilled under its film of sweat. She dropped to
her knees; she lowered her forehead to the needles. "Oh yes, I
have been. It's so cold and lonely and dark in that place where the
drugs take you; please, Singer. Don't tell the priests. I could not
bear to lose my memories and the light. Not again."

"Singer!" By her cheek his hem swirled; needles glittered into
the moonlight. "Gods, what have I been saying?"

Cassia's face heated. She had known she should not listen!

The earth under her arms and knees grumbled and dropped.
Heart thumping with fear, she listened to stones rattle; the sobbing
furbushes wailed.

She swallowed and tried to ignore the quake. "I beg pardon. I have no excuse, except I—I was afraid. Of the drugs, or if you found I was conscious and told . . . of sale . . . Sacrifice. But I would not repeat what you said. I understood nothing, I have forgotten all, truly!" The ground's shaking slowed.

"Enough, child. I've been deprived of my dignity before, I expect I shall be again. And I have no intention of going to a priest, or anyone else." The rock beneath them stilled. "However, we must find a safer place to wait out the night. Not there!" he said as Cassia jumped up and started toward the river's glow where the slavers' firelight showed through the trees. "Panicky troops wakened by an earthquake aren't safe. According to them the watercourse will continue to be relatively unmoved. We'll go upriver."

Guiding on the orange flicker, he led her in and out of moonlight and shadow. "You named me back there, did you not?"

"Oh." How like a master to insist on propriety at such a time and place! But she repressed her sigh, lowered her glance, and recited, "'A beast knows not its master's name, for to a beast, all possible names are master.' I beg pardon. It slipped out."

"Never mind that!" He motioned her toward a colony of furbushes. "Call me by name as often as you like. Just don't address me as 'Singer.' It's a slave name, like 'Tumbler,' 'Pretty Boy,' 'Sweetums.'"

For an awed moment she contemplated the forceful personality that could call this dignified man "Sweetums" more than once.

"But as long as I'm free"—he approached the furbushes; they swayed— "my name is Jarell."

"Singer, the bushes!" she warned.

"Jarell," he repeated. "Use it, if you wish a reply." Mouth compressed, he ignored her second warning and frantic gesture toward the slavers' camp. He stepped on a leaf; it thrashed. He kicked a stalk; it yipped. The bushes around it rippled, whimpering. "Gods!" He jumped away. "No wonder highlanders are few. Even your flowers hide dangers!" He made a wide circle around the buds.

Cassia hung back, telling herself not to giggle. As he moved away from her, a desperate anger crawled toward her like a miasma. *Mine?* She shot a hard look at Jarell: the leashed rage and anguish clenched from him. Her hands clenched, all laughter draining out of her. *Oh, not that, not now!*

"Take this other ear from me, Goddess!" she breathed. Jarell's distress; her nursling's terror at demondreams that woke Cassia long before the child crept to her for comfort; her master's jangling panic that wracked Cassia's peace before he came looking for her or the boy, with a whip . . . She did not want them! These small masters already owned her actions. Must they also replace her feelings with their own?

But even as Cassia rebelled, she embraced the man's fears, his needs. She smoothed his knotted suspicion of the highlands forest, his doubts of survival in it, his despair at a life mislived and better scrapped. His erect silhouette paused beside a torchpine. The mats of mold curtaining it made it a dark, lofty triangle above him. He looked back.

By Cassia's foot, a white barkhider the size of her finger crawled from under a stone.

"Come," Jarell mouthed and pointed toward the slavers' camp below them.

She looked from him to the barkhider and its tree. The insect's legs bent under its weight. Long before it reached the trunk they would break. Spoiled by the plentiful food beneath the bark, its kind could no longer fly but only soared to progressively lower branches to feed. Helping it would take just an instant. Anyway, she tended to bump into things while her mind was busy with healing. Focusing on Jarell, she knelt, and set the bug on her palm.

She could feel Jarell minutely relax as she lifted the barkhider to the ghost tree. In her mind, the insect's spark of trust lightened her dread, and lit the small man's ebbing anguish. The barkhider scraped its smooth wing against its serrated one, chirped, and whisked behind a white shaving.

"It is my lot and joy to serve," she answered courteously, and accepted the last of Jarell's agony. She cradled it; she soothed it. When it was quite gone, she looked up.

"Well, come along, Beast!" he said from the shadows beneath the pine. His voice sounded lighter. Even his stance looked easier.

Cassia's glow of pleasure was only a craftsman's satisfaction, she told herself.

He climbed down an embankment. "I can't call you 'Beast' all the time. What's your name?"

"Cassia." She jumped after him. Just beyond lay a last drop-off, the bluff above the river.

"Cassia. It's meaningless, or a pallet name. Your besotted master gave it to you?" Scouting for a way down, he glanced back as her chin lifted and she made the sign against Abomination. He added smoothly, "Or perhaps a child's house name used by its family. Is there more?"

"I never tell it." She squatted, waiting for him to climb down so she could follow. When he looked at her inquiringly she admitted, "Well, once I did. But the other beasts laughed. Some of them strutted around with their noses in the air."

"Why? What did you say?"

She almost started her usual answer: *I don't remember.* Then her loneliness and need made her burst out, "You're from the lowlands, my book scrolls come from there, you might know—I want to find out who I am, where I belong!"

His tone was guarded. "A reasonable ambition."

"I—I'm Ricassia Addiratu."

He stood quite still. His dark eyes blazed. "Ricassia!"

For an incredulous moment she thought he would embrace her. Then he raised an eyebrow. "You're not. You heard the name. Or the slaver called you that to increase your value."

"No! He wanted to call me Stripey, because of my hair. I hated his name for me. I even stamped my foot. Kateeb—I was young, not even past my first Thitamanit. I still had all my milk teeth. But I'm not supposed to talk about it. It's—it must be the songfruit. 'Beasts have no existence before their lives with their first master.'" She primmed her mouth.

"Never mind that! Tell me when the slaver came. Was it day? Night?"

Should she trust him with one of the few cherished memories left her by the Obedience Drugs? She glanced up. Only the first pastel folds of the Veil tangled with the stars. Dawn lay half a night away and the drink ran warm in her blood. Perhaps this Kakano, soon gone, might be a more satisfactory listener than a great carved Ear of the Goddess. Set in a mountain shrine, an Ear was visited only by the wind, or by those with secrets too shaming—or too explosive in the small, tightly-knit highlands communities—for living ears.

Temptation won. "It was night," Cassia whispered. "Lamplight woke me. It lit the pink shell by my pillow. I kept it to remember a perfect day. I don't remember who gave it to me or what we did. I just remember happiness."

Beside her Jarell drew in his breath.

"A tall woman pushed through the door curtain and opened her fingers around a lamp. My mother, I think. I know I loved her. She was wrapped in black traveling veils—she gave some to me, then knelt and helped me with them, and kissed my forehead. We left my rooms and went outside without an attendant." She paused, wondering if he would laugh at a beast having such a thing. But Cassia thought she had not always been a beast.

The small man did not laugh.

"After a while I dragged my sandals and begged to be carried. I cried for her to knock on a roof in the Kakano quarter and buy me a sweet or a roll, but she would not. She wouldn't tell one of her riddles or sing.

"In the dawn we came to a rock as high and wide as a palace —two palaces. Pink and gold streaked it. From the sunrise shining in the dew, I suppose." Cassia swallowed. She did not want to remember the rest.

Jarell hunkered down. "You describe the Rock of Sacrifice outside Qaqqadum. Where tall Rabu rid themselves of bastard children who do not grow, telling themselves their infants' starvation or enslavement is the gods' doing. And then?"

"She left me." Cassia flattened her voice so it would not quiver. "I cried. I ran after her. The third time, she took off one of her head veils and tied me with it to a jagged part of the rock. She said I must wait for someone from my father, or from the goddess. Her face was calm, but her cheeks shone with tears. And she was strong, she never cried."

Cassia bit her lips to stop their trembling. "So I stayed. The sun got higher. I played with some stones. I pulled the veil over my face and slept. It smelled of her—I could pretend that nothing bad had happened, nothing had changed.

"The sun dropped behind the city to a long blue line . . . the sea? I got thirsty and I sucked on the stones. Hungry too. A slaver came—he had a black beard and his striped robe pulled over his stomach. He took a cake from his sleeve. It was stale and bitter, but I ate it."

Cassia looked at her listener defiantly. Night and the shadows swallowed his face; only a little light from the river gleamed in his eyes. "I expect you think that was foolish. Even then, I guess I knew it was. But I hoped that if I was very good, and did everything I was told—because I didn't always—she would come back. It was still daytime when I swallowed the last crumb of the cake but soon the air got cold and dark. I could hear the slaver telling me to come, and I wasn't going to, I wanted to wait for her. But I *did* it."

She brushed her sleeve across her eyes. "Why am I saying this? I've never told anyone, not Tadge, not even my—"

"And yet, you say you loved your mother." Jarell stood; he moved back into the darkness, but not before she saw his lip curl.

When he spoke his voice was smooth. "So your name is a true childhood memory?"

"Yes. All right, I told you. Who am I? What does my name mean?"

His laugh was harsh. "I will tell you in Qaqqadum. And may you get more joy of your past than those of us not granted your forgetfulness.

"As for the boy, he must wait as you waited. Though not for so long. Come." Leaping over the brink, he skidded down the bank. Dust smoked into the moonlight.

"But—but I thought—" She twisted her hands and looked toward the slavers' camp. Almost certainly this man knew something of her past. She might yet coax a hint, a word from him. Then, tonight—surely tomorrow—they could free her nursling.

She moved her shoulder. It felt well enough. Her steps hesitant, then eager, Cassia started down toward the river.

Chapter Seven

The Mindstone held by one, or by two with unfinished minds and flesh, channels thought and feeling. The Mindstone held by two adults, their persons and intellects in harmony, grants vision into each other's worlds and all of time's worlds from eternity's dawn to its night. But the Mindstone forced on one unwilling can give the weaker partner death's desires, and to the one who denied him Choice, it brings shared evil, addictive dreams of a thousand times a thousand worlds, and the mark and curse of Sassurum.

EXCERPT FROM BAZAAR TALE, QAQQADUM.

Cassia bent low in the underbrush, tension squeezing its fist in her belly. Just behind her the river's roar drowned all other sound. The afternoon sun spread its cloak of heat across her back, easing the ache of her Night Demon bite; the bite had grown steadily worse as the night progressed.

Pushing back a stab of dread, Cassia peered over the bushes

and down the wide, curving beach. There, slavers snored between
the scoured bones of drift trees and an occasional rockfall, sleeping off their night of earthquakes and fear.

Across the stretch of sand and gravel stood the bluff where
Cassia and Tadge had hidden. Cassia scrutinized it for movement.
Falls of red clay had ripped stripes from it; crumbled mounds lay
at its base. On top of the bluff, uprooted trees poked through the
ferns. A wind stirred them and the undergrowth, blowing spores
and pollen into the sunlight. Everything appeared quiet.

She shook her head in disbelief. No lookout above, no open
eyes among the snoring, bruised, and bandaged slavers; not even
Jarell's owner was awake where he lay by the dead fire, his
waxed blond curls splayed across a pack.

Once more Cassia went over Jarell's argument: if they wished
to escape with Tadge, they must distract the boy's new owners.
That distraction might end in deaths.

Still reluctant, Cassia wiped her sweating palms on her sleeves
and located the captives. They were bound by common ropes and
slept in three rays of an incomplete star. One row aimed toward
her and the river at her back, the others pointed to opposite ends
of the bluff. A boy with a mop of copper curls lay nearest the
captives' stake: Tadge.

Tears muddied his cheeks. His grimy hands pillowed his head;
ropes bound his wrists.

Cassia looked from her nursling to his strapping captors; her
hands flexed into claws. All hesitation gone, she straightened and
waved.

Beyond the driftwood and sand, through the woods' moving
light, a shadow in a torn blue robe flitted toward her. In one hand
he held a stone; in the other a knife.

The haft of the folding dagger fit with rough comfort into
Jarell's palm. As he ran through the trees to the beach and his
sleeping owner, he tightened his grip on the knife and, in his other
fist, the rock. He swerved to avoid a torchpine bearded and curtained with mold.

In the open he slowed, making his steps noiseless. If a Rabu
woke and Jarell had to kill one, the slaves and captives would be
slaughtered in case they had helped. Even if he escaped, their
relatives and the dead Rabu's would hunt him down. He wove
between the driftwood and dreaming slavers.

Jarell's owner lay at his feet like a felled tree. Salimar's pale
blue robe shimmered as his arms as large as trunks moved with

his dreams. Jarell knelt. Mind blank as he could make it, he delicately untied the poison sack at the giant's waist, and threw it into the trees.

A pebble scraped, and Salimar muttered. Lifting his gray hand the size of Jarell's head, he groped in Jarell's direction. "Singer?"

Jarell dodged away, packing his thoughts with surface glints of leaves and sky and the distant skeleton of a burned torchpine. Still Salimar reached out; with unerring aim he hooked Jarell close. For Salimar carried the Mindstone that Jarell had stolen for him —an artifact, nothing more. It strengthened Salimar's mental powers but it was not supernatural; it could be circumvented. It must be! Jarell submitted to the giant's embrace. "Good," the other grunted.

As Salimar fondled him, sweat trickled down Jarell's ribs; he raised his mouth to the throat like a stump, and wondered, *If the beast still watches, will she run away, shocked?* Not that he cared for her opinion. Finding another beast would be inconvenient, that was all. At the caress, his owner's knotted biceps eased.

Jarell leaped free. Holding his breath, he eased his hand into his owner's chest pocket and drew out the manskin pouch that held the stone. Below it he glimpsed a metal circle—the circle Jarell had last seen in a flying lizard's jaws before dawn while he clung to the side of Sassurum's temple in Qaqqadum. That ring was the Mindstone's setting—its lodestone, tradition said. Probably superstition. Still, on the chance that the Firstmen who shaped the circlet had used their lost science to implant in it a directional device, Jarell must take the ring too.

Moving quickly now, he slid from the manskin sack the porous Mindstone with its two pinkish knobs connected by a central bar sparkling with white crystals. He shoved the river rock he carried into the emptied pouch, whipped its drawstrings shut, and pushed the substitution back into Salimar's pocket. In Jarell's hand the Mindstone seemed to warm and turn.

Impossible—it's only a rock. He hurried the Mindstone into his chest pocket.

He straightened, squinting down at his huge owner, remembering other awakenings, other dreams of setting a point just there, giving it a quick, hard shove.

Jarell bent over the blond Rabu; the stone in his pocket swung forward. He pushed it back, thinking wryly of the slave woman's disappointment if he died before freeing the child. But his life was a small thing to trade, he thought, his hand tightening on the stone, for the satisfaction of revenge. Revenge on Salimar; revenge on all betraying Rabu. Jarell pulled back the dagger.

A whirlwind seemed to snap away the dark. He found himself jumping up and racing from his owner. A warm urgency pushed him toward the sunlit captives' stake, the child, and life. A silver gaze seemed to go with him, as tangible as the sun's heat. He risked a glance in its direction.

The woman awaiting him by the river brushed back her long loose hair; it blazed gold and copper in the sun. Her lips curved in the beginning of a smile.

He felt straightened; cleared. He started an answering grin. Her tarnished gaze left him for the boy. Jarell blanked his expression, reminding himself how little he cared for those who bound themselves in willing slavery to another.

Only much later did he remember that he had left the white-metal ring in Salimar's pocket.

Cassia stepped back into the river's mist and the shadows, breathing in the hot, pine-scented air. Her head echoed from her mental shout of *No!*

Desolation and death had seemed to loom like a thunderclap in the goddess's busy green silence, startling a cry into Cassia's throat. She exhaled, willing her heart to slow. Lucky she had not shouted aloud; she would have awakened the camp. As it must awaken now.

Across the stretch of sand and driftwood, the singer fell to one knee by Tadge's rusty curls. He put his hand over the boy's mouth and lifted him; he slid the knife between the boy's tied wrists.

Tadge opened his eyes—which darkened with a new reflex of fear—and tried to twist free.

Watching, Cassia husked, "It's all right." She hurried to her nursling, angling across the beach, darting between uprooted stumps and boulders to the captives' stake at the end of the bluff.

Tadge's eyes rounded. Watching her approach, he lay still.

The rope at his wrists parted. The one at his waist fell to the ground. Cassia grabbed Tadge and held him, her demon bite, the Law, and the child's new dignity forgotten. Pain seared her back.

"Cassia! I knew you'd come." Tadge pushed his face into her neck.

At her feet Jarell frowned upward. "Quiet," he mouthed, and waved her toward the forest. He scuttled to the next sleeping prisoner.

Above him Cassia pressed her check to her nursling's curls.

When she could breathe again she drew in their smell of sweaty little boy, dust, and a hint of foaming sand. She helped Tadge onto her good shoulder.

As she eased past a slaver's prone form, she glimpsed Jarell behind her, cutting a farmer's bonds. Jarell shook him awake, laid two fingers over his lips, and sent him tiptoeing to freedom.

Cassia neared the charred remains of the fire. On its other side, a large Rabu slaver sat up; she blinked at the stirring prisoners. Afraid to draw attention to herself and Tadge, Cassia stood still, watching the slaver woman push a hand through her cropped gray and yellow hair, rub her weathered face and look again, then leap to her feet, pointing and cursing.

In a moment the beach rang with screams, yells of "Run! Freedom!" and staccato orders as prisoners lunged separately or in tandem to the woods and the river.

A brawny merchant levitated into wakefulness. He raced in a circle, his roped companions bumping behind him like a lumpy tail. On Cassia's shoulder, Tadge repeated, "Let's go, Cassia; I want to leave—come on!"

She glanced back for instructions from Jarell. Movement in the clearing's center caught her eye.

Beside the charred logs, Jarell's owner stretched and unfolded until he stood above them all. He set his taloned hand on a lump in his chest pocket.

With slow inevitability, as Tadge jiggled on Cassia's shoulder, Salimar's translucent gaze swung to hers. She froze.

A cold alien will crept along her nerves and muscles. The clank of swords and mail, Tadge's shrilling, Shamash the Sun God's golden arrows shimmering down in waves of heat—all grew muffled as the invader stripped her thoughts, fingered then discarded her dreams, desires, and few scattered memories. Unsatisfied, it began slipping from her. She shuddered. *Did the singer also endure this violation?*

The intruder paused. Swarming along her senses, it found her mental picture of Jarell's dark eyes, their hurt and cynicism. It saw the cave—and their plan. Triumph suffused the intelligence like flame; it demanded more. At the edge of her frozen vision, Cassia glimpsed the singer's dark glance intent on her; he touched his chest pocket. A little strength flowed into her. She reached into herself for more.

From that unplumbed well, a dark green transcendence rose to crack the barriers of her mind and memory. She strained against the other's will; the barriers broke. She gained new eyes—Salimar's.

For a long astonished moment she looked through them. Salimar's pent feelings whined, screeched, then screamed, ripping his indifferent mask, engulfing her in his hopeless loneliness behind it.

Instinctively, as she would with a sobbing Tadge or a snake that struck from fear, Cassia reached out. *Soothe,* she thought. *Heal.*

A pale frightened eye looked back at her. Behind it, mental walls slammed down. The eye vanished.

Aware of the beach once more, Cassia watched the giant float toward her in a haze of light centered in his white, blazing eyes. Behind him Jarell, looking at her no longer, shooed more captives from the beach to the woods.

Tadge urged her to run; he climbed to her hurt shoulder. Flame wrapped Cassia's spine and belly.

As she struggled for breath, Salimar loomed above her, groping for a poison pouch that was no longer there. Behind him sped the last tied pair of slaves.

With a shout, the pair rocketed on either side of Salimar's legs. Their common rope hit the backs of his knees, bending them. The captives sailed toward each other, howling as their noses smacked his shins.

Salimar's grip on Cassia's mind vanished. For an awed moment she stared upward as he spread his massive arms and toppled. At his feet the pair of slaves shot horrified looks upward, rolled, but unfortunately toward each other: they knocked heads.

Salimar roared. With an earth-rattling thump he flattened the prisoners.

Cassia hurried toward the forest, glancing back with appalled pride at the chaos she had helped create. Beyond the tangle of bodies, dust fogged the beach. It was loud with coughs and sneezes, moans, and bellows of rage. Footsteps pelted toward her.

"Don't gawk, run!" Laughter choked Jarell's voice.

"You're enjoying this," she accused, but a laugh bubbled into her own throat.

"Go-o!" Tadge cried, his fingers cold against Cassia's scalp.

Adjusting her balance to the child's, she pushed after Jarell into the spicy secrecy of the pines.

Chapter Eight

The Fosbury Flop is a method of high jumping in which the athlete goes over the bar backward and head first. It has developed spontaneously on most 1-G humanoid-inhabited planets, when its beings reach the level of athletic expertise typified half a millennium ago by Sol III's Olympic high jumper who gave the technique his name.

INTRAGALACTIC TRACK & FIELD: SEMI-MILLENNIAL EDITION.

Tadge grew heavy on Cassia's shoulder as she followed Jarell even deeper into the trees. At last the man stopped in a glade's afternoon shadows.

Easing her robe away from her throbbing Night Demon bite, she said when she had caught her breath, "I've been trying to tell you!"

Jarell ignored her. He stooped by the ferns at one side of the meadow. From under them he pulled the screen they had woven that morning, and dropped it by the ditch they had dug with shovels of split stone from the nearby cave.

"What's that? What's he doing?" The boy wriggled against Cassia's neck signaling to be set down. She knelt; he jumped onto the lush green starred with white and lavender flowers.

Sitting back on her heels, she kneaded her shoulder and inhaled the forest's cool scents. "It's a hole for us to hide in, and a screen to pull over us, Tadge," she said when no answer came from the small man who was busy beneath the trees. She raised her voice. "And we can't use it."

Coming out of the woods, Jarell stared at her over his armload of ferns. "What did you say?"

"Salimar knows of it. We'll have to think of something else."

Jarell looked at her narrowly through sunlight thick with spores from the uprooted fronds. "Had a good conversation about it, did you?"

"No, he—" Cassia's face burned as she remembered the giant's plundering of her mind. "But he knows. And about the cave too. If I were tricking you, I wouldn't tell you any of this!"

"Possibly." Jarell crossed the ditch, kicked the screen over it with one of his flimsy entertainers' sandals, and dumped the ferns on it. "Nevertheless, you'll stay here where I can watch you. And this time the plan will be mine alone."

As Tadge looked, eyes wide, from Cassia to the small man, Cassia got to her feet and waited for her orders.

Cassia's fingertips were scraped and bleeding. Putting down a last boulder, she brushed the rock dust and fine gravel out of her cuts, then wiped her hands on her robe and glanced around the rockfall where the cave had been. It looked different in daylight —smaller. Jarell's broken zanglier, hastily dug up, lay at a drunken angle among the stones. Yiann—the last of his store— dripped from the keys and ran down a golden string to puddle in the zanglier's black, splintered base. The reek of yiann over-powered the fragrance of sun-warmed rock.

At one side of the avalanche, rather battered furbushes whis-pered under a torchpine whose tip disappeared in a haze of sun and sky.

Jarell nodded toward it. "We'll go up that. It's high enough for us to locate our pursuers, and they won't be able to see us behind that parasitic growth."

"No! That's a torchpine." Cassia pointed to the tree loaded with cones, its shape almost obscured by the mats of gray mold hanging from the ends of its dark green branches. Threads beaded with resin netted it; where the sun hit them, they glinted with streaks and globes of amber light. "Look at how thick the mold is, and all that resin. In this heat, with the cones open and the spores already flying—"

Jarell's face hardened. "If you object, that decides it. We take this tree. Where I know my loving master will not expect us."

"Cassia's right." By the cave Tadge stopped in the act of pocketing a colored stone. "It could burn."

"And besides, the furbushes will cry out," Cassia said simulta-neously.

"More and more the two of you determine my course." Jarell's dark eyes glittered. "We climb the tree. Now."

The command in his voice took Cassia halfway across the rockfall.

After a pause to assure Tadge he need not fight the man for

control of his beast, she hummed the ruffled furbushes silent; Jarell watched, a peculiar expression on his face, and muttered about sound vibrations, plant nervous systems . . . Cassia interrupted with a last protest.

Fiercely Jarell hushed her. "Did you hear that? Up!" Using Cassia for a leaping post, he took a running jump, and flipped backward into the torchpine.

Over the soughing of wind in the boughs and the creak of opening cones in the surrounding trees, she caught a Rabu's deep rumble and a harsh contralto answer. Obedient to the man's urgency, she hesitated only a moment before boosting Tadge into Jarell's waiting hands. Then she too hurried up the tree.

Keeping to the fire-resistant trunk and comparative safety, Cassia followed the others. The late afternoon sun slanted through dark nets of fungus, turning the bark to checkered gold. Light trembled in the threads and tiny amber spheres festooning the tips of the boughs. Fear edged through Cassia. No sap was dripping down the smooth bole; the pine's cycle must be complete. Today, tomorrow, fire would cauterize the outer branches so the main stem could pump juices once more. *But not yet. Please, goddess, not yet.*

She climbed higher. The sunbeams swarmed with pollen. Cones squeaked in nearby pines, the males opening to puff the yellow grains into the air, the females spreading their wooden petals for it, then clacking shut over the quickened seeds that would take two or three cycles to mature. Then, one spring, the tree would turn to a pillar of fire whose heat would cause the release of the seeds.

Cassia glanced at the cones on her own tree. Only a few shriveled males from earlier cycles swung, darkened and empty, in the breeze, their pollen sacs in transparent tatters. The female cones hung plump and heavy with two or three cycles' gestation. She breathed in the rich smell of the fermenting mold wrapping the cones. In the full sun, that shaggy bundle— Did she imagine its curl of smoke? Greater unease crept through her.

"This tree is about to flame," she called upward.

"Shut your teeth!" Above her Jarell and her nursling had stopped climbing. They looked down through the spiral of branches.

On the distant gray and yellow fog that was the ground, Cassia saw the foreshortened figures of two slavers: a lean old man in the black robes of a priest of Salimar, and a square woman with cropped gray and blond hair. Cassia squinted; the woman looked like the slaver who had given the alarm during Tadge's rescue. Her open mail vest clanked as she strode behind the priest.

Her back to the zanglier planted in the rockfall, the woman put her fists on her hips, and surveyed the collapsed cave and the furbushes and torchpines on either side. Her forthright tones floated upward, only occasionally lost in the sighing wind and the creak of wood. "It's all here. Your so-called God-priest may be an arrogant, incompetent sirdar, but his Foreseeing is strong enough, for all that it's blurred."

The woman jerked her head in the direction of the glade where Cassia and Jarell had dug their ditch. "We can collect his manikin you're so jealous of." Watching the Rabu priest narrowly, she took a brass firebox from her sleeve, blew on its pierced lid, then shook red coals into a bowl. Smoke curled into the spore-laden sunbeams. The smoke's sweetish scent mixed with that of resin, fermenting mold, and— Was that burning wood?

On the branch beside Cassia, Tadge whispered, "Look. Smoke."

Jarell's hiss cut through the creak of opening cones on the surrounding trees. "Yes, joy smoke. Hush!"

"No. That smoke. And that." Tadge stabbed his dirty finger toward the gray wads baking in the afternoon sun. The jewels of resin strung around them glowed like captured flames. Cassia's bough swayed as her nursling landed beside her. "We've got to get down!"

With a slithering sound and a streak of blue robe, Jarell clung to the branch on Cassia's other side. "Silence that child or I'll strangle him."

The priest's exclamation from below cut across Tadge's angry answer. "Jealous!" the priest said. "Of a scum of a Kakano pleasure slave? Watch your tongue, Captain." The old man paced toward the woman, his bony hands flexing. ". . . know my Dark Lord well. I was first to recognize his telepathic talent . . . showed him the goddess's falseness . . . owes me everything and he knows it. He's like a son to me."

"Son! He's a lover who's discarded you." The woman fanned the bowl of joy smoke; gray vapors spilled over its sides. She breathed in the fumes and offered the bowl to the priest. "Go on," she said when he was slow to take it. "Protection against this demon-eating pollen . . . relax you . . . strung tight; following your sirdar deeper and deeper into the highlands' quakes on the say-so of his fancy little Kakano robe tosser." She snorted.

"If you ask me, your Lord Salimar doesn't care where he

goes, just so he's out of Qaqqadum, out of reach of the civil guard and the temple's Unravellers of Secrets. Bought commission... Talks treason: says he and the Dark One will topple the goddess. Troops have had enough!" She paused to sniff and hold a finger under her nose.

The priest was standing quite still; without having used it himself, he returned the bowl and waited for her to inhale more of the vapors. When she had done so he signed for her to go on.

Cradling the joy smoke against her side, she sniffed again, clanked over to him and flung an arm around his shoulders. "Tell you what. We march home to the lowlands. Tonight. And leave Salimar here—get a new sirdar, one that's earned his commission. But if your Salimar walks out of here, we stand a better chance in the courts if the mutiny's unanimous."

As she spoke, she looked over the priest's shoulder at the rockslide and the broken zanglier. "Look! The manikin's been here, all right, and may still be, poor scum." A few quick steps and she had the zanglier freed. She dug into the slide.

"You'll bring the hillside down on us." The priest skirted the avalanche until he stood near the furbushes at the base of the torchpine, far below Cassia. The furbushes swayed uneasily; the half-opened blossoms nearest him folded shut. As the woman persisted in her digging, the old man took an impatient step backward; alarm scurried through the flowers like wind. "Mutiny. Tonight, you say?"

"Right." She squinted at the sun. "At about the time we get back if we leave now. We'll just be able to circle around and check the ditch they're supposed to have dug. Though it's more likely he's here. Sure you don't want the Kakano's head or hands to wear at your waist? He's your enemy. Admit it. I've seen you staring at him and your leader at night, across the fire."

The old man released his breath in a snarl. "By the gods, I have! Since the singer arrived, my lord has changed. You can see it! His hands used to be white, fine. Only after their first meeting did his fingers twist into claws. The Kakano prates of 'hysterical arthritis.' But no twisting disease makes a man neglect his off-world investors or his lieutenants, just so he can pallet-thump with a pleasure slave. I think it's enchantment—the singer's an agent of the goddess."

The priest shifted his feet; a broken furbush flower screamed under his sandals. As his voice had grown louder, the furbushes had swayed. Now, as the damaged flower passed its hurt along to the others' feeder roots, they squalled.

The priest crouched; a dagger from a concealed wrist sheath flashed into his hand. Like an ancient turtle he turned his head, quartering their surroundings.

High above him in the torchpine, Cassia held her breath. If he glanced up, his view of them would be clear.

Tadge dug his fingers into her wrist. He leaned out, peering down through the chasm of light and shade. "Cassia, Cassia, don't let them . . ." He canted further over the empty air.

"Watch him!" Beside Cassia, Jarell's voice sharpened.

She whispered, "Tadge. Sit back."

"What?" The child jerked around, teetering over the void, his eyes gray and unfocused.

From below, over the priest's invective against the highlands and the caterwauling of the blossoms, came a contralto snort: "Mott take this pollen! I hate spring. Ah-choo!"

Tadge jumped; his clutch on Cassia's wrist vanished. "Ow! Cassia-a!" He sprawled on the empty air, arms and legs wide, his robe flapping in the wind of his fall, fingers catching at the branches flying by him; he halted, slipped, fell again.

"I said, watch him!" Agile as a house lizard on a screen, Jarell launched himself into space and dropped after the boy. Snagging a branch, he thrust out his hand, grabbed Tadge, and shoved him behind him into a nest of cones. Needles and crumbs of mold and bark rained down. The quieting furbushes squeaked. Beside them, the priest looked up.

"You!" The old man's burning gaze locked with Jarell's. He lifted his arm. "Come down."

Jarell shook his head.

On the rockfall, the woman shaded her eyes, and looked along the priest's arm into the sunlight and mold and changing shadows. "By the gods, the Kakano! Well, if he won't come down, I can get him." She strode into the furbushes; their caterwauls increased in volume. "These things don't bite, do they?" She looked the priest up and down. "Or you can get him. You haven't said you'd join us. This will keep you occupied until it's too late to betray us to your lord."

As the woman spoke, Cassia looked toward Jarell for orders —and froze. Beside him, heat shimmered around a cone, flaring yellow at its edge. Fire crackled up a nearby amber thread; its beads of resin exploded into yellow flame. Cones squeaked open to receive the heat and shoot fat, winged seeds like arrows into the air. Below Cassia, Tadge whispered her name and stared at the miniature blazes and flying seeds.

On the ground, the woman also noticed the burning cone and the others smoldering nearby. "Or leave him! Let the tree have him." Retreating, muttering curses aimed at the highlands vegetation, she started toward the forest.

Behind her, the priest wrung his hands as he looked from Jarell to her solid back and then at Jarell again.

Above him Jarell grinned and swung upward to another branch.

The old priest clenched his fists and hissed, "I would kill you with these! But I must warn my dread lord." He hurried through the bushes, accompanied by furbush squawks almost loud enough to drown the creaking of the forest's opening cones. At the edge of the furbushes, he paused.

"And may you burn until your flesh sizzles and cracks from your sinews! If you leave that tree, I'll hear them"—he indicated the furbushes—"and I'll be back—with this." His wrist dagger flicked into his hand. "Salimar rules!" He hurried after the woman.

Chapter Nine

Naphar's phonosynthetic plants known as furbushes use sound energy to spin filaments that protect them from too much noise! Like the products of photosynthesis, the threads (or fur) that fill the blossom are made from carbon dioxide and nitrogen, but they're simultaneously fixed in a unique biosynthetic process in the head of the flower.

The carbon dioxide and nitrogen also are delivered in a singular way: sound vibrations beyond the plant's range of tolerance stimulate the hairs fringing the opening of a spherical air sac below the flower. The hairs signal the plant's nervous system to collapse the sac, forcing air up the stem into the closed petals. Whatever air is not needed in the manufacture of the "fur" exits through the slit below, making a sound my Napharese guide described as that of babies crying.

Too much fur and the plants will smother. Since they do not react to the calls of native lizards and insects, more than one exobotanist has speculated that furbushes evolved in the voiceless days before gods or humans appeared on Naphar.

PICKING AND PLUCKING MY WAY THROUGH THE GALAXY:
MEMOIRS OF A FLOWER LOVER, BY RETIELE T'CHU (PRIVATELY PRINTED).

As the slaver and the priest of Salimar vanished into the forest, the cries of the furbushes beneath the torchpine quieted to uneasy murmurs overlaid by the crackle and snap of flames. High in the burning tree, Cassia pushed herself against its bole, ready for the long slide down.

Jarell signed for her to wait. "You said the trunk doesn't burn —we'll be safe here for a while?"

"Not for long, not with this breeze. The oils in the bark won't protect us from flames blowing inward." Cassia looked up. At the pine's tip, fire sparkled through the golden net of resin. As the heat above her increased, a cool wind whooshed upward, lifting her hair. Instinct screamed, *Leave!* Training chained her to the small man and the tree. "It's spreading. Please. Let us climb down."

"You can argue if you want. I'm going!" Beneath them, Tadge wrapped his robe around his legs and started to slide.

"Wait!" Jarell slithered downward, grabbed Tadge, and clicked open his knife. "You!" he called up to Cassia as the child kicked and tried to bite. The knife pricked Tadge's throat; he went rigid. "Go ahead of me," the man told Cassia. "And if those bushes down there make a sound, I'll kill the boy."

Tadge: dead. A chasm of loneliness seemed to gape before Cassia. Hands stiff with fear, she slipped and swung downward. "What if I can't calm them, or if the fire spreads to them before I can get there?"

"You can calm them. You must."

She clung to the lowest bough, Jarell and Tadge just above her. Fire sheeted through the pine; sparks and winged seeds sailed past her face. Gathering herself for the final drop she summoned all the calm, all the reassurance and pity of a lifetime. She sent it in waves toward the flowers, and began to croon.

She hung full length from the branch. The ache in her shoulder spread in a fiery column from her back to her head. "Oh, goddess! What will happen to me?" she whispered. Terror swept her —for herself, for Tadge—and her concentration broke.

Below her a half-opened flower hooted. A bud beside it whimpered. Unease rippled through the blooms rustling among their stiff pointed leaves. Sparks rained onto the immature buds and they gave husky cries.

As Cassia's sore fingers slipped, she glanced up at Tadge's white face and at Jarell's dagger. With his other hand the man touched his chest pocket. *You must* echoed in Cassia's mind. Beneath Jarell's fingers she seemed to see the Stone that once the goddess had offered her in a dream: pinkish ends, white central spindle.

Strength flowed into Cassia. As she sent downward thoughts of peace and solemn joy, the furbushes stilled into listening quietness.

Her song filled her throat and she dropped into the flowers' whispering welcome. She lifted her arms for Tadge. Setting him, stiff and furious, on her shoulder, she hesitated then reached up for Jarell.

He flicked her with his dark glance; something moved in his eyes. Distaste, she thought. Unaided, he dropped to the ground as above them the creaking and the thunderous burning rose higher. Sparks bit Cassia's cheeks and hands. At Jarell's signal, she raced across the avalanche to the forest.

When the woods enclosed them, Jarell halted among the slanting pillars of sunlight dense with smoke and flying seeds and pollen. He gave Cassia a straight look. "My apologies, beast. I have read of thermophyllic molds and the heat-induced release of seeds. I simply did not recognize either one. I am sorry to have frightened the child. But it was necessary," he added.

Apology. From a master. Cassia stared down at him, her anger and fear dissipating in her astonishment.

His tentative smile faded. Curtly ordering her to follow, he headed downhill.

Cassia wanted to stop, to cradle Tadge against her breast and soothe his rage. She wanted to thank the lowlander, and explain. She wanted to laugh. But she did none of those things: her training forbade it. That, and her sudden realization that none of them mattered—after tonight, neither she nor Tadge would see Jarell again.

With new surprise she swallowed. She had tricked a master into rescuing her nursling. She had won! So why did some of the brightness seem to have gone from the day? Hunching her shoulders for the comfort of her rider, she followed Jarell to the river.

Chapter Ten

And the Sky Goddess wept, lamenting, "How can I live without my lover, Iammu the Sea God? Yet how can I forsake my father the sun and the stars my brothers and the ordering of the winds and light that I know, to follow my lover beneath the tides? For there I have no duty, no country, no honor; I would be forever outcast, my roots and roof dependent on the whim of strangers."

Know, oh my children, that for eons she has not Chosen, though between each day and night when she lies on the horizon with her lover the sea, her jealous father Shamash the Sun God consumes them in sunset's flames. For know also, my own, that Not Choosing is also a Choice.

TRANSCRIBED FROM STORYTELLER'S TALE, BY JIEN NAGOYA,
OUTREACH ANTHROPOLOGIST,
GALACTIC CENTRAL REST AND RESEARCH STATION,
QAQQADUM, NORTHERN NAPHAR.

Cassia's back itched. She leaned against a drift log, contemplatively rubbing her good shoulder against the bark. She wondered if she could persuade Tadge to leave this beach by the river and start back to the farm now, before the moons rose and their doubled shadows changed the look of the mountains and of the way home. So far the boy had refused to talk. If only they could be gone before Jarell returned; then she could avoid telling Jarell that she would not go with him to the lowlands.

Her nursling was kicking his heels on the log beside her; she edged out of range. Her bitten shoulder throbbed as if it had been hit by the avalanche. But if she did not acknowledge the pain, she could not die. Ignoring her illogic and the fright that prompted it, she prodded her nursling again. "Shall we wash your cuts in the river? The Lathon is supposed to be healing. . . . Were the slavers very bad?" she burst out when he still did not reply.

The little boy scowled at the red sun sinking and flattening on the smoky western horizon. Only a scarlet bean poised above the

54

purple ramparts of the Fire Mountains. The scent of the river and of growing things breathed through the bright brown dusk. The strengthening brilliance of the river sent scurries of light into the shadows under the trees and the tangled drift logs.

Fiercely Tadge examined a dusty russet stone. He licked it and held the patch of crimson to the light, then dropped it in his chest pocket.

"I hated their food." He glanced up at Cassia, his eyes green with anger. "They slopped it into crusty bowls—didn't even wash them! And when there wasn't enough, and the grown-ups fought over it, the slavers laughed."

"Oh, Tadge! You haven't eaten?" They could wait. She could find some wild food in the forest. They might even stop for something Jarell brought.

"No. I'm hungry now but I ate yesterday. That big musclehead with the yellow hair"—he shot Cassia a defiant look and she swallowed her wince at the term—"he fed me. And kept patting me all over with those ugly gray hands. I told him he'd better stop or I'd throw up on them. Pretending he didn't know the Law!"

Cassia's stomach contracted, her wish to leave forgotten. "He —did he do anything else?"

The child's mouth jerked as if he held back a sob or a laugh. "No. He just smiled." Tadge leered. "Like that. *I* did, though. He was feeding me olyos, see? When he kept shoving it at me I saved up some bites and—and I spit them at him!" Tadge darted Cassia a naughty look, his eyes sparking green and blue in the deepening twilight. "It went *splat* all over him—brown and drippy. So it looked like—well, you know."

Frightened laughter filled Cassia's throat. "And then? What did he do then?"

"Nothing. He just stood up, and up. He—he was like a tree, Cassia." The boy swallowed. "He said, real slow—and he's got such a deep voice—'I'll remember you.'" A stray sunbeam lit the boy's copper lashes and the spatter of freckles on his cheeks.

Cassia gripped her hands until they ached with her need to shelter him, and her knowledge that for his dignity's sake, she must not. "I would have been so scared," she ventured.

"I was." He took a deep breath. "For a little while, anyhow. He's nothing like the beasts at home—not like you, Cassia! All the time I was tied up, I kept thinking about you, and—and looking for you—" Shutting his eyes, he lunged for her and flung his arms around her neck.

She twisted to meet him; fire leaped through her bitten

shoulder. Rage blinded her. She would never forgive Tadge or the lowlander for causing her this anguishs, for causing . . . her death.

"Thanks for getting me," Tadge said into her neck. "But now I—I got to think of something else."

"Think of what?" she asked when the black waves of pain and anger receded and she remembered her purpose, but the little boy only shook his head. "Kateeb, never mind," she said carefully, "we can go home now, or when you've eaten. You'll soon forget—"

"I'm not going back, Cassia. Ever."

"But—but there's so much to do; your father—"

"I mean, can't *you* take me to the lowlands?"

"The lowlands!" First the small man, now Tadge! *I have a place here*, she thought. *I am cared for, my master gives me freedoms another might not, and I have my nursling.* "I— It's too far, and we have no coin. Come, let's find food. Then we'll go home." She jumped up and strode across the beach to the woods. After a moment, the boy trudged after her.

Cassia stood knee-deep in the ferns in the forest's murky shade. She squinted into the last of the sunlight streaming through the rivertrees. Still Jarell had not returned. Impatiently she waited for Tadge to pause for breath as he held forth on a favorite subject.

"And the spacers' ships going over are different shapes, Cassia! Balls, disks, columns—I think the marketplace storytellers are right, they come from different stars. If we went to the lowlands and the spaceport, we could ask them! We could even go see. Don't you want to? They say the spacers free any slaves that can get to them," Tadge coaxed when she continued to snap off fern heads without replying.

Cassia looked at the green dark splashed with amber sunlight. She drew in a breath spiced with loam and pines. She thought how much she wanted to see more of the goddess's creation before becoming One with her—in a sennight? A season? But she could not tell the boy that. Not yet. Perhaps when they were safely home. "Are you ready, Tadge?"

He set down his fern tips and shook his head. "I got to tell you. I can't go back. I found out just before we left the farm. Pa won't let me." Jerkily at first, then faster, he poured out his story.

Tadge was not his, his father had shouted when he forbade him to attend First Rising. The boy had been conceived in the lowlands before his parents met and were hurried into partnering;

his mother had confessed when she lay dying and feared to go down the River of Death weighted by a lie.

"He said every time he looked at me he saw her flaunting red hair and her lying green eyes, and felt befooled all over again. He'd see me sold or Sacrificed before he'd give me another fingerlength of what was his."

"But—but you came early from the goddess's realms. Your mother's shock caused it—we witnessed a public flaying that day. My babe too was born!" She swallowed.

But Tadge was not listening. "Cassia? Is it true what he said: I'm demon spawn and that's why I'm so bad?"

At the sight of the woebegone face at her knee, she consigned conventional doctrine to Ailessu the Wind God. "Oh, no! She was no demon! She was just young, afraid of your father, and heart-yearning for her lowlands." Assuring Tadge that his mother went fully veiled like any Protector of the Unborn and could not have taken Shamash the Sun God as mate, nor could she have borne one of the god's accursed misshapen children, Cassia repeated the stories of the days before his birth. His mother talked to Cassia, she said, not realizing that Cassia was just off the Obedience Drugs and could understand—

"She talked with an accent!" Cassia interrupted herself. "She spoke the way the singer does, every word sharp and clear. That must be why he seemed familiar. Master, do you think they came from the same place?"

Tadge did not answer. He looked past her and scowled.

Stones rattled and she looked up.

The dying light rimmed Jarell's dark hair as he bent over his armload of battered-looking rounds of bread and hacked sausage ends in red and black casings. Purple crunchroots peeked from under one sleeve, their white fringes lacy against his robe; around his neck hung a string of gray and white tear roots.

His robe swayed. Even in the forest Cassia could hear it clunk over the burbling of the shallows. The sour yeasty scent of yiann cut through the river's fishy-wet and the pungence from the fern tips overflowing her spread skirt.

Jarell. Who would own her future? But perhaps she and Tadge could become temple workers. Only, the workers were so thin, so silent . . . *It's not fair,* Cassia thought with a rebellion that belonged to her dreams and shards of memories, *how these little masters' problems are complicating my last precious days!*

With sudden shyness she watched the man who might, after all, be her new master set his spoils on the trunk she and Tadge had vacated. She started to call out, but stopped. Beasts did not speak to adult masters uninvited. The phrases that would tell him where she stood flicked through her head; she saw the route to his feet where she should kneel and await his orders: she did not call, she did not move. She found she did not want to. He cut through her surprise with news.

"The slavers have gone, and in a hurry," he said. "Look what they left! Drying cloths, and foaming-sand too, at their pool upriver."

"That's the man with the knife! Don't let him see I was doing beasts' work!" Tadge's red head appeared among the ferns; he threw his curled fronds into Cassia's outstretched robe.

"He's already seen." Dumping the tips on the pile nearby, Cassia dropped her hem modestly toward her sandals and pushed toward the clearing, sending spores flying into the sun's flat rays. She had forgotten how well the lowlander saw in the dark.

As she and the boy approached, Jarell glanced up from slicing rounds of sausage onto the capsized tree, then looked again. "Highlands fern tips! We shall dine like the Ensai's court tonight. Or we would if we had a cooking pot."

"I've got a firebox." Tadge reached in his sleeve. He had been watching wide-eyed as the lowlander tore off wedges of bread, stuffed them with sausage, and gathered up the crunchroots to wash them. "Cassia can do that, and she can roast our ferns. Go get the stones, Cassia." He pointed to a beach downriver where a past spring flood had heaped rocks.

Jarell looked up swiftly, eyebrow rising.

He snapped his mouth shut when Cassia murmured, "Yes, master." She piled her greens beside the sausage ends, returning her life to normal, her rebellious words unspoken. But some-day. . .

Soon she had a hollow in the sand lined with rocks. The coals at its base drenched the curled greens with fragrant smoke. Her bitten shoulder ached from the digging and the hauling. *Please, Goddess,* she bargained silently, *if I keep Tadge safe, take away the poison.* She knelt by the covering layer of leaves, and watched the wisps curl around their edges, then drift upward through waves of heat to the encroaching shadow. She picked up her turning stick as Jarell came toward her.

He shoved bread and sausage under her nose; in his other hand he sloshed a jug. Pale vapors curled from its mouth. In them, blue sparks wavered upward into the smoke.

Cassia glanced over her shoulder to her little master skipping rocks into the darkening shallows in explosions of light. She looked back at the jug with longing, but shook her head.

"It's all right! Before long you'll be posing as my owner. To Mott with what the youngster thinks, or any small Kakano!"

"No, I— Water is fine." *How can I make him take Tadge to the lowlands, and guarantee his safety there?* she thought. *How can I be sure he will not abandon Tadge if he proves difficult or if I die? He does not love my nursling as I do. No, the temple is best.*

She lifted a leaf; smoke poured out. Shielding her face, she prodded the nearest fern with her stick. It gave a little. Almost done. Raucous whirrs made her look up.

By the river, Tadge had progressed from throwing stones at the ripples to throwing them at Night Eyes of the Goddess—great brown moths swinging through the dusk, their furred wings spread two handspans across, and painted with luminous circles like eyes. When hit they rattled out metallic screams.

Curtly, Jarell told him to stop. A startled Tadge obeyed. "Curse the boy!" the lowlander muttered to Cassia. "Sound travels over water. I look forward to his departure. A child—particularly that one—can only be an encumbrance."

"I can't leave him." Cassia did not dare look at Jarell as she searched for words of explanation about the temple.

Jarell too was silent. Then, as she started to speak: "If he goes with us, he could cost us our freedom! And he's a master. Would you risk your life, your liberty, for one who orders you about? Yes, of course you would," he answered himself. "If you were not content with your slavery, you would not obey me. So. Where the child goes, you go?"

Cassia held her face rigid. *It's not slavery I love, it's Tadge!* she wanted to cry. "The temple—they'll take us," she stammered.

"I can't allow it. I need you. You won't reconsider?"

Heart beating hard, she shook her head. She braced herself for a clout.

"There's no help for it, then. I must attach him." Jarell started up the beach.

Cassia pulled her feet under her. Tadge must not go with the lowlander, it was dangerous! *Goddess, help me find the right words. Remember our bargain!* The smell of singed greenery floated upward.

"The ferns!" Cassia threw off the covering leaves and flipped the juicy tips onto a flat stone, pausing only to blow on her fingers and shake them. Just a few edges had turned brown.

"Who are you?" By the river, Tadge stared belligerently at Jarell, then at the hand that had held a knife to the boy's throat.

Cassia brought the steaming greens to the log. "He's the singer from last night. Master, we could go to the temple." She set down the ferns.

But Jarell was rising from his full court bow. "Allow me to introduce myself. I am Jarell. I regret the incident with the knife, but it was necessary for our escape from those who would retake us. Like you, I have been captive. But now I am on my way to the coast, Qaqqadum, and the sea, where I plan to take passage on a starship, outward bound." Dark eyes smiled with great charm into wide blue-green ones. "Would you, perhaps, care to come along?"

Tadge stared up at Jarell. "You'd help me get out of here?" He caught his breath. "To the stars? Me?" Ending in a squeak, he sprang toward the lean, elegant figure, arms wide, and yelled, "Sure!"

Gently, the lowlander caught the boy's wrists and held him at arm's length. He winked at Cassia, who rushed into speech.

"That was foul! You didn't tell him—" Controlling her fury, she said to Tadge, "It's not safe, Master. Your father might take us back. He needs us to strip the bark off the logs, haul it to the temple tanneries, sort the seed grain. Or if we went to the temple, you wouldn't miss priest's school."

Tadge exchanged a conspiratorial look with Jarell. "I don't care about being safe, Cassia. And I sure don't care about any old lessons." Longing naked on his small face, he raised it to the twilight sky where a single star trembled, a light on the golden horizon beneath the translucent, darkening green. It reflected, tiny, in his eyes.

Beside him, Jarell cleared his throat. "I can do little about your farm's spring rites, but as for his studies, *I* can teach him." His lips twitched as he glanced from Tadge's dismay to Cassia's open mouth. "I doubt it will too greatly tax even my meager resources. Come!" He clapped Tadge on the shoulder and as quickly released him. "If it's her price for the trip? And if I promise that the moment your studies bore you, we'll stop?"

"Well . . . I get to say?"

Jarell nodded, his face solemn. Two pairs of eyes, one light, the other dark, looked expectantly at Cassia.

"I—I—" *Oh, goddess, I said all the wrong things, what have I done? I must stay with my nursling.* Fright at the thought of her short but suddenly wide future made Cassia turn away from her persecutors. Neither one stopped her as she walked ever more quickly upriver, dismayed to find her distress lit by a small, growing spark of anticipation.

Chapter Eleven

Naphar's moons are as stable as its civilizations. Shaped from dust ringing the newly formed planet, its two moons coalesced over the tidal bulges they helped cause. In return, the tidal bulges' greater gravitational pull locked the moons into place. This stability, called the McDonough Effect, is tested once each century when Naphar is passed closely by an escaped moon. For some years that dark body's approach causes erratic behaviour in the planetary moons, until for a season they become geosynchronous, then wander behind Naphar to be forced into parallel orbits while the dark moon passes. Released, they reverse their behavior, returning over the years to their stations above the tidal bulges.

Their extraordinary performance is reflected in northern Napharese society: individually flexible, it has not changed for millennia. The dark moon's influence may actually account for Naphar's lack of global war, the traditional reason for cultures' eradication and rebirth. Thus, nature provides battle's periodic destruction, population control, weakening of the social fabric, and chance for individual advancement and adventure. Whether the cosmic engineers terraforming Naphar planned these social consequences and deliberately fine-tuned its moons' orbits...

> "Astronomical Determinants of Social Change."
> Paper given by Orla t'Negri,
> Third Astro-Historical Congress, Luna City, Sol III.

A last ray of light cut through the water's brown depths. In them a shadow slipped, became a speckled fish darting to safety beneath one of the boulders that dammed the bathing pool. Cassia gazed into the amber ripples below her and moved her knees on the log. She pushed back her hair that a last flat ray transmuted to a copper and gold screen, and glanced with longing at the slavers' forgotten drying cloths. They fluttered on nearby branches like displaced spirits from Arob Shamsi, the shadow land beneath the setting sun.

An itch made her glance over her shoulder—beasts must not draw attention to their Different bodies in a master's presence. Seeing no one, she gave her hip a long, satisfying scratch. Soon other prickles clamored from her scalp to her toes.

She bent to rub between her sandal's thongs; she breathed in the cool breath. She drew her hand through the ripples. The water was warm—or at least warmer than the farmyard's well. Light coalesced around her fingers. When she pulled them out, it dripped from her nails in fiery splashes that lit the green mossy underside of the log.

She glanced from it to the other end of the pool. Beneath a fallen limb stood a clay bowl filled with glimmering foaming-sand.

Cassia looked from the bowl to the pool beneath her. Scratching her head vigorously, she listened. She heard only the tumult of the river, the scrabble of a lizard's claws, and its victim's buzz. She was quite alone.

Her lips quirked. Hands flying, she loosed her robe's inner tapes, pulled it over her head, slid out of her undergarments, and dove into the pool.

Cassia floated on her back, watching the sky's afterglow of fragile green flood with purple and spark with stars. Radiance blazed around her wound, nibbling and tingling, lessening its ache. Her workcloth gown hung over a branch, no longer dripping since its rough fibers retained their oils and shed water quickly. Beside it lay her dried and folded undertunic. She was considering getting out of the pool when she heard voices.

"Look! You were right, there's her robe. Ho! Cassia!" Tadge hailed her.

When she answered, footsteps crunched toward her. She spread her clean hair around her as Tadge's head and the lowlander's appeared above the log.

"Oh, prime! I want a swim, too!" Tadge pulled one arm inside his robe, then the other, straining the seams.

"You found the slavers' pool, I see. We wondered when you

were gone so long. Have you any objection to our joining you?" Jarell glanced at the night that turned his face to harsh angles and shadows, and reached for the laces at his throat. The boy hopped beside him, struggling to get his imprisoned arms down to his sides.

Jarell would see her Difference—he would talk no more of freedom. "No! I mean, yes! I'm all through. If you'll wait over there, I'll get out and you can have it."

Jarell backed away, a startled expression in his dark eyes. "Certainly. Come along, Tadge. Modest, by the gods!" Jarell muttered. Grasping one of the red-faced child's empty sleeves, he drew him backward.

"Wait!" the boy said, wriggling to regain his balance. "I don't want to go this way!"

The small man murmured something to him, then called to Cassia, "Enjoy your repast—I hope it meets with your approval." A drying cloth sailed toward her.

Cassia grabbed it, splashed out of the water, and scrambled over a log. Crouching behind it, she swiped at her Different breasts like sand melons, so unlike Tadge's, who was a master, and her own smooth ribs from the days when she had been free. She gave a quick rub between her legs to the Different blond and red fur like a Night Demon's that betrayed a demon's lusts, and her need for the smooth masters' passionless control. At least the priests said they were smooth, and neither Cassia's stern master, nor her glimpses of highlands women cocooned in veils, had hinted otherwise.

Less than half dry, she yanked on her damp robe. Her cheeks burned. She ignored the question in the small man's eyes and her nursling's squeals as he raced, a bare pink streak, to the pool. Turning away from them, she followed the river's glow back to the campsite and lastmeal.

Cassia felt comfortably full as she leaned against a fallen trunk. Her shoulder's ache was little more than a memory as she gazed into streamers of flame backed by the radiant curve of the river, and listened to Jarell talk of the stars.

He looked up, the strong angle of his chin and throat showing a leashed eagerness; his voice held a timbre she had not heard before.

". . . the difference! A culture that does not use its people for labor, pets, or food!" he was saying.

Cassia glanced uneasily at Tadge, his eyes wide and bright with reflected firelight, as he drank in the Kakano's sacrilege.

". . . precise and repetitive work, as well as lifting and hauling —all that is done by machines."

Machines! The goddess forbade machines since machines had brought the colonist gods to Naphar. Their machines had erased the Winds that Circle the Sky so they could no longer protect the plants and people from the full fury of the Sun God; then their machines had carried the gods away from the earthquakes, tidal waves, and storms that followed. The survivors had promised: never again would machines be allowed to ruin Naphar. Cassia lifted her palms to cover Tadge's ears. But the singer had changed to another subject.

"When I was your age, Tadge, I'd beg tales of the spacers; of worlds like Ch'ai, over in the fourth quadrant." He gestured toward the northern pinnacles glistening with starshine. "Living things share consciousness there. Imagine—perfect understanding, from the smallest plant to the highest tree, as well as from the creatures burrowing beneath its roots. You'd never feel alone again." Jarell's gaze settled on Cassia; she felt an unexpected twitch of curiosity about that planet. Expression bland, he nodded as if he had accomplished what he had set out to do.

The fire popped and collapsed with a shower of sparks into red and black embers, as the singer's stories took on the quality and privacy of dreams, and "abomination" became only a whisper from absent day.

". . . machines teach, build, care for children with unruffled tenderness. In one star system they compose mathematical music for one another, write logical poetry, send each other intricate, sharp-edged drawings . . ."

Cassia watched an amber star shoot toward the horizon. *A scoutcraft?* she wondered. *Or the first of the lowlander's meteors —the Burning Tears of Sassurum—that marked spring's end?* Sleepy, content, she stopped listening to Jarell's words and instead thought how the rise and fall of his voice recalled a musician's cadences; she regretted the lost golden-stringed zanglier. In a pause tinged with smoke and the smell of water, she asked idly, "Why don't you sing?"

The night's stillness became intense; only the barkhiders' silver chiming drifted on the rising wind. Cassia turned her head, and the dream broke.

Eyes narrow, Jarell stood. "I sing at no Rabu's command. Not while I'm free." With a swirl of robes and firelight and shadow, he stalked into the forest's night.

Across the burning driftwood, Tadge stared after him, his curls like polished copper in the shifting brightness. "What's the matter with him? He sings. I heard him that first night. And what did he mean, Rabu? You're not. You're just my old beast, you—you're not one of them!" he ended shrilly over a gust of wind and the volcanoes' grumble.

"I look like them," Cassia whispered. She glanced up. And for the first time, she saw fear of her in her nursling's eyes.

A rumbling woke Cassia from a brief sleep. The moons' white curves hung above her, tangled in the river trees. The blot beside them—was it bigger? A gust of wind from the mountains sent the leaves' doubled shadows lurching across her pallet.

Cassia's heart beat faster as she gripped the sticky pine boughs. The roar of falling stones in the hills and the volcanoes' dull explosions competed with the nearer slosh and rattle of the river, but as Jarell had predicted, the banks held firm beneath her and the sleeping Tadge. She licked her lips and made herself relax her hold.

A crackling came from the forest's edge. A hunting lizard?

A blot of shadow separated from the swaying black; Jarell stepped into the moonlight. Of course! Tadge's need and her own returned to her as Cassia blinked away sleep's last gauzy threads and slid to the earth. It heaved; spores fell around her like snow. "I beg pardon," she began.

She had stumbled through less than half the formal phrases when he cried, "Don't!"

She sat back on her heels, pushed her hair off her face, and stared into his eyes, a handsbreadth from her own. His lashes lowered like shields.

"But I forgot a beast may not ask a master anything, and that you do not want to sing. Though I wish you did—I love it so." She waited, wishing her last words unsaid, and stared over his shoulder to the midnight sky. An avalanche blurred a northern peak, its banner of ice white against the stars.

"I know. I knew almost immediately. But I find I have a taste for walking, even in these very inconvenient woods of yours. Also, I wished to be certain that the slavers had not returned. No, sit still, they're gone. The child's safe."

He looked from her to the groaning hills rippling with after-shocks. Voice a little strained, he added, "What's the boy's name, anyway? You never did say, and I have no intention of calling him 'Master.'"

"Tadge. His name is Tadge. I did not say, because you spoke to him before I could!" Cassia heard her voice rise, dropping the grammar and vocabulary of respect. "And I don't just call *him* 'Master,' I even call *you,* 'Master.'" The earth stilled.

Jarell's grin flashed white in the darkness. A barkhider chirped; another answered. Jarell rubbed his palms in the whispering sound of night applause. "So, you do have spirit—and opinions! I thank you for the title, but I think I have not requested it, though I expect to return the compliment once we're in the lowlands. I take it you are coming? So far you have avoided my attempts to secure your promise."

"I—" Cassia jumped up, the barkhiders around her in full choir. She strode to the river, Jarell's footsteps sounding behind her. "What would I do there?" She stared at the horizon where the black clouds above the Fire Mountains flickered crimson, their reflections floating red lozenges on the river's currents; she looked down at her image in the water and saw only her Difference that condemned her to slavery. "I'm stupid, lazy, ugly—I could not earn coin."

"Who told you that?" Jarell picked up a stone, weighed it, and threw. "You can retrain yourself," he said more moderately as it spun into the shallows, and light fountained. Smaller explosions skipped toward the rapids. "The temple schools will help you there. Though much is wrong with the goddess and her priestesses, they are dedicated to Change and Choice, after all. And what of your past? Does it no longer interest you?"

"I . . . yes!" Cassia stooped; her fingers curved around flat, smooth edges. "To have a name, two of them, like a person, not a slave or a child. But more than anything, I want . . ." Her throat constricted and in her turn, she threw.

Like a Moon Screamer pursuing Night Demons, her stone skimmed the shallows, touched with a splash of light, rose, and skated into the rapids, to be lost in their confusion of brilliance and shadow.

"I want to remember!" She thought of the tall nameless warmth of long ago that she was almost sure had loved her. The familiar rage enfolded her at the One who had snatched that love away. She pushed it down. "I want to know where I belong." She saw Jarell staring at her clenched fists and blurted out defensively, "And Tadge can't travel alone."

Cassia looked at the moons and their lightless companion, sentinels of destruction and rebirth. Could they somehow transmute her too? No, of course not. Her Difference lay in her blood and bone as did her looming death. But for the moment, she felt well. Hope sang thin and sweet through her resignation and fear. "Goddess forgive me," she whispered. "Yes! I'll come."

Chapter Twelve

Dear friend, you must discover who has started these rumors you report: that the approaching body is the face of the Dark God; that after this passing he will rule the goddess as he rules her daughters, the dawn and dusk moons...and related nonsense.

You and I know that the Dark One is black because our fierce young sun showers the methane and other gases in the atmosphere of this escaped moon with corpuscular, X-ray, and ultraviolet radiation. This results in a perpetual snow of the dark organic compounds—from which life can come, not destruction!—that cover its surface.

The creator of the fantasies you mention is worse than a mischief-maker. Already the people fear quake and tide damage. They are made uneasy also by the renaissance of the Salimar cult, the well-subsidized training of its soldier priests, and its preaching the overthrow of the goddess, its wish to replace her with the Dark God and his priests. Thus, the gossip you describe is not only dangerous, it is treasonous. So long as it is believed that the Dark One's approach is evil and deadly and releases similar forces within the human heart and mind...

> CONFIDENTIAL SCROLL FROM PHIKOLA EN,
> HIGH PRIESTESS OF SASSURUM IN QAQQADUM,
> TO HER CHIEF UNRAVELLER OF SECRETS.

Cassia moaned when at last she slept, the rush of the river in her ears. She dreamed of pale eyes searching, the mind behind them reaching, touching. Not her, but the man asleep on the pallet of boughs beside hers, a hand on his chest pocket.

Come. Bring back to me what you have stolen. The blond giant's words thrust into Jarell's mind where Cassia heard them.

With Jarell, Cassia winced. *For the thing you hold is mine as you too are mine.*

With Jarell, Cassia suffered the despair that pushed him from his pallet, and drew him, still sleeping, toward the river.

Outrage knifed through Cassia's dreaming mind; within her once more, the green shadow stirred. *No!*

The invading consciousness turned to her in surprise. She fell toward a gap in its defenses—and plummeted through the gap. She looked out through Salimar's eyes.

He stared down at the slavers working in another part of the forest where pines were few and the leaves of the many ghost trees hung on older, stiffer stems. His minions replaced the poison lost with his stolen pouch.

With Salimar, Cassia watched the troops grind and press blackened seeds to remove their oils, then soak the resulting cakes of contact poison in salted water, filtering it through silken cloths held gingerly by the hems.

He had always been alone, Salimar thought as he sat on a drift log by the southern Lathon, weary to the marrow from controlling his rebellious soldiers. He knew nothing of what men called friendship; he could only command. He remembered . . .

Abandonment by his parents so long ago that all that remained of them was a fragrance, a snatch of song . . . the brief, bright days of his childhood running naked on the Fire Mountains' vivid slopes, companioned by the shy tree hiders, and flying lizards like guileless, winged jewels, delighting with him in his growing ability to guess their thoughts and sometimes to guide them . . .

"Dread lord, the first poison cakes are ready for parching; will you choose one on whom to test them?" The firelight reflected red in the old priest's eyes.

I will test them on you! Salimar wanted to howl, *you who wrenched me from my hills to lead your cult against the mind-speaking priestesses of Sassurum; who coaxed and bribed and reasoned with me to no avail, then put me in a box alone until I wept and broke and learned your ugly spitting tongue and took your Dark God and his cause and name; who brought me to your pallet with promises of love when all you wished from me was power, and who led me into this endless cold and lonely dark. You, whom one day I will kill!*

But not yet. The old man was still useful. It was he who had told Salimar of the slavers' mutiny, he who helped order the slavers now that Salimar could no longer use the Mindstone to increase his mental strength. For Salimar's only aid now came from its lodestone, the ring that had held the sacred Stone.

"Choose whom you like." The blond giant waved away the priest, a spark of anticipation warming his belly.

Behind Salimar's eyes Cassia watched, unable to move, as the chosen soldier struggled in his companions' hold and the priest scratched him with the poison.

The man clawed his mouth and throat as if it burned; staggering blindly, he gasped, "Water! Help . . . me." He retched. Gobbets of olyos shot from his mouth and nose, spattering the troops, then surges of yellow curds until at last only green slime dribbled from his lips. He clutched his belly; moaning, he writhed in the dust. Bloody feces gurgled down his legs and robe. The other men drew closer and reached for the moon. Above them the Dark One hung beside the growing moons.

"You can't have him . . . he's mine!" Salimar rasped. Reluctantly the rest moved back; beyond them the priest signed dedication to the Dark God. Not wanting to breathe for the stench, Cassia bent with the giant, felt him grab the man's slippery thighs and spread his buttocks with his thumbs. Salimar paused, excitement beating in his loins. Then as the death god shook his bones in the other's throat, Salimar plunged into the man's hot slickness.

Horror jolted Cassia. Wide-eyed, she returned to her place on the island by the sleeping Jarell and Tadge. Her lids closed. Salimar's grip on her senses pulled her back . . .

She could neither watch nor listen as, satisfaction slowing his words, he told the priest, "The poison's good enough," and the slavers hauled away the body.

"Set the cakes in the drying pans and assign someone to stoke the fire all night," Salimar rumbled on. "In the morning, before we march, the cakes can be ground and screened and ground again. Meanwhile you may work another poison pouch for me from the kerchiefs in my pack. And a funnel so that touching the poison will not kill more of my Things. As for the rest of my faithless minions . . ."

A whisper entered Cassia's darkness. *He and the others are wrong, my daughter, as many of my children are wrong. But they are still my children, as are you. And in the end, it matters little how you come to me for healing and to be reborn.*

The goddess's stern comfort dissolved the edges of Cassia's shock and unwanted self-knowledge. For, goddess help her, during one shuddering moment she had joined in Salimar's pleasure. Her scalp prickled as he ordered the slavers, "You will search the highlands for my Stone and the ones who took it from me. And when my Foreseeing clears and I direct you to them . . ."

Like talons, Salimar's nails drew blood from his palms as his peace fell away and inside him he screamed for the Mindstone, and the one who shared it and its addictive evil dreams.

Chapter Thirteen

And when Lagash the Wanderer woke, his robe and hair were stiff with salt, and strange beings with strange garments and manners and speech surrounded him. He had washed ashore on a far northern island, the Papermakers of that place told him with signs. They had found him while gathering the fibers and stiffened foam caught on the marsh grass after a storm.

He stayed many sennights on those sands, shaking off his bitterness, harvesting fiber and foam, gleaning it of shells, washing it, pressing it onto screens where the sheets green with algae dried in the sun, then cutting them into scrolls of the sea paper we use for impermanent messages and drawings and the efforts of children. And while Lagash the Wanderer labored, the goddess's peace warmed in him like yiann, and the Chief Screenmaker's daughter, with hair like moonlight and night-colored eyes, taught him her tongue, and much else besides.

> TALE OF LAGASH THE WANDERER, FOUNDER OF CITIES.
> RECORDED DURING WINTER NET-MAKING IN QISK,
> A FISHING VILLAGE NORTH OF QAQQADUM,
> BY JIEN NAGOYA, OUTREACH ANTHROPOLOGIST,
> GALACTIC CENTRAL REST AND RESEARCH STATION,
> QAQQADUM, NORTHERN NAPHAR.

Cassia opened one eye. Above her a green and gold flutter of leaves latticed the morning's shell of fragile blue. Once more Shamash the Sun God had risen from the goddess's dark loins, yawned, and exhaled light and color across the void to re-create the sky, his daughter.

Under Cassia's shoulders and hips, branches rasped as she squinted into the horizontal rays fanning through the pines on the bluff. Smokes climbed through them; between the insubstantial pillars, brightly patched robes swirled above children's bare feet. They darted around cooking tripods, baled trade goods, stacked pots, packs, and barrows.

Awake now to the aroma of boiling meseq and the sizzle of sausages, Cassia felt a touch on her bitten shoulder—the touch tightened and shook her.

Her back felt incandescent with pain. So, last night's respite from the Night Demon's wound was only that. Cassia bit back her disappointment and blinked upward. Tadge looked down at her. The sun laid white fire on his copper tangles.

Small boys and girls crowded behind him, their grins contrasting with the black stares of lizards peering from their ragged collars and black curls, or clinging to their scratched wrists and ankles.

"Cassia, the potmenders are here!" Tadge said. "And it's the Dajo's tribe, only he won't let me tell Jarell we know them." A boy nudged Tadge. "They want me to go fishing—they'll teach me how to charm lizards! Only, would that Jarell leave without me?"

The potmenders. They had cures, and found more on their travels. Of course, brewing them could take time. "We could catch him up in a day or two."

"No! Pa can be here by nightfall! I'll ask Jarell."

"Wait, where's the Dajo?"

"With him." Tadge and the children hurried across the beach. Before the bluff, Jarell and a white-haired man talked by a fire, their backs to Cassia. Both stood a head taller than the potmenders scattered among the boulders and the logs, eating, hammering barrow wheels, or carrying washing to the shallows where, robes kilted high, they pounded it with rocks and foaming-sand.

As Cassia watched, she drew her hair over her shoulder and combed it across her breast with her fingers, her mind clearing of the night's strange dreams. Jarell faced Tadge; the man with white hair also turned, his eyes very blue in his brown, seamed face.

The Dajo! Cassia divided her hair for braiding. She jerked in the first few plaits. Her lips curved, anticipating the old man's beaming welcome.

By the fire, Tadge pointed to her. Across the driftwood and smokes, the old man's gaze pinned her.

"D-Dajo?" she faltered, raising her hand in tribal greeting.

Still unsmiling, the old man started toward her. The others followed, the potmender children slowly stroking their lizards.

Cassia glanced from Tadge's scowl to her hands, knotting braids as they had for thousands of mornings of conscious slavery. *Jarell told my nursling not to go,* she thought. *But last night he called us free.*

She paused; then undid the plait she had begun.

She was spreading her hair on her shoulders as if the goddess had unbonded her for festival, when Jarell and the Dajo stepped out of the shafting sun. Pollen drifted through its wide, flat beams thick with smoke and flying drops from the river.

"Little Flower!" The old man's yellowed teeth gleamed. "So it *is* you!"

"Dajo! I greet you with a daughter's joy. I ask help, advice—"

"Hah! Enough of your ritual requests! It is my help that your, ah, fellow traveler here has refused. So. Come to my fire. Drink! Eat! I bring news. We have much to discuss."

Cassia sucked in a breath. "But first—" She gulped at her daring and tried again: "Perhaps Tadge could go with the others while we talk?"

Behind the Dajo, the singer's eyes narrowed.

"My own suggestion," the old man said.

"No, there's no time!" Jarell burst out.

But already the Dajo was whistling, and shouting in his harsh language.

At the signal, Tadge clambered over the drift logs. His eyes were bright with excitement as he hastened downriver after his companions.

The Dajo lifted a smoky pot from the embers of his cooking fire and poured a cup of the dark red brew. As Cassia knelt between him and Jarell, the old man undid a pouch at his waist and carefully shook honey crystals into her drink. At last he handed it to her. She blew on the smoking fluid, savoring the aroma of 'seq and burning driftwood carried on the warm breeze.

"Cassia?" Jarell's dark eyes held a peculiar expression. "You two know each other?"

"Oh yes! Since I first gained consciousness. He taught me to read."

She told of the Dajo's tribe quartering in her shed. Picking up one of the tribe's bookscrolls, she had unrolled it, then asked in surprise why anyone would keep records of lizard tracks, and how they trained the creatures to walk in such straight lines. "They laughed, but then the Dajo showed me how the tracks made my name—my first lesson."

She glanced down. She would not—could not—speak of her

first meeting with the Dajo, almost two hands of cycles past when she had awakened to her adult self, naked, in the highlands breeding pens, her last memory her abandonment on the Rock of Sacrifice. She had been weeping and incoherent when she had heard a voice cry, "Stop!" She had looked up to see an old man fighting toward her, wielding his staff among the enormous snarling creatures she would learn to call beasts.

It had been his turn at paternity witnessing, he told her as he threw his cloak around her and called for the tablets to declare her unfit, her name to be chiseled from the list of public breeders on the stele in the marketplace. She would never go to the pens again, he had promised, and she had not.

Now Cassia huddled closer to the Dajo's fire and sipped. The drink scorched down, spicy and bitter and laced with the crystals' syrupy sweetness.

The old man cuffed Jarell's shoulder. "It is as I said! We Anadajoie know everyone. We see all. We hear everything, but speak only when we please. We go"—his arm's sweep included the sky as well as the horizon—"everywhere."

"Nice for you." Jarell turned to Cassia. "I was just telling your old friend, here, that your master commissioned me to deliver Tadge without delay to Qaqqadum's temple school, and you to market before your mind flickered out from too many cycles of Obedience Drugs. I should have remembered, I talk too much."

The old man peered under a lid; steam rose into the sunlight. He dipped out a cup of simmered grain as he shook his head at Jarell. "No, my friend, it was a good lie! You were not to know. And you have proved you have the dishonesty this one lacks and that you will both need to survive."

"Thank you." Raising an eyebrow, Jarell took the cup.

The Dajo offered Cassia a similar one and a wedge of bread, pulled a twist of soft green sea paper from his sleeve, and thumbed it. "As for you, Little Flower." Crystals showered onto Cassia's simmered grain. She dipped her bread through a sparkling crust of salt, "Your master's rage at your flight is equaled only by his dread of your neighbors' opinion should he neglect his prayers to bring you back." The old man's chin and nose met in a grin. "But to the less pious he offers gold for your capture and that of your companions, as does a lowlands priest, tall as a god and as beautiful—except his hands are lizards' claws."

"Ah. Gold." Voice even, Jarell touched his chest pocket. "I can outbid them, I believe. Do you speak for your tribe?"

The old man drew himself up. "Am I not the Anadajo? Or Dajo to the Little Flower, here?"

Stopping her chewing, Cassia waited for a tirade against bribery like that in the Dajo's bookscrolls. She heard only the river's many voices, the snap of the fire, and the sluggish bubbling of the grain.

"Then look," Jarell said into the impossible silence.

On his palm, firecloth fell away from a clear stone laced with cracks. A ray lit it; in its gelatinous center, something moved. "The gem rids itself of the sun's energy in the form of coherent light," Jarell said softly. "It projects it on the smoke to form a natural holograph of fire." His fingers opened; sun flooded the stone. The smoke and pollen thickening the morning air vibrated with black and purple flames licking upward from the gem. Sheaves of orange wove through them in a tapestry of flame.

"A flame gem. And a fine one." Beyond the old man, the wind in the pines hummed accompaniment to the potmenders' cries and laughter.

Jarell's closing fingers shadowed the stone; the brightness in the air above it trembled to a green flicker, died to the blue of a mountain tarn, then faded until, once more, the stone was only a cracked clear rock. He wrapped it in the firecloth.

The Dajo teetered back on his heels. His blue eyes glittered behind his white lashes. "These are registered with the stone cutter's guild in Qaqqadum. They are less valuable if stolen."

"Unless they can be smuggled to the spacers for their experiments with light," Jarell agreed. "But this was a gift from a . . . a grateful patron. I will scribe the papers over to you."

"Patron." The Dajo scratched in his white stubble. His glance traveled from Jarell's high-arched feet in flimsy sandals, and his somewhat clinging robe, to the smooth curve of Jarell's hair so black it glinted blue in the sun. Last, the Dajo looked at Jarell's sweep of lashes and the flush creeping along his beardless jaw.

"Patron." Jarell lifted his chin. "Granted, I may not be a mother's preferred companion for her gently-reared daughter, but then, this beast has no mother who cares for her. Has she?"

The Dajo stopped scratching.

Cassia held her breath. Now the Dajo would explode in righteous anger, offer Cassia a home—

He snatched the stone. "I like you. Done!" Whacking the singer on the back, he stowed the wadded firecloth in his sleeve. "Only, for this, we do more. We build you a boat!"

"But—"

"Hsst! You tell of sailing the Western Islands, and the fjords above Qaqqadum—you will know how to use our gift. I go! We finish in the winking of an eye. Or perhaps by afternoon."

"I haven't sailed since I was a child, and the time it will take to build—"

But the Dajo was striding away, shouting orders.

Jarell's mouth tightened. "I will not allow that old fool to dribble away this day and another and another while my owner hunts me. He is near. I am minddeaf but I have felt his touch too often to mistake it. We must leave now. Last night I dreamed—"

"I dreamed, too." Cassia stared into her cooling 'seq. But it had been just a dream. As had been her belief in the Dajo. Now only Tadge had not betrayed her. Tadge. She shook her head. "My master needs this time with the children. He's been so lonely."

Jarell set his face close to hers. "And I need my life! If this is what the boy wants, leave him. Come with me." 'Seq spiced Jarell's breath. Between his lashes lay her twin faces, bright with sun.

She swallowed; she sat back on her heels. "I can't. Besides" —her voice firmed—"whatever else the Dajo is, he's not a fool. If he says he can build a boat in an afternoon, he can. I have heard," she added carefully, "that sorcery like your owner's cannot follow over water."

"Nonsense!" But Jarell's lashes lowered. "Very well. I'll wait until afternoon. Then, whether or not the boat and the boy are ready, you and I go."

Cassia bent her head and told herself not to smile. She had won time—for Tadge, and for herself to find a cure.

Chapter Fourteen

For the Anadajoie were old when even the gods were young. Our island refuge destroyed by the Great Mother's anger, we must ever wander, ever atoning for our Great Wrong; outcast forever from the salt tides, when even our name means People of the Sea.

ANADAJOIE LAMENT.

* * *

The noon sun poured light between the spindly trees lining the river. Cassia's question beat in her, still unasked. She squinted along the old man's finger to a pointed rectangle of logs bobbing in the shallows. Potmenders splashed around it, inflating waxed lizard skins and lashing them beneath the raft.

"No, no, Little Flower," the old man answered her protest that she could not accept the precious hides, "you only borrow! When you reach the lowlands, give them to a tribe going upriver—they will return them to us. Always the Anadajoie travel so."

Behind the old man, sweating potmenders trooped down from the bluff, calling to the Dajo in their strange sharp tongue. The mast was ready, he translated as he led her across the beach and into the forest's dappled shadows.

When they emerged from a stand of ghost trees, he halted Cassia before a torchpine. By its stump lay the felled trunk stripped of its branches and bound with a few ropevines. "Where are the rest of the pulling ropes?" the Dajo asked, "and your halter?"

The boat was nearly finished; Cassia must not wait longer to ask her question. She took a steadying breath, then plunged. "The Anadajoie are such an old people: you travel, you gather knowledge from many nations, you build boats." She glanced downhill, where men balanced on tripods, binding rivertree trunks into arches for the stern shelter. Her heart beat faster. "You have remedies, even for. . ."

The Dajo paused in kicking the drifts of ghost tree bark in a vain hunt for the missing vines. "For what, Little Flower?"

"For . . . for Night Demon poison?"

He thumped his fists onto his hips. "Hah! So even you believe those old tales! We Anadajoie brought no secret potions from our sunken island kingdom. Only Those Who Come By Night—the lowlands healers—can reverse death and the Night Demons' changes. And should you find one, and that one is willing, the price may be more than you wish to pay. For healers always cure, but they always collect their high fee. In coin if you have it, or your freedom, or, some say, your life blood."

Death. Certain death, unless she could get to the lowlands. Cassia's lungs seemed stuffed with furbush spinnings. When she could speak again, she called, "Wait! Are you sure—"

But the Dajo was hurrying away. "I tell the others you are ready—and to bring more vines!"

"These will do," Cassia said, but to herself, for he was gone.

She knelt by the mast; ghost tree bark fluttered into the air. Her nostrils clogged with the bitter scent of loam. Soon she would be one with it. Ah, goddess, no! To feel her hands and feet cooling, and watch the world darken as the frightened blood pooled around her stuttering heart! Anguish swelled in Cassia like tears. "Help me, goddess," she whispered.

And the hairs on her nape rose, for behind her a presence seemed to form like smoke.

There is another side to death, my daughter.

Cassia drew in the scent of cold earth and decaying leaves. And she seemed to watch her transparent bones and flesh sift down, down, through the soil and rock of Naphar, her pulses slowing to match the surge of volcanoes and seas, her breath sighing with the wind, from the waves to the ice of the highlands' peaks. She dreamed that her spirit huddled in the rock and pale roots of Naphar, gaining substance and strength in the long unchanging dark. It uncurled; through the wheeling centuries it drifted upward, gathering cartilage and sinew from the warp and woof of the world to emerge at last, reborn.

This is my promise, my daughter, the smoke whispered, then thinned and blew away on the warm spring air.

A little comforted, Cassia looked up at the sound of footsteps and a burst of laughter.

Jarell came toward her. Surrounding him were potmender women carrying ropevines and giving him sparkling glances. As they dropped their green burdens, they scattered toward the river, calling, "Come, help haul the mast."

Something in Cassia twisted as Jarell smiled after the invitation in the women's fluid walks. Then a branch cracked behind him, and he whirled.

Cassia followed his stare. She had forgotten their shared danger. At any moment she might see the slavers' jingle of mail, Jarell's avenging tall master, his waxed curls on his shoulders like stacked gold coins . . . A beetle whirred; insects clicked. Peace. She glanced up, braced for her new master's jeers at her fright.

Eyes blank, Jarell lowered himself to the brown winter leaves and hid his face in his hands. So: all this day he too had been afraid—not of death but of a return to slavery and his master.

As Cassia slid out of sight, her foot scraped the ghost tree bark; white fountained into the air.

Jarell looked up, saw the flurry, and her. He shut his eyes, then laughed shortly. "You can get up. The show's over."

She blushed. *He looks tired.*

"Am I so fascinating, or are these encounters all accidents?" He stood.

"I'm sorry, I'd never spy—I didn't mean to see you."

"Don't apologize all the time." He picked up a ropevine and stripped its leaves. "Actually, it's rather restful, having one person with whom one needn't pretend." He began twisting the vine into a halter. "That's as good a definition of a friendship as any, perhaps. We have a long journey ahead. It will be easier if we're not at odds. So shall we? Be friends?"

Cassia stared at him—and potmenders surrounded them, shoving wreathes on her head and Jarell's, impaling more on the mast. She started to rise.

"Don't get up or I can't reach you. Well?"

Warmth from his body touched her face, her throat. Color stained his cheeks. *Jarell, blushing?*

Friends—with a beast! "I—all right." She felt oddly breathless as his color returned to normal and he motioned in a proprietary way for her to raise her arms; he slid the green sappy vines over them. She took her place at the head of the mast.

The Dajo's shouts of "Pull!" bumped the log onto the beach. A jug of songfruit pressings was opened; as the released vapors rose, blue lights winked like stars over the pines.

Downriver, the children straggled toward the smoking pits. All carried fish. Puzzled, Cassia saw Tadge did, too, but he was scowling. The Dajo called, "Heave!" and she forgot the boy.

The raft was almost finished; few earthquakes had halted the work. As the potmenders pulled the mast upright, helped by the ropevines at its tip, the mast drew wobbling circles on the afternoon sky.

Cassia squinted upward, her heart pounding. She grabbed a breath—it tasted of broiling fish and smoke. She blinked sweat from her eyes and hauled harder on her vine.

"A line's breaking!" someone screeched. "'Ware!"

A humming swish; a great whip cracked her bitten shoulder. Pain sprouted through her; before her eyes, a black lake spread across the sun.

"She dropped her line— Ill omen!"

Someone cursed.

Cassia was supported to a log by anonymous arms. The fish she had eaten heaved in her belly.

When the potmenders had twisted the many vines into four ropes stretching from the tip of the mast to the raft's bow, both sides, and the stern, Jarell and the Dajo hurried toward Cassia.

"What is it, Little Flower? I think you are more than hurt!" Beyond the old man squatting by her feet, young men and women unpegged the green square of sail they had woven.

"You're still in pain. Why?" Jarell's glance raked her shoulder and the arm she cradled.

If she told him, he would leave her. "I'm fine." She got up and stretched her mouth in a smile. "See?"

He looked at her skeptically.

Footsteps pelted toward them. Tadge scrambled over the log. Grease and a dab of honey smeared his mouth. "I saw what happened, Cassia! Poor old beast, want to hold my lizard till you feel better?"

"Oh, Tadge, you found one! Have you named it? Him? Her?"

"No—I can never tell with a lizard. But look, Cassia! They showed me how to charm it."

He thrust out his fist squirming with a tail and claws. Opening his fingers, he stroked a blue, featureless belly. The lizard jerked its tail, then let it dangle. It sprawled on its back, fragile legs wide.

Tadge giggled. "See? He loves it. Anybody can do anything with him now."

"Don't!" Jarell's voice was harsh. "Keep it or let it go, but—don't!"

"Sure, Jarell." Eyes wide, Tadge spilled the creature onto the log. "It's only a lizard. It doesn't really like me. It'll run off in a little, just like all the others."

The torchpine smoldered on the bluff, ready to flame and erase all evidence of the raft. The Dajo led Cassia and Jarell to the river. "Night nips soon at the heels of day; if you wish to make camp before sunset, you must sail now."

They splashed into ripples of reflected blue shot with sunlight. Cassia's anxiety melted into pleasure. The water felt cool and silky and it led to a world of possibility she had thought closed to her.

She sat on the raft, excitement drumming in her. As the potmenders cast off, she scarcely listened to the old man.

"These are troubled times. You could possibly have chosen a better moment for your journey. In the capital, a sacred relic is lost. Without it, in this spring of springs, fear will call back the festivals' ancient craving for blood." Glancing at Cassia's inattentive smile, the Dajo pressed her knuckles to his forehead. "But it is more than time that you left.

"You will do well!" he shouted from the bank as Cassia waved, and Jarell, who was on the stern, frowned at a lowlands invention there, a handle connected to a steering paddle underneath the raft. "Remember only that a river is not an ocean, you have no keel, and the nearness of the banks allows little room for error," the old man called. "But it also makes it very hard to get lost."

The potmenders pushed them out of the shallows. "I'll keep it in mind," Jarell yelled over the din. "Old fool," Cassia heard him mutter.

"Hah! To be young once more," the Dajo called as they swung toward the deep, swift current in the center of the river, "and adventurous, and never, never to heed advice."

Above them the torchpine burst into a sheaf of flame; the raft whirled around the bend, and the encampment was gone.

Chapter Fifteen

So the colonist gods, oh my children, continued their sweep through the galaxy: terraforming, gene-splicing, re-creating their cindered world. Choosing not to acknowledge that its thread and their own had been snapped by the Weavers of Destiny. Here they selected, as always, a G-type star, but one closer to an F-type in luminosity. Thus our moon-bright nights are as light as Sol III's far northern winter days.

In their arrogance, the colonist gods wished to temper the sunlight that produced free radicals in their ailing bodies: they tried to deepen and widen the Winds That Circle the Sky which the off-worlders, my own, call the Van Allen Belts.

But something went wrong, as often happens with those who depend on machines, and instead the Winds scattered. More radiation flooded our planet, so women who Choose to bear children must go veiled against Shamash the Sun God's advances.

Drowsing in the hot sunshine, Cassia leaned against the mast. Above her, Ailessu the Wind God filled the square green sail and blew the raft toward the lowlands.

"Look!" Tadge said from behind her. "Another road of the gods. Can we climb up and explore? I'm tired of never stopping to see anything. We don't even get off the raft to sleep."

Cassia glanced over his head to the volcanoes' hazy purple cones towering above the river; she peered into the green hung with flowers that swathed the volcanoes lower slopes. At the water's edge another clearing of red clay slid by, this one planted with scrawny songfruit vines.

They were sailing along the Fire Mountains now. Between the boles of the huge trees, Cassia's gaze followed Tadge's finger to a crumbling road that ended, perhaps, at an underground palace, one collapsed millennia ago when the goddess expelled the colonist gods from Naphar.

A strand of Cassia's hair tangled in her lashes. She pushed aside the lock that two sennights of sun and water had bleached to white shot with reddish gold, and lost interest in the flotilla she had been watching on the other side of the river. She and Jarell had looked for the tall heads of slavers, but agreed that it seemed made up only of small highlanders on their way to a partnering. The pillars of moving veils on the women's raft made no sound, as was proper, but on the men's raft that towed them, every *thump* of the drums and *screech* of the flutes drifted across the water.

Behind Cassia, Jarell winced and steered closer to the bluff and its deep, slow current. "No, we will not leave the raft," he said to Tadge. "I sympathize, but we do go ashore to bathe, and scout the river ahead. That should suffice."

"Why not? The Dajo says the potmenders climb up to the roads of the gods. He's found pieces of statues—and once, gold!"

As they argued, Cassia shut her eyes against the glare. The sun seemed brighter each day that they journeyed south.

"That road, if it is a road, would take a hand of days to reach.

And though it's difficult to believe in danger up here, we must get to the lowlands, and soon. These fair winds can't last forever." Jarell flexed his shoulders as if they cramped, and glanced back at the northern peaks nicknamed the Weathermakers, now a distant glitter against the blue. "But if you're bored, tell me about the roads' builders. And mind the cadences."

"Oh, *legends*. What use are they? I know." Tadge scowled and mimicked Jarell's precise speech: "On a scout ship, how can I understand what other worlds believe if I have not practiced by learning about my own?"

Jarell appealed to Cassia. "Do I really sound like that?"

She swallowed a smile, shook her head, and breathed in the fishy breeze that carried the scent of loam and leaves, and the sweet hot smell of the raft's bark.

Beside her, Tadge waved at a band of potmenders trundling their barrowsaround a curve in the riverside path, crossed his legs in a storyteller's pose, and began.

"... phrases to sing you ... I understand the lightning ..."

Cassia's eyes closed in one of her increasingly frequent naps. As she seemed to drift away from the knock and slap of waves against the logs, she heard Jarell's clear tones giving the off-worlder's explanations of the myths and history Tadge preferred to skim over or hurriedly chant.

"Colonist gods mixed their seed with Naphar's first mammals' ... created the large Rabu and small Kakano ... labored for the gods beneath Naphar's fierce sun ... gods poisoned by a metal in our creatures' flesh ... neutralized by their machines ... Machines broke ... Hungry, the gods demanded their Rabu and Kakano children for their tables. . . ."

Cassia slid into a trance that was not quite sleep; Jarell's voice merged with that of the wind and the waves.

"... gods gave their Kakano children their own sight; those children have their small size from their other parents, Naphar's diurnal mammals ... From the gods the Rabu inherited great height, but the mammals' dimmer vision ...

"Myth says, 'The angry goddess threw the gods and their machines back to the stars. They left behind their Rabu and Kakano children who, like the gods, their parents, could not eat the native life.'"

"'Blinded mothers wept over monstrous babes,'" Tadge interrupted Jarell with relish as Cassia nodded toward dreams. "'They staggered, convulsed, and died. We gave up the hunt, husked our grain ...' Um—"

"'Deprived of protein, since our plants have none'—not enough to utilize, anyway. When the 'gods' left they took their extracting machines," Jarell prompted.

"Oh, yes! 'A new death found us. We grew lizard skin . . . hair striped and loosened . . . we bloated and again we died . . . We found the gods' own cure. Through ritual Sacrifice, we eat each other.'"

Jarell's chanting became a pallet-song:

> "From the slain god's body, Kumar drained the blood away,
> Mixed it with the Apsu's waters and its clay.
> Thus from the sacred caverns, he emerged with—"

"Man!" Tadge's triumphant chortle and bounce startled Cassia awake for an instant, then rocked her over the edge into sleep.

In Cassia's dream like the other dreams that came to her more often now, in a vast dark space a thousand watchers held their breaths. Before them in the torchlight, brass tripods winked, their incense rising straight and high to the goddess. Cassia bent her head and peered through the eye slits of her wooden mask at the black, oiled curls of a kneeling king.

The goddess stirred in her; the invocation rose to her lips:

> "I speak of Sassurum's three: the song of the stars,
> the wisdom of the Stone, the strength of the tree.
> Star, Stone, and tree are yours to command. What would you
> ask Sassurum through me?"

From the man crouched by her golden sandal came a husky question.

When the goddess had given her last cryptic answer, the king, head still lowered, crawled backward and another took his place.

The multitude sighed. The incense eddied, expanding in the yellow torchlight. It changed to the golden shimmer of sun on Cassia's lashes.

The raft jerked. Cassia surfaced from her dream as the sound of bare feet splatting toward her paused, and a small brown body catapulted across her into the river. Spray exploded from the waves.

She was brushing off her robe when Tadge, shiny with water, surfaced by her foot. "You're not asleep, are you, Cassia? Jarell said you were and not to bother you, but I knew you wouldn't mind. Want to swim? It's getting so hot!"

Jarell's voice came from the stern: "Rogue. If she wasn't awake before, she is now. You should show more respect for your future mistress."

Tadge scowled around a laugh and scooped water at him. Drops, individual as jewels, glittered through the air to vanish in the river.

Cassia watched them fall, a fragile sweetness like happiness stealing through her. She caught at it, but even as she grasped it, it slipped away.

"Race you!" Tadge called to Jarell. "Loser cleans up after lastmeal."

The lowlander shook his head, teeth white in a face tanned by the fourteen days of sun.

"You never swim," Tadge complained. "You're as modest as Cassia, or else you don't know how."

For answer Jarell flicked water at the boy.

Tadge gurgled and dove under the raft.

When he burst through the blue and white ripples on the other side, Jarell shook his head. "Someone has to watch the currents while keeping us on course, and it won't be you until you're a more accomplished scholar. Though you're progressing. Come aboard!" Behind him, as the craft followed the river's slow curve, the bluff smoothed into a hill filmed with new grass.

Tadge heaved himself onto the logs; Jarell tossed him his robe and a drying cloth. As the boy struggled into his faded brown robe, Jarell quizzed him on the word for man and for woman in the Old Language.

"Adapa?" At Jarell's nod the boy added, "And adattu!"

Ignored, Cassia watched the hill increase in size behind them. She wriggled against the mast until it fit between the two increasing lumps on either side of her spine. Only her daily swims relieved their itching and burning.

Surreptitiously she spread her hair over them; her long hair and her loose robe had kept her nursling and Jarell from noticing the lumps. That, and their absorption in learning. Cassia watched the hill loom larger.

But it was you who withdrew so the singer might grow fond of the boy, fond enough to care for him if you're gone, her mind whispered.

Cassia's mouth tightened. She dipped the bread cloth in the river, wrung it out, and draped it over the crock again while Tadge continued to recite.

He never worked that hard when I helped him, she thought as the hill drew closer and the river vanished beyond it. Still Jarell did not look around. Cassia glanced at her nursling to see if he had noticed Jarell's oversight.

But Tadge frowned at his feet in concentration.

"When she birthed man, Kumar's mother got eight midwives to help; then she and Kumar got drunk and she bet Kumar she could wreck all his plans and make man useless." The boy paused for breath.

"You lack meter, and you definitely have your own style, but essentially you are correct." With a series of clunks Jarell set down the tablets of mathematics disguised as problems in navigation. He picked up tales he had scribed in the Old Language of the Betrayal of the Gods and of their minions' revenge; he raised an eyebrow at Tadge's rows of wedges, dots, and slanting lines of translation. Jarell nicked the clay by an error; he found another.

"Seven times she made a monster." Tadge watched Jarell out of the corner of his eye as the raft swept into the hill's shadow. "For each one, more horrible than the last, Kumar found a place. For the black-winged immortals, Beloved of Membliar, he found dominion beneath the moons and in the earth. For the menfish swimming in the sacred sea, and for the great and the small—Do you want all seven?"

"No." Frowning now, Jarell smeared a line with his thumb, pulled a stylus from his sleeve, and wrote. "Where did he fail?"

"On the eighth—old age. That stopped even Kumar. You know, he's supposed to be the youngest and handsomest of the gods, but he's so tricky! Somehow when I picture him, I always see the Dajo."

Jarell set aside the corrected tablet and picked up another. "You must tell him. The old charlatan will be delighted."

"It's funny how he calls Cassia 'Little Flower,'" Tadge went on. "She isn't little—she's big." At last he looked up at her.

She glanced over him to the river. Were the ripples getting higher and deeper? "He's always called me that. I don't know why. Do you think we should stop, because—"

Behind Jarell, the waves were like floating black mirrors. "Don't you really know why he calls you 'Little Flower'?"

Cassia shook her head.

Beyond the hill's curve, wind riffles flashed with sun like the shields of an invading army. She shifted uneasily but did not finish her sentence. It would be satisfying if, just once, Jarell did not seem to Tadge to know everything.

"What an ignorant girl you are," the man murmured.

Cassia's last scruple vanished. Fists clenching, she took small notice of Jarell's narrowing gaze.

"He's translated your full name, of course," he said deliberately. "In the Old Speech, Ricassia means Little Goddess of the Flowers."

Cassia's jaw dropped. "But . . . No! Anyway, there's more. Addiratu."

"That's simply your title: Lady of the Palace. Very good," he said as she gasped. "Almost, I believe you did not know."

"But I've never told him—or anyone—my full name! Just you and those beasts. And 'Lady'! A beast *couldn't*—You're laughing at me. You must be!" Anger and hurt constricted her throat.

"I assure, it's true." The raft spun into the turn. Between the closing sweep of his lashes, Jarell's dark eyes glittered with reflections of the water. He stared at the logs by his crossed knees, unaware of the raft's progress. Too bad! She would not warn him, ever!

Tadge snorted. "Cassia, a court lady?"

Tears prickled behind her eyes.

Jarell lifted an admonitory finger.

Above their heads, the sail thundered—bellying, falling slack, and snapping full again in the changing wind.

Tadge sprang to the lines. The raft whirled past the hill into a blaze of sunlight.

They rocked, waves slapping across the bow. Jarell swung the tiller, stared straight ahead of them, and exclaimed.

Chapter Sixteen

Cassia shut her eyes, dazzled by blue above and blue below. The river had become a sheet of water stretching to the horizon, bounded on either side by the now-distant Fire Mountains and low green hills.

A chill crept up her arms. *What if this lake had been a waterfall?* She must make her peace with Jarell.

"Careless!" Behind her, he echoed her thought. "I should have scouted. Well, by the gods! Look."

The bow dropped. A low island bounded into view: white beaches, clear shallows, and above them the green and silver flutter of rivertrees.

In the stern, Tadge leaped up. The raft tipped; water slopped over its sides, darkening the bark and adding its wet smell to that of hot wood. "Oh, luck of the goddess! Let's explore!"

Cassia's stomach tightened. Her life was forfeit if they slowed. "We can get farther today—"

"Check if it's deep enough," Jarell said simultaneously.

As Tadge gleefully counted off knots on his weighted line and Jarell grinned, Cassia looked from them to the shore. *Kateeb. Perhaps for an afternoon . . .*

She secured the sail with half hitches, an improvement on her first day's knots that had had to be picked apart while the sail exploded overhead. After Jarell had asked with restraint that she not help so much, Cassia had found she rather liked indolence.

Now they glided under a canopy of rivertrees; she tied up at a beach strewn with driftwood. With a cry of wordless joy, Tadge splashed by her to vanish in the thornfern. She followed more slowly with Jarell, who carried a pole and hooks.

As Cassia watched him search under a rock for stream grubs, she pushed down her jealousy and said how well he handled Tadge.

Jarell cast the long green shred of ropevine. "I expect his father beat both him and you. Which accounts for the child's belligerance and your withdrawal. I strike no one."

Cassia dropped onto a scoured log. "H-how did you know?"

"My dear child, I am slave, too. How could I not know?"

"I was afraid it was my fault! Tadge did and said the wild things *I* wanted to. As if he knew how I applauded inside. But my interfering made it worse! I'm sorry; I talk too much."

"You talk far too little, Cassia. And don't apologize! Not for kindness, a quality I never thought to find in a Rabu." Jarell concentrated on his growing handful of fat reddish worms.

Cassia hesitated. When she had started to ask earlier about her wound, he had interrupted, saying coldly it was too late to avoid him by feigning illness. Now . . .

She opened her mouth. But he was skewering a grub on a bone hook and saying, "As for the boy, he likes activity, entertainment, praise. I provide them. However, if I deny him something, or the weather changes, I will reap what his father and the priests have sown."

Watching the bait drift across the ripples, Jarell remarked that Tadge was the child he would like to have had, "if Naphar and my life had been different. Or perhaps the spacers' anti-beard injections have not made me sterile, and such a son exists somewhere. I would not be told." He moved upstream.

Cassia stayed, letting her hair slip over her hot cheeks. For the first time she had imagined Jarell with one tall like herself; she had wondered how they managed. And her long-dormant body woke.

She gazed at the pink grubs heaving on her palm, no longer able to block her memories.

She had been very young when her mate saw the Dajo lead her from the breeding pens—she had only recently had her Time of First Blood. Unkempt, weeping at her ugly new body so different from the six-cycle-old self she remembered, she cringed from the huge naked males forcing painful immodesties on her. Even so, her mate had wanted her. And his master had seen.

After the Dajo left, the two masters had agreed: in exchange for conjugal visits to settle the recently captured beast, Cassia's master would have the first whelp.

Her mate had hated his desire for her that chained him to his slavery—more and more his feverish tenderness turned to blows. She never equated what they did together with love. Fear; pity; rage, as she tore at him to hurt him as he hurt her; rarely an exhausted comfort; but never love. That came after his death when with disbelief she read the Dajo's scrolls of poetry, myth, romance. And, filled with regret, began to dream.

In the meadow that topped the island she again met Jarell. Above the new grass, booming pollen snatchers darted through speckled shade; sunlight glinted on their dark blur of wings and the pollen dusting their purple fur. Reluctantly Jarell said it was time to leave if they wanted to be dry by night. "For only you may wade to the raft unsodden. And I have had enough of sleeping in wet robes."

She followed his glance to the murmuring joy vibrating from the earth at their feet. The wide bed of sun followers bobbed in the insects' wake. Their yellow petals seemed to flatten and stretch toward the sun, their communal energy shimmering over them like heat.

Cassia shelved her embarrassment, her aching shoulder, her urgency; she moved toward the flowers. "Oh, couldn't we sleep here?" Her steps shook through the sod of the blossoms' feeder roots. The nearest blooms rolled into green and yellow spears and began their day-long descent into the loam.

"It's tempting."

She searched the grass for the deep blue tassel bells coaxed to life by the sun followers' emanations.

"To stretch out at night; to be able to walk . . ." he went on.

She threaded the flowers through her hair. Unmentioned by either of them was the stern shelter's crowded dark; his jerking awake with a cry or a muttered curse; his thrashing ashore to hunch over a fire and a pot of 'seq turned thick and black when Cassia and Tadge joined him at dawn.

"Let's ask Tadge," she said hastily. "Where is he?"

"I've not seen him." Jarell halted her rush to find the boy, and pointed to the flowers. Only the ones they had disturbed were rolled into green and yellow candles. "He'll be here. And he knows the dangers as well as you do. Meanwhile, if you need someone to protect . . ." Jarell's grin seemed almost shy.

Impossible! Cassia thought. But she smiled to herself as she gathered stones and wood for the night.

From the hillside below came panting and the snap of branches. She straightened. Jarell glanced downhill from their almost-completed oven and waved her back.

Tadge burst into the meadow; several rows of sun followers rolled green leaves around their stems and started underground. "Cassia! Jarell! Look what I found!"

Behind the boy, a shiny black and white lizard as high as Tadge's knee waddled out of the ferns. It's stout body was propelled by stubby legs ending in retracted black talons. Raising its triangular head, it blinked a dull lower lid over its eyes; it curved around Tadge's legs, forked tongue flickering, rubbing its brow ridges on his robe.

"A kotellue, by the gods!" Jarell looked up from the fire he laid in the oven. "They're worth a fortune in Qaqqadum."

"I'd never sell him! He likes me—I didn't even have to charm him. He wants to come with us." Dropping to his knees, Tadge leaned his head against the lizard's thick neck.

Cassia took a step toward them. "Tadge, be careful."

"It's harmless." Jarell held a firebox to the curls of shaved wood and blew. "The nobles and wealthier merchants prize them as pets. They're even teachable if you're willing to repeat your-self five or six hundred times."

Tadge looked from the curl of smoke to Jarell. "Don't you laugh at my kote—kolet—what did you call him?"

"Kotellue." When the fire was crackling, Jarell stood and re-placed the firebox in his sleeve. "Tadge. If he's your friend, you won't take him from the only life he knows. How content will he be, restricted to a raft or a city's ruts or closed in a starship? Besides, he lives up to his name."

The boy's lower lip jutted. Cassia intervened: "What do you mean, lives up to his name?"

"He sings it—three notes—all night. In the palaces they're let into the entrance garden at dusk, well away from the sleep chambers. For excellent reason."

"I don't care! I want him. And he wants me."

Jarell looked from the boy's face to his whitening knuckles. Leaf shadows studded with sunlight blew over them both. "Then he may come," Jarell said carefully. "Though I hope he catches his own meals—we haven't food for four. And now I must un-load."

As he left, Tadge asked, "Cassia? Is Jarell taking off my stuff and leaving me here because of the kotellue? Pa would."

Now I can pry them apart, she thought. But when she died or Changed, the boy would have only Jarell. And she found she could not betray the man to the boy. She explained.

Tadge's widening eyes were like green fire crystal and as full of light. "Do I want to? I'll help! Come on, kotellue."

Biting back her envy of his vivid life, and feeling very alone in her dying, Cassia sighed and started toward the cove where she and Jarell had agreed she would swim.

Cassia had finished her daily bath in the river and was hunting a twig to pound into a mouth scrubber, when she heard Tadge's shout.

She stuffed her damp hair down her back where it cooled her swellings; she squinted up at the capering silhouette. "It's Jarell—hurry!" She hurried.

On the other side of the island Cassia lay in the thornfern, her heart pounding from the easy run, and looked where Tadge pointed.

On grass cupped by boulders and the roots of a few ancient trees, Jarell faced them. Jarell—unhurt, unmenaced, and naked but for a loincloth bulging with his Difference.

Sweat gleamed on his smooth tanned skin as he stretched, then brought his hands forward. His flat belly tightened; muscles bunched in his legs—

His legs! Blushing, Cassia yanked her gaze to his workcloth robe, almost dry on a limb. He rubbed a yellow lump on his palms—the scent of resin drifted toward her. She started downhill. "Tadge, if he's all right we shouldn't watch."

Jarell leaped, tucked his knees into his chest, and flipped backward, his hair glittering with sunlight. At the trees, his face intent, he jumped for a horizontal limb, then rotated around it, his glistening back crosshatched by glare and shadow.

Tadge hissed, "Isn't he goddess-great?"

Resentment tightened Cassia's belly. Jarell had first stolen Tadge from her with his charm, then his knowledge; now this. *She* had no leisure to acquire such skills.

Jarell dropped and snapped into a spinning ball. He landed, skidded, and thumped onto his back. The air *whooshed* out of him; his mouth opened in what looked like a soundless cry for help.

She jumped up to follow Tadge. The man sucked in a breath, laughed—and saw them.

"That was prime! Can you teach me how? And Cassia?"

Face set, Jarell flowed upright. Cassia shrank back, feeling large, awkward, and unwanted. Tadge faltered, "I—I was looking for a fishing hole. I know you always swim alone, but I thought just this once—Don't look at Cassia like that! I said something so she—she thought you might be hurt."

"Did she, indeed? Remind me not to be present when you attain your full powers of persuasion." Jarell raised his hand. Tadge dodged as if from a blow. "So. Trust ends that easily." Finishing the motion, Jarell pushed at his hair, and turned away.

The afternoon sun lit his back as fully as a priest's mirrored lantern illuminates a god-puppet about to speak. On Jarell's shoulders and spine, inflamed ridges crossed white seams over a tracery of older, puckered scars.

"Gods! What happened, Jarell?"

"I ran. I was made an example."

"But those aren't from just one beating!" Cassia blurted.

Jarell's dark eyes looked dead as he explained: a marked pleasure slave became an Exotic, "revolting to normal individuals such as yourselves, but much in demand by"—he glanced at Tadge—"others." Who recouped their investment by passing him on, and on . . . "More questions? Comments?" He pointed to blue reflections below. "I shall bathe now. There, if you wish to observe." Hands not quite steady, he reached for his loincloth.

"No. We don't. Goddess forgive me, I envied you!" Eyes hot with unshed tears, Cassia fled down the hillside.

Chapter Seventeen

Naphar, on the other hand, is an angler's paradise. Its rivers teem with large sporting fish since the Napharese eat only fingerlings of less than four seasons' growth. The sporting fisherman's larger catch, however, must be detoxified before consumption since fish that have seen more than one spring have absorbed fatal quantities of selenium, leached from the soil and washed into the watercourses by the annual floods.

THE COMPLEAT INTRAGALACTIC ANGLER, 62ND EDITION.

"Cassia, wait!" Tadge pushed through the thornfern at her knee, demanding the reason for Jarell's anger.

"He was ashamed." Cassia's voice was low.

"Kateeb, don't cry—he didn't. He's a coward!"

"Only a master would say that!" Cassia raged. "What choice did he have? 'A slave who runs steals the body his master owns and punishes as he wills.' He's smaller, weaker, has no say."

"Don't be a stupid old beast! The new laws forbid—"

"They're for workers, like me." She quoted: "'The tribal courts don't rule on love.'"

"Cassia, are you going to be sick—over *that?*"

Ignoring him, she scrambled blindly toward the river.

The smell of baking bread drifted to the beach. There Cassia readied a lapful of greens; at water's edge silvery fingerlings twitched by her nursling. The kotellue lumbered toward them.

Tadge dropped his pole and grabbed the lizard. He hauled it onto his lap and hid his face in its neck. Cassia sailed a stem over them to the water.

Hissing, the creature wriggled free and waddled after it. At the river, stem forgotten, the kotellue nudged the fish. One flapped across its nose slits; shaking its head, the lizard skidded back.

Cassia glanced at Tadge, amusement loosening her anger.

"Cassia? I get so lonesome when you're mad. Oh!" Tadge's pole arched black before the gold ripples and yellow afterglow. "It's big! Even if we can't eat it I'm pulling it in!"

Tadge released the arm-long pink and green fish, asking the Lathon's Dragon God to grant it edible young. "Cassia?" he said as she gestured response and started uphill with the greens. "Will Jarell feel better if I tell him he's free—so he won?"

Shall we? Be friends? Jarell had said. She told the boy, "We should at least apologize." He nodded.

But as he and the lizard scrabbled past her she heard him whisper, "Hear that, kotellue? Jarell won. Only, *I* would have killed them."

Lastmeal over, Tadge was throwing sticks for the kotellue to fetch—as predicted, it was not a fast learner—when Jarell stalked from the moving dark, robe laced to his chin.

"Come on, kotellue." Tadge faded toward the trees.

Jarell tore open the last round of bread and stuffed in the soggy greens and the fish—heads, tails, fins, and all. He took them and a cup of opaque 'seq to the meadow's edge, turned his back, and stared into the dark. The river's glow rippled on the trunks of the trees and the undersides of their branches.

Before she too could change her mind, Cassia marched to Jarell, knelt and peeked upward. A fish stared whitely back. "I couldn't not look. Any ugliness is in those who hurt you. You were... beautiful." Passionately she wished for an anonymous wooden mask to make these very personal remarks bearable. *If friendship requires this, no wonder it's so rare.*

A long moment passed. He stroked her cheek. "Why will you not look at me, my sweet child?" He tipped up her chin.

Above her, his dark eyes brimmed with moonlight. His breath was sweet; it smelled of 'seq. Her lips parted.

From the edge of the meadow, footsteps: Tadge catapulted between them, flinging his arms around Jarell, gabbling apologies, questions.

And Cassia sat back on her heels, wondering if she had imagined the moment just past.

"... hurt only if I don't oil them when it's dry." Over Tadge's head Jarell gazed at Cassia.

She led Tadge to his blankets by the fire, then she lay down, too, though she felt strong, alert as she seldom did by day. And for the first time in two sennights no raft rocked her into dreams.

The embers hissed as Jarell emptied his cup across them; he strolled toward her. Closing her eyes, she tried to breathe naturally. After a while his blankets rustled and he too settled for the night. But not, as it chanced, to sleep.

The moons and the Dark One climbed higher, firing the volcanoes and shaking the earth; the myriad southern stars fizzed behind a thin, high haze. Below the campsite waves crashed into the driftwood, clacking it together, then squeaking it apart. A call belled through the night, ending in a quavering howl.

Cassia jumped, staring at the kotellue who was raising its snout to the heavens. It called its name three more times into the barkhiders' respectful silence, then dropped its head on its forepaws.

Again Cassia shut her eyes and drifted toward dreams. An alien anxiety threaded them, one that seemed outside her, casting about in the night, hunting her.

The goddess-cursed secret places of her body ached with fear and desire she could no longer deny; once more in the dark she awaited her mate's touch.

She moaned. She turned onto her stomach, embracing the ground and the ferns that cushioned it. In her dreams her mate grasped her, hissing that he would not make a child to be a slave but, gods help him, he wanted her. More, he was afraid he loved—

His touch changed. And the thrusting hurt Cassia remembered became a gentle sureness driven by strength, and a knowledge of her that set her drifting on waves of delight. He drew up her robe. He whispered, "Oh, how beautiful," and her name.

Beautiful! Lashes wet, she felt tenderness melt, burn, and expand in her as he made her move, shuddering and drawing harsh breaths. Catching his head in her hands, she drew it down to kiss—eyes, cheeks, mouth, throat . . .

His grip shifted; it closed on her bitten shoulder. And she threw back her head and screamed.

But in the way of dreams, it emerged only as a gasp. The world turned to buzzing blackness and she fainted.

When she woke she sat propped against a rivertree at one side of the clearing with Jarell beside her. The anxiety was back. Was it another's? Hers?

She glanced down, but no, she wore her robe, it was tied at the throat—all was as it had been. Of course it was all a dream. A pang of loss shot through her so sharply she caught her breath. She licked her lips, swollen and warm with the memory . . . But nothing had happened. She schooled her expression.

"You're ill. You have been, ever since we stepped the mast." Jarell's voice was uneven. He indicated her hurt shoulder. "May I look? The Academy gave me some medical training. In an explorer ship one must be one's own healer."

She stared at him. Masters could do as they wished. As he untied the laces at her breast and drew down her robe his touch seemed warm, familiar. Heat fingered through her . . . It was a dream!

Behind her he touched the legendary slitted wound. "A Night Demon! I thought in that cave I heard wings, but you said nothing. So much simpler to assume I imagined it. Gods! I'd seen holos of the things—I should have known them, sleeping."

On the shore below, a wave thumped, its flare illuminating the trees at the meadows edge. He jerked her robe together; dread knocked at her skull.

"Don't look like that. The lowlands has healers. And there's the river."

He began a lecture full of spacer words he must know she couldn't understand: . . . phosphors digested her wound's poisons and stopped the spread of infection . . .

"But you knew that. You've been punctilious about bathing. Why did you not tell me? Why, Mott take you?"

Cassia's resentment mixed with the fears lashing her. "You'd have left us. And later, you didn't listen!"

"Gods. Ricassia, I swear—" He glanced at her. "Kateeb. Better to see how long we have. How's your night vision?"

Cassia glanced at the wash of scarlet dripping from thorn and frond and leaf and pouring from a sky-wide billow of Veil. It winked with stars: red, white, gold, blue, green. "Fine!"

Above them the kotellue yodeled. When Jarell could make himself heard over the noise, he asked, "And your day sight? You've been squinting."

"It's brighter here!" The dread pounded at Cassia like waves.

"Chills? Fevers? A rash? Itching? Strange dreams, or waking ones that seem real?"

"Sometimes."

"Sometimes. Even a few symptoms of serum sickness are too

many. And yet, you seem well. Could some quirk of the genes have made you one of the few who do not die?"

Cassia heard only the words that gave her back a future; she did not notice his lack of joy. "Then I'm glad I was in the cave to be bitten! Or I'd have missed this"—she gestured rather wildly at the night—"these sennights on the raft with you, and—and Tadge, of course." Cassia looked up.

Jarell seemed very close. "You're a nice child, Ricassia Addiratu. Those eyes like silver spangles—they see a better world than I do, I think. You call the pain and danger I have inflicted on you gifts! Perhaps in this peace—this relative peace," he amended as the lizard again took up its cry, "I may give a greater pleasur to us both?"

Cassia's indignation drained away. She scarcely dared breathe. Could—could she not have dreamed? Eager, fearing, she reached out to him with her mind; she opened it to him . . .

And, out of the darkness, Salimar struck.

Chapter Eighteen

Cold. Fear. Salimar felt them both in the minds he grasped. He flamed with triumph.

The female slave's startled white radiance folded into rays of green and blue and gold. His exploring tendrils thrust deep, surprising her confusion, her desire . . . *Nothing!*

Salimar tossed away her aura; he reached out to the one beside it. With his hand on the circlet that sought its lodestone, he eased his control along the smoothed, familiar paths of his runaway manikin's sinew, arm, and breath. He moved his male slave.

His! Found after sennights of mental searching. To hold, to extract revenge, to retrieve the Mindstone . . .

Salimar shouted to his sleeping minions: "Rise! Come, I will touch you with my poison to ensure your return. I will give you more for those you seek. Quick-march upriver. By dusk bring me news of the Rabu and Kakano—perhaps another—who stole from me. When I tell you, take them captive. Poison them. Carry them here to me. Do this and you may receive the antidote. Fail, and you will surely die!"

Salimar's bellow of joy bounced from the peeling murals and chipped columns of his borrowed provincial palace. The slavers' faces were drawn, their hands bore fatal scratches, as they scattered to do his bidding.

Chapter Nineteen

Walk!

At the top of the island, above the river that lit the night, Jarell touched the Stone in his chest pocket. Stiff with rage and the desire to weep, he felt his numbed legs obey. "Yes, Salimar" whispered through his lips.

Jarell left the hillside's red and silver light and doubled shadow, he crossed the beach. Water lapped his ankles.

He pulled on a rope; he fumbled with its knots while staring downriver toward his destination, hidden by the night; the night, owned by Salimar the Dark God; the night, when Salimar was strongest.

"I come!" Jarell shouted interrupting the annoying voice behind him. His voice emerged as a croak.

Then warm hands pulled his from the Stone and the rope. They were hands roughened by work. Engulfing hands, Rabu hands. But Jarell felt no nausea at their touch—quite the contrary.

On the horizon false dawn grayed the northern peaks and the ragged hem of the sky. The voice resolved into words: "No, it's not time to leave, not yet. Soon, when first light comes and we can see. The water will be blue then, sun will light the rocks and shoals, travel will be safe."

The voice breathed a fog of radiance into the black shield of will enclosing Jarell. Feeling seeped into his feet and into his hands, rubbed, he discovered, by the larger, warmer ones. They persuaded him away from the raft and fear, and soothed his fingers still twitching at the mooring rope. His legs no longer jerked, urging him toward the road on the other side of the river where he must meet—

Jarell's skin crawled and he blinked. A face swirled into focus. Delicately modeled, a stubborn chin, great silver irises shadowed by lashes that would be golden in the sun; moonlight awash on tumbled light and dark hair . . . Cassia.

His loins grew heavy, and he remembered. Heat, then clammy cold suffused him. What had he been thinking of, up on that hill? How could he have forgotten, even for a moment, that Cassia was Rabu! Giving even a little of himself into her keeping could destroy him.

And what could he offer her? He belonged to Salimar as utterly as did a knife, a rock, or any of Salimar's other tools. Instead, Jarell took from Cassia. Again. Shame ignited in him. He pulled his hands free.

"Thank you." He examined his feet. Beside them on the beach, lost stars winked in puddles and slowly the night retreated. "I was going to bring him—"

Jarell paused. He should tell her what he carried. It endangered her too. But with the Mindstone to barter he could leave this planet and his inadequacies behind. The off-worlders believed the Stone was a relic from a prehistoric civilization, one that could tap the energy powering psi phenomena—energy that did not obey the inverse square law, and was unaffected by distance or time. For the key to the Stone's power, they would pay well. Or the temple would, to keep the Stone. But Cassia was so demon-eating upright! She would insist on his returning the Mindstone profitlessly. And that he would not do. Already their association was strained. Perhaps later . . .

"I was going to bring him something," he temporized, "and— myself. But as always, you were there to see. And act." Though chagrin wormed through him, a corner of his mouth quirked.

Cassia drew back into the windy shadows. "I—I beg pardon."

"Your goddess curse my clumsiness! It's all right, child. I'm perfectly aware that this too was an accident. For me, a fortuitous one. And stop apologizing! You're not responsible for all my ills.

"How is it that Salimar does not control you too, I wonder?" he mused. "Can it all be due to the coming dawn and the waning of Salimar's strength?" He looked up at her. She was tall, and thus Rabu. The whoring priestesses of Sassurum who were sensitives were Rabu. Might Cassia secretly be a Sensitive, and amusing herself with him?

But in her wide metallic gaze he saw only distress and an

absence of guile. The knot in his belly loosened; tenderness flooded him, and desire. "If only..."

Waves crashed beside them, showering fiery drops onto his feet and Cassia's. An unearthly warble floated downward.

Jarell started, then smiled faintly as Tadge's sleepy voice said, "Oh, hush yourself, kotellue."

Cassia took a step uphill; stopped; and turned back to Jarell—hovering, he thought, like a mother lizard torn between two clutches of eggs.

His smile twisted. "Let's get some sleep. Even Salimar can't do that twice in a night—I hope. But after this I shall stay on the raft, on the chance that there was a grain of truth in your remark about sorcery not traveling over water."

"I—I'm sorry—" A glare from Jarell stopped Cassia in mid-apology.

As they huddled in their blankets, waiting for the light, Jarell stared up at the lopsided moons and their companion. Was that a faint color at its poles? And in between—sparks? What had he learned of it from the holo tapes long ago? It had an atmosphere? He shrugged. It hardly mattered, for another tape he had watched at the Space Academy was replaying itself in his head.

He had been sitting on his pallet, projector beside him, studying. A silver-helmeted, white-caped lecturer on comparative parasitology had stood on its tumbled blankets, only her foot in his steaming cup of Learning Tea betraying the fact that she was a holograph.

Sipping the pale green broth of neuro-transmitters, he had listened to her illustrate the Neo-Classic Evolutionary Theory that large structures were created from smaller ones, by describing the workings of Night Demon poison.

"While drawing blood, the Night Demons' viruslike parasites go into the victim's bloodstream and take over the cells' deoxyribonucleic acid. During a honeymoon of no more than sixty days, if the subject has not died, these cells change, producing a life form—half human, half Night Demon—with which the parasites may enjoy the same symbiosis they had with their original host."

A great sadness filled Jarell: if Cassia died or Changed, his scheme must fail! But there was the slight hope of finding a healer: they would; they must.

His peril and Cassia's thrumming in his mind, Jarell waited impatiently for the night to end.

Chapter Twenty

Nowhere is the difference between goddess- and god-centered two-sex societies clearer than in their attitudes toward the taking of life.

A patriarchal god not only condones beingslaughter, he often glorifies it, in some cases granting special privileges to the killers, such as speedy entry into an afterlife of luxury and honor. In extreme examples he even confers ghostly nobility or sainthood upon those who take their own lives in his service.

Societies that worship a matriarch, however, usually define her as the sole giver and taker of life. Thus, unsanctioned murder of another or of one's self is considered a crime against the goddess—against the life force that has been deified and placed at the society's ethical core—and is the most heinous crime of all.

> "THEOGENY: A DISCUSSION OF ITS SYMBOLS."
> SPEECH GIVEN BY URT T'PING ON THE OCCASION OF THE OPENING
> OF THE CONFUCIAN-PONTIFICAL INSTITUTE.

The kotellue splashed into the river and stopped, breast-deep in slow-moving ripples layered with the white mist of dawn. It *chirruped*, darting looks from Cassia to Tadge, who sat on her shoulder. Tadge clicked encouragement to the lizard.

Cassia smiled faintly and stepped into the water. "Come."

And the little creature plunged after them, swimming hard, its spine and tail a black and white riffle arrowing through Cassia's wake. In the shade of the green and silver trees, both trails glowed with the light of a thousand phosphors.

The raft tipped when Cassia set Tadge and the kotellue near the bundles Jarell was knotting to the mast.

The kotellue scrabbled for purchase as it circled the logs, then stretched out in their center. From under its brow ridges, it watched Cassia loose the moorings and push the raft away from the island, its black eyes narrowed in unknowable lizard thought.

The raft moved into the lake, lead-colored under a paling sky.

* * *

Cassia leaned against the mast. She had scoured the brazier, taken it part, and stowed it. Now she tried to think only of the midmorning heat that smelled of water and pines, the slosh and gurgle beneath the logs, and her own full stomach.

She rubbed the lumps by her spine and looked down at Tadge and the kotellue asleep beside her. The grease from the fish the boy had eaten glistened around his mouth.

Jarell was at the tiller, scanning the low hills cupping the lake. Cloud fuzzed the sky. "There must be an outlet or the current wouldn't be this strong. But where?" They sped on.

Their talk was desultory. Of the kotellue Cassia said, "Tadge has so little to love and to love him back."

"He has you." Dots and a clacking sound spiraled out of the sun's white eye.

"Oh, but mothers are part of the landscape! Wasn't yours?"

"Mm. But you're not one. Or has your memory improved?"

"No. I'm not." Cassia's throat shut on the words. In her mind, once more she tossed in her straw, breasts aching and swollen with useless milk, keening for her babe born dead, unkissed, unheld, unloved. Again the cold tears slid down her cheeks as she sealed it in the coffin she had woven, covered the laden basket with black wax, and cast her motionless babe into the River Lathon. Her babe, so little, so alone, forever...

One of the fliers skimmed toward her, green fur rippling. Its abdomen was as long as her arm and trailed a powerful thorax.

"'Ware!" Jarell jumped up as the flier's two sets of wings fanned Cassia's face. But she only cupped their rainbows in her hands and stared into the insect's faceted golden eyes. Its alien innocence touched her mind, hinting at other lives, self-absorbed...

I can care for none of them as I did my babe! She covered her anguish by chattering that it was only a green needle; they lived on spores and insects, leaving the upper air from curiosity or to escape a storm; in the fall she and Tadge climbed the cliffs to gather the green needles' huge green eggs for winter carving. The insect zoomed up to its fellows circling the mast. "And where is *your* mother?" she asked, further changing the subject. "In Qaqqadum?"

"Dead. By her Choice." The sail flapped overhead. After a while Jarell added softly, "I do not blame her, though I think of her sometimes, sealed in her reed casket, bobbing in Membliar's sunless sea where man began and will one day end."

Ritual suicide. Cassia shivered. The goddess cut self-murderers from Naphar's womb, never to merge with the slow heartbeat of the centuries, never to be reborn. The Weavers of Destiny pulled their snapped threads from the Tapestry of Fate as if they had never been. Cassia tried to understand; she said, "Once, when death seemed everywhere, I also— But she had you!"

"I killed her." Jarell's hurt and anger beat in her.

Afraid to speak, afraid not to, she lay on the hot, rocking logs, the sun heating her aching shoulder that must go unbathed.

When Cassia woke, an afternoon sun glared in her eyes, shooting long shadows from the purple volcanoes to the bobbing raft. Beside her Tadge slept on. "Hasn't he been awake at all?"

A wave splashed coolness across her hand; Jarell eased the tiller aside. "He swam. Ate. It seems he didn't sleep well last night." Brief amusement lightened the strain in his face.

Behind him the highlands mountains wore black shrouds of cloud and veils of rain. At the river's edge, watery sunlight glinted on the barrows and gaudy wares of a band of potmenders scurrying for shelter in the hills. Waves hit the raft with hard little knocks.

Cassia started to smooth Jarell's tension. She paused—it was his tension, after all. Again she remembered his idea of friendship, swallowed, and asked, "Do you want to tell me about your mother? Sometimes if you talk about a bad time, when you think of it next, it's as if the one you told was there. You're not so alone with it anymore."

"A wise child," he said after a moment. "Very well. You shall have your story. And I, my companion." He hooked his arm over the tiller, and began, "My father was a fisherman . . ."

When his father drowned, the poverty that followed ended his mother's songs and tales of wonders. She sold his sister to Ynianna. "I've heard my sister is happier now—in my lowlands many servants of the love goddess at first are unwilling."

Above them, wind thumped into the square green sail. Tadge jerked in his sleep. The sail bellied; the raft skated over the waves; the hills before them grew larger.

Phikola En, head of the Temple Space Academy, "gave my mother gold and promises. And I agreed to my sale! My mother spoke of favors for us from visiting nobles."

Jarell's tale of good fortune blended with the rush of the strengthening breeze. Under the raft, white swirled with red.

"A fellow bond student became a friend; caring for Phikola's baby daughter eased my heartyearnings for my family; nobles favored me." He had no tutor, the coin for one had gone for a fishing boat share, better housing, a few pretty things.

The colors in the waves became a fish with a nose like a flute; it shot toward the surface. Cassia envied Jarell his easy slavery and the lessons he neglected: she watched the fish.

So Phikola complained, Jarell said. "My tired, once-pretty little mother wept: I must get my flaws from my father, she could not face my grandfather or her friends. When I clung and begged for a tutor or to leave, she pushed me away, saying I contaminated her. And on that sunny afternoon she walked to the Temple of Sweet Repose, drank its waters, and died."

The fish spread ribbed wings, flipped from the water, and blinked a blue eye. "A dragonfish, and it winked! That's good luck!" Cassia exclaimed. Then, in the breezy quiet, Jarell's words echoed. "Oh, goddess forgive me, I—"

"You have neither heard nor understood one word I said, have you? This time, *listen!* When a great lady invited me to her palace for sweets, after her first words, a tutor—a children's guardian—would have stopped her. But I! I went."

In that lady's palace, Jarell had simpered at her praise as he perched on her thighs taking delicacies from her lips. "Each time she fondled me and I shivered with delight, she laughed and popped a sweetmeat in my mouth. After, my new finery crumpled, my arms heaped with gifts and coin, I thought, *So much for so little!*

"I served her often. And her friends. Then their fathers, companions, brothers." Still he did not know what he did. "Until a student called me a name. And that night I demanded and got my first fully earned jewels and coin. At dawn when my . . . admirers . . . returned me to the great sleep chamber I shared with the other students, before I crawled onto my pallet I bathed. I dressed. Last, I met my eyes in my new, polished gold mirror."

"I had guessed some, but—all Rabu? And so much older. Men too? Obscenity!" Cassia breathed. "Tadge would have killed—"

Jarell looked startled. "Obscenity? Oh, I see. My lowlands puts no boundaries on love, child. The wrong was that there was none on either side, only a wish for profit." His face was haggard as he added, "I fear I lack my mother's and your nursling's courage: I killed neither myself nor my patron; I only moped. In those days, I was a sensitive plant. Gods! How I can babble on so, and to you, with your lack of experience, your distaste—" He paused, an arrested look in his eyes. "I had thought distaste. But you surprised me. Only now, you—can you have thought it did not happen?"

"You're still sensitive!" Cassia interrupted.

He lifted an eyebrow. "Hardly. Bad-tempered, perhaps. I think you mistake me. I did not stop. I, an object, determined to be a valued one. I caught up with my classmates' studies and surpassed them. Each patron left me, satisfied. And *paid*."

Jarell breathed as if he had been running as he rammed the tiller to one side. Wind slapped into the sail; the craft skimmed across the waves. Spray drenched them. The logs tipped; Cassia dropped to all fours as the sail swished murderously overhead. It emptied, then exploded full as they rocketed down the center of the lake. The encircling hills grew tall.

Cassia brushed water off Tadge. He wriggled against the sleeprolls, curling around the kotellue.

"I—I wondered . . ." She glanced behind Jarell to the clouds boiling over the northern peaks and flashing with lightning. She thought of the torrents of rain, and of the highlands' filled run-off ponds, their dikes already shaky from the frequent quakes. "It's raining! The floods—"

But Jarell lowered his black brows. He looked forbidding. "Yes? You wondered? What did I leave unclear?" She tried to remember. "Oh, ask! Innocent young ladies enjoy these discussions—one of the few ways they may safely satisfy their curiosity."

Cassia lifted her chin. The storm was distant—probably local. The passionate childish self she remembered wouldn't warn one who spoke to her so! Instead she replied, "I am *not* innocent. I only wondered why you didn't complain. If you were, ah, too busy to study, you couldn't complete your bond and the temple would lose its gold."

Jarell's edgy look softened; his mouth twitched. "Practical as well as innocent. That is not the sort of question I expected. Kateeb—I did complain." But Phikola En asked only if he led his noble friends to favor the Academy. Though Sassurum as goddess of the stars sponsored it, the conservatives wished Naphar to remain as it was before the off-worlders came: alone in the universe.

To Cassia's protest he replied, "She did mean it. My fellow bond student refused his admirers. She auctioned him. Moments before his new owner arrived I found him gently swinging. Dead.

"When I maundered on about it, Phikola asked why did I not

change society? With these, I suppose." He held up his hands. Beside him the vines strung from mast to logs began to hum.

Cassia's hem and sleeves snapped in the wind. Its chill ached through her shoulder; she shivered. "Did she hate you?"

He shrugged and she stared, unseeing, at the foam flying from the racing blue heads of the waves.

The raft bumped against the surges' increasingly deep cups. Spray hit Tadge. He gulped and flailed wildly in his sleep.

Cassia looked ahead of the raft to the long shadows that the setting sun cast across the hills and water. It was time to find a place to tie up for the night, yet still the raft sped down the middle of the lake. The hills loomed closer; they shut out the light.

Jarell made a surprised sound deep in his throat. When she looked back he frowned and shoved on the tiller. "The rudder doesn't answer." He pushed again. "Mott take these new inventions! What I wouldn't give for a steering oar."

The craft swept closer to the land and its unbroken ring around the lake. A glimmer of beach rushed close; Cassia braced herself for the crash. She reached down to shake Tadge awake.

The wind thrumming in the lines mixed with a new thunder just ahead of them. In a cleft where two hills plunged into the shady darkness of the water, Cassia saw a white ruffle—it snapped into focus: a strip of foam punctuated by boulders.

She pushed back her whipping hair and pointed at it. "Rapids!" she screamed over the roar. "The current—the wind—they're pulling us straight for them!"

Chapter Twenty-One

In contrast, the central assumption of Northern Napharese law is neither guilt nor innocence but change. This reflects the Napharese philosophy that nothing is forever. Not slavery—bonded and owner agree on its extent at the time of sale and file the record in the slave courts where one of twelve tribal judges periodically reviews it; not adoption—that too is a renewable contract; not leadership—even the ensai's rule, though usually served in serial terms, is officially limited to seven springs; not partnering—its many versions last only as long as both parties are satisfied and, in the case of children, until they are independent; not guilt, which is seen as a facet of personality to be restructured or ended, not punished; not life; not even death.

SURVEY OF JURISPRUDENCE
IN PRIMITIVE AND POST-INDUSTRIAL AGRARIAN SOCIETIES.
GALACTIC CENTRAL UNIVERSITY PRESS.

"Sail, Cassia!" Jarell's shout was thin through the rapids' roar.

She sprang for the line and whipped it free of its cleat. The coarse green fabric swished to the deck, where it bellied and snapped and threatened to blow into the waves. Cassia dropped to her knees and bundled the sail against the mast. She wrapped a line around the sail and rocked back onto her heels, poised for her next order.

None came. Cassia looked back, a whine of alarm edging through her. Jarell was tying the useless tiller in place. He straightened and bounded past her, holding a coil of green rope.

"What are you doing? We'll crash!" In the roar of wind and water he could not have heard. He knotted the line around him, glanced up, and threw his folding knife into Cassia's lap.

"Push the knob on the handle." His eyes were bright as he glanced forward. Only a few manlengths to the rapids. His mouth curved.

Cassia remembered his rescue of Tadge in the slavers' camp. *He's enjoying this, too!* she thought savagely. Clumsy with anger, she fumbled at the knife. Its blade snicked out.

"Push on the edge," Jarell called through the roar.

Stupid, Cassia thought as the blade folded in. *What does this have to do with sinking?*

"You can pry logs from the raft with it. Swim ashore," Jarell shouted. He tied himself to the mast.

"But if we turn over, you'll drown."

He grinned and hurried more line around himself. "I'll drown anyway. I can't swim."

"But—" She reviewed Tadge's past accusations and Jarell's evasions and believed him. "Don't you care?"

He looked surprised, then frowned. "Not really. I expect I'm too old to do much with my freedom, even supposing I won it." He glanced at Tadge. "Wake him."

Dazed with sleep, the boy tightened his grip on the kotellue as Cassia pointed to the rapids. Every freckle showed on his pale face. "Goddess great, Cassia!" Glancing at Jarell, he gave a shaky grin. "What a ride!"

"Good boy!" the man said. Tadge's smile broadened. Suddenly, unaccountably, Cassia's eyes prickled with tears.

Through them swam the heads of rocks two armlengths away . . . one . . . With the detachment of terror she counted chartreuse patches of moss, their tiny white and lavender flowers.

The wind snatched her hair and took her breath. The bow hit the first boulder. Cassia's teeth jarred together and a breathless laugh bubbled up from her toes. She was still alive! She grabbed for the logs, Tadge's cries in her ears.

Boy and kotellue slid past her; Cassia threw herself across her nursling.

"Hold your breath!" Jarell shouted. She shut her eyes. *Goddess!* A dropping sensation made her look.

The raft soared into the air, banged onto a whirlpool. Spume exploded around it, sluicing Cassia's hair, face, robe. The soaked folds snapped in a chill wind as the raft whirled downstream. She grabbed a breath. The logs slammed into a barrier of rocks. Cassia's head jerked down; splinters showered into the sky. Still, incredibly, the raft held together.

For a moment it stuck. Cold water rushed over Cassia.

"Push us off—we'll break up!" Jarell shouted.

As if they still floated on a sane river, she obeyed his order, set her palm on the cool, gritty boulder, and shoved.

The craft tilted; they hurtled around a bend on swift-smooth current, the shore a blur beside them. Tadge wriggled free. "Look. Are we in the lowlands?"

They were on a broad ribbon of water that glinted silver in the failing light; it snaked the valley's length through a patchwork of fields. Some squares were yellow with winter grass, others were ploughed and brown or hazed with green.

As the boy crawled forward and Cassia sat up to wring out her hair, she glanced at the white houses dotting the fields. Golden-thatched, or roofed with red tiles, they were connected to each other and to the river by a tracery of dirt roads. She looked beyond them and gasped. "That must be a city!"

On the horizon a mound hid the setting sun; light blazed around it. Behind the wall crowning the hill, domes and spires glittered with gold and shone with tiles. It was nothing like the enlarged crossroads market she had imagined.

"A provincial town, not large," Jarell said. "With luck, it may support a healer. If not, we go on."

Cassia bit her lip. Overawed like an ignorant beast; to forget she was going to die . . . Blindly she stared at the dike and the few dejected furbushes scattered down its sides.

A ramp sloped from its top to a dock bobbing at its base. Climbing the ramp was a richly dressed farmer. Behind him, servants carried a boat, its oars, and a rolled sail; a chosen few led a Dreamer of the Goddess. A Dreamer! Cassia studied the tall woman.

The priestess's unfocused eyes and robes the color of fog proclaimed her ability, when helped by ritual herbs, to relive others' lives. In her hand was the blue-green staff of healing, the sign that she would find and unknot the pain and fears in a living person's history. If she had planned to uncover an Old Soul's rebirths, she would have held the white staff of knowledge.

But Dreamers were rare, their health fragile; they seldom reached the highlands, never Cassia's northern wilderness. How had she recognized one? The ramp's use struck her and she forgot her question. "That's what we should have done!" Cassia nodded toward the farmers and the priestess. "There must be a portage above the rapids—we just didn't see it from the middle."

One hand on his chest pocket, Jarell grunted without looking up from the bright knots at his waist. He jerked on them; a loop of ropevine fell free.

Cassia looked for Tadge—*he* would agree with her!

The boy was sprawled in the bow, stroking the kotellue. Black and white scales dull, the little creature lay on its side, stubby legs extended. It rolled with the motion of the craft, nictating membranes congealing its blank, black stare.

"Oh, Cassia, is he . . . he isn't . . . ?" Eyes suspiciously shiny, the boy leaned down and whispered in its earholes.

"But the kotellue swims. Just water shouldn't do that!" As Cassia watched in growing concern, the wind wrapped Jarell's robe around her arm. She seemed to see into the kotellue's darkness; there, as in her dream, the goddess offered a knobbed, pinkish rock. Cassia sensed a spark. With her inner eye on the stone, she willed the spark to strengthen; it flared to a candle's flame. The kotellue twitched a foreleg; it gave a faint *chirrup* that was almost lost in the shouts of the farmer's retainers on shore.

"Oh, kotellue, you're all right!" Tadge hugged the lizard.

Making a god sign, Cassia glanced toward the shouts.

The farmer and his helpers had abandoned their boat. They scooped up the priestess, and ran across the top of the dike, then jumped down its other side into the fields.

"Why do you suppose they're running?" Cassia turned to Jarell, who was picking at the last circle of line holding him to the mast.

"Cassia, might you hand me the knife? This knot's—"

She stared behind him.

Far above them poised a brown wall of water. Logs, branches, and rocks studded the great wave.

"The storm in the mountains—it flooded! Tadge!" Cassia groped, but could not reach him.

Jarell whipped around to look.

"Hang on!" Cassia screamed.

And the wave thundered down.

Chapter Twenty-Two

The great wave broke over the raft, turning the wind and sky to water.

"Tadge!" Cassia snatched a breath to scream again; her mouth filled with cold and the taste of mud. A surge pitched her off the logs, forcing her down through the tumbling currents. Her face ground into the bottom. Bark scraped her, and hardened vines. Her heart pounded in her ears as she peered through the murk at a rectangle. *The raft?*

Cloth swirled over her arm. Something solid pulled the cloth away. *Jarell? Tadge?* She caught at the fabric; it tore.

She closed her hand on an arm, felt upward to a muscular shoulder that did not move when she pulled. Jarell, then, still tied to the mast.

Fear for Tadge keened in Cassia's head as she grabbed the knife Jarell had given her and slashed. Jarell floated free.

Lights popped in and out of Cassia's vision. She kicked upward, her lungs convulsing with their need for air.

Her head broke through the waves; breath tore into her lungs. Sobbing, choking, with weighted arms she hauled Jarell to the surface. *And Tadge?*

Dirty water slopped over Jarell's rolled-up eyes. They were

white and staring behind his wet hair. Muddy water trickled from his mouth. *No!*

Pocketing the knife, Cassia started across the currents.

"Here, Cassia!" The distant voice was small over the sound of the wind and the river.

"Tadge!" She scanned the streaming figure on the dike and the kotellue crouched beside it.

Her bitten shoulder and swollen back ached with sudden pain as sharp edges bumped her. She glanced around and saw tied logs behind her. The remains of the raft!

She slapped Jarell across the logs and kicked toward Tadge.

"My kotellue saved me, Cassia! He's my best friend forever." Tadge's irises bleached to gray as Cassia flung Jarell at his feet. Jarell, whose chest did not move, whose lids did not close over his white stare. "Is—is he dead?"

"No! I won't let him be. Go—go get the raft!" She hardly noticed when her small master hurried to obey.

"Goddess, help me." She dropped to the mud and pulled Jarell across her knees, cradling him as if he were a child. Arm on a hard lump in his chest pocket, she ran her finger inside his cold mouth and throat. Clear. Cautious hope warmed her. She shut her eyes. Behind them the darkness became the goddess's black stare. Slowly she offered the stone of Cassia's dream. Cassia reached out—an umber shadow flickered, glowed to faint life . . . The goddess turned to tattered shadows.

Shaking her head, Cassia bent Jarell over her arm and struck his back. Nothing. In her mind the umber light dimmed that was his life force. Outrage consumed her, releasing her childhood stubbornness. "Live, goddess eat you!"

She found a memory of an infant Tadge choking on an unripe songfruit. Turning Jarell upside down she pounded his back, dimly aware of an increased silver light and distant wails.

His robe fell over his face, baring his body. Mud and stones showered down with a tinkling, rattling sound. She thumped him again. He coughed; he shuddered; he took a rasping breath.

"Oh, thank you, Goddess!" Cassia's whisper shook.

With arms weak as riverweed she lowered Jarell's breathing body to her lap. His hair dripped over her sleeve. Below his sodden loincloth he seemed all legs. She averted her eyes. She was fumbling Jarell's torn robe over his legs when Tadge heaved the remains of the raft to the top of the dike and hurried toward her.

"Is—is he—? Oh." Tadge looked at the man taking the boy's

place on Cassia's knees. "You'd better move Jarell before he wakes up. You know he doesn't like being touched."

Cassia nodded, eyes widening. For beyond Tadge, floodwater stretched to the encircling hills. Through it, lines of refugees made for the dike and the city on the mound, its silhouette purple against the sky's yellow and silver afterglow.

Cassia shivered as a chilly wind breathed across her drying robe. The wind rattled through the furbushes whimpering on either side of the dike. Jarell pressed against her, his back and shoulders shaking with tremors.

Reluctantly she lifted him from her lap and set him against the logs that Tadge had positioned against the breeze. When Jarell's warmth left her, she felt bereft.

His lashes were stuck to his cheek; he opened his eyes, failed to focus and closed them again. "Always saying thanks, Cassia," he husked. "Foolish . . . loyal to my father, proud of sailors not learning how to swim."

She laughed, wiping the tears that kept sliding down. "If I just could have done it better. I was so scared!"

Jarell shook; his teeth chattered. "Cold, so cold," he whispered.

"Me too, Cassia." Tadge leaned against her; shudders were running through him.

Cassia looked at the nearest refugees shuffling far in front of her; the closest cottage looked a quarter-day's journey off. It sagged with water, its whitewash gone and its windslits dark; no sparks swarmed from its smoke hole.

As her thoughts scurried like frightened lizards between what must be done and her wish not to do it, evening's tarnished light deepened to violet, and night's chill crept from the shadows, sharpening the edge of the wind.

"Cassia? Remember the priest telling Pa about men falling in the holding ponds up there—getting so cold they died?" Tadge nodded toward the northern peaks. "Will we, uh, die, too?"

"No!" Telling the boy to strip the bark from the logs, Cassia marched to the furbushes. When Tadge had a pile by Jarell, and she had gathered all the curls she could, she untied the inner tapes of her robe—it was almost dry—and pulled it over her head. "Take your robe off, too," she told her startled nursling.

Cassia shivered in her thin undergarments, refusing to think of her ugly round breasts and the patch of fur above her thighs that marked her as slave. They were all too visible in the waning light.

She removed Jarell's robe and spread it on the clay. "Now, here's what we'll do . . ."

Soon they lay folded together on their sides, Jarell's torn robe beneath them. Tadge and the kotellue were against the logs; Jarell curled around the boy's back, with Cassia on the outside. Her robe and Tadge's covered them and a layer of warm, dry furbush curls; the bark on top insulated them from the wind.

Dismay edged through Cassia at how little her undergarments shielded her and her Difference from the man's chilly back. It was only in dreams that her Difference was—was beautiful. Cassia swallowed, pushed down her unease, and gathered him close.

She dreamed she woke in the night to a pink and silver world lit by two lamps hung high behind luminous clouds, the Veil a shimmer of rose behind them.

She dreamed that the earth shook and rocks tumbled in the hills while the kotellue tolled its name, making her start, almost waking her from her slumber. And that Tadge murmured lovingly for it to stop, hiccuped, then resumed his gentle snores. She fell deeper into sleep.

She dreamed that she was well and in her cubicle, her mate's lean angles overlapping her, his heartbeat strong against her own. Softness brushed her throat—his hair, so silken, so black—he turned his head on her shoulder and groaned.

"Ah, gods help me, I need you. Just this once." He pressed his feverish lips to her throat. He cupped her breast and kissed it, he found her hot hidden places, and touched them until she cried out. He murmured, "Sweet . . . lovely . . . darling, darling child."

And he was as she had so often wished: alive but transmuted, his resentment at his wanting her gone, along with his curses, his rough hurried touch, and her flinching desire.

Hungrily she pulled him to her. Their bodies were slicked with moist heat as they moved together in the age-old heart-stopping rhythms; incredulous delight stretched in her until she thought she must shatter into tears and crystal shards of joy.

Sated, glowing with well-being and utter peace, she curved around him, listening to him whisper her name, and slipped into many-colored dreams.

In the white light of morning, Cassia woke alone, her breath puffing smoke like an Ice Dragon's into the frosty air. The robe and the strands of fur covering her were warm against her skin.

Someone had tucked them around her. Who? She hoped no one had seen her Difference. And she had dreamed . . .

Tingling with remembered pleasure, Cassia sat up. Her robe's outer folds and the bark were rimed with frost. As cold knifed into her bitten shoulder, she forgot all but its ache.

Dressed, she leaned against the logs, waiting for the pain to lessen. She felt sore but relaxed in odd places. Because of her unexpected swim, she supposed. Unless . . . No, of course it had been a dream.

Cassia looked across the fertile valley of the day before. On the shallow lake that now covered it, nothing moved but the wind. From the silver sky a few flakes drifted down, to melt on the clay at her feet, or hiss into the drowned crops below. A freeze, she thought. It would finish the destruction that the flooding began. No wonder the refugees wailed. Stiffly she went in search of her companions.

On the other side of the logs she found Tadge walking up and down the dike, slapping his arms and rubbing his hands above the rock and mud buildings he had constructed on the ridges of yesterday's labor. Tadge picked up a stone. The kotellue waddled over and licked it, revealing a streak of scarlet. Boy and lizard were more uniform; the mud covered them.

Thanking the lizard, Tadge crowned a tower with the stone. He paused and hefted a larger one, knobbed at both ends and connected by a central spindle; one end's curve seemed to fit comfortably in his hand.

He started to put it on a topless tower but the kotellue nudged a nearby rock. Tadge laughed, dropped the knobbed stone in his pocket, and used the lizard's choice. Then he saw Cassia.

"Ho! I thought you'd never wake up. Jarell and I already had firstmeal." He made a face and waved at the limp seedlings below.

Beside the seedlings, at the water's edge, Jarell paced and stamped, the worst of his mud gone. He expelled a frosty breath as he methodically searched and re-searched his torn front pocket.

He can't forgive this indignity too, Cassia thought. *Oh, why wasn't I the one to be turned upside down and thumped?*

Well, best to get the moment over. With false cheer she called down, "I can mend your robe. I still have the knife. I can whittle a needle and pull a thread from your hem."

He stared at the river and shook his head. "So can I. It's not my robe that concerns me." He let go of it to gesture; the torn folds whipped wide in the frigid wind. "It's every gem, every section of chain—gone. Even the—even the most valuable one. They're all there, but where?"

"Gems?" Cassia stammered. "Oh. The ones from that first night? But you don't wear them. Do you really need them?"

He swung around. Did she imagine that his dark gaze softened? "Yes I need them! Why else, in that cave while I waited for you to wake, would I have broken them up and hidden them in my robe?" His laugh was harsh. "Where did you think the jewel came from that paid for our raft and supplies? And in the lowlands did you suppose we would live on air and nectar? Here we must pay. For everything."

Savagely, he gestured at the valley that could offer them no work, no food, no aid. "The river has it all. I cannot buy you a healer's services, nor fare for a single day, let alone passage on a starship."

He slanted her a look compounded of misery, hope, cunning. Or was it a trick of the shadowless light? But she thought he added under his breath, "However, you must and will be saved. You are all I have left."

Chapter Twenty-Three

Cycle: (1) Napharese unit of time corresponding to a Sol III Standard Year. Measured from spring to spring, perhaps because the violent Napharese springs uproot many lives.

NAPHARESE VOCABULARY LISTS:
GRINELDA MAO-VANSCHUYLER, ACTING ANTHROPOLOGIST,
GALACTIC CENTRAL REST AND RESEARCH STATION,
QAQQADUM, NORTHERN NAPHAR.

The city on the mound floated like a dream in silver mists. Below it, water covered the valley floor; only the dike beside the river drew a dark line through the floodwater to the city.

As Shamash the Sun God breathed his vigor and heat and light into the day, the mists turned to gold, then hazy lavender. On the dike, the trickle of refugees grew to a stream. Their dark hair and eyes looked exotic to Cassia, who was used to highlanders colored like dried grass and the dusty mountainsides they tilled.

As green needles spun bars of iridescence across the waters, she greeted a family of potmenders, using the tribal signs. She begged needle and thread from them to mend Jarell's robe, and repaid the favor by helping repair their barrow's plank wheel. They traded news.

There would be many cheap slaves now, the young man said as they pulled off the wheel. Those ruined by the flood must sell themselves and their children to pay their creditors. Buyers— butcher priests and slavers—crowded the town.

Cassia hammered an iron band around the wheel with needless force. *She* had been sold away from home, from love. It was wrong!

"A priest from the capital," the young man said, "tall as a god and as beautiful, but with lizard hands, cries reward for two escaped slaves and a boy." Cassia's breath stopped. *Salimar!*

She hunted for Tadge. Her nursling must be kept safe! He lay in the barrow's shade, fondly scolding the lizard that again had failed to return a stick. The boy reached into his robe for a pinkish knobbed stone, hefted it, and met Cassia's glance as she mentally called, *Help us!* to Jarell, thinking she spoke aloud.

Jarell went on sewing and joking with the potmender's mate.

But he must answer—he was Cassia's; she needed him! She lifted her chin, imperious as her old childish self; she seemed to fall into Tadge's eyes until she saw only the rock he held—and the goddess behind it who frowned.

Mentally Cassia reached; she touched hazy amber sureness with thoughts moving in it like small strong fish. Behind it, in gold mists, drifted rose dreams. She pulled.

The laughter drained from Jarell's face; he took a step toward her—another. He looked as he had on the island at night.

I did that! Cassia felt grass blades of pride thrust up in her. Then, nauseated, *I am no better than Salimar.* And she released the russets and ambers that were her friend. They scattered like veils in the light and dark chambers of her mind.

"Salimar's here!" she said as Jarell shook his head like one waking. He told the potmenders he had no coin to buy their silence.

"We have no love for this new dark god who slaughters the

Anadajoie as unbelievers. Gladly we help his enemies," the young potmender told them.

More callous taking of life! More fuel for Cassia's anger.

"Was that you?" Low-voiced, Jarell broke in on her thoughts.

She blushed. "I—I think so. I won't do it again."

After a long moment he gave a snort of laughter. "What have I loosed on Naphar and on myself? 'Just another mindless beast!' Almost I believe in your goddess, and her sense of humor."

The potmender woman tugged at Cassia's head-wrap of trade-cloth; she tucked in a curl. Straightening, Cassia thanked her for the partial disguise and the globes of bread and curd. She sighed as below, Tadge slapped mud on his curls she had washed that morning. Only Jarell had refused to change, saying with a shrug that Salimar could find him any night he wished.

As they parted, Cassia asked, "The town—what is it called?"

"Kaladussa, lady. The City of Joyful Sounds."

"Way!" a man called. "Way for the Lady Anatta!"

The crowd on the track parted. Behind the forerunner came a chariot driven by a young Rabu, her black loops and plaits flashing with jewels. The refugees knelt before her like a field of immer in a high wind. So did Jarell. Cassia, following his coaching, stood with the other Rabu. By her knee Jarell shoved a protesting Tadge into a puddle where the kotellue lay submerged.

Cassia stared at ten light and dark Kakanos pelting toward them pulling a white and gold chariot—its wheels had spokes!

"I've heard of lightening wheels that way, but my master wouldn't try." The team pounded by. Sketching a salute to Cassia, its driver shouted for more speed, her white tunic whipping around her thighs. Cassia's shocked look met Jarell's amused one. His eyes widened as he glanced over her shoulder.

"Move, Cassia!" Jarell grabbed Tadge and dove for the verge.

A chariot crusted with red, green, and brown gems exploded through the crowd. Its team of ten blond Kakanos scattered the refugees like chaff from a thresher.

"Kotellue, my kotellue!" Tadge plunged in Jarell's grip, his anguished gaze on the lizard deep in the puddle. Its eyes were opaqued, its earholes tightened to pinpricks. It was blind and deaf to danger.

Beyond them the cursing driver jerked up a runner just before she fell under the wheels; then he dropped his reins and disappeared onto the chariot's floor, still yelling at his team. In spite of

the stocky leader's efforts, the team veered toward the puddle.
The dike rained screeching Kakanos. Cassia gathered herself.

When Jarell did the same, Tadge pulled free. He snatched the
kotellue just as the chariot sliced through the puddle.

The lizard gave a rising sound like a woman's scream; muddy
water tinged with pink arced to the sky. The chariot barreled
down the track, sending more travelers flying. Tadge held onto
the lizard and danced into the road. "Insolent beast!"

"Shut your teeth!" Jarell glanced after the chariots as the
woman driver turned in time to intercept his scowl. She frowned,
swerved around a dray, and raced on.

Tadge waved a bloody tip. "That rolling dung ball!"

"I'll not be whipped or flayed or Sacrificed for a lizard tail,"
Jarell cut in. "Keep shut or go home. Understood?"

Tadge poked a sandal in the crusting mud. "Sure, Jarell. You
want me to crawl and beg for a kick like you."

Over Cassia's angry gasp, Jarell said, "Well? You knew the
conditions. Will you stay and crawl with me? Or go!"

The boy glanced at him, then up at Cassia; he swallowed. The
kotellue plumped down between Tadge's feet; it hissed defiance.
He patted it. "Stay, I guess. Sorry."

Cassia's heart melted at the bent tousled head and small
shoulders sagging so far below her. Jarell, however, appeared
unmoved. Without a backward look, he trudged on.

Chapter Twenty-Four

Sight and perception are inextricably bound. Can we compare our world to
that of a pollen snatcher crawling through a blossom on paths invisible to us but
clear to it in the ultraviolet light it sees by? Can we compare the brilliant days we
bask in to those same days' intolerable heat and brightness and radiation that drive
underground our off-worlder instructors evolved under older, darker stars? Can we
compare the nights we blunder through with those traversed with sureness by our
large-eyed nocturnal tree-hiders and Those Who Hunt by Night? Can we even
compare all these various days and nights with those of the colonist gods who
preceded us, fleeing inward from the thin-starred edge of the galaxy, forever hunting a world like their lost one circling their dead, red sun? Or for that matter, do

even Rabu and Kakano share this world at night? Outside these walls it is forbidden to whisper that Kakanos inherit their vision from the alien gods our fathers, and see well under the Veil's scarlet light—while Rabu look with the eyes of the goddess our mother, inherited from her diurnal mammals, whose furthest ancestors have gazed only at the light of a yellow-to-white star. Yet all these worlds are still Naphar.

> PERCEPTION OF BEING: PHILOSOPHY OF FIRST CONTACT.
> TEXT FOR SCOUTSHIP CREWS,
> TEMPLE SPACE ACADEMY PRESS. FOURTH EDITION.

I

Thunder loud as collapsing palaces woke Cassia in the night. Lightning ripped the clouds; through their scudding black the Veil glowed fitful red. As her nocturnal strength and the lumps on her back grew, Cassia found greater color and detail in the dark. Because she became more Night Demon, less human? She winced from the thought. The downpour drummed toward her, replacing the sharpness in the air with the smell of rain. Behind her, Jarell hugged his pulled-up knees.

Tadge wriggled closer; his head lay on her shoulder like a heavy flower. "I love you, Cassia," he murmured sleepily.

"I know." Her unbathed wound throbbed and ached. The rain sluiced down. "Will you shelter with us?" she asked Jarell.

Sheets of cold fire blew across the floodwaters; their reflections filled Jarell's eyes with flames. "What are you offering me, Cassia? Mothering? Pity?" He shook his head. "I'm enough in your debt as it is."

She hid her hot cheeks in Tadge's curls. She could not give more! The memory of her dead mate's dark, bitter gaze and their stillborn babe floated before her like specters. After a long while, she slept.

II

The rain fell too in Kaladussa, thrumming on the tiles of Salimar's borrowed palace. One who had led a long, full life had willed the palace to the goddess, wishing thus to avoid that life's consequences. When no visiting dignitary required the palace's echoing rooms, Oprekka Enna, Kaladussa's thrifty head priestess, used it as a warehouse. Consequently, bits of crates, torn lizard-skin pouches, and a prizing tool strewed the audience chamber.

A lamp lit the chamber's gloom, shedding a yellow glow over a table stacked with coins, scrolls, and the remains of a meal. Salimar stood behind the table, surveying his red-eyed priest and ranked, unmoving minions. He cleared his throat; he picked up a scroll written in Oprekka's tidy hand on the backs of requisitions for the temple kitchens.

"Here is our spy's plan for overthrowing Qaqqadum's Ensai and the decadent goddess cult," Salimar said. "'Forty crunchroots, hairs intact; eleven warted lizard skins baled for scrubbing.' Bah!" Salimar slapped the parchment onto the table. Then he turned it over. He ignored a snort from the darkness as he read out names, places, and times. He ended with a list of grog shops by wharves, academies, and the Southern Gate, where militia ould be recruited cheaply for a few days' fighting.

Salimar called up two slavers. He eyed their blank stares and beckoned to the old priest.

"Go with them," Salimar told the priest. "Set up communications, leave the slavers in charge, and report back to me." At the older man's protest, Salimar hissed, "I need coin. Promise the off-worlder the Stone, crews for his company's unshielded ships, *anything*, but bring coin. This she-beetle, Oprekka Enna"—Salimar spat at a broken box—"prates of poverty and gives me nothing—*nothing!* While I, Salimar, high priest of the Dark God and the Dark God incarnate, am reduced to begging and fending off creditors, while daily in the beetle's antechamber her simpering priestesses say only, 'She returns from the capital soon, dear man'!"

Salimar ended in a falsetto that sent the priest from the room. A titter came out of the darkness. Salimar glared at a square-jawed woman with cropped gray and fair hair. She straightened her smile. "You dare to laugh at me?" he growled. "Come!"

He hurled his mental thunderbolts and watched with satisfaction as her eyes unfocused and she marched to him.

He cuffed her backhanded and cuffed her again. Until, wearying of his sport, he let the thing leaking blood and tears crawl from him. "Go!" he screamed to the silent slavers, and watched them shuffle to their posts on the roads surrounding Kaladussa.

Alone, Salimar leaned against the wall cold with rain, and dropped his face in his ruined hands.

Just two possessions—one slave, the other the Mindstone—had solaced this demon that rode Salimar, sucking light and color and taste from his days: Jarell the Singer, who brought music to shake the soul, and laughter in the night; and the Stone, whose visions held terror enough to blank all feeling.

Soon Salimar would own slave and Stone both—and Naphar. He saw possibilities in this rebellion that Oprekka and the priest did not. They sought to use him; they would find themselves used! For Salimar's energy and mental strength were greater than theirs, and he lacked their scruples. He could not return to his mindless life with the lizards and voiceless beasts on the green hills above Qaqqadum, for who can refuse knowledge once it has been gained? Instead, he would stand on command's frozen pinnacle with only the wind and the sun for equals. There he would possess power so great, this terrible loneliness must end. Lonely . . . Salimar lowered his hands.

His hands! Once so white, so graceful they earned an Ensai's compliments; once they held a singing man; a Stone . . .

Loss rang in Salimar like iron; he saw his demon's face.

With a howl Salimar clenched his gray talons. He grabbed the prizing tool to smash the walls; the table; the earth, his mother, that had betrayed him. He wept, shaken by pain and fury and a child's panic as outside, the night burning with lightning wept icy rain.

III

Rain fell, too—a fine, penetrating mist—in wheel-shaped Qaqqadum, the white and amber capital of Northern Naphar, perched on the cliffs above the Western Sea.

In the city's hub, water dripped from the Ensai's palace of whitestone and gold, it trickled down the great stone blocks of the Temple of Sassurum, it stood in shining drops on the house of Sassurum's high priestess, which was set between them.

In the high priestess's house, Oprekka Enna slipped from her guest's cubicle, its yellow curtains scarcely moving behind her bulk. Once more she had put off her departure, this time pleading rain and muddy roads. She stole noiselessly as a hunting lizard toward her high priestess's rooms. Oprekka scanned the corridors, her nose twitching.

Plain! she thought. Good materials in the tapestries and sculptures, but where was the flare of gold and flash of jewels that proclaimed Phikola En's importance to the world? Nowhere! That tasteless creature should never have been high priestess.

Oprekka, now, *she* had imagination. Mentally she hung the

walls with trapperfish silks, luminous with seasonal dousings of salt water. Lovely really, and so saving of lamps and candles! Oprekka imagined herself alight with jewels; she added a train of deferential foreign and off-world courtiers . . .

Oprekka started—she had almost passed Phikola's entrance. Lucky her old classmate had that low, loud voice. Hm. Whom could she be entertaining at this time of night?

Oprekka breathed excitedly through her mouth as she tiptoed to Phikola's door; she applied one pale blue eye to the gap between the entrance curtain and the frame.

The anteroom to Phikola's sleep-chamber shimmered with lamplight. A tall creature all in black stood by the windslit; the creature held scrolls in its black claws. A manlength away, Phikola En, High Priestess of Sassurum and religious ruler of Qaqqadum, sat on cushions on the tessellated floor. She pored over a document weighted open with heavenstone ingots. Pointing to a string of wedges, dots, and slanted lines, Phikola counted off, "Cytosine, quanine, thymine, adenine. This combination looks promising. The New Children will not be noticeably different from the other orphans in our Homes of the Compassionate Goddess?"

Partway through her visitor's answer, Phikola raised her head. She rose, rang a bell of fire crystal, and called, "A messenger-lizard's mindcall, Yanna!" A scarlet flying lizard shot through the windslit. It dropped, spent, into Phikola's arms.

She bent over it, stroking mud and scales from its blunt head and heaving sides. Ignored, her tall visitor wrapped his cloak around him like silence and leaned against the wall. Nictating membranes similar to the lizard's climbed his eyes.

In answer to Phikola's call, an elderly serving woman bustled in exclaiming, set a golden bowl on the table below the windslit and departed, still exclaiming.

"Well done!" Phikola crooned to the lizard. "To reach the highlands, find my Chief Unraveller of Secrets, and return in so few days and nights!" She tipped the bowl's clear pink liquid invitingly. "Drink. It is nectar, and redfruit squeezings to revive you."

The transparent lids dulling the lizard's eyes snapped down. With a hiss it plunged its snout into the fluid, blew ecstatic bubbles, and gulped more.

The high priestess balanced lizard and bowl with care as she

sank onto a floor cushion, her pale nightrobe billowing about her.
She communed mentally with the flier.

   . . . In a nearby courtyard a caged lizard sang of lonely heartbreak; a watchman's call twined with it, and drunken laughter. A
door slammed. The scent of rain and smoke and early flowers
breathed through the windslit, mixing with the warmth of the
room, the smell of lamp oil, and the lizard's musky heat . . .

   When the bowl gleamed empty, the flier hissed and snaked its
head toward Phikola's.

   "Come," she said. "You must tell this to the Ensai."

   In the tunnel, the lizard perched on Phikola En's shoulder, its
tail curled around her neck. The lizard hissed in subdued alarm.
With its claws it kneaded the surplice covering Phikola's nightrobe.

   She held the stone lamp high; the light in its sides glowed like
a captured sun. It illuminated the passage leading from her house
to the Ensai, secular head of Qaqqadum.

   The scarf of flame and smoke thinned; Phikola passed the
lamp over a sand-colored wall, watching the shadows fly across
antique picture writing, underlined by modern wedges, dots, and
lines.

   The lizard hissed and pushed its head beneath her chin. Absently she scratched its throat while computing the time of year,
the state of the moons, her own rank and girth. She murmured a
prayer for accuracy, set her fingers in the proper niches, and
pulled.

   With an oiled rumble, the wall began to open; a massive
counterweight swung outward to poise above her head.

   The flying lizard on Phikola's shoulder started; she stroked its
unfolding wings. The gap was almost wide enough . . . now! She
darted through it.

   Behind her the wall slammed shut; the counterweight crashed
to the passage's floor with a muffled boom.

   The lizard's claws dug into Phikola's shoulder. It chattered
about the noise, the vast chamber, the guards in the four corners
holding smoking lamps, and the absence of windslits. *How may I
escape?* it screeched in her mind.

   It was true, Phikola thought, reassuring the lizard. Only this
chamber and a few others in Qaqqadum had escaped the zeal of a
past Ensai. Delighted with the holes cut in his walls by imported
southern craftsmen, he wanted similar ones everywhere he went,
so he set taxes that doubled the price of any construction or re-

pairs that did not include windslits. Now only the very wealthy and the very poor could own an antique dark.

Phikola addressed her consort, who lay behind red and blue banners depending from the ceiling. "Brother, I bring—Oh!"

From the shadows beyond the silken panels sailed a black man-sized ovoid set with eight red eyes. Four pairs of hairy legs doubled under it as it sprang; in its gaping mouth, fangs dripped venom and opened to engulf Phikola's head.

The flier on her shoulder shrieked and levitated. It looped toward a pillar, and darted under the finial, one of the sparkling stone boughs that supported the roof.

Phikola's heart tripped over her breath. She dodged the spider's charge. "Dass! Return to your post. It is I!" A similar order rapped from behind the silks.

The great arachnid shot past the high priestess, crunched into the wall at her back, and plopped to the tiles. It rose on six of its legs; tufts of black hair stood up in embarrassment so strong the spider lost its ability to mindspeak. Silently Dass limped around the streamers to twin portals leading to halls dank with the breath of rain.

The boy waiting at the portals looked from Dass to his blade wet with fresh poison. The boy wiped the blade, and returned it to his sleeve.

The spider's black cephalothorax quivered. Facing the high priestess, it started the Begging of Ten Thousand Pardons.

The arachnid—its size, age, and intelligence a legacy of the vanished gods who had hoped to use its kind as draft animals— was on its eleventh plea and clambering aboard the boy's shoulders when a pale hand emerged from the banners. From behind the banners a melodious voice said, "Enough, Dass. The fault was mine. Lost in joy at our visitors, I failed to give your signal.

"And now, welcome, my sister, my consort my love. What brings you here to beguile this tedious night?"

The spider's apologies dreamed into silence. Its lifelong communion with the boy resumed. Above them the flying lizard's circles tightened; the lizard settled on a chiseled twig.

"The pain is still worst before dawn, my brother?" When the hand flipped the banners impatiently, Phikola said in harsher tones, "This messenger has news of the Stone."

"Tell me. Mind speech, even with such as yourselves, is too much for me tonight."

Phikola shrugged and stepped into the lamplight. The light

shimmered the yellows and bronzes of her floor-length surplice. She nodded toward the guards. "I trust your mutes do not read mouths. Simply: my operative has located the Mindstone. He asks whether to retrieve it, or to arrange for its thieves to bring it here. As for which off-worlders caused this treason—"

The hand waved. "No names! I have not your mental shields. As for your alternatives, I like the second one, sister mine; it has your subtle touch. The Stone cannot be lost?"

"Impossible. Veteran fighters surround it. The one who holds it—"

"Enough. I trust you. Our interests lie together in this.

"But of late, and wakeful in this rain, I find I miss other of your attributes. You know my mutes repeat nothing. So if you and your messenger are in no hurry to return?" It was as close as Phikola's consort would come now to the begging that once he had not been ashamed to employ.

Phikola considered. Dass's attack was not all accident, she thought. Even when they were children her older half brother, son of two rulers, had shown an invalid's spite toward her and the other exuberantly healthy offspring of the concubines. And as yet he had offered no apology for her fright, when once her smallest discomfort had brought tears of distress to his eyes. She stiffened her back. "I am very tired, my brother."

But I have played my own tricks, she thought, *while taking with both hands all that he can give. Even now my old friend spins more than one scheme for me in the highlands. And shall I not share my plenty with one who, in himself, has so little?*

Besides, the pallet was an excellent place for the sniffing out of secrets. Smoothly Phikola continued, "But my mind races with this news. I cannot speak for the goddess's own."

Above her, the flier launched itself toward the doors. The hand in the silks gestured. The boy opened the portals; the messenger banked through.

Phikola nodded toward the closing doors. Her voice was husky with the familiar welling of revulsion, wary pity, and tenderness, as she said, "Sleep and the nesting tunnels in Sassurum's dome call there, I think. But I am wanted nowhere for some time yet, my love. And I, like you, have little expectation of rest before dawn."

She listened to her consort's quickened breathing as she glided across the shadows to the banners and the one who lay behind them, her golden sandals whispering with the sound of rain.

* * *

Oprekka Enna yawned and rubbed her aching back. With a bleary eye the head priestess of Kaladussa measured the predawn light filtering through the dripping windslit of Phikola's private apartments.

Gone all night! No need to ask what her old classmate was doing! But those documents on the floor, now—if only Oprekka dared scan them, just for a moment.

Again she squinted at the strengthening dawn.

Almost here. Wherever Phikola was, she could not return to her rooms, then go to the temple, before the Sun God peered over the horizon. As high priestess of Sassurum, Phikola must welcome the day's New Beginning on the steps of the temple, even as her trumpeters heralded it from the dome. So there should be time.

Oprekka Enna gave an excited snort as she shoved open the door curtain. She ran into the apartment with a lightness surprising in one of her size. As she knelt in front of the scroll her knees creaked. She whistled air through her teeth; she rounded her eyes.

"Genetic diagrams! Of Rabu." She yanked open a second scroll. "And Kakano." She pursed her small mouth as she studied the two documents, then let them snap closed. She stared, unseeing, at the brightening rain. "Infamous," she hissed. "To tamper with the goddess-ordained sizes of our people! If Phikola En succeeds there will be no difference between Rabu and Kakano, slave and free, noble and plebeian. Is this what I have labored for? To climb to a place *that woman* would make no place at all?"

Humming sounds came from Oprekka's nose. She added, "Not that I care for myself! Oh, no. I'm nobody, only a humble priestess, doing her duty as best she can. But for my Ibby, with his noble blood, to be no better than the lowest dung peddler!" Oprekka flexed her hands as if she crushed the parchment.

Instead, after a moment, she smoothed it. She took a wax tablet and stylus from her sleeve and wrote quickly, glancing often at the streaming windslit and the door behind her.

Carefully she left the scrolls as she had found them; she got up with a minimum of popping of the joints. She peered into the shadows beside the windslit and started.

She hurried down the hall muttering, "Forgot about her visitor. Just leaning there, meditating, eyes covered with that transparent lid— Gave me palpitations; I'll never be used to them, never! But there. They don't interfere, and even if they did they wouldn't dare tamper with *me*, not if they want to leave their city, or enjoy their nightly nourishment."

With a snorting giggle Oprekka pinched awake the diminutive priestess lying across Oprekka's doorway. Oprekka set the girl to packing. On top of everything went provisions: a napkin of pastries and sweets pocketed at banquets in Oprekka's honor. "Only a little stale—and so saving!" Her voice echoed in the emptied guest chamber. "Now get my litter and extra bearers. I must be in Kaladussa by moonrise. I bring news of treason!"

"Perhaps this will galvanize that deep-voiced lump, Salimar," Oprekka muttered as the priestess hurried away. "Dear, dear, the Mindstone's prophecy was an inspiration, but such work! Spreading rumors about the Dark One being the Dark God; finding a buyer, and Salimar . . . who won't fight but whines for coin—from *me*, a poor woman alone and with a son to raise. But I'll not complain! Only after the revolution succeeds, perhaps I'll be rid of Salimar. So much thriftier doing accounts for an undivided rule."

In her litter Oprekka munched her sweets and eyed the dawn, impatient to begin her return journey to Kaladussa.

Chapter Twenty-Five

The primitive forests of Naphar resemble the Tertiary ones of Sol III: they include pines, large fern trees, deciduous ones, and other flora, some with unusual properties.

> GUIDE TO NAPHAR
> (TO BE KEPT WITH PASSPORT BY ALL VISITORS TO
> GALACTIC CENTRAL REST AND RESEARCH STATION,
> QAQQADUM, NORTHERN NAPHAR).

On the road through the flood, the rain stopped before dawn; the water began to recede. After a meager firstmeal Cassia and Tadge again followed Jarell toward Kaladussa.

The morning warmed. Sunlight shafted through billowing clouds; ground fog rolled into the valleys. A breeze dried the track to a cracked brown ribbon connecting muddy farmlands to copses, and to Rabu and Kakano royals' villas whose high walls were traced with vines. In the fields, shards of blue flashed like spare summer skies; between them colors frothed.

With a smile, Cassia pointed from the distant colors to the familiar springtime miracle at their feet. "Look, Tadge. Bubble riders."

A break in the dirt pouted into a mound. Antennae, little feet, then a beetle's drab brown shell broke through. Grains of loam still clung to its back, when it started blowing a translucent bubble, bright as flame. The bubble inflated to palm size; the beetle clambered aboard.

A breeze took the bubble, bouncing it along the tussocks and skimming it over puddles, its creator sprawled on top, still blowing. On the next bound, the wind from the river caught the scarlet and orange sphere and lifted it high to join its fellows of green, amber, blue, on its chancy journey to the highlands.

"Have you not been this before, child?" Jarell spoke from behind Cassia.

"Oh yes! Always, at home on the first warm day after a rain. It's the same!"

"A great many other things are not." Jarell shielded his eyes with his hand. "Now that I have no treasure to ease our way, I wonder if you would not be safer waiting for a healer in your highlands where you know the dangers. So long as you bathe in the river and your spirits remain high, I think there is time."

Cassia was hit with disappointment. The highlands bubble riders would float across the valley, past the volcanoes to the Western Sea. And she would not? "I—I thought you needed me." Tadge ran past the steaming fields where bright balls, each with its little passenger, bounded through ramparts and palaces of fog.

After a while Jarell said, voice low, "I do need you." His eyes were hooded as he stared up at her. "Remember: I tried to pay my debt." He started down the track.

Feeling unreasonably happy, Cassia followed.

Cassia shifted Tadge, who was asleep on her good shoulder. Her bitten one ached steadily now. She glanced back at Jarell. He walked like one drugged for Sacrifice. A sandal was missing; only a part of the other remained. Amber light from the setting sun heightened the lines of exhaustion in his face.

They came to a wood. At its edge was a stele carved with the broad wings of the Misbegotten, signaling danger within.

Cassia peered longingly at the trees. *Food, shelter, a place to hide. And only superstition keeps us out.* She hardly faltered. As the refugees settling on the verge murmured disapproval, she soothed her flutter of fear with a gesture asking the goddess's protection, and left the track.

In a stand of pines Jarell slumped to the needles and slept. Shadows dimmed the air; the sun glided into the smoke above the volcanoes, turning the amber sunlight to red. Cassia pulled Tadge onto her lap and shut her eyes.

When they woke, night was fully upon them.

They finished the last crumbs, curd, and wilted seedlings. Tadge wandered off to hunt for tender needle tips.

Jarell looked around. "Stay—these woods aren't safe."

But Tadge and the kotellue had vanished behind a tree. Cassia hurried after them. Wearily, Jarell followed.

Through the branches Cassia glimpsed the round faces of the moons edging over the distant peaks; their dark companion emitted an eerie glow tipped with fire. White radiance glittered on the needles. Cassia made the sign against demos.

The volcanoes rumbled; from either end of the wood came the crash of stones and muffled cries. She tensed, heart thudding, unready as always for the quakes that must follow—but among the pines no wind blew, and the earth lay as steady as if it rooted in the center-post of the world. A fragrance of warmth and feasting breathed through the boughs.

Cassia's pace slowed. She came upon Tadge looking in a pine cone for seeds. By his knee the kotellue flicked its tongue; it swung its blunt head toward the teasing aroma. Its throat pulsed in a mournful cry; it lumbered into a run. Tadge sniffed.

"What's that? It smells good!" He hurried after the lizard. Its markings blended with the moonlight and shadow.

Ahead of them Cassia glimpsed something white. She breathed in the scents and hurried toward it.

Behind her Jarell shouted. Cassia didn't heed it. She burst into a glade washed with moonlight. In its center stood a ring of pale, motionless flowers. The kotellue galloped toward them as a breeze sighed across the grass, flattening it to silver. The luminous blooms never moved.

Cassia smelled spice cakes and honey, grain mixed with cold well water and eaten raw from the palm, redfruit bursting with juice. Her belly tightened with hunger. She ran toward the blossoms.

The lizard was ahead of her. With a quavering call it braced its forelegs against the nearest white stem, which broke with a tiny pop. The bell-shaped flower tipped; spores showered into the moonlight, covering the lizard and the ground like snow.

Cassia stopped beside the lizard and grasped a smaller stem. Light, spongy, it snapped easily. The spore cases dripping from it jiggled but stayed intact. She raised it to her lips.

"Cassia! Don't!" Jarell broke from the trees and leaped. He knocked the flower out of her hand; he shook another from Tadge's.

Cassia licked dry lips. She cried, "Oh, why?"

"Demons eat you, Jarell!" Tadge shrilled as he struggled in the man's grasp. "It was fried sausage, cakes with pinksweet syrup—"

"But," Cassia protested, "I smelled grain, redfruit—"

"Did you breath any spores? Swallow any? They sting, then numb, so you want more." Jarell's voice was harsh.

Cassia shook her head. Tadge said bitterly, "You saw."

At the edge of the glade Jarell dropped clumps of grass in their laps. The moons outlined him with pale fire. "Wipe your hands. Every child knows of the Death Flowers of Membliar and runs from the scent of banquets in the forest at night."

Cassia swallowed. She wiped her hands again. "A flower? A flower wouldn't—" She remembered the Green Priestess's circle of plants in the courtyard of Sassurum. Flowers did kill, and more. Yet how could she know? Those plants did not grow in the highlands. She was recalled to the glade by a weak chirrup.

"Kotellue, my kotellue!" Tadge dropped his handful of grass, and ran back to the clearing.

The lizard was on its side. Spores and shattered stems were white around it. Tadge knelt. "Kotellue?" He stroked the lizard's broad forehead; he scratched its eye ridges.

The kotellue let its tongue drift across Tadge's hand. It peered blindly toward him, raised its head, and hissed. It jerked, became rigid, stubby legs stretched in front of it.

"What's the matter with him? Will he get better?" Tadge's voice was thin. He petted and petted the lizard's neck.

The kotellue flicked its tongue, questing: it called the first two notes of its name; its head thumped to the grass.

Tadge gave a hard little sob and dove toward the body.

"No! The spores!" Jarell carried the screaming boy into the trees.

When Tadge's sobs were less frequent, Jarell still held him. *Jarell looks spent—old. Older than I*, Cassia remembered with surprise. *And he never touches. Perhaps the moons do bring changes.*

"I regret, Tadge, I could reach only you and Cassia," Jarell was saying. "For your kotellue it was too late the moment the first spore hit his tongue."

"No! It's not!" Tadge wrenched out of Jarell's arms.

When Cassia stood beside Tadge in the center of the glade she thought for a moment the kotellue lived—breathed. Its plump side rose, swelled; it split. The tip of a bell emerged, blackened by trickles of sluggish blood.

With sucking noises the flower grew swiftly, its dark-smeared head reaching toward the Dark One and the moons. At its base, white tendrils bored through the lizard's corpse, feeding, lacing it to the turf, passing its nutrients to other, less fortunate blooms.

Jarell pointed to the ring's foundations. Each blossom grew from a skull—small Kakano, a lizard, huge Rabu. Bleached, eyeless, they stared at the sky, ribs pushed wide by the roots of the lovely, insatiable plants.

"The Death Flowers call with scents of the food we love best." Jarell touched the boy's shoulder. Tadge breathed in quick, shallow gasps. "At least you were with your friend. He did not die alone."

The boy whirled. "You let him get killed! You never wanted him—you're glad he's dead. I hate you!"

"Tadge!" Cassia exclaimed as Jarell reached for him.

The child dodged. "Don't you touch me, you—" He named a much-ravished cup-bearer of one of the less respectable gods. "The potmender boys told me about you. I wanted to fight them. Because I thought you were—" he dashed tears from his eyes. "I was wrong! You're just a cowardly slave like Cassia."

"He doesn't mean it," Cassia whispered.

Jarell stood as still as inked stone. Overhead the moons and the Dark One floated free of the trees. "I am also alive. Which none of us will be if you continue to speak and act as you please. You go to the highlands with the first potmenders we see."

"No! Pa—I won't! And you can't make me, you—"

"I can," Jarell said clearly. "Whatever else I may be, I at least know my father's name."

Tadge opened his eyes wide. He stepped back and fled.

"No, don't go!" The doubled moonlight confused Cassia as

she hunted her nursling in the woods. On the road that the trees and the moons changed to cobbled shadow, she turned back.

She stood again in the clearing where the flowers bloomed. Near them Jarell scrubbed at his hands. "I tried to free the kotellue for burial; couldn't. Roots too strong. Pheromones are potent, too. Tempted to eat the flowers, myself."

"I can't find Tadge. If we both looked for him . . ."

"You believe he would come to me? He'll find you. Take him to the highlands."

Cassia sank to the grass. "But why? Because of what he said? He—he's like that when he's overtired, hungry."

"Hungry! The gods save us from his starvation."

Cassia looked up from the holes she was punching in the turf. "You listened when he told me about his father."

"I did. My welfare was involved. I've done worse. I will not change to fit the requirements of a prudish highlands beast." Jarell stood with an athlete's easy grace but his breath came fast, as if he were running a race. "Go back where it's safe, Cassia," he breathed. "I don't want to do this."

"But I want to stay with you, learn from you!"

He prowled toward her. "You wish my more informal learning—which you seem so unaccountably to have forgotten?"

But he hated to be touched, while she . . . She remembered her mate's hard, hot body, his waves of self-hate when he lay with her. "I can't . . ." Why did Jarell cause her this anguish? Why not? He was small, a master. Even if he were a beast like her—with his evasions, his sly maneuvering, how could she ever be certain of him?

He waited. The moons lit strange pale lights in his hair. His robe smelled of clay. *But if this is his price?* He moved closer; his robe stroked her hand. A wave of desire moved in her. "I—if you need me." She shut her eyes and reached.

He was not there.

"No! Not like that, child. I would not have you sully the principles you so plainly hold." He spread his ringless hands. "I find I miss my ornaments. Since I plan to return to the craft that Tadge described just now with such learning, I do not care to dispense my favors to a coinless, forgetful, unbathed Rabu."

Fury scalded Cassia's eyes. As she reached in her sleeve for her childhood's dagger, she leaped up. Impotent, raging, she clenched her empty fist. "Kateeb, I don't want your favors! I was willing to suffer your fumblings, just to stay. And to think I worried—pitied—was being so careful." She would not blink—he would not see her tears! She'd kill him first. She strode to the edge of the clearing.

"Cassia."

She swung around, hoping. She shivered with self-disgust.

Jarell held out two round white objects. "Give these to Tadge. And watch for the healer I will send to you. Soon."

On his palm were globes as colorless as the Death Flowers.

His mouth twisted. "They won't harm you. Tell the boy not to let them get cold."

She snatched the leathery things. They were warm from his touch. As if they burned her she dropped them in her robe and hurried away from him into the pines.

Chapter Twenty-Six

Cassia walked on the road beneath the pines. The brilliance of the river beside her dimmed to brown as Shamash the Sun God raised his fiery head above the northern peaks. The trees ended.

She was encased in heat. It clenched around her to become the burning fist of the Sun God himself.

Her skin seemed to catch fire. Warm dust circled up to meet her. On her hands and knees on the cracked clay, she crawled toward the shade beneath a clacking bone bush. The morning grew intolerably bright; her eyes shut and she slipped into the comforting dark.

She heard footsteps scuffle up the riverbank on the other side of the road. More came and passed her, blending with the roar of the river.

Water, Cassia thought. But she could not move her tongue to say it.

She heard a pair of footsteps slow. A motherly voice said, "Look, under that bush, a pile of rags. Oh. Is she dead? So young! Couldn't we—?"

"Too big. Can't even help ourselves."

The footsteps moved on.

* * *

Cassia felt the touch of small hands patting her robe. The patting slid furtively into her chest pocket. Other footsteps tramped near—the patting vanished.

Someone wearing studded sandals kicked her ribs. "Rabu filth! May the priests grind your flesh for meat, your bones for flour."

Hot eyes too dry to weep for her lost happiness, Cassia embraced the darkness. It enveloped her.

"Cassia, wake up. Cassia?"

She felt water trickle over her lips. Life stirred in her, centering in her thickened tongue. It reached out, licking, searching. Sensation returned like a thunderclap—heat slammed down; her shoulder ached and throbbed; dust grated under her eyelids, caked her nostrils and mouth.

"Good, child; again." More water dribbled over her teeth.

"Mama?"

The hands sponging her face became very still. "No. Can't you guess?" He sounded amused and a little shaken.

Jarell. She wanted to turn from him, to run.

"Gently, child. If you are ready to rise and find the boy, let me help you."

Tadge! How could she have forgotten? She tried to pull her feet under her.

"Can you not open your eyes at all? Gods! If only I had started out sooner. Then when a band of potmenders said they had seen neither of you on the northern road and I wasted precious time searching the wood . . ."

Jarell was in front of her, smelling of sweat and clay, his hands pulling hers over his shoulders, lifting—she wavered upright, fell.

"Sorry" she got out.

He staggered; she leaned on him. He sagged. She pulled away with another muttered apology. "It's all right, little one, just getting my balance." His voice quivered.

Laughing! She blushed, then gave a hysterical giggle. "Why help?" she croaked.

"You fished me from the river. It seemed a poor return to leave you under a bush. And you take me very little out of my way. I had thought to avoid the city, but if we're together it should be

safe enough. We shall hope that the boy is there. And a healer."
They started down the road.

She tried to withdraw her hands. He clamped them in place.
"But you fear touching," she protested.

He gave a crack of laughter. "So you find me shy. You have
selective recall, my child. But——kind of you to spare my
blushes." He chuckled again, as at a private joke.

Talk became a memory. Only the road existed, and the heat.
Cassia felt trapped in it, incandescent with it, seared by a fire that
never consumed. She slid into dreams.

She stumbled.

He caught her. He was talking. ". . . slavery, Sacrifice, still
with us after millennia. And Sassurum, the all-loving mother goddess 'to whom nothing is permanent but Change,' allows it! She
doesn't exist. If she did, she'd be an obscenity."

Cassia roused, as she supposed he intended. "But I've seen
her; become her. I know she's real!"

His voice was gentle. "An imaginative, motherless child,
lonely—it would be odd if you did not."

She slumped at the verge while he climbed down to the river
for water. Her back felt as if it must burst open. In the lumps
there, something bunched that she could almost control with new
muscles. Frightened, not wanting to think what the lumps must
be, she asked at random when he returned, "Do you believe in
any gods at all?"

"L'h, perhaps. 'The one. He Who Is Nameless.' "

She sucked muddy water from the cloth Jarell pushed between
her lips. The water tasted flat. She caught herself yearning for
something salty, thicker, hot, torn from smooth flesh. She leaned
closer to him, predatory . . . *No!* She shuddered. *Goddess!*

"L'h, the father of the first gods, whose shrines are empty rock
shelters on the mountaintops; who created the universe and set it
in motion. And then, I assume, retired or strolled away." Jarell's
voice resumed its usual dryness.

But Cassia did not hear him. Light as a bubble rider, she
seemed to be floating up into the breathless blue, drawn by the
sun's white eye.

Silky dust pillowed her cheek. She could not move her tongue
to lick the water dripping over her face. She felt deft fingers open
her robe, familiar fingers. As from a great distance she heard an
indrawn breath.

"How could it grow so much worse, and so quickly!"

The voice urged her to rise. She could not. It coaxed, ordered. Then it was gone.

Alone, left to shrivel in the sun and hot breezes, Cassia tried again to weep, but no tears would come. She contented herself with a sniff that was overtaken by a desperate yearning for her nursling. *Goddess!* she prayed as she drifted toward unconsciousness and Membliar's lightless seas. *He's so little. See him safe!*

The air around her seemed to darken and swirl and form a pillar; it became a tall woman with hair that whipped around her like night and whose black irises smiled from whites like bowls of whitestone. Her deep, warm voice formed inside Cassia's head. *The child is well, my daughter, but soon he must make some interesting decisions. Look.*

Sassurum's black locks spread across the dark, and thinned and coalesced into color and light. Cassia dreamed.

In Cassia's dream, Tadge's red curls bounced as he rode in a Rabu farmer's cart, pulled by sweating Kakanos. Beside the little boy sat a large, comfortable Rabu woman. She put a redfruit in his outstretched palm and a slab of baked grain. His other hand lay against a lump in his chest pocket.

"Cassia," he was saying, *"she* made cakes like this."

"Poor innocent," the woman fretted, interrupting him. "Walking all alone, no nursemaid to care for you, so small, so helpless! What would your mother say?"

Swallowing a grin, Tadge looked up soulfully. "My mother's dead."

"Oh, the pathetic wee babe!" As the woman petted the child, her mate glanced back with a speculative look and remarked that Tadge's red curls were a rare sight in the lowlands; see how the passersby stared. The boy might fetch a good price as a fancy slave, or a dance troupe might buy him. At the least, that hair could go to a wigmaker for enough to buy seed grain.

"Hsst!" the woman said. "Not before the child! Anyway, I won't let you."

"Those little Kakanos don't understand more than a lizard— they only mimic human speech."

But as his mate's protests continued, he yielded with an ease that surprised Cassia, and promised to stop by a forger's outside the city gates to buy Tadge a pass to get him inside Kaladussa.

Tadge watched the exchange with the wide, uncomprehending stare that Cassia had learned long ago to distrust. He moved his hand from the lump in his chest pocket to slip it trustingly into the farm woman's capacious one; the vision faded.

Cassia was satisfied that her nursling was not only safe and cared for, but that he had the situation well in hand. She tried again to weep a dusty tear over the fact that she seemed neither wanted nor needed anywhere, failed, and completed her slow slide into darkness and unconsciousness.

Chapter Twenty-Seven

Naphar's poetry and myth describe their Dark One as being wreathed in fires and alight with thunderbolts. We assume that the fire they're talking about is auroras circling the approaching dark moon's magnetic poles. Auroras, of course, are made by a solar wind's energetic particles knocking out the atmosphere's gases. Different energies hit at different depths, so there can be a lot of layers and colors of auroras. A fast proton hitting nitrogen, for instance, gets green. Landing a scoutcraft on that dark moon would be really something! Diving through auroras of blue, orange, green, red; thunderbolts sizzling at every level. The Dark One's atmosphere is thick, so the Napharese only witness the outer storms — there would be more, all the way to the surface. Can you imagine standing on that moon's black snow and looking up?

> LECTURE BY RUD CHEW-MCCOY, FLIGHT COMMANDER,
> GALACTIC CENTRAL DIVISION OF PLANETARY EXPLORATION (RET.).

"Stop, you jokes of Kumar's drunken mother!" a deep voice bawled.

Cassia roused from her stupor. As she lay at the side of the road, dust and a pungent smell swirled by her nose. Wood creaked, harness jingled, and the shuffle of many feet halted. Small bodies plopped onto the clay.

"This her?"

"Yes, Cushy Harpay, Lord, if you would be so kind." Jarell.

"You'd better make it worth my while! Go, you lazy sons of Mott!"

In the back of a jolting wagon Cassia floated in and out of consciousness. The wagon bed smelled of absent grain and musty hay, and strongly of the night crocks of manure sloshing beside her. Farm-bred Kakano dung was prized for its hearty effect on city gardens, she heard the deep voice tell Jarell.

She soon stopped listening to their muttered conversation, to snatches of jokes, to chanties sung in a clear tenor. The sun's full kiss absorbed her, lighting fires beneath her skin. She moaned. Someone fussed with the sides of the wagon; shade came between her and the burning heavens. She sighed . . .

. . . and dreamed of diving into a pool lined with amber rocks where a speckled fish hung, its sides pulsing in the cool, sweet current.

The chill of ending day breathed through the heat. The wagon had stopped. Reviving a little, Cassia made out long blue shadows cast by a few rivertrees precariously rooted in the dike.

Clumsy footsteps approached, followed by lighter ones. Jarell's. At her feet a chain rattled and the tailgate of the wagon clunked down. Horny palms dragged her across the planks. The reek of yiann and tearroot blew past her face. "Just don't try coaxing favors out of me ever again, because I won't do it!" The Rabu's broad chest smelled of sweat. His huge arms opened, and she fell, her knee and shoulder striking the road. White-hot pain enclosed her.

"Go, you pestilent scum, before I sell you to the priests for demonbread!" she heard the driver shout when she could listen again. His wagon trundled away, leaving behind the sound of the wind and the river and the slow step of an occasional passerby.

"What was the matter with him? And where did this come from?" Cassia asked Jarell when she had drunk great drafts of silted water from a pottery cup. She slid it in her pocket.

"Mmm. Our host was feeling generous." Smoothing wetness over her face and neck, Jarell tweaked a curl, murmured that if all else failed he might set up as a ladies' maid, and removed her head kerchief. He snapped the dust from it, then began rebraiding her hair. "He wanted to adopt me. I'm afraid I laughed."

Their host had borrowed heavily from the temple, Jarell explained; the flood had wiped him out. With Jarell's help he planned to invoke the goddess's law prohibiting foreclosure if a child existed whose living depended on the mortgaged property.

Jarell chuckled as he helped Cassia to her feet and set her hands on his shoulders. "He didn't seem to think anyone would notice that I'm Kakano and he's enormous even for a Rabu. Or that I'm at least as old as he is. He even rehearsed me in the Eight Filial Duties."

Cassia listened, walking more easily after her rest. And as Naphar turned its face from the sun's blue envelope of sky to the ever-present night, Cassia's trickle of returning strength became a stream.

". . . defend his good name," Jarell went on, "quite a trick, considering Kakanos are forbidden hostility toward a Rabu . . ."

Cassia's nose twitched. An appealing warm, metallic scent tinged that of the dust and the river. It started a hunger in her that had nothing to do with food.

". . . lead him home from the grog shop when he's had too much yiann . . ." Jarell was still talking about a son's duties.

They moved into deep shade—the sun must be setting. The lumps at Cassia's back stirred, trying to break through her stretched skin, to unfold. Horror crawled through her. But this was only a waking demon dream. It must be.

". . . repair his roof in the Time of Mud, wash his clothes in the Time of Slime. Shorthanded after the flood, I expect, no idle sons for him—" Jarell stumbled.

The scent was stronger. She associated it with him. She dug her fingers and nails into his shoulders and leaned over him hungrily. "But you belong to me! I mean, you said you'd say that, And if he had no coin—"

Jarell's breathing sounded labored but when he spoke his tone was casual: "I'm afraid he's an unprincipled rascal. He proposed leaving you in the sun for another day or two, thus saving him my purchase price." He patted her hand. "I sense disapproval. Quite right. Even I felt his plan involved a certain disloyalty on my part. And there were other considerations."

The scent and the craving writhed in her like serpents. "'Other'?"

He hesitated, then laughed. "You're a religious child, head stuffed full of the god's outrageous activities. Perhaps you'll not be shocked. He had a little godlike incest in mind. t was when he announced that renewal of my adoption papers depended upon my satisfactorily sharing his pallet as well as his provisions that I laughed, told him once was enough, thank you, I preferred my mistress. So I made an enemy. Always a mistake. But he was angry, wasn't he?"

"Once!" Cassia's mind crowded with images of Jarell tumbled in the dust by a stinking Rabu in return for a cup and a ride. She yanked out the pottery thing and threw it. "I would have hit him! Killed him!"

"You would?" He sounded startled. "I was afraid you'd take it badly. But you're used to honest toil. As you recall, I'm not. And of course, you're Rabu. You might get away with it."

The barkhiders' first hesitant chirps announced the sun's setting. Cassia left one hand on Jarell's shoulder for balance, straightened, and opened her eyes.

The squat towers and flat roofs of Kaladussa bulked large before her. The city was blue with dusk and black with shadow; in it, light bloomed here and there from flickering torches and the shine of lamplight. Behind Kaladussa the green afterglow faded to a deep blue sparked with stars.

Snaking toward the city was the River Lathon, spilling its thick light across squares of farmland where huts glimmered. The houses stood closer together now. Between them lay estates, the trees behind their walls obscuring the villas and palaces within.

Jarell stumbled. Cassia looked back. Dark smudges spotted the dust. The enticing scent was strong.

"Your feet are bleeding!" She ran the tip of her tongue over her lips.

"They'll toughen. Couldn't tie any more knots in my sandals. Tossed them." Reluctantly he added, "I've seen no sign of the boy, and with our ride, we should have overtaken him if he's walking."

Cassia recalled her vision. "Oh, he got a ride, too. He should be in the city by now. The goddess showed me."

"Mmm." Jarell's murmur was skeptical. With false-sounding cheer he added, "Then there's no cause for worry. The potmender girl told me tonight's the start of the Festival of the Full Moons when your goddess is encouraged to ward off the Dark One at the time of its closest passing. Any escaped slave or criminal in the city or its shadow can't be retaken for a sennight." He stumbled again.

But what if Tadge strayed from the farm wife, or her mate sold him? Cassia tried to hurry their steps. Jarell tripped; swayed. Reluctantly she asked, "Do you want to stop?"

"I think I must. And soon."

It would be wrong to leave him. Chafing inwardly, she watched for a place to rest. Tremors and distant rumbles announced the moons: slowly the great white disks slid from behind the northern peaks. Beside them loomed the Dark One; green fire circled its poles; lightning cracked over its face of swirling black. Making the sign against demons, Cassia looked away.

An estate loomed large before them; an oddly attractive one. Behind its walls, trees tossed their shaggy heads at the stars. Below them on the white mortared blocks was a crude drawing of the Misbegotten. No travelers leaned against those stones. *This time I won't leave the road,* Cassia thought as her hunger rose in her, *and we'd be alone. Undisturbed.*

At the wall Jarell slid to the ground, asleep, the hot, sweet blood coursing just under his skin. Cassia bent to his throat where a pulse beat; a strange half-heard music made her pause. She straightened and peered over the wall.

It formed one side of a spacious rectangle. Inside, pines and fern trees met over neat graveled paths, their branches twined with Night Blooming Star Flowers' glossy leaves and tiny white blooms. A wind blew the flowers' cloying scent to her, a mossy fragrance, and a rustling that almost resolved into melody.

Broad wings darted across the moons and their dark companion. Far too large for a Night Demon, the winged creature dove low to disappear in the treetops. Leaves thrashed; a branch cracked. The shadows moved and swayed, calling with soundless, compelling voices.

Understanding and love flowed into Cassia like yiann. She set a foot on the base of the wall; eerie harmonies called to her of dark happiness and an unearthly peace that dissolved the boundaries of self, shared all Choices, and even preordained them.

Relief rushed through her. She need not Choose, or bear responsibility. A tune of her own chimed within her, weaving with the others. A tall shadow separated from the clustering dark and drew her with a clear obbligato.

Yes! she answered, *I renounce . . . I come!*

A burst of delight met her as she reached for the top of the wall. Ravishing descants clashed wild around her; she swung herself over . . .

Pain burst through her shoulder and tore into her back.

Gasping, she fell. Sanity returned. She could not, must not enter the garden, she had to find Tadge, every dark whisper of her remembered life said the winged shadows lied. *But they were so fair!* She huddled by Jarell, her knuckles jammed into her mouth to smother her sobs.

Many-directioned breezes fanned her. Dry rustles, the mossy

scent, and a cascade of song wound around her; a promise breathed on a wind sweet with flowers. *Not yet, my sister, Beloved. But soon.*

Something dry and warm skimmed her shoulder. The song faded to a thread. Slightly comforted, she slept.

When Cassia woke, the full moons had set and the earth was quiet. On the horizon, above the volcanoes webbed with flame, only a tip of the Veil fell through the stars. At her side Jarell still slept. By her other elbow stood a jug beaded with moisture, and a basket covered with a clean cloth.

The dark liquid in the jug reflected the night and smelled tart. From under the napkin wafted the aroma of freshly milled grain, yeast, and spices. So her suspicions had been wrong. Jarell stirred. "Look," she said. "They've brought us food."

He sighed. As he blinked up at her she raised the sweating vessel and drank. When she had downed half of it, she set it beside him and licked the last drops from her lips. The drink blunted her other craving. She reached beneath the cloth and pulled a disk from the basket. Honey crystals sparkled in the starlight. A bite, a gulp, another, and the pastry was gone.

She was curling her tongue around her fingers and the corners of her mouth, searching for crumbs, when Jarell asked, "Cassia? Where did the food come from?"

"They left it for us."

He looked up, then down the empty track. "Who, Cassia?"

"Them. In there." While she fumbled in the basket she gestured toward the wall with its drawing of the Misbegotten.

"By the gods!" He scrambled up the blocks to look. When he dropped to the ground beside her, he flinched.

Cassia bit into her second cake, her other hunger further receding. From the corner of her eye she watched blood, like ink in the moonlight, ooze from his feet. They must hurt him. He said, "There's no light, no house, no one. Who are 'they,' Cassia?"

"The singers. Of the song."

"Singers?"

"Dark shapes, tall, beneath the trees." She fingered a third pastry. It smelled delectably of redspice. "And they give peace . . ." Her voice trailed off. It did sound a little unusual. "But I couldn't have imagined it! Because how else did that get there?" She downed the cake and pointed to the jug and the basket.

"Your logic is indisputable." When she reached under the napkin he captured her wrist. Her pulse strangled under his fingers. He flicked a crumb from her mouth. "You've eaten."

"Well, not all! I left you some. But your feet! Let me see them."

"Never mind that. Cassia, do you never suspect anyone?"

Her throat ached with unexpected tears. *Only you.*

He grasped her chin. "Look at me, child. This is a preserve of the Beloved. Their offerings can heal, or they can lead to the Death Worlds of Membliar, but they are never innocent. Do you understand?"

She pulled away. "No! They bring peace. They're not demons. And I feel fine. Try it!"

He looked from her to the basket and the jug. He hesitated; he drank deep. A scout ship hummed overhead. He watched it until its yellow spark vanished over the horizon. With a thoughtful expression he fumbled a pastry from under the napkin. He reached for another.

"You ate. I didn't think you would."

He shrugged. "Either it kills or it doesn't. Any more?"

She lifted the cloth. "No," Cassia said in a small voice. Cheeks heating, she became very busy tearing strips from her hem for his feet.

He grinned and leaned against the wall. "I knew another greedy child, once. Caring for her was part of my bond service— her mother headed the Academy. That little one loved a jelly winking with phosphors extracted from the light glands of the riverfish. She called it 'eating stars.' In one sitting she could polish off hers, mine, her mother's—"

Cassia reached for his foot.

Jarell's expression changed. "Don't serve me!"

"Why not? You helped me." Dirt and pebbles impacted the sores on his feet. Her stomach lurched. Blood oozed from the cuts. Her strange appetite crept back. She dropped his foot. "These should be washed first. I'll fetch some water."

He got up and limped across the road.

"Don't! Your feet!" She was ready to say more but when she joined him at the river's edge she took one look at his closed eyes and straight mouth and bit back her comments. She knelt by him, fire from the river's phosphors dripping down the soaked cloths; it shimmered in a trail behind her. She dabbed at the first cut. At random she said, "This will hurt. Talk some more about the child." The blood ran free. She swallowed.

Voice carefully conversational, he said, "She also liked shells.

She kept a pink one by her pallet—I found it for her once when we climbed down the cliffs to the sea."

Tightening her lips, Cassia wrapped strips around the padding until she could no longer see or smell the blood. Her hunger dimmed to a faint clamor as she smoothed and smoothed the bandages over his ankles and long straight toes. His feet seemed cold. She warmed them with her hands. After an initial resistance they moved wherever she wished, touching the inside of her wrist, stroking down her thigh . . . She looked up.

Lazily he watched her. "I'm glad we're friends again, Silver Eyes. Have I told you recently they have a light of their own? But cool, like rain at sunset. I missed them in the wood. And you." He smiled and lifted his hands. "Come," he breathed.

For a moment, vividly, her dreams came back to her. She remembered her mate and the glade. "Friends! Are we friends?"

"Certainly. And more, if you wish it." He regarded her steadily.

She jumped up. His feet hit the clay. With fierce satisfaction she saw him wince. "And do friends sell their charm—their beauty that catches at the heart?" She wished she hadn't said that. "Their learning, their intelligence, their humor, for gems and gold?" Blood seeped through the bandages. It spread, its scent sharp on the moist river breeze.

Jarell struggled onto his elbows. "Oh, that. I thought you realized—"

Her craving beat in her like wings. "And if I come, will you send me away again?"

"My dear child, I see I must explain—" He glanced up; he stood. "Was that movement?" And he was gone, taking with him the scent of blood and his false tenderness. Or was it real?

When Cassia reached the road, opposing hungers dinning in her, she leaned against the wall of the garden.

A wind rustled across the trees and graveled paths. *Stay with us, share our peace*, its many voices whispered.

In the shadows, dark forms stood, blackness folded behind them in double points. The column she had seen earlier stepped into the Veil's light. She glimpsed its palely beautiful masculine face. Cropped curls surrounded it; they glittered in the red and silver glow like whitemetal. The column moved toward her, black cape spreading and billowing. As the being moved into the starlight, its eyes flashed with silver. *Stay*, the choir of whispers sighed. Invisible hands pulled her, the wind breathed caresses.

Footsteps padded near; the strange, jangling music broke.

"Cassia," Jarell said, "they can't have you, not yet. There's humanity in you still. Come, Tadge needs you. And there's danger. I saw nothing ahead, and yet—"

Tadge. When Cassia took one longing look back, the shadows had become just shadows; the mossy fragrance was gone. The wind whispered only of drying fields and pine boughs and flowers.

Cassia had followed Jarell for some time when they rounded a curve. She saw with surprise that against the lightening sky Kaladussa's silhouette hung above them less than two hands of man-lengths away. Then she saw Kaladussa no longer. For beside and behind her, gaunt sleepers raised their heads as one, rose, and closed in around them.

Jarell exclaimed and shoved his way to her side. Breath shortening, Cassia recognized the woman with the square jaw who had stood beneath the torchpine, and her partner, the tall old priest with burning eyes.

"Slavers!" Jarell hissed. "They were waiting for us. Run!"

As they fled, the sound of feet tramping in step made Cassia glance back.

Faces impassive, the sleepers herded behind them, staring straight ahead, eyes white with starshine. All their lips parted. In a many-voiced chord they husked, "The Ruler of the Night calls. You will come."

In Cassia's mind icy tendrils of thought plucked at her barriers, seeking entrance. Beside her, Jarell stiffened and slowed. Over his head she glimpsed a tall form striding toward them across the fields, its waxed curls pale under the fading stars.

It was Salimar.

Chapter Twenty-Eight

Stop! Bring me the Stone, Thing. Salimar's thought was aimed at Jarell. It echoed in Cassia's head as she ran. Beside her Jarell shuddered and fell farther behind. At their backs, the slavers pelted nearer. She glanced ahead.

The track they ran on lifted to climb the mound to Kaladussa; its turrets and walls embraced the sky. Sanctuary—if only they could reach it! Beside them the blond giant seemed to skim the muddy fields, one hand on his chest, his black robe and red surplice flaring wide around him.

"No, don't stop!" Cassia spoke aloud as Jarell checked and turned toward his owner. Above him whipped the gray locks of the priest—the old man's black rusty sleeves flapped—he reached for Jarell. In desperation Cassia grabbed Jarell's arm, slung him around her neck, and sped away.

No! He's mine! In Cassia's head, the lax tendrils of Salimar's mind turned to snakes. They struck; they burrowed under her defenses; they found fear. They became bands of whitemetal, stilling her thoughts, probing them, finding her breath and forcing it and her feet to slow.

Cassia's lungs tightened with panic. She glanced back. In spite of her burst of speed, the old priest and the square-faced woman raced less than a manlength behind her, their frozen faces and their robes bright with the coming dawn. In Cassia's throat a pulse jumped. In an instant, sunlight would flood the dike and her strength would fade. She would lose Jarell, and all hope of finding Tadge. She choked on a sob as her vision clouded with black spots. But superstition said the Dark God too was weaker by day. If it was fact and she could run just a little farther. . .

Help! Goddess! she cried inwardly.

In Cassia, the green strength stirred that Salimar had freed so long ago in the slavers' camp. Behind the spots, in the shadowy air, a point of radiance grew, brightened, and resolved into forms, colors. She saw Tadge.

He stood in a curving stone chamber, one hand on a lump in his chest pocket. He reached between jars of grain to snatch a pastry; he slid it into his robe. Over his shoulder he whispered to someone, "This is the kind Cassia likes. I miss her! I hope she hurries." He paused. He stared past the jars; he seemed to look straight at Cassia. His eyes widened; he tightened his hold on the lump in his pocket.

Power flowed into Cassia. A tendril of the alien intelligence swarmed through her eyes; it surrounded her vision of Tadge. Behind her she heard a roar. She glanced back. Salimar bounded up the dike.

Above the track his smooth blond head appeared, then his pale eyes. He leaped onto the road. "Halt, beast! You cannot escape me. But I have no quarrel with you or the child. Throw me my Thing and I will let you go." Salimar's grip on Cassia's mind thinned; still holding the slavers, he poured more of his will into Jarell. Effortlessly, Salimar began to run.

No! He'll possess us as he does the slavers! Fear whipped Cassia. Not thinking to break the link with her nursling, she darted to the verge, where a Rabu family slept. Most of her pursuers gave scant attention to their feet; they tripped. But Salimar darted around his rolling minions and the family. Energy seemed to storm from him.

On her shoulder Jarell convulsed, then struggled with the slow jerky movements of a puppet. He kicked; he shoved away from her; he tried to slide down.

"Look: day's coming. Hold out!" She grabbed his flailing arms and knees. In desperation she summoned her new strength —Tadge's braided with it—and Salimar's bonds on her mind snapped.

The giant's shock jolted her. He changed his thoughts' broken chains to vipers. She swept them away. Fizzing with exhilaration, she laughed breathlessly. She could beat him—they had a chance! She glanced back. Dawn's first pink rays stained the northern peaks and the sky.

Salimar was silhouetted against them. He put his fists on his hips and shouted, "You can't do that! No one can! Not unless you hold the Stone. It's not in your hand." She felt his mind leave hers to scurry through Jarell's, it returned to hers. "Neither of you have it! My Stone!" Salimar's wave of anguish hit Cassia. His bellow cut off. *There's still the child!* he thought. In Cassia's head, Salimar's attacking serpents melted to warmth and light and flowed outward, following her vision to Tadge.

The giant's shout of triumph burned along Cassia's nerves. *Tadge! Hide!*

I know how, Cassia! His excited voice echoed in her mind. *I just hold the stone and think—!* Then the boy vanished.

Salimar howled. Through his eyes Cassia glanced at the brightening sky.

"Catch the beast and its burden!" he screeched to his slavers running steadily as priests' dolls in a drama. Mental lightnings seemed to crackle around them. As one, his minions sprang forward. Light edged the road's curve and widened.

Cassia headed toward it. A brassy flourish made her look up. Beyond the dawn trumpeters, the first rays of sunrise gilded the tiled domes of Kaladussa, painted its towers with white dazzle and blue shadow. They flung a circle of darkness from the walls to the crowd waiting to enter. Cassia burst into the light—it struck her like a blow. Through her closing lashes she watched the great carved gates of the city glide open.

Pushing back her dizziness, Cassia settled Jarell more firmly across her aching shoulders and raced toward the shade. In it milled refugees, farm carts, and a pair of chariots. But her weakness had slowed her. As she stepped into the dark, from behind her came a deep-voiced growl, she smelled sweat and dead flowers, and a horny hand like a lizard's closed on her arm.

Chapter Twenty-Nine

"You see that white speck high on the mountain behind our city? That, my dear sir, is a convent housing our Purity Priestesses. Every Northern Napharese town has them—a small population but a noticeable one, particularly to wrong-doers. The priestesses define the wrongdoing, of course. They are celibate—in itself a remarkable habit since our society eschews sexual politics, preferring those related to size. The priestesses confine themselves to their mountain fastness for most of the cycle, praying for an end to wickedness. In pairs—each keeping an eye on the other, you see—they wander about our bazaars and feasts, denouncing improper acts, descending en masse only once each cycle, usually during some festival or other in the spring. Then they not only discover error, they offer it Sanctuary in our city, and the goddess's Second Chance. Since the priestesses' numbers are understandably limited, they employ local matrons as Volunteers."

CONVERSATION WITH A NAPHARESE NOBLE
RECORDED BY SYNLIN t'KRILL, CLUB SITE EVALUATOR FOR
INTRAGALACTIC FUN! FUN! FUN! INC. REJECTS FILE.

Women in white robes and headcloths streamed from the opening gate. As they spread out in a great circle an arm's length apart and stopped at the edge of Kaladussa's round shadow, Salimar tightened his hold on Cassia, grasped Jarell, and began the ritual

Claiming of a Slave. Cassia struggled, but Salimar's grip was as steady and as impersonal as a tree's. Despair knotted in Cassia's belly; her eyes streamed with tears. They had been so close!

"My dear sir, may I ask what you are doing?" a woman's voice inquired beside them.

"She stole the body I own. I reclaim as mine: hair, toenail, and bone; spirit, loyalty, and mind." Salimar relaxed his mental grip on Cassia and Jarell. Groggily Jarell lifted his head and looked around.

A soft thumb and forefinger twitched Cassia's arm. "You! Dry your eyes, girl. Tell me what this person does."

Blinking away her tears, Cassia looked up. Before her stood a neatly coiffed and perfumed Rabu woman dressed in a swirl of white robes and veils, their almost invisible stitching betraying the hands of a host of Kakano seamstresses. Again the woman shook Cassia's arm. "Speak! Unless you're witless."

"He Claims him as his slave, Lady, but he escaped!" Upside down on her shoulder, Jarell poked Cassia. "I mean, he's *my* slave, not his!"

"Oh, you people lead such messy lives." With discreetly avid glances the woman eyed Cassia's dishevelment and what she could see of Jarell. The woman dropped Cassia's arm, and drew a gauzy handcloth from her sleeve. Briskly wiping her fingers on it, she recited, "Escaped slave, possible obscene attachment, disputed ownership—It's enough.

"Permit me. Permit me!" She reached up to tap Salimar's shoulder. "You can't do that."

Salimar, Claiming finished, interrupted his calling on the binding gods to turn to her with a snarl.

"The Kakano on this woman's shoulder is eligible for sanctuary. Remove your hand."

To the giant's shouted objections, the white-robed woman's answer remained firm: "All that may be, but I have just taken every fourth afternoon from my extremely busy schedule to memorize the Thousand and One Impurities. (And very interesting they were, too.) I am a fully qualified Volunteer Auxiliary Purity Priestess. The law is quite clear. During the sennight that we observe the Festival of the Full Moons, no slave or criminal may be retaken within the goddess's city walls or their shadow."

Jarell's chest moved against Cassia's back; she heard a stifled snort. He could not have laughed!

His weight vanished. Releasing Cassia, Salimar had snatched

him. "By the gods, you idiot woman, I'll take this up with the masters of the city!"

The Volunteer Priestess skipped sideways; setting her golden sandals against Salimar's manskin ones, she fixed on Salimar's black robe and red surplice. "You go too far, sir. This is the goddess's city. The servants of her rivals may not enter until Festival is past. Now set down the manikin and go away. Go!" She flipped her hand.

Bellowing, Salimar tucked a kicking Jarell under his arm and shoved past her.

His adversary sniffed. "Ruffian!" Pulling a golden bell from her sleeve she rang it. Out of the gates filed twelve burly Rabu robed in the goddess's blue-green. The Volunteer pointed at Salimar.

Though the giant clapped his hand to his chest and hurled mental thunderbolts, the guards plucked Jarell from his arms, set him down, and hustled Salimar away.

The white-robed woman called after him, "And do please remember: the fine is ruinous for tampering with the goddess's shielded servants! Only Sassurum's priestesses may use mindtouch.

"Now, go along. You've caused enough trouble. Here's your Grant of Immunity." She handed Jarell a scroll of green sea paper. "And if you feel moved to rob someone, please stay away from the Street of Rigorous Joys and *my* house. You—wait!" She fumbled in her sleeve as Cassia started after Jarell. "You dispute ownership of the Kakano. Therefore you must report to the slave courts. This entitles you to freedom of the city, but only after your case has been heard at Festival's end." Over Cassia's head she dropped a clay tablet on a thong. "Now, who's next?"

As Jarell and Cassia worked toward the gates, Jarell said to Cassia, "And again, my thanks for my life and freedom, child. Now I'm comparatively safe, best forget me and throw that away." He indicated the tablet. "With luck you can claim flood loss and gain the city without a pass. I think you cannot wait a sennight to find a healer." He glanced toward their goal where priests joined the sentries before the gates and started the dawn's Litany of New Beginnings.

"Oh, but we'd have papers, you'd be safe! I'll be all right. Yesterday it must have been the heat."

Jarell shook his head and edged around a red-robed butcher priest absently tapping his calipers with his Sacrificial dagger. "Once in the Slave Courts, nothing and no one can get you out

before the appointed time. Nor will they send for a Temple healer
—you have no coin to pay."

"But not to have to lie or fear!"

When Jarell again shook his head, Cassia's lips tightened. He
could not always know best.

"Way for the Lady Anatta!" From behind them came a
woman's strong voice. "And Ibby, Lord of the Town." The man's
nasal tones were plaintive.

Jarell glanced over his shoulder. "Move back, Cassia; don't
draw their attention. I've met provincial nobles like these. Too
much power, too little scope."

Farm wagons rumbled between Cassia and the noble pair,
blocking her view of them and drowning out the priests' and sentries' chanting at the gates. The eye-watering smell of ripe manure overlaid that of dusty seed grain and vegetables. The guards
and priests had finished Blessing the Day's New Beginning; they
secured the timbered portals. The wagons jockeyed for position;
crocks sloshed. The smell grew powerful. Chariot wheels scattered the gravel just behind Cassia.

"Oh, lizard fry! Pull up, Ibby. The farm carts haven't gone
through yet." The Lady Anatta's contralto rose effortlessly above
the noise of the Kakano teams, the rumble of wheels, and the
chatter of the crowd.

Jarell murmured to Cassia that she must let him do any speaking to the nobles if it became necessary.

"But—" Cassia glanced back at the tall young woman. Glittering combs secured her black hair; it contrasted with her white
racing tunic. Hastily Cassia looked away from the woman's short
skirt and amber thighs. She would never get used to the lowlands'
nudity, never! Still, the two nobles intrigued her.

"I know their sort," Jarell was insisting. "You don't. Promise
you'll let me do the talking."

Reluctantly Cassia nodded. At least she could listen.

"My team will get stiff, waiting. Let's go in," the young man
fretted. "Claim privilege, Anatta. Or I will. Ho, guard!"

"No, Ibby. Supplies for the city have precedence over pleasure
vehicles. We should obey our own laws! Anyhow, they're already
Asking the Question."

At the gates, a guard thumped his spear on the packed earth.
"Who asks entrance to Kaladussa?"

"We ask!" Jarell answered with the ragged chorus. More carts
rattled into position. A heavy acrid smell settled around them.
When the young nobleman called for a Scenter, and a ragged

child hurried toward them swinging a pot of incense, Jarell glanced at the cause. "By the gods. Of all the chances!"

But even as he put Cassia between him and the wagons, a Rabu in the manure cart beside them bounded to his feet and pointed. "Stop him!" he howled. "Escaped slave. I Claim him!" The voice was Cushy Harpay's, their driver of the day before.

Motioning for Cassia also to disappear, Jarell slid under the nearest cart. He emerged at its other end and he tried to lose himself in the crowd.

"There he is! Catch the Owner Killer!" the driver screamed.

The crowd parted. Jarell changed direction; he jumped over a wagon tongue and stumbled. Blood reddened the cloths on his feet. Cassia stared at the growing scarlet blots, her hunger stirring. The outcries around Jarell turned to growls. Rabu and Kakano alike moved toward him. He backed away.

"Owner Killer, you say?" Behind Jarell the tall woman snapped a whip. Her team moved as one.

As Jarell lunged away from the wagon and flipped toward the next one, Anatta's chariot wheel closed off his escape. He slammed into it. Doubling into a ball, he rolled from the impact, snapped to his feet, winced, and for an instant wavered off-balance.

Above him Anatta slapped her reins into one white-gloved hand, bent, and grabbed his shoulder. "Got him!"

Cassia's heart beat hard; she wanted to disobey Jarell and speak. Instead she watched as the Rabu woman effortlessly held him. Chest heaving, head drooping, he whined, "But I have amnesty, Lady." He reached into his robe for the priestess's sea paper scroll.

Anatta waved the scroll away and pushed at a slipping braid. "I've seen you before, clod. I'll remember where in a moment. Fool!" she said to his accuser. "Have you forgotten it's Festival; escaped slaves are immune to arrest?"

Cushy Harpay rolled his mud-brown eyes. "But not seditionists! Oh, he's a bad one. Wanted me to kill his mistress! And I gamble that's not his first try at owner killing. He's tasted the manwhip—you know that's only used for serious crimes. Here, I'll show you."

The woman tightened her grip on Jarell.

"Aw, Anatta, this will take so long!" Ibby complained. "Let the scum go, or this driver can have him!"

"It's true the goddess doesn't forgive a threat to her city." Anatta snapped her fingers. "I know where I saw this one! He was looking thunder at me on the road. He could be a rabble rouser. They flourish in times like these. Still, I didn't see him actually do anything. Well, the slave courts can decide—the gods know our fleshpots need filling. Ho, guard, take your prisoner!"

Jarell raised his head to gaze at the sky, his face smoothing into tranquility.

"Uh, Lady?" the sentry called. "If he's convicted and Sacrificed and his owner appears after Festival and complains, who'll pay? Mistakes come out of the arresting officer's salary. I've a young family to feed."

"Oh, very well. I'll stand surety. Hold him for me." The young woman pushed Jarell toward Ibby. Voice cold, she said to Jarell, "Don't run. What's mine stays mine. And I don't forgive." Stripping off her gloves, she leaped from the chariot and strode toward the guard.

Jarell's glance found Cassia's. He motioned her away.

She shook her head. There must be something she could do. She ignored his second and more urgent gesture, and wriggled closer so she could see. She caught a glimpse of Anatta.

The guard handed the young woman a tablet. From the neck of her tunic Anatta pulled a carved cylinder on a thong, and rolled it across the damp clay. She borrowed the guard's stylus. As she wrote, she remarked, "Any trouble and you can reach me at the Temple of Sassurum. I'd have been there already if it weren't for him." She jerked her head toward Ibby. Her heavy braids and smooth locks sagged toward her collar. "Running over a parked team, dispatching my forerunner . . . I'd had that one a long time, Ibby. He was useful!"

"You can buy another, half sister mine. Or take this one, free. Call it a partnering present from your future consort."

In spite of Jarell's instructions, Cassia turned to look. The young man flicked Jarell's cheek—it left a white mark that blossomed red. She hardly noticed. She saw Ibby. She stared at his yellow tunic and the fillet of gold leaves in his light brown hair. He looked very fine. And familiar. Perhaps it was his highlands coloring.

"Don't let your mother's ambition overcome you, Ibby. I haven't agreed yet to partnering. But . . ." Anatta was eyeing Jarell as a thrifty housepartner might a bargain fish she wanted, but suspected of being not quite fresh. "Hands!"

Anatta ran a thumb over Jarell's palm and fingers. She tipped up his chin. "You're no farm clod-leaper. You're too pretty. A musician, maybe. And I saw you run—a tumbler. What else can you do?"

The serenity ebbed from Jarell's face. He stared at his bleeding feet, mouth tight.

Cassia watched the scarlet brighten and widen; she swallowed

At last Jarell answered smoothly, "Whatever pleases my lady. Not all my skills require me to stand." Languorously he looked up at her through his lashes.

"You've hooked a live one, Anatta. Now what? Or if you throw him back, aim him my way!" In the charged silence, Ibby's whoop was loud.

Feeling ill, Cassia opened her mouth to speak. She hesitated. This was what Jarell had said he wanted. She began to back away.

"Name?" Anatta rapped out.

Jarell's smile was thin. "Singer, Lady."

Cassia remembered a crumbled cave in the moonlight, "No," she whispered. "You can't want this." She opened her mouth to speak.

Jarell's dark glance moved toward hers. He shook his head.

But Cassia was intent on the chariots halted by the creeping yellow line of sun. She gulped in a breath and called, "You can't have him. He's mine!"

Noble half brother and sister stared at her. Ibby rounded his green eyes. Hesitantly, he nodded at Cassia. Jarell's shoulders sagged. "Is she your owner?" Anatta asked him.

Jarell hesitated. "Yes, Lady," he said at last. Ibby looked from Cassia to Anatta and back to Cassia again. He pulled his lower lip.

"Do you Choose to return to her, Singer?" The Rabu woman's question was edged as a battle knife's.

Jarell gave Cassia a hunted look. Then, "She is nothing like you, Revered One."

Anatta relaxed. Stooping to pat his bottom she said, "I'll get you out of this. Come here, girl! You could be Sacrificed instead of him, you know, for training an accused seditionist. But I've got nothing against you. What'll you take for him?"

Cassia shook her head. Rays of sunlight heated the air beside her; they turned the chariots' spokes to molten gold and made her dizzy.

"Besides the coin, I mean." Anatta's voice seemed to come from a distance. "I'd like to give you a present. How about a gold mirror chased by my craftsmen imported from the South?"

Cassia's wound ached. Dried sweat and clay on her robe

chafed the swellings by her back and made them burn. Something struggled in them, crying for release. Fear sang in her ears.

"I know: a robe," Anatta said. "Amber? Or maybe blue with silver needlework on a gold panel? Match your eyes and hair. You could be quite passable, you know, cleaned up." She grinned and thumped Cassia on her bitten shoulder.

Fire shrieked through Cassia; black curtains seemed to sway around her. A chariot squeaked; she fell into large moist hands that caught her.

"I could have done that, Ibby," Anatta complained. "What's wrong with her? I was just being friendly."

Through a hazy dark Cassia gazed up at her savior. How handsome he looked. He searched her face with his green gaze; above his eyes, the gold leaves of his fillet set lights dancing in his curls and on his finely modeled face.

"She has not your glowing health, Lady," Jarell answered Anatta. "She needs a temple healer. Soon."

"I'll get her one." Ibby spoke with suppressed excitement. "Now my mother's back, I'll make her do it."

"But the race?" Anatta asked.

"To Mott with the race! I concede it. Meet you at the temple, Anatta."

The farm carts trundled through the gates. Over the sound of their plank wheels Cassia heard Jarell's captor remark, "With any luck, Ibby will leave your owner someplace and forget her. Then our problem will be solved. And how will you like that, my little manikin, eh?"

After a long moment, Jarell chuckled. It sounded forced but Cassia was beyond making such distinctions. Her rage at his betrayal made her clench her teeth until her throat ached and her eyes burned with the tears she would not shed. Masters! With their goddess-cursed Difference, a beast was a fool to trust any of them. Sassurum was right. Loving them was obscenity!

The chariots rolled into the city.

Chapter Thirty

In the cone mosaic, blunt-ended cones of red clay are packed, base to base, on a flat surface, usually a wall, and allowed to harden. They are then painted white, and decorated with figures or geometrical designs in all colors. Since the paint covers the cone, as the viewer moves or as the light does, the murals seem to do so too, appearing three-dimensional and alive.

ARTS AND CRAFTS OF NAPHAR: A POCKET GUIDE FOR VISITORS.
GALACTIC CENTRAL REST AND RESEARCH STATION,
QAQQADUM, NORTHERN NAPHAR.

Sound and color and smells assaulted Cassia. As Ibby strolled beside the chariot holding the reins, she crouched in the shadow of the chariot's high sides, and squinted where he told her.

Around the outermost circle of the city, she saw a portable market being set up. She smelled unwashed bodies, charcoal smoke, and hot oil. On one side of her, striped awnings unrolled, vivid lengths of spider silk spread aloft on poles; on the other side apprentices hung up strings of reeking white tear root, or they stacked pyramids of rather spotty redfruit and shrunken sand-melons. In a neighboring alley, past a line of braziers laden with spitting sausages and circles of breadscoops, a woman squatted by a tray, laying out metal shells to slip over the ears.

As Cassia breathed in the aroma of freshly brewed 'seq and the yeasty scent of dawn rolls in what Ibby told her was the Street of Satisfied Appetites, shouts, chatter, a crash, and squawks dinned in her ears.

"Halt!" Ibby shouted. The chariot stopped.

In the team's path stood an old Kakano man, and a middle-aged Kakano with black hair and mustache. Beside him a young girl peered through her tangled white-blond hair. The trio brandished the chalky coils of a wormcase flute, a pink fluted shell rozzer, and, in the girl's dirty hands, brass cymbals.

"Musicians," Cassia breathed.

"Them? Ownerless bazaar players are musicians?" Ibby raised

his whip. "Begone or I'll set my team on you." The men paled
but lifted the white and pink shells to their lips. Ibby shouted; the
team started forward.

"Oh, no!" Cassia blurted. "You'll hurt them. Please—let them
play."

". . . the same. Compassionate Voice of the Goddess . . ."

Staring down at her, Ibby caught the thong of the whip in his
hand. "I'll show Anatta who's smart! She never recognized—" He
touched a curl that had escaped from Cassia's headcloth, grinned,
and dug into the silken pouch at his side; a handful of minute
whitemetal coins showered through the air. "Play!" he cried.

Squeals, clashes, and blats canceled all other bazaar noise.
Ibby bent down. "Like them?" he shouted over the din.

Through an increasingly fixed smile Cassia said, "They're,
um, very enthusiastic."

Ibby's yelp of laughter made her straighten; as she glanced
over the side of the chariot she surprised a smile on the ruddy face
of the team's lead man. The Kakano saw her looking at him—his
expression blanked.

"Enough, you're giving me a head pain," Ibby grumbled. As
the players bowed, then scrabbled in the dust for their coins, he
started the team.

With the concert over, Cassia was overcome by tiredness that
came from the relaxation of fear; she shut her eyes. She would not
cry over Jarell, she had cried all her tears long ago! She lapsed
into a doze.

She woke to the drumming of wheels beneath her and the
chariot's bouncing. She wriggled into a sitting position and
caught her breath. The team ran in step, shoulders back, blond
caps of hair flying. Ibby aimed the chariot toward a group of
prosperous free merchants, both lowlands Rabu and visiting highlands Kakano. The merchants were strolling and talking with their
backs to the oncoming chariot. Above their striped robes, the men
jiggled their waxed beards, and, the women nodded their oiled
braids, oblivious to their danger.

"Look out!" But the strollers did not hear Cassia. Ibby's lead
man glanced back at her, frowned, and slowed. At her side, Ibby
cursed and snapped his whip. The lead man's white tunic spotted
with red. The team gained speed, ploughing into the merchants.

Bodies flew. A tall man and a miniature woman hit a redfruit
stall—poles swayed, the awning crumpled; the rickety wooden
structure collapsed. The pair vanished in its ruins, with bouncing
redfruit and large and small apprentices flailing in the wreckage. The

merchants' striped robes slipped high; legs kicking, they displayed to the interested bystanders that in their haste to arrive at the market, they had dispensed with the goddess's modesty garments.

"But they're made the same as beasts—and they're free!" The image of the pair's nakedness painted itself on Cassia's mind as Ibby burst into the full sun and she fainted.

"A gold Ensai-piece on the Whiz Bug with the blue stripes!" Ibby's voice penetrated the heat blanketing Cassia. A bare tree's fragile shade threaded it; Cassia looked around.

The chariot was parked in the circle lapping that of the bazaar: fallow lands that had been leveled and left to the weeds to be fired as a second ring of defense. The furtive gardens of the poor and an occasional battle practice circle were visible between the dead brown stalks; just beyond them lay Kaladussa's third circle of orchards. Green misted the low twisted trees; a few had burst into bloom.

In a rectangle of earth, Ibby knelt beside his chariot, intent on a Whiz Bug race. He and a motley group of bazaar companions stared from a plank to the streaks zipping toward it. One by one the colorful little racers splatted against the board accompanied by the watchers' cries of anguish or occasional joy. The owners retrieved their squashed Whiz Bugs and threw the carcasses aside. They reached into their sleeves for reed cages of more of the fast, straight-running beetles.

More cries . . . Ibby's voice . . . Cassia slipped back into unconsciousness.

Someone shook her. Cassia's shoulder hit the chariot's wooden sides. A scream built in her parched throat.

"What are you doing in my chariot? Out, you wilted soup leaf!" The sun shattered into a thousand flames, fractured on the trembling leaves of Ibby's gold fillet. Below the fillet, his green eyes narrowed as recognition seeped back. "Oh. Oh, yes. Surprise Anatta. And my dear mother." Again he took up the reins.

The chariot creaked into the broad Avenue of Triumphal Ingress. Trees lined it. With a sigh of relief Cassia embraced the dappled shade and slept.

Softness brushed Cassia's cheek; gossamer touched her hand and tumbled away. A wind rustled the trees, changing the light on her closed lids; more little wings showered her face and robes with breathless kisses.

Cassia blinked at a sky filled with ferns and magenta blossoms.

As the wind blew, and the fronds brushed against each other, they curled into fists. The breeze carried with it the gurgle and drip of a fountain and the smell of water. Cassia rolled onto her side.

She was alone in the chariot; the team was gone and so was Ibby. The flagstones of a courtyard lay beneath her; blossoming curl-up trees surrounded her and a central pool and fountain. Around it, planter beds marched in orderly curves, alternating square beds for the goddess's medicinal plants with round beds for her ceremonial herbs.

Scanning the weedless beds, Cassia nodded. Sassurum's Green Priestess of the Plants did well. Cassia was checking off the healthy seedlings of fireplant, dreamleaves, and feverbane—a few even had flowers—when Ibby pushed through the double row of trees.

"Can't find Anatta, but my mother's here. Come along, let's surprise her!"

Ibby was still helping Cassia navigate on her shaky legs when they emerged from the trees. She stared in surprise at a squat golden hive of a temple, its sides spiraled with windslits. Fronting it was forest of black, red, and white columns. They supported a wide triangle of roof. Before the columns stood several lines of Kakanos, interspersed with a few Rabu.

Ibby stopped by a sturdy Kakano man with smooth yellow hair that covered his ears. Behind him other fair Kakanos waited.

"Why, it's your team!" But where were their erect carriages and seeming youth? These men and women slumped, their eyes were hollow, and on their skins she saw bruises, welts, and old scars.

"Yes. My team. And my lead man." Even as he spoke Ibby pulled the sturdy older man toward him, spread his hand on the man's chest, grabbed, and twisted. Staring into the smaller man's face, he smiled. He released him. The man's skin flared from white to angry red. "That's for losing my race. And for disapproving when I scattered those merchants. You're not my tutor any more, you're just one of my slaves. Mine. You obey *me* now. I'll remind you again tonight."

A dull flush crept up the lead man's throat. Before Cassia could look away, a surge of his feelings washed over her: shame, resignation, a reluctant anticipation— No! She did not want to feel, not any more, she could not bear it!

As Ibby giggled and helped her onto the loggia's shallow platform, Cassia looked back. Ibby was cruel—but to her he had been kind, and she liked him. Shaking her head, Cassia decided to wait and see. Jarell had said the lowlands were different. She smelled food; she looked in its direction as Ibby towed her past it.

Deep in the shadows, in front of the temple's wooden doors, priestesses stood behind a long table, tearing wedges from stacked round loaves of bread, or ladling soup out of great pottery urns from which steam curled. It smelled thick with vegetables and the darker undertones of meat.

They neared the end of the platform. At its end, in the sunlight, a tall stout woman stood with a group of older priestesses.

"Going to meet my mother. That's her. Surprise, surprise," Ibby chanted as he pushed Cassia behind him and slowed.

Over his shoulder Cassia studied the woman with interest. Her unbleached Robe of Humility was fronted by a surplice embroidered with silken threads. They glinted with gold and silver and carved gems. Above the surplice, the woman's blue eyes reminded Cassia of shiny flat shells, the kind found in spindrift, scoured of their inhabitants. The woman seemed most interested in a very small priestess, scarcely larger than a Kakano, who stood on tiptoe to reach into a soup crock with her ladle and whose long reach across the table was done with enormous care.

The woman stopped her scrutiny of the Kakano to confer with the other priestesses; Ibby halted. As he bounced on his toes and hummed tunelessly, Cassia looked behind the servers.

At first she thought she saw dancers in the changing shadows. Between bands of brownish red and black, kilted figures connected by scarlet ribbons capered in motionless, elaborate poses. Looking more closely, she saw that the scarlet ribbon connecting the dancers issued from gaping holes in head and heart and neck. Shuddering, she realized that the dancers partnered large with small in strange, unlikely positions; both sizes interacted with Naphar's mammals, fish, and insects. *Abomination!* Cassia's face heated.

And yet, the priestesses who allowed such obscenities also gave food to Rabu and Kakano, well dressed and tattered alike. In the highlands, where such acts were forbidden, if a Rabu or Kakano was hungry, he must sell himself into slavery for coin to feed his family, or send them to Sacrifice.

Cassia looked again at the dancers. They were not real! They had only seemed to move when the trees swayed in front of them, changing the light. But now Cassia saw that the apparent movement came from the play of shadow on painted fingerlength cones of clay packed together base to base.

"Here! Didn't haul you all this way just to gawk at my great-grandmother's bawdy pictures! Interesting though, aren't they?" Ibby snickered and pulled Cassia forward. "Brought you here to meet my mother. She's stopped talking now. It's all right."

He led her down the ramp ending the platform; he shoved her into the light. It hammered at Cassia, taking her breath. "Here she is. My mother, Oprekka Enna, head priestess of Sassurum—here in Kaladussa, anyway. She got back from the capital last night. She's part of the wall tapestry there."

As Ibby's mother glared at him, her brindled brown and gray coronet of braids flashing with jeweled flowers, Ibby gave an excited little laugh. "And here's your homecoming surprise, honored mother. Recognize her? *I* did," he said with simple pride.

Cassia's eyes were watering; she blinked and squinted down at the ground where the light should be less intense. She heard a sharp intake of breath; robes rustled; a knee joint cracked.

And through the gold glitter of her lashes Cassia saw not the courtyard's paving stones, but a plump aging face staring up at her, mouth open, pale blue eyes wide.

Oprekka Enna shut her mouth and swallowed. "Princess! Addiratu! You have returned!"

Chapter Thirty-One

Oprekka Enna looked around the busy courtyard. "Have I your permission to rise, Addiratu?"

Cassia nodded, dumb with astonishment. *Addiratu. Princess.* Her dreams on the raft flashed through her mind, and Jarell's explanation of her name, his laughter . . . Grief tore at her. She no longer cared about her identity or her past. She wanted only her unthinking joy that was gone.

Oprekka surged to her feet and beckoned, arching her plump fingers as if to claw the earth. "Come into the temple, if it pleases you, Addiratu. We may speak privately there." She stood back, bowing her head toward her knees.

"Mother," Ibby squawked. He tightened his grip on Cassia's elbow. "I want to go, too! *I* found her. I remembered, Anatta didn't, how she used to give me sweets when Anatta left me. And she needs a healer. That's why I brought her to you."

"A healer! Ibby Adon"—the priestess's irises were chips of ice— "unless you have the treasure to pay for it, leave this to me, son of mine."

"Oh, Mother!" Ibby glowered and scuffed his golden sandal on the flagstones. His face emptied. He dropped Cassia's elbow, and slid from his sleeve a black handwhip bright with cloissoné flowers. He swished its three lashes through the air. Without a backward look he started down the loggia calling for his team.

"Well, that's resolved. Children can be so difficult, don't you agree, Addiratu?" Oprekka bustled behind Cassia, herding her toward the platform and its hot shadows and silent dancers.

Oprekka wet her fingertips in the blackstone basin just inside the door, sketched an obeisance, and gabbled the antique formula, "Praise to Membliar where life began and will one day end, as manifested in this Apsu. And praise to Sassurum, goddess of death and life, as manifested in her temple, round as her womb is round, that bore Naphar and all its creatures."

Cassia in her turn dabbed the sacred water to her head, hands, and feet, and followed the priestess into the gloom of the temple. Cassia took a wary breath of the air smelling of old dry wood and age—then blinked and stared.

From the walls of the great circular chamber, God masks gazed down on her. In their garish colors gold glinted; more outlined their empty eyes. Beneath them in the room's center loomed a crimson wooden altar. Flanked by two thrones atop the altar, a whitestone blood basin long enough to hold a man glowed in a stray beam of sunlight; a golden cage stood behind it, bars gleaming in the breathless dusk.

At the altar Oprekka said, "This is far enough, Addiratu," and looked at Cassia from behind her white lashes. "How much do you remember?"

Cassia's vision roiled with waves of dizziness. "Some," she got out. Her shoulder's ache seemed to envelop her. Wanting only to ask about her nursling, she started to add the woman's name as courtesy demanded. But—"What should I call you?" Mother, as Ibby did? No. Oprekka? Enna? Both?

"You don't remember," Oprekka said. When Cassia shook her head, the priestess smiled and led the way to the high curved and gilded thrones. "Come, my dear, let us be comfortable for our chat."

Oprekka hitched herself onto the high seat, puffing a little.

Cassia perched on her chair's edge to avoid hitting the swellings throbbing on her back.

"You may call me Oprekka, since that is my name, or Oprekka Enna if you wish to be formal and use my title. Enna is given to priestesses of noble blood, or, in my case, who have borne a noble child. I could earn the recognition no other way! However diligently I worked for Sassurum, the high priestess in the mother temple in Qaqqadum would not allow— But there, it's all past, and we're the best of friends now, as you and I will be, my dear." The woman pursed her small mouth in a smile. Abruptly Cassia decided to wait to ask her help in finding Tadge.

The crisp thump of war sandals approached the doors. In their rectangular glare a tunicked figure paused. Anatta strode in, slapping her white gauntlets against her thighs. "So there you are, Oprekka!" she said without obeisance or salutation. "You and your son have interfered once too often. Now Ibby's come between me and the ownership of a manikin I fancy—for spite, or because you put him up to it!"

Oprekka flowed to her feet. "Anatta, dear, may I present the Addiratu? Incognito, of course."

Cassia tried to rise and found her legs would not support her; she dropped back into her seat.

Anatta stared at her and the head priestess. "What game are you playing Oprekka? I know who she is. She crawled out of the dust just now by the city gate. I could have bought her off, gotten rid of her, only Ibby had to interfere and bring her to your temple —for a healer, he says." The tall young woman snorted. "Healer! A Night Demon bit her, my manikin told me so, and everyone knows you don't recover from that. No offense," she said to Cassia, "it's just the way it is. You call her 'Addiratu'?" Anatta said to Oprekka while scanning Cassia's tangled hair and robe smeared with clay. "As well give a title to that little Kakano pallet thumper she says she owns. You and your schemes!"

Cassia shut her eyes as the young woman marched forward to stand nose to nose with the head priestess. A trickling made its way down Cassia's back. She tried to ignore it and her throbbing shoulder. Anatta went on, her voice more suited to a parade ground than the confines of a temple.

". . . warned you . . . Ibby's laughing at me. I won't have it! Not for a full sennight of playing goddess to his god, day, night . . . So I'm through—finished!" Cassia's deepening trance was broken by Anatta snapping her fingers.

"Get yourself another goddess!" With a swirl of her tunic Anatta wheeled and marched out. At the doors she called over her shoulder, "Ask that one to be goddess, maybe. Your Addiratu—an Addiratu's even higher born than I am. That should suit your ambition." Anatta laughed—it was a joyous contralto that seemed to come from her toes—and was gone.

Leaning forward, surreptitiously pulling her wet undergarment away from her backbone, Cassia met Oprekka's flat gaze. All thought of amusement fled Cassia's mind.

The woman tightened her mouth. "My dear, you must forgive the impetuous girl. These provincials!" Oprekka laughed lightly. "Her father governs Kaladussa, so she is of the highest birth in this small city; always excepting my Ibby, of course. She believes herself superior to the rest of us. Even me." Oprekka made a moue.

"But she had an excellent thought. Would you consider—dare I hope—could you be our goddess for just the few days of Festival? We have no one else of sufficient birth who is also of the right age. It means so much to the people, you know, especially now.

"Ibby—dear boy, so compassionate—said you have a Night Demon bite! My dear, so serious, only one of our best temple healers can help you."

The rage, fear, and betrayal radiating from Oprekka mixed with Cassia's dizziness to become a roaring in her ears. Cassia breathed in long shallow gasps and leaned her head against the back of the throne while the woman's talk battered her.

". . . a healer's services . . . costly . . . such a long climb to our temple from the healers' city, I believe. Of course we will be delighted to pay, though in these difficult times . . . resources strained . . . prefer to spend on the truly hungry and needy. Still, we will be so happy to help you, dear Addiratu." Oprekka halted and drew breath. "Where was I?"

Even through her pain, Cassia had been to the crossroads market with her master too often not to recognize bargaining when she heard it. She snatched a breath and answered evenly. "You were telling me what I have to do to get a healer."

Oprekka clasped her plump hands. She gave a trilling laugh. "Oh, Addiratu! Such a comical way you have with you. But truly, it is so little! You will simply personify Sassurum in her aspect as bringer of fruit and flower. Very pretty, really. You greet the populace from a cart decked with whatever blossoms and produce and grain we can find at this season."

"I've read about it," Cassia said into the woman's pause. The trickling was stronger. She leaned back, trying to wipe it with her robe. "Who takes the part of the god?"

"Oh. You *know* the ceremony. Why, who but our present city governor's son and probable heir? My own dear Ibby."

Darkness seemed to fall from the ceiling's scarlet and black arches. "And the consummation and sacrifice—how far . . . how far do they go?" Cassia heard herself ask as from a great distance.

Oprekka fluttered her hands. "Oh, ceremonies, miming, a demonstration in the temple for the citizens. First, of course, we would bring in a healer this very night. You would be well, my dear."

Well. To have the fear gone, to plan beyond the moment, or a day. And perhaps as she was driven about Kaladussa, to find Tadge. "I . . . all right." *I can always withdraw*, Cassia promised the small voice of apprehension inside her. *Annatta did*.

Oprekka smiled, her large square teeth very white in the oppressive heat and dark, and clapped her hands.

The little priestess who had been dipping soup appeared in the glare of the open door. "Yes, Oprekka Enna?"

"Take the Addiratu to the gods' apartments. Prepare her according to ritual. You will serve her for the length of festival. She is to take the Lady Anatta's place." Oprekka rose from the scarlet throne. "Until later, Addiratu." She moved swiftly from the room, her bulk almost silent on the dark shining floor.

"Yes, Reverend Handmaid of Sassurum. If you will come with me?" the younger woman said to Cassia and hesitated. "My head priestess did not say, Addiratu, but I am called Huraya."

Huraya led Cassia to the back of the cavernous room and a small door, almost lost in the carved black and red panels. It opened onto a corridor.

There, Cassia leaned against the wall taking deep breaths, readying herself for the climb ahead. Through blots that obscured her vision she saw priestesses hurry by carrying bags of immer, crocks that sloshed, and bowls heaped with winter roots, vegetables, and a few shriveled fruit.

The corridor slanted upward, following the curve of the squat tower. Cassia glanced into a room divided by curtains and filled with pallets. Stained bundles sat by some, women and children lay on others. The room was cluttered but quiet with the repressed quality of vanished hope.

Just short of the corridor's second spiral, Cassia smelled food cooking. Through an arched doorway she glimpsed great clay ovens, chopping tables, and a wall hung with knives, cleavers, and stirring blades. Flour hazed the air. Kakanos, old and young, moved about in frenzied purpose, supervised by a tall Rabu priestess working with stylus and tablet.

As Cassia and her guide completed the next circle, the walls of plastered stone cut off the gabble of voices, the thump and scrape of wood and metal.

To Cassia's left in the tower's core, the curtains led to senior priestesses' cells, Huraya told her. Across from them on Cassia's right, infrequent windslits admitted the sun's dusty rays. The rays illuminated chipped murals in red and black and white of the doings of the gods, gods who seemed to point at Cassia and whisper. But it must be her imagination, that and her tiredness and the drumming in her head.

By the time they reached the top of the tower, Cassia's breath was rasping and she leaned against the murals every few manlengths, waiting for her sight to clear.

Beside her the little priestess wrung her hands. "I cannot support you, Addiratu. I am not of the Sacred Royal Blood."

The spirals ended. Cassia blinked at a round mosaic floor at the top of the tower. She stood in its center on Sassurum's sign: an intertwined tree, star, and stone. Through the white chips set with gold and the goddess's blue-green, the symbols of the other gods radiated like spokes from Sassurum's hub.

Cassia's eyes stung from the light. She glanced up and shut them. Her lids were printed with the image of a narrow windslit framing the valley, river, Fire Mountains, and thick blue southern sky.

When she could look again, Huraya was pushing a key into a wooden portal bound with blackened iron also twisted into the goddess's symbol.

Cassia did not remember entering the semicircular audience chamber behind the door. She only knew the chamber was filled with unbearable light. Tears poured down her cheeks as she listened to Huraya's patter of sandals, and the clack of shutters on the many windslits.

"You can look now, Addiratu," Huraya said, "and here is a seat."

Huraya guided Cassia to a throne near the outer wall. Ignoring the wetness clinging to her back, Cassia looked around her.

The room was rich. Carved and inlaid stools and tables, cushions, and padded lizardskin rugs strewed the floor. On the walls between the shutters hung tapestries picturing the history of the goddess.

When Huraya vanished into an inner chamber, Cassia gazed at

a hanging of midnight blue sewn with crystal stars. It showed the mating of the goddess—a shadowy figure formed by gold and green emanations from the earth's curve—with L'h, the Nameless God of the Spaces Between the Worlds.

Cassia glanced at the vibrant yellows of Sassurum's coupling with Shamash the Sun God; she ticked off the gray and black and silver of Sassurum's battle with Mott, God of Death and Sterility. She was counting the goddess's eight children by mortal rulers and the crafts they represented, when Huraya threw back the green curtain leading to an inner room. Its rings jingled, the first loud noise Cassia had heard since they left the kitchens.

"The Apsu is here, Addiratu, if you would like to bathe."

Cassia leaned against the door opening, and stared. Perfumed lamps floated in a great black pool set into the floor. The pool's raised edge of blackstone was set with a mosaic that flashed like jewels in the uneven glow. This, an Apsu! Cassia thought of the highlands entrance basins and buckets wreathed with flowers.

Huraya said nothing about the wetness of Cassia's robe and undergarments when she removed them. Perhaps Cassia had exaggerated the extent of her perspiration or whatever the trickle had been. The little priestess bundled them for discarding.

"Oh, don't!" Cassia protested. "They've been part of me for so long, in so many places! Can't I keep them? Just for a while?"

Huraya looked at her with pity and hung them on the wall at the foot of the Apsu. "Of course, Addiratu."

Huraya's every phrase began or ended with Addiratu, Cassia thought. The strangeness of the title and its nagging familiarity made her uneasy; she associated it with childhood and imperiousness and temper. As she stepped into the pool, astonishing warmth lapped her.

"It is heated by the Fire God who lives beneath those mountains, Addiratu," Huraya explained. She added scented oils and salts to the dark water streaked with lamplight.

Arrayed in a new yellow robe with a silver panel, Cassia awaited first meal. She sat in the chair in the room she had first entered. Huraya rubbed her hair with length after length of drying cloths scented with mountain flowers' light fragrance. At last the priestess threw her hands in the air.

"It is so thick, Addiratu, the locks curl out of my fingers as quickly as I can catch them. We must let nature do it."

"It's the dampness in the air," Cassia apologized. "The same thing happened in my highlands after a rain."

Huraya was spreading Cassia's hair over the back of the chair to dry when a double knock sounded on the door. Huraya opened it; two huge metal trays gleamed in the dusky corridor. Their bearers moved forward.

At the height of the lock, a blond head appeared; it belonged to a Kakano child, a girl with gray solemn eyes. Just behind it bounced red curls atop a Kankano boy's beaming freckled face. "Ho, Cassia!" the boy said.

It was Tadge.

Chapter Thirty-Two

Naphar: (1) Total. (2) The second planet on which humans and other sentient beings live, circling First Quadrant Star G-782. (3) Philosophical concept: The world, complete; ecosystems and psyches in harmony. A not-always-realized ideal.

> NAPHARESE VOCABULARY LISTS:
> GRINELDA MAO-VANSCHUYLER, ACTING ANTHROPOLOGIST,
> GALACTIC CENTRAL REST AND RESEARCH STATION,
> QAQQADUM, NORTHERN NAPHAR.

Tadge slammed the tray to the floor; he raced to Cassia's side. Scrambling onto her lap, he gave her a neck-cracking hug, then slid down again, scowling as if he dared her to notice that he had embraced her.

Blinking away her dizziness, Cassia studied his scrubbed face, damp hair with the comb marks still in it, and his rounded belly. "Oh, Tadge, thank the goddess you're all right!"

"I almost forgot how your eyes flash in the dark, Cassia. I guess I missed you, some. Once in a while I—I even pretended I saw you, talked to you. This is Talley," he finished gruffly. "She's my partner here; she's pretty smart." He pulled forward the thin Kakano girl with long yellow hair who had preceded him into the room and who still held a tray. He picked up his; the pair carried both laden trays to a table under the windslits.

While Cassia finished a bowl of jellied redfruit and licked the last flakes of the pastry scoop from her fingers, Tadge devoured her sausages, drank her broth, and explained how he came to be there.

A farmer had brought him into the city, determined to sell his hair or him, he said. While the man was haggling with a potential buyer and his mate was scolding, Tadge had slipped down from the wagon and hidden himself in the crowd. He followed a mourning procession, hoping to pick up some of the coins thrown to the spirits of the dead, and found himself in the temple court-yard. There he had discovered unlimited food.

When he came up for his third serving, the Rabu priestess handing him a wedge of journey bread told him he looked too healthy to eat without working for it. Furthermore, if he did serve the temple, he could have a place to sleep.

He volunteered to help in the kitchens; there he met Talley, who had whispered to him what to do.

"I remembered you were coming here for a healer, Cassia, so I just stayed and ate a lot and waited for you. I heard about you when that Ibby Adon brought you in—I was almost sure it was you—so when you went by the kitchens I made sure to watch, and sure enough, it was my good old beast! And being called 'Addiratu' just like that Jarell said. Thinks he's so smart. Well, Talley's smarter!" Scowling, Tadge stuffed a meat roll in his mouth.

Cassia groped for a less painful subject; she glanced at the little girl waiting by the door, her hands folded under her white starched front panel. "Talley. That's the rain goddess. Were— were you born in a storm?"

"No, Addiratu. I was born in a drought. But when no rain came my father decided the goddess was angry at his presump-tion, so he sold me to the temple for a quarter cycle's supply of irrigation water."

More selling of children, into servitude, starvation . . . Cassia's old anger returned. Through the humming in her ears she could hear only parts of Talley's explanation.

". . . didn't mind . . . kind here . . . read . . . make characters . . . want to be scribe . . . Already I have two languages . . ."

In Cassia's ears the humming grew to a buzz as Tadge de-scribed how the other kitchen helpers teased the girl about her ambitions. He described a fight with regrettable relish, and how Talley had coached him to imply that they did not want to be the ones to carry heavy trays to the top of the temple. Thus they had been made Cassia's servers by popular request and without a battle.

As Cassia's eyes crossed with the difficulty of focusing on Tadge and Talley, Huraya stepped forward and suggested that it was time for the children to return before someone came to look for them.

". . . And Cassia," Tadge said as they went out, "don't tell anybody that you know us. Talley and I have a secret way of getting news. She found out in the courtyard just now that something funny is going on and Oprekka and Anatta are in the middle of it. But don't worry. We'll protect you."

When the two were gone, Cassia rested her head against the throne, her anger draining away, her tiredness rolling over her. Huraya felt Cassia's hair and nodded. "Would it please you to sleep now, Addiratu?"

She led Cassia to a semicircular chamber behind the Apsu. Cassia glanced at the mural covering its walls, and got an impression of a great deal of green, many pink and brown people, and plants heavy with pollen. Just below the ceiling's green painted sky, god masks flashed with jewels and mirror mosaics.

Under the gaze of the masks' empty eyes, Huraya turned back the green cover of the great round pallet in the middle of the green floor. Ignoring the light green and dark green flufflower blankets piled at one side, Cassia shoved back the green cushions heaped on the pallet, stretched on her side, blinked once at the hanging pots of green ferns and vines above her, and slept.

She awakened to the crash of wood against stone and a contralto voice calling her name.

Cassia fought her way through the dark tides of unconsciousness. "Here," she got out.

Anatta strode in, splendid in a dark yellow robe and chains of gold and amber that clinked when she walked. She exuded a musky fragrance and her black hair was again piled high. Already the glossy coils drooped over one ear.

"Get up. We have to talk." With a sweeping look around the room, Anatta left.

Anatta strode into the audience chamber. She glanced out a windslit, checking on the state of her valley. Long blue shadows gave anonymity to the city streets and rooftops and the courtyard trees that moved and whispered like secret gods. There and in the fields beyond the walls, the encroaching dark hid the broken paving blocks, the thatch chewed by lizards and not replaced, the land too muddy to bear, crying out for the Flood Seed developed in the capital, and farmers who could be brought to try it.

Murmurs from the inner room and the whisper of robes told Anatta the girl was coming. Anatta plunged her hand into her pocket and grasped the sweets she had brought. Mentally, she reviewed whether ownership of the Kakano singer was worth the trouble she was about to take. If Anatta freed or killed the girl, Oprekka would become an open enemy. Did the prize balance Anatta's risking an open feud between temple and governor's palace?

In the Room of the Apsu, water splashed. Anatta glanced from the pink afterglow above the Fire Mountains to the outbuildings below, swallowed in violet dark. Oprekka kept them in repair, Anatta gave her that, even if the coin *was* skimmed from public works. The head priestess was getting too powerful, though, and cronying with that Salimar cult. Someone should stop her. Oprekka in a fury would make a lizard laugh . . . Anatta liked battle.

Still undecided, Anatta watched the peasant girl shuffle in; Oprekka's tame half-breed novice fluttered after her. Anatta dropped into the only chair; it was reserved for the room's noblest blood.

With a long look at Anatta, the peasant girl slumped onto a stool.

Anatta stiffened. She hadn't asked permission! Was the insult intentional? Unless she really was royal. Anatta eyed the other's blank silver stare, the blue circles under her eyes, her flushed cheeks. No, she was no royal, she was just a fool.

"It's better in here." Anatta put a disarming friendliness into her voice, in case she decided to go forward with her plan. "That sleep chamber! Oprekka has terrible taste. It's what you get for mating with the proletariat, as I've told my father more than once. Kateeb, he won't reply, but I notice he never goes to her apartments if he can help it. She's relentless with blue. Someone must have said it matched her eyes."

The girl's faint grin made her abruptly beautiful. Anatta thought of the singer watching that face, and felt a queer twist in her middle. And decided: *I'll do it! He's promised he'll hold back nothing if I see her safe—I'll try that first. But just in case . . .* Jumping up, she dropped cross-legged in front of the peasant girl. "I heard you're playing goddess. With Ibby as god?"

The other nodded, her striped hair catching the light.

"Don't." Anatta help up a finger. "One, Ibby has nasty habits. I can handle him. You can't."

"But it's just ceremonial," the girl broke in.

No one interrupted Kaladussa's First Dweller. *But the peasant is only ignorant!* Unclenching her teeth, Anatta explained, as if to an idiot, that that was true for the daughter of a provincial governor. "But all we know of *you* is that Oprekka calls you Addiratu. Not your family name, or who will speak for you. So Oprekka can give you to Ibby, or to a proletarian consort, or to Sacrifice, and no one will say a word. Except possibly my father, if I tell him to. Oprekka! Always maneuvering for advantage."

Anatta muttered that she wished her father had Chosen twenty cycles ago to frolic with someone less ambitious as she watched the girl through her lashes and dug in her robe. Anatta's heart beat hard. *This backup plan—will it work? Of course it will! Doesn't the god speak to me in the clash of arms? And it is his voice, it's not my mother's legacy of madness—it's not!* She held out the golden sweets. The peasant took one. Triumph burned in Anatta like lightning; she pulled out the honeyed nuts she had provided for herself.

Wiggling a comb higher, Anatta chewed companionably. "Listen. If you're really an Addiratu, Oprekka will make Ibby consummate the mating. Then you'll be partnered to him, as well as to the god he represents, and Oprekka can rule in Qaqqadum through the pair of you." Anatta offered a second foil-wrapped morsel.

Murmuring thanks, the other took it. "But what can I do?"

Innocent as a lizard! The true god's sureness was like a wave under Anatta. She spat a shell through the windslit and tapped the girl's knee. "You won't have to. This spring Oprekka needs potent magic, old traditions—like the Scattering of the Parts."

Behind Anatta, someone caught her breath. *Demon dugs! I forgot Oprekka's pet half-breed.* Shoving back the sweets, Anatta rapped, "I need yiann. So does she. Go get it."

As the priestess obediently gathered a tray and cups, Anatta pushed at a coil—it slipped further—and chatted, "I'm parched. Ibby talked me into practicing with our war bows—it took forever. People kept getting in the way. But when he wanted to use them for targets and called for my poisoned golden arrows, I quit! Oprekka's ruined the boy. He used to be well enough as a child, always tagging after me." The door shut.

Anatta sucked nut pieces from under her nails as she stood, walked to a windslit, and delved for more sweets. She eyed them critically as she offered them. They were a little battered. But with a shy smile, the girl took one. Exulting, Anatta said she hadn't wanted the priestess to hear her warning.

"You'll rule for a sennight," she told the girl. "New robes, processions, feasting, even proclamations, mostly about holidays. Nothing useful like free scribe schools, or broader-based admittance into the craft guilds. Then you're Sacrificed. In the temple, wearing the sacred jewels, but you're still dead."

Anatta strode to the room of the Apsu—good! No one was watching. "I don't know about you, but I like being alive."

The other looked up blindly with her strange eyes. Coolness crept over Anatta's arms. "But without a healer, I'll die anyway," the girl husked. "If it helped . . . and it's in the Tapestry of Fate . . ."

"Bah!" Anatta made a demon sign. "Our life's what we make it. If you want something, take it, even if it's life itself."

In the thickening shadows the door opened. The half-breed priestess offered a tray of red and white enamel. On it, dew beaded two silver vases faced with gold, and a silver carafe. The tart smell of yiann mixed with that of stone and of cooking drifting upward on the cooler air of evening.

Anatta gulped her drink; she twitched the sagging coil—it plopped to her shoulder. She looked at it in vague distaste and told the priestess, "Wait in the bedchamber until we're through.

"I'll make a bargain with you," Anatta said when the priestess was gone. "Sell your manikin to me, and I'll get my father to sign a scroll calling for a proxy to die in your place."

"Someone dying for me? No!"

The Kakano had said she'd object. "They're criminals! Our punishments are harsh; they wouldn't be convicted unless the tribal judges were sure they're guilty with no hope for rebirth."

The girl's breathing was shallow, her look blurred. "Is this what my servant wants?"

Hers! "Singer?" Anatta made herself ask casually. "Kateeb, he did suggest refusing Ibby, and asking for a volunteer from the people. Said you were always one for Choice. But—"

"May I ask my servant if he Chooses to be sold?" the girl asked.

Anatta bit back a killing rage at the second interruption, the second reminder of ownership. She leaped up. "No! That's my bargain. Don't wait too long to decide."

* * *

Cassia stood at the windslit, not really seeing the activity in the kitchen courtyard below. The creak of rope and pulleys drifted upward as water was drawn from the central well; children squatted beside the trenched stream running diagonally through the courtyard. They were gossipping, shelling greenglobes, and peeling the root hairs from purple crunchroots.

Anatta appeared, her hair now slipping in back too. She held a pair of long red ribbons—they were tied to Jarell! As he bounced into sight, Cassia tightened her grip on the stone sill and leaned outward, watching him hop and dance, his rapid speech accompanied by smiles while Anatta's chuckles grew to laughter that made her lean against the wall of a storage shed. Above them, Cassia turned away. When she looked again, the pair was gone.

As behind her the priestess swept up shells and scrubbed at sticky finger marks, Cassia's glance caught a familiar red head and a fair one close together. Their owners sat beside the refuse pit, two buckets next to them. They looked tense—and solemn. Glad of the distraction from Anatta's unwelcome Choices, Cassia watched. She eased her wet robe away from her back. It was while Anatta talked that the trickling had begun again.

On the shadowy ground below, Tadge pulled two handfuls of rocks from his robe's chest pocket. He and Talley arranged them in a circle, then stepped inside it. The boy took a final large pinkish rock from his robe; he held one knobbed end in his hand while the fair girl took the other. They closed their eyes, playing a guessing game, Cassia thought. She waited to see what forfeits they would pay.

She did not find out—a woman called from the kitchens. Hurriedly the children put all the rocks back in Tadge's pocket, carried the buckets to the stream, and started scrubbing the brown and white roots they held.

The pink sky faded to purple. Cassia stared at a single spark above the smoking Fire Mountains. Someone scratched at the door.

Huraya opened it; Cassia turned to greet her visitor.

Oprekka Enna stood in the corridor, but in spite of Anatta's accusations, Cassia gave her no more than a glance. For beside the woman stood a tall, tall being. His black cape hid shoulders that rose almost as high as his round ears set on top of his dark furred head. His slit of a mouth opened in what might be a smile; it revealed crooked rows of teeth. Above it Cassia could discern no nose—a fleshy pinkness with holes in it took its place. Her incredulous attention centered on the being's eyes in which no irises or whites showed.

She stepped back, glad of the wall's support. The creature looked very like the descriptions she had heard of the Misbegotten.

Oprekka bustled into the room. "Addiratu—your healer has come."

Chapter Thirty-Three

Oprekka stepped into the windslits' dying light. It brightened every solid curve beneath the priestess's gown of shiny green. "Here is your patient," she said to the healer. He stood in the doorway like a manifestation of the temple's inner dark.

Silently he bowed his tall head and glided through the door toward Cassia. She heard a rustling sound, like wind among winter leaves; she smelled a familiar mossy fragrance: *the Garden of the Beloved!*

The healer bent over her. His cloak parted; he extended a black claw and tipped up her chin. In smothered, hollow tones he asked Huraya for a light.

Huraya sprang to bring him a lamp—he thrust it into Cassia's face.

With a cry she covered her eyes. When she could see again she peered up at him through her fingers; he motioned to Huraya to open Cassia's robe. Cassia shrank away but, *There is no Difference,* she remembered, and submitted.

The healer moved close behind her. Surrounded by his pungent fragrance, she waited for his verdict, her throat tightening with anxiety.

With a dry touch he outlined the pain of her wound, then the swellings beside her spine—by now quite large. She sucked in a breath as he sliced one, then the other. The tightness in her back eased and uncurled. Something wet slipped down her sides and clung to them.

Behind Cassia, Huraya gasped; Oprekka made a guttural sound.

The healer lifted his talon to the light. Blood glistened on one of his curved black nails. From his sleeve he pulled a brass box with a solid top, opened it, and reached inside. When he withdrew his claw, the blood was gone.

Muted night sounds floated upward—the clink of meals being served, the calls of children. Before Cassia, the healer straightened and reached into his robe.

Oprekka surged forward, her face white but determined. "Remember our agreement."

He looked down at her with distaste. "I do not forget." Cassia knew that voice. The memory winked out as she watched him draw from his sleeve a handful of crystal vials and a packet of sea paper. He extended them on his leathery palm to Huraya.

Huraya glanced at Cassia; her eyes were dark—with fear? Slowly Huraya took the packet and vials.

"Drink." The healer pointed to the tubes' golden fluid. "For pain." He gestured from the sea paper to Cassia's back.

Putting the philters into her robe, Huraya retained one; she ran a nail around the wax covering its transparent stopper.

Cassia gazed at her nails: ten pink transparencies over the hot, sweet blood beneath. The wetness along her sides stirred.

Huraya intercepted her stare. At arm's length she held out the vial. "Drink, Addiratu. Soon I will bring you another." Her voice sounded strained.

Cassia looked at Huraya. Lines in the young woman's face made her appear hard, disillusioned; perhaps it was the light. Cassia drank. As the liquid's burning faded from her throat, warmth spread through her belly.

Huraya touched her back. Cassia winced from the delicate smoothing of the priestess's fingers, then let out a long breath. The pain had vanished. "Oh, thank you," she whispered.

High above her in the growing dusk, the healer nodded. Like a scent, like a broken melody, words caught in her mind, familiar words: *Soon, Beloved, if you will it.*

The Garden, Cassia remembered.

With a rustling sound, his cloak swirling around him, the healer flowed toward the darkness of the door to merge with the corridor's night, and was gone.

Oprekka remained, standing near the wall. "I am so happy to see you looking better, my dear Addiratu. I hear darling Anatta has been visiting our invalid. So nice that you girls get along, in spite of that awkwardness over the little Kakano, hmm? Anatta has had trouble finding companions of her own station in this dull provincial backwater; such low horrid people she has taken up with in consequence. Her father is so indulgent! He only laughs when I point out the dangers. But there!" She shook a playful finger. "Fathers can be foolish about their daughters, especially those as lovely as our dear Anatta!"

Oprekka's smile vanished. She leaned toward Cassia. Her breath smelled of perfume and yiann. "What did you talk about?"

Warmth from the healer's liquid spread to Cassia's fingertips. Joy shimmered through her. She felt a new certainty that Jarell and Tadge and Anatta, and oh, everyone in this lovely marvelous world, would soon be as beautifully and perfectly happy as she was now—as she had been when she was an imperious child. All it took was a little decision. She remembered Anatta's advice, stretched and laughed. "Why, we talked about my Choice of consort, Oprekka. I have just Chosen. Kind as Ibby has been to me, I cannot force myself on him. Instead, I shall give him and everyone else in Naphar the goddess's Choice!"

Huraya moved to Cassia's side; she touched Cassia's arm in warning.

Cassia laughed again and shook her head. She was tired of feeling frightened. "Huraya, here, is my witness," she said to Oprekka's congealing stare. "Your Addiratu—who outranks you and so cannot be gainsaid—wishes to invoke the old laws and advertise for a consort from the populace." Cassia's memory stirred. Long ago hadn't she waved her hand in this airy way? It felt good. "Go along," she said to Oprekka. "Do it!"

The priestess stood very still. "You reject my Ibby?" Her mouth tightened; she turned her stocky body and stumped from the room. Very softly the door closed behind her—and locked.

Chapter Thirty-Four

APSU: A sacred container of water ranging in size from a hand basin to a bathing pool. Located at the entrances of Northern Napharese homes, shrines, and temples, it reminds the citizens of the sunless seas of Membliar from which, according to tradition, all life sprang and in which it will end. Scholarly argument divides as to whether this refers to the amniotic fluid of the mammalian womb, or an area protected by radiation where life did indeed begin, or an actual body of water in the caverns that riddle Northern Naphar.

INTRAGALACTIC ENCYCLOPEDIA.VOL. 12: AO–AQ.

The next morning Cassia sprang from the great round pallet, scattering cushions across the green floor. She padded through the room of the Apsu to the audience chamber and leaned against a windslit. Cassia breathed in the morning air, tainted only a little by the sulfur of the Fire Mountains. She stared into the daylight, and smiled. It didn't hurt her eyes; she could see! And she had slept well. Even the earthquakes brought by the moons had not wakened her.

In the door behind her a key snicked. Cassia started to frown, her heart thumping. Then the healer's golden joy from the night before bubbled through her and her moment of dread vanished. She laughed aloud in welcome and pleasure as the tall priestess from the kitchens held open the door for Tadge and Talley. The two children carried trays again loaded with firstmeal. This time the trays were brightened by a slender vase of blooming herbs.

Cassia looked at the herbs with interest, then recognition. They came from the Green Priestess's beds in the courtyard, she was sure. There were the long explosive leaves of the Fire Plant, used for lightning flashes in the temple braziers just before the goddess appeared in her mask; cough root for clearing throats and congested chests; and a froth of white buds from the Night Blooming Star Flowers, closed now that Shamash the Sun God ruled the skies: but under the moons when the open flowers were dropped into hot water and consumed, they induced sleep.

She thanked the children—Talley blushed and Tadge scowled with pleasure—and set the vase on a low table out of sight and breathing distance; it was only the pollen of the coughroot that induced a barrage of sneezes and streaming eyes.

Cassia had eaten most of the fruit and all of the pastries when Tadge, finishing the last sausage and meat rolls, was nudged by Talley.

"Tell her," the little girl whispered.

He nudged her back. "No, you."

"Tell me what?" Cassia asked.

Tadge blurted, "Salimar's here."

A chill shivered through Cassia's delight in the morning. "In the temple?"

"Yes. He's wearing a citizen's robes but he can't change his size or those hands! He was talking to Oprekka."

"Have you told anyone else?"

"Not Jarell! Not as long as he prances around in those red ribbons."

Cassia remembered the white globes Jarell had given her for the boy. Instead of trying to explain actions she herself did not completely understand, she said, "Wait. He gave me something for you."

Her robe was hanging where Huraya had left it, in the room of the Apsu. Cassia searched its pockets and gave a sigh of relief. They still held Jarell's knife and what he had given her by the circle of Death Flowers. She returned, and held out the white spheres. "He said to keep these warm."

Tadge's eyes rounded. "Lizard eggs—I'd wager anything. And big ones! When did he give them to you?"

Cassia told him. The boy grabbed the spheres, his eyes luminous with excitement. "Kotellue eggs, by the gods! They've got to be! But I thought the kotellue was a boy. Well, it's hard to tell with a lizard!" He scowled when Cassia laughed. He ended, "Anyway—thanks, Cassia."

"They're from Jarell."

"Well, but . . ." Tadge shifted his feet. At her continued silence he burst out, "How can I talk to him after what I said back there? And I've been giving him the handsign every time I saw him."

"Oh, Tadge! In front of the priestesses?"

"Besides, he knows about me," the boy said in a low voice.

"Who does? What are you talking about?" Talley broke in.

When, haltingly, the story had been told, the little girl said she thought both Tadge and Jarell had been very silly, so both should apologize, and why didn't Tadge go first since he was rude first.

Tadge agreed to think about it. The tall priestess returned and beckoned to the children.

The sound of the door locking after them started fear creeping around the edges of Cassia's joy. Huraya brought another vial of fluid; Cassia sipped it. Rapture fizzed in her veins, drowning her brief anxiety.

"Addiratu," Huraya told her, "it is time to dress for the first procession."

* * *

All day Cassia bowed and smiled and bowed again from carts decked with flowers and drawn by Kakano teams, by temple guards, and once by priestesses dressed in the green of spring. In the shadowy temple she changed between processions, each new robe richer than the last. And before each change, Huraya wiped and powdered and strapped Cassia's back in private, and administered another of the healer's vials.

The plank wheels of Cassia's wagon rumbled from an alley that circled Kaladussa's hub. She started down the straight thoroughfare leading from the temple in the city's center to one of the four gates in its walls. Before her was a spreading roar.

The people lining the street looked at her with hunger in their eyes. And as always, she rode in a great bubble of silence, the only sounds those of the crowd's breathing, the creaking of the wagon, and the straining of the team. Behind her the hush lifted; she heard growing ripples and eddies of comment and shrill chatter.

That night the sound of Festival and the moving flicker of torches filled the city below. It reached even to the inner room of the Apsu where Cassia lay, her mind tumbling with memories of the day, unable to rid herself of its febrile excitement. Even Huraya seemed possessed by it. Her soft steps were quicker, her gestures sharper as she spread a final pool of scented oil on the dark, ever-changing water of the Apsu.

Mist from the water curled a wisp of dark hair against the priestess's neck. A pulse throbbed beneath it. Cassia found herself staring at it. When Huraya bent over her with a pouch of scrubbing sand, Cassia laid a finger on the fluttering vein, conscious of a wish, a desire. "I—I'm thirsty," she said, but that wasn't it, not exactly. A new ribbed softness stirred on her back, sliding along her sides and hips.

Huraya's eyes darkened; she jerked away. A moment later she brought Cassia a dish of redfruit and her favorite honeyed sweets wrapped in gold. The priestess backed hurriedly from the room.

Listlessly, Cassia chewed and swallowed. She was reaching behind her to investigate the odd addition to her back when Huraya returned.

"Look, Addiratu!" She held up a long, full night robe.

Cassia gave a gasp of pleasure. The fine cloth of the gown was pale gold as a field of immer. Yellow flowers and tendrils of green embroidered its square neckline. More green leaves twined through the blossoms cascading down the folds, their colors shad-

ing to orange, red, then violet. Flowers so blue they looked purple stiffened the hem and banded the wide sleeves.

After Huraya applied the healer's powder and Cassia swallowed another vial of liquid, Cassia felt the gown drop over her
head. She twirled, reveling in the heavy swirl of cloth. She was
pacing the audience chamber, her head humming with song, when
Oprekka unlocked the door and entered, swathed in a green
dimmed only a little by the metallic surplice flung over it.

"Addiratu." The head priestess's tone was hard. "As you de-
creed, we have advertised among the people for a consort."

"Oh, then they're ready for me to Choose—"

"The sole volunteer will be with you shortly. Because of his
station, the contact between you can no longer be a symbolic one
between the gods. However, that is your Choice."

"But I didn't mean—only one volunteer?"

Oprekka continued as though Cassia had not spoken. "By
midnight, when the moons hang overhead, the Mating must be
completed; the Viewing of the Sacrifice will begin. Until then,
Addiratu." Oprekka trundled from the room, her silver panel with
its golden sheaves of immer swinging and whispering against her
robe.

Mating. With a stranger. Sacrifice. After all Cassia's striving,
all her hopes—was this how it ended?

"Here, Addiratu. Drink this. It will make it easier." Huraya set
another vial by Cassia's hand and backed away.

Cassia was sitting in the tall chair by the windslits, watching
the ebb and flow of light from the lamps on the sills and tables
and floor of the audience chamber when a click made her
straighten.

Two touseled heads, red and yellow, peered around the door.
With a word to the kitchen priestess in the corridor, Tadge and
Talley hurried in, carrying trays.

"There's a fair tonight. Half the cooking staff is drunk and the
rest are gone. As soon as you've eaten, we're going, too." The
boy looked out the windslit into the blue night.

While Talley set out the dishes and bread scoops, Cassia
looked down at the increasingly noisy streets below. Torches
streamed scarves of black as revelers ran with them and tossed
them in the air. The flickering orange light illuminated jugglers,
tumblers, magicians, dancers, and even a few priests carrying
their puppets and folding theaters to the temple.

"I see," Cassia said when her nursling pointed to them. She

felt increasingly remote from the people below, people who could predict the span and flow of their lives.

Tadge reached up and patted her hand. "Don't worry, Cassia. I did what you and Talley wanted. On the way here, that beast with the loud voice who calls herself Lady Anatta sent me to her rooms for more of her sweets you like—those." He pointed to the tray and its silver dish of tiny packages wrapped in gold.

Cassia took one. Nuts crunched. Dried fruit stuck to her teeth. Smooth syrups ran down her throat. She took another.

"This time Anatta told Jarell to go with me. First I wanted to fight him. Then Talley kicked me so I remembered and told him I was sorry. Jarell just said I was right when I called him those names and he, uh, 'would not waste energy on anger over something that was true.'" Tadge shuffled his feet. He brightened. "We made some plans! Uh, Cassia," he said when she remained at the window, showing little interest in his words or in the food they had brought. "If we call the Priestess of the Kitchens, she said we can go to Festival and come back later for the trays."

The sounds of Kaladussa's Festival were muffled inside the temple's stone walls. Salimar crouched in their musty dark, straining his eyes and ears as he hunted for an exit. He had taken a wrong turning among these accursed secret ways, and must get to his meeting place soon or that she-beetle, Oprekka Enna, would tire of waiting.

Salimar straightened to ease his back, and hit his head on the stone above him. The dirt of centuries and miscellaneous crawlers showered onto him. Cursing, he alternately snatched at the wrigglers and rubbed his head.

"Oo-hee! So there you are. Dear man, this way!" Oprekka's voice fluted through the darkness.

Salimar was amazed at the depth of his gratitude at hearing her hated tones; he hurried toward Oprekka. He emerged into a blue twilight. It danced with torches and was loud with cymbals and pipes and calls. As he adjusted his brown citizen's robes, a pair of Kakano children strolled by, a redheaded boy and a girl with yellow hair. The boy seemed familiar . . . Oprekka spoke and Salimar forgot them.

"You're just the tiniest bit late." Oprekka tapped her little foot. "Of course, *I'm* not important, my needs and convenience don't matter, but one has heavy duties at this time of year, I owe promptness to my people. So this must be short," she said over Salimar's erupting growl. She glanced at the Festival-goers. "And speak in the Southern tongue. We have listeners. Did you get the coin?" she asked in that lisping speech.

"Yes, I have it," he answered. "I give half now, half when our work is under way and I again hold my Stone."

"Oh, but dear man, we still have the Banquet of Atonement before us; of Forgiveness; the Royal Procession and Recession; the Blessing of the Fruitful Womb. All must be done beautifully and *differently*, for with each familiar sight the Addiratu will remember more, until— Dear, dear, the erasure of her memory was not as effective as one could wish. But there! I'm a poor woman, I did the best I could. With an Unraveller of Secrets due at the temple next morning, ready to accuse me of snatching the child, of using a Sensitive for profit . . . Lies, of course; I *rescued* her, was tender with her as if she were my own daughter! But it was simpler to be rid of the chit than explain. Kateeb, such a rush! It was not as though I had the time or the coin for a healer's block, as *some* did."

At Salimar's growl, Oprekka found her way back to her original subject. "But these ceremonies are in *your* interest, too, dear Salimar! They soothe the people, readying them for your appearance as glorious Saviour; your rule must seem inevitable! And that is not done in a shambling, helter-skelter way. Or cheaply, of course. So give me the coin, we can discuss later—"

"Now!" Salimar thundered. At Oprekka's "Hsst!" he looked around and lisped, "Tonight, when my power is strongest, kill them! Or if you or your puppets delay, *I* will do it. I'll have no more of these self-serving schemes of yours! The people must be committed to me through an irrevocable act against their goddess and their rulers!" He slapped the coin pouch from his waist into Oprekka's outstretched hand. "Half now—half when they're dead. And if you fail, nothing! We will proceed without you."

"But—but my dear man, I'm speechless! That you would think I might betray—"

Speechless. With a burst of intense joy, Salimar whipped his robes around him before she could rally, and pushed into the crowd, for once leaving Oprekka standing at its edge, her mouth opening and shutting like that of a beached fish.

When the children had gone, Cassia nibbled at a few dishes, the vials' building delight warming her belly, then ringing through her brain. Its tide effervesced into her hands and toes and skin until she could not sit still. *Mating*. Kateeb, it might not be so bad. It could be like the dark excitement of the breeding pens, or the first driving, breathless nights with her mate—or like her dreams.

Humming, Cassia held out her skirts and stumbled through a dance step she had seen on beast holidays.

Someone knocked at the door.

A memory that vanished even as she caugh at it produced the formula for welcoming unknown noble equals: "Enter, Honored Stranger and Future Confidant."

Keys rattled; the door opened.

A small, dark-haired man stepped into the room. He wore a robe of deep blue shot with silver.

Though she clapped both hands over her mouth, she could not stop peal after peal of laugher.

It was Jarell.

Chapter Thirty-Five

"Listen, fool, and learn! Each of my simples is ruled by Sassurum, goddess of life, and by Salimar, the Death God. That powder you now confess you gave to a blind soldier for his old mother—yes, it dissolves killing clots in veins and in the lungs, and yes, he may have reason to bless you, but not necessarily for the reason you think. You will learn in this trade that those who come to us are not always what they seem. Eaten in larger amounts than you ordered, and regularly, it causes bleeding within and soon releases its user from this misery we call life. If it is given to one who bleeds already, that bleeding will not stop. Even the healthiest slave blood, added to the bleeder's veins, also will be infected. Well may you look dismayed! Next time refer our charities to me! But first you will scribe fifty times on this tablet: 3-alpha-acetonylbenzyl-4-hydroxycoumarin is dangerous."

HERB WOMAN TO HER APPRENTICE IN KALADUSSA'S LOWER BAZAAR.

Cassia sat primly in the high-backed chair before the windslit; Jarell leaned against it.

"I'm glad to see you looking better, child. They did send a healer?"

"Oh, yes." Cassia described him, then smoothed her dress. "Isn't it pretty?" She got up and whirled slowly around the room, no longer alarmed at the thought of her consort, whoever he might be. With Jarell's help she would manage this threat as they had the others.

"Very pretty, child. Those are the flowers of Naphar—both hemispheres. Your full name translates as 'Little Goddess of the Flowers,'" he reminded her when she stopped beside him to grasp the chair for support. "Perhaps Oprekka is not so ignorant of your origins as the Lady Anatta believes."

Cassia's ears were ringing. Not really listening to Jarell, she slumped into the seat. Along her spine, more wetness trickled—only perspiration, surely. And the tension and pain of the two lumps there were gone—she was well! Her pleasure came bubbling back. "I'm so glad to see you!"

"Is that why you laughed? Disconcerting of you."

She watched the room circle her in a golden haze, dipping toward her, retreating; she remembered why she had not seen Jarell for some time. "When we were in the glade, you lied, didn't you?"

He looked remote.

Into his silence she said, "I've had days to think. In the highlands you talked only of freedom. You never said you wanted *this!*" As she waved at his robe, jewels, and leading ribbons, she straightened and covertly pulled her wet robe off her back.

Eyes hooded, he said, "I will not justify myself to you. My dignity or lack of it are my affair."

"I think you said those things so Tadge and I would hate you and go back to the highlands and be safe." When he did not deny it, she whispered, "You took away our Choice. Even beasts and slaves have that. By deciding for us, you made us nothing." She gazed at him through a film of tears, and thought he looked startled, that he apologized.

He bent his head. His loose fine hair fell forward and Cassia wondered how something so black could catch the flames and reflect them almost undimmed.

She was caught once more in the twinkling nets of dream. A breeze smelling of damp and smoke and flowers flared the candles behind him; she saw with a little shock that he was rouged as the nobles were for Sacrifice. His dark eyes looked brilliant in his fine-drawn face. Around his head a flame spread a halo. *From where can this enchantment come?* she wondered. *It's only a candle and my friend.* Her pulses beat weak and fast.

He took her hand. "We have spoken enough—too long, perhaps. It is time to go into your sleep chamber."

Cassia's eyes widened. "You're the consort!" Her pulses hammered with fear as he led her into the room of the Apsu's glimmering dark. She heard only snatches of how he had bribed the others to withdraw. The consort should be someone she did not know, could not—could not love! "But Anatta!" she blurted.

"She accepts it," he said with finality.

In the sleep chamber, Huraya waited; Jarell signaled for her to go.

Cassia looked with surprise at the lamps glowing on the floor, on sills, in niches, and their reflections in the mirrored and gilded masks. Ribbons of pale and dark green fluttered between the windslits, echoing the verdant floor, cushions, and ceiling with its trailing vines.

"By the gods, who did this place?" Jarell glanced away from the mural's pink and brown people brandishing leafy fronds and doing inappropriate things with them. Surveying the rest of the chamber he said, "Let me guess. Someone who likes green."

Cassia swallowed a giggle. "Anatta doesn't like it either."

"Whatever else the Lady Anatta may be, she possesses excellent taste."

"I like her!"

"I thought you might. So do I, in a way." He sank onto the pallet, settling his open hands on his knees.

Cassia hesitated, then wavered down to sit a distance from him. She stared at the blue lines inside his wrists and swallowed.

He looked up at her; twin flames burned in his pupils. "Cassia, Anatta is different from you. You cannot trust her to do as you would, partly because of her birth; in part, I think, because she is a little possessed by the divine madness, and partly"—he shrugged—"because she is Anatta."

Cassia was not listening. At his familiar amusement, then his lecturing tone, her fright had died. She forgot his betrayals, his witholdings, his cutting words; she recalled only that for sennights on a rocking raft he had been her friend, and that she wanted him. And—a load seemed to fly from her shoulders— there was no Difference!

She looked tenderly at the smudges beneath Jarell's eyes. He had not had an easy time with Anatta, she thought. Well, she would make it up to him. She knew how. She remembered nights with her mate . . . She leaned toward him, a sweet ache budding and growing in her. In her skin a thousand mouths seemed to open, all whispering Jarell's name . . .

He broke off.

She cupped his jaw. The muscle was firm. Watching her, he swallowed; his cheek clenched in her palm. She stroked it; she traced his ear; she slid her fingers into his hair. Like warm silk it drifted across them. Under her fingertips his pulses quickened. *Here are his memories*, she thought, *his hopes, his despair, and his wry laughter—all that make him Jarell.* For a golden moment, time paused.

"Cassia." He shut his eyes. Turning his head, he kissed her palm.

It felt very odd. She giggled.

He opened his lids, dazed. He frowned. "Look at me, Cassia. Now at the candle."

In the niche behind him, a flame bloomed; the room vanished in a cascade of gold. She gazed and gazed at the wonder of it.

"What is your maid's name?" His voice was harsh. It seemed to come from a great distance.

Recalled from the beauty and her clamoring senses, Cassia objected, "She's not a maid, she's a priestess. Why? You're mine, not hers! Huraya," she said grudgingly when his scowl deepened. Beneath the rouge a flush stained his cheekbones. She thought of the hot, salt blood coursing there; a darker heat built under Cassia's desire. Her stare became predatory. He did not notice. He looked toward the doorway.

Huraya stood in it, the darkness of the Apsu behind her.

"What have you given your mistress?" he asked.

"The healer left a philter for her, and powder for her back."

"Powder and a philter! And that was all? You are her priest-ess-intercessor—you did not question it?"

Huraya's glance evaded his. "I am on sufferance here. I am half-breed, tribeless. Oprekka Enna brought me to the temple from Ynianna's Bower of Blossoms for Weary Travelers, a poor one by the southern gate. If I gainsay her or her healer, she will send me back."

Jarell tightened his mouth, deepening the lines around it. "I see. My sister once served the Love Goddess in such a place. Cassia, let me look at your shoulder."

At last! He remembered her! She would make certain he con-tinued to do so. She focused on a pulse beating in his neck and thought of licking it, biting deep, drinking— *No*, a dark new voice whispered. *First arouse his more conventional desires. Then when his senses are rioting and he will allow anything . . .*

She fluttered her lashes as she had seen beasts do on holiday, and untied her robe. With one finger she eased it down, baring her shoulder and a great deal else. At her back something long and wet slithered over her ribs. A rich salt smell permeated the room. The wetness twitched. Watching him she shivered, and not entirely from the cold.

Jarell's expression darkened. He yanked up Cassia's gown in front, and scrambled behind her. After a moment of stillness he began a monotonous string of curses. "Bring me a basin and cloth," he ordered Huraya, "and some prebattle salve, the one made from warriors' livers. Or any coagulant."

Again Huraya, not her! Cassia twisted around. "Why—?"

He slid his hands behind his back, but not quickly enough. They dripped red with blood.

The sparkling mists opened; Cassia faltered, her tongue slow with shock, "Is that mine?"

He hesitated; he gave a quick nod.

"I'm not cured?"

"No, curse them for liars!" Jarell turned to the masks above their pallet. "Do you hear that, you withered, greedy hags? We're not performing, not tonight or any night!"

"What—are you talking to the masks?"

"To the witnesses looking through the peepholes behind them."

As Cassia stared at him, only partly understanding, Huraya carried in water in a silver basin, its sheen beaded with dew. She set it down, glanced at what Jarell did, and froze.

Cassia gazed, fascinated, at the candles' reflections in the basin. They glowed in the silver like flames in fog. A moment ago she had been afraid and on the brink of knowing— What? She could not remember.

Huraya's face was wan as she pattered back to the door. She stood there, breathing quickly. Water splashed; metal clinked.

"Is this clean?" Jarell asked.

"The artesian well carries away the bathwater and all in it each quarterday, Adon." Huraya fixed her gaze on Cassia's back. "Does she know—?"

Brusquely he shook his head. "Singer is what I go by, here. Did you bring the salve? Cloths?"

Huraya nodded; at arm's length she gave him a pot of unguent. "Drafts and potions are outside the door by the cabinet of drink, and the hot water pool." As Jarell spread salve on either side of Cassia's spine, Huraya drew a handful of rolled lengths of fabric from her sleeve. She dropped them on the pallet, and retreated.

Jarell folded some into pads. Setting them against Cassia's shoulder, he told Huraya, "Help me strap them."

The priestess knotted cloths together. Gingerly she tied them over Cassia's robe and back. Again she hurried to the door. The trailing things along Cassia's spine felt imprisoned; she could not move them.

She paused in her staring at the marvels of real and reflected light to peer behind her. She mourned, "My beautiful gown. Is it ruined?"

Jarell grunted and pushed against her back. Unresisting, she fell forward. "Lean against my hand!" After a while he said, "I think it's slowing. What made the blood flow like that? It could have killed her! What did you give her?"

Killed. Cassia's palms moistened. She began to listen.

"Only this, but twice the dose. She was afraid." Huraya took one of the healer's crystal vials from her sleeve; she pulled out the stopper. Its clink sounded above the muted cries of the revelers below, the soft breath of the flames and the rustle of ribbons in the wind.

He sniffed. He made a strangled sound. "Do you know what this is?"

The priestess nodded. "In the House of Blossoms some others used it when the life was too much for them. I did not—it was too unpredictable. And costly."

"Not so costly as a cure." Jarell's tone was bitter. "It gives strength for a day—perhaps two. Then—" He threw the vial on the floor. It shattered, winking in the candlelight like dew on a dawnspinner's web. "I had thought the healers, at least, were honest! So it was all for nothing." He slumped on the pallet beside Cassia.

As Huraya left the room, murmuring that she would find a brush, Cassia touched Jarell's sleeve. "Am I going to die?"

After a moment, he nodded. "I won't lie to you again."

Grief cut through her, shoving home the dagger of her desire. She slid her hand down his arm to his wrist. She fingered his pulse. "Then, please . . ." She gestured toward the pallet.

"No! The drug is in you, child. It's not you who wants this, or I; it's them." He gestured toward the masks looking down with black, empty lids.

Behind one she thought something moved. In another an eye,

perhaps, gleamed and was gone. She shuddered. Bright vapors of bliss overcame her revulsion; she searched her memory for what might make him touch her, use her, cleanse her of this wanting. "I love you," she said, and moved closer. She could smell the hot blood gushing under his skin.

He gave her a straight look. "You feel liking, friendship. Forcing it into more—or less—could lead to hate. Besides, you're hurt. We might start the bleeding again. Cassia, don't."

"Please," she said craftily, "it's comfort!" Tears balanced in her eyes. When he still shook his head, she caught at a memory strayed from her childhood. Gazing down at him she thought sad thoughts; she became them; the required drops slipped down her cheeks.

"Gods. Never once have I said no and made it stick. Why begin now?" Jarell tipped her back onto the pallet. It reflected green into his eyes. He smiled down at her. "Well, perhaps if we're very careful. Witnesses and all?"

Joy reached into her fingertips. Behind his head the candle-light grew and brightened. "Yes, please."

He raised an eyebrow. "Only if you call me by name. I've noticed, you know. You don't use it."

"It seems presumptuous. Beasts don't—"

"Cassia, child, what we are about to do is definitely presumptuous. Say my name."

"Yes, Jarell."

Smiling, he touched her mouth with his forefinger. "Again."

"Jarell . . ."

He replaced his finger with his lips. They felt warm. With infinite gentleness he settled himself beside her.

It was not enough. On Cassia's back the ridged bundles jerked in their strapping. Breathing hard, she encircled him with her arms and tightened them; she dug in her nails.

He grunted with surprise, then the heat and excitement took him too.

The conventional pleasures forgotten, she licked, kissed, bit; her robe fell away, and the strapping. She stretched her freed back; above her something snapped like sails hit by wind. She sunk her teeth in his lip; they rolled. His strength answered her every charge—she lunged at his throat. Her back arched. At her sides the ridged scarves vanished. They rose and spread and flapped, veering the flames.

He shouted aloud, "Ah, Cassia, gods! Look!"

She followed his gaze. Above her shoulders poised crumpled

silver wings. Blood dripped from them. She shrugged; their scalloped segments rippled, their short silvery fur scintillated with
lamplight. She hunched and tensed; the wings clapped upward
with the sound of banners in the wind. Shock caught her, and she
collapsed over Jarell. Her wings dropped with her, covering her
and Jarell with taut warmth.

Cassia gabbled apologies; she felt on the floor for her robe and
struggled into it. In the Audience Chamber the door crashed open.

Jarell had just time to pull his clothes into a semblance of
order and whip the strapping around Cassia and her robe, impris-
oning her wings, before Tadge and Talley burst through the door
curtain, followed by a protesting Huraya. The curtain's rings jingled, then jingled again.

"Oh, good! Jarell's here, too. What are you doing to Cassia?"

"Very little, at the moment." Beneath Jarell's blandness he
sounded shaken. "Tadge, hasn't anyone ever taught you to
knock? You never know what you might interrupt."

Beside him, head whirling, Cassia rolled onto her belly. She
stifled a mad little laugh in the crook of her arm.

"Oh sure, but this is important!" The boy came close to the
pallet. "We can only stay an instant—the kitchen priestess is outside waiting for the trays. But when Talley and I went to the fair
just now, we followed Oprekka like we said we would." He told
of her meeting with Salimar. Talley had learned the language in
scribe school that they spoke, Tadge said, and repeated their conversation. "When we found Oprekka again she was wearing the
goddess's mask—I knew it was Oprekka because she's fat. She
said everybody should come to the temple at midnight to hear the
goddess and get a share. The crowd got so excited, I asked Talley,
'Share of what?' Tell them, Talley."

The little girl stepped forward, her thin hands folded, and said
in her precise voice, "They've revived the old Spring Sacrifice. I
learned about it last cycle when we studied the Accursed Misrep-
resentations of the Goddess. Whoever is enacting Sassurum is
impregnated by the god's substitute—she has to be or the magic
won't work. Then he and she are Sacrificed. It's especially good
luck if a butcher priest doesn't do it; if instead the Frenzy of the
Goddess descends on the people and they converge on the altar to
tear the living gods to pieces with nail and tooth." She broke off
to explain: "The farmers take the bits home and plow them into
their fields so they'll get good crops. It's not very effective. They
would do much better using farm-bred Kakano fertilizer."

"A sensible child. You should go far." Jarell sent her out of the room, explaining that she should know as little as possible since she meant to stay with the temple. Huraya followed her. "Tadge, come into the room of the Apsu."

Cassia still refused to think about what had just passed. She followed them in.

". . . the second plan," Jarell was saying when she entered. "And remember, Salimar can't seem to find you if water or its image is between you and him." He waved Cassia away.

"Rest," he told her. "You'll need your strength later on. Besides, with the drug, your mind is open to Salimar. And Cassia," he said as she retreated, "think of curses."

Talley and Tadge had gone, and Cassia was standing in the Audience Chamber, watching a serpent of torches coil outside the temple, when Huraya answered a pounding at the outer door.

Oprekka sailed in, splendid this time in a yellow-green that brought out a similar shade in her skin. Priests and priestesses crowded behind her, carrying pots of incense and caskets and two folded scarlet robes covered with rainbow stones. The room filled with the scent of their bodies, perfumed oils, and aromatic, eye-watering smoke.

"It is time." Oprekka sent the priests with Jarell to the sleep chamber.

Cassia's red robe and panels were laid out and her golden sandals opened. Lamplight glowed in their buckles, each carved from a scarlet jewel. Oprekka bent over Cassia, her eyes like flat blue snail shells. "So, you were too fine for my Ibhy, were you? Now that you are about to die, will you remember? Shall I help you? So I can tell your mother, if she asks in her patronizing way if we had a good Sacrifice, that her daughter was very useful to me, as she was not? Your mother who thought cycles ago that she had you safely spirited out of Qaqqadum in a time of danger, but who believed me too stupid to understand her plan? I sent my own slaver to bring you to *me*, not to your father. I outmaneuvered your mother, your mother who despises me and denies me honor because I haven't her psychic abilities! Your mother who plots treason, and who refuses me my proper title and power in Qaqqadum, who isolates me instead in these provinces. Kateeb, I have used what crumbs she let dribble my way—I've had my revenge on her through you, and the very profitable use of you as a Mouth of the Goddess! Ah, do you recollect now, Addiratu?"

Cassia stared up at the woman. She found pictures, memories, and feelings exploding from behind the mental barrier. The bar-

rier had been formed, she discovered, at Oprekka's order, by a
bazaar herb woman. Cassia shook her head at Oprekka's flow of
honeyed venom.

"Your mother believes you deceased, you know. Perhaps it
was something I said? Oh, dear, dear, have I upset our goddess on
her night of nights?

"Put that over the other dress and the strapping. Thanks to
Salimar there's no time to undo those bindings now. It will be
bulky but it won't discommode her for long," Oprekka answered
a priestess's whispered question.

Cassia's emotions were tumbling as she allowed herself to be
turned and moved like a puppet in a temple drama. The priestesses dropped a scarlet robe over her head. The rainbow stones
sewn on it flashed colors into the shadows.

"The red is so effective in disguising fresh blood, my dear,"
Oprekka murmured.

But Cassia had no room left in her for fright. Rage crackled
around her rocketing memories, burning away the lovely mists
and the last rags of her hungers and desires. She had been a
naughty child, she remembered, and willful, and had played
many tricks. But she had been privileged—and she had been
loved! All, all had been snatched away—by Oprekka!

The priestesses circled her, patting here, tucking there.

Cassia knotted her fists. She wanted to scream, to stab, to
watch Oprekka's blood gush, her face twisting in agonies like
Cassia's own. But how? There was Jarell's knife. The problem
was getting it secretly. And stealing close enough to use it.

Cassia-the-child was still planning, her older beast-self watching in shocked fascination, when Jarell returned. He was dressed
in a scarlet robe shimmering, like hers, with rainbow stones.
Above the robe, his face looked grim.

Her childish self fully in charge now, Cassia stared past him
thoughtfully. She glimpsed the low table, hidden from her visitors
by the room's curve, where she had placed her vase of ritual and
medicinal flowers. Tadge and Talley had brought it to her on that
first morning, which now seemed so long ago.

She drifted toward the flowers, smiling vaguely, slipping into
her new role of drugged Sacrifice as easily as she had into her old
one of drugged beast.

When Cassia saw that Oprekka was absorbed in giving Jarell
his instructions, Cassia rubbed her hands in the whispering Night
Applause. She simulated her former happiness when she caroled,
"Huraya, yiann for our honored guests! It will be the last time,"

she added pathetically and listened, pleased, to her visitors' sympathetic murmurs.

Oprekka did not hear her—she was talking. No one countermanded the order; Huraya padded out.

When Huraya returned and the company's attention was on the crystal decanters of blue flashing liquid and on Oprekka telling Huraya to put them away again, Cassia knelt before the bouquet's low table. Keeping between it and the others, she stripped the Night Blooming Star Flowers of their narcotic blooms and palmed them. She held her breath against the coughroot's pollen as she shoved the rest of the bouquet into her deep chest pocket, then joined Oprekka and Huraya.

"Oh, let me," Cassia said, lifting a sealed crystal jug.

"No, fool of a girl! We've no time!" Oprekka pulled back her hand for a slap.

With a show of clumsiness, Cassia yanked at the flask's clear stopper. It came out suddenly. The yiann sloshed forward, splashing Oprekka's silver front panel and its embroidered golden sheaves. The panel flooded with blue sparks, lighting her face from below with an unearthly shimmer. The reek of yiann filled the air.

"Oh, a thousand pardons, Oprekka Enna!" Cassia smiled beatifically in the wrong direction. "Cloths, Huraya! And hot water to kill the phosphors before they set. And perhaps some meseq to refresh the company while they wait. As well bring two crocks of hot liquid as one," she explained.

With a doubtful glance, but waved onward by an incoherent Oprekka Enna, Huraya sped from the room.

When Huraya returned with a tray of cups and steaming jugs of 'seq and hot water, Cassia set Huraya and the priestesses to helping Oprekka while she bent over the cups. On the bottom of each she scattered the Star Flowers, then poured the 'seq on top of them. Its heat would bring out their sleep-inducing qualities, she reasoned; its aroma would disguise their cloying scent.

Cassia handed out the 'seq, staring vacantly and seeming unable to move until each priest and priestess took a portion.

"Oh, very well, do as she asks, it will be faster than arguing or explaining to her in that condition, and my panel is still too bright. Not to mention the smell. If it wasn't priceless . . . Hurry, girl. The moons are almost high. We shall have to shorten the ceremony as it is," Oprekka snapped at Huraya, who sprinkled the head priestess's surplice with more hot water and rolled it in drying cloths.

When the 'seq had been drunk, the priests and priestesses clustered around Oprekka. Her front panel was no longer brighter than the torches, they told her. Its aroma would be mostly overcome by the incense.

Behind them, Cassia picked up the empty vessels. When she was sure her visitors' attention was elsewhere, she carried the cups into the room of the Apsu and dumped them into the dark, warm pool. The cups sank, taking their flowers with them. *And before the night's over, they'll be washed by the artesian well to the fiery gods below,* Cassia thought with satisfaction. She crossed to her old robe of unbleached workcloth, took out Jarell's knife, and hid it in her sleeve.

As Cassia returned to the Audience Chamber, Oprekka was announcing her panel was satisfactorily cleaned. The priests and priestesses formed columns on either side of the door.

Another priestess led Cassia past Jarell. She thought he muttered as he had once before, "What have I loosed on Naphar and on myself? 'Just a mindless beast!'" He must have seen what she had done. She met his glance. In it she found a gleam of laughter —and fear. Of her.

"Now, at last, we may go down," Oprekka said. She glanced out the windslit. "The Full of the Moons is upon us!"

She prodded Cassia from behind. Cassia's fingers worked with their urge to use Jarell's knife as she followed the head priestess down the torchlit spiral of dark. Outside the wind rose; the Dark One's face and the perfect globes of the moons rose high.

Chapter Thirty-Six

Cassia's heavy wooden mask smelled of its former wearers: stale perfume and sweat, and old dried blood. Through its eyes she watched the torches weaving through the night, leading her in the final procession around the outside of the temple. Quakes flung dust into the moons' light in the surrounding hills. Cassia had not noticed them in the temple; she had been too busy.

Again Oprekka jabbed her from behind.

Cassia left the protection of the courtyard trees, and started up the ramp. The dancers on the temple walls swayed and leered. One flapped phantom wings—*no! Impossible!*

Her red spangled draperies brushed the mural's cones; shadows rotated around them as the torches moved. The dancers' life was illusion. *So are wings, all wings—they must be!*

The guards swung wide the great carved temple doors.

Inside, the crowd waited. On the red and black columns in the center of the room more torches burned, casting their flickering orange light over Rabu and Kakano Bearers of Children. Swathed in veils, they held up blood vases to the scarlet wooden altar. Far beyond them, under the god masks on the walls, candles glimmered in shrines dedicated to the goddess's lesser aspects and to her progeny.

Images of their flames wavered on jewels set in nobles' bordered hems and sleeves, or hung on merchants' striped robes; they winked on brass pots of perfumed coals swung by children who, for whitemetal coins, kept the crowd's stenches from noble noses. Through the resulting smoke and incense, candlelight sparked on soldiers' medals, brooches, and daggers. It shed a yellow glow on the faces of the elderly, draped and cowled in black, as well as on those of the younger builders, reed-cutters, apprentices, sweepers, smiths, and diggers of clay, both Rabu and Kakano, who watched and waited, their children asleep on their backs, cuddled in the hoods of their robes.

"The goddess. The goddess comes—and the god!" Whispers ruffled the crowd. It shifted and sighed like a great leashed brute; then parted, as Jarell's procession joined Cassia's. Oprekka, her face rigid with a swallowed yawn, backed against the altar. She motioned for Cassia and Jarell to enter the great golden cage.

The people filed past.

"Die well, love; bring us good harvest and shield us from the Dark One's vengeance!" A motherly woman pushed withered stalks of grain and a loaf through the glittering bars.

Above the woman, in the windslits, the dazzling heads of the moons and the Dark One's green flames edged over the sills. The cage floor moved; deep in the earth, rock scraped; antique dust from the rafters sifted onto the crowd. From the rear of the temple a chant to Salimar began. Silenced, it started in another part of the room.

A man screamed: "The wrath of the goddess—blood Sacrifice

to appease her! To Mott and the Dark God with reforms. Return to the Old Ways!" A baby cried.

The woman who had given Cassia grain and a loaf muttered propitiations, gazing avidly at Cassia's throat where a pulse beat hard and fast; she signed for all wrongs to transfer to Cassia, and passed on.

The Viewing continued.

The Dark One hung suspended above the sill. Green fire wreathed both poles; lightning shot through the black clouds boiling across its face. Murmurs and cries rose from the crowd. The light of its companions, the moons, silvered the windslits. Arrowing through the smoke, outshining the torches' radiance, the moons' twin white fingers crept toward the altar.

There a tall Bearer of Children approached the cage, remarking to a friend, "I hope she has enough blood for us all. I don't want to just smear it on my belly, I want some to drink too. The bazaar herb woman assured me that this child will arrive safely if only I can..." Still talking, she gave Cassia an assessing look and passed on.

Cassia shivered, anger scorching her horror. She would not look at the next two very small Bearers of Children nor would she listen to their whispers. With sharp gestures (of disgust?) the miniature pillars of veils made their way to the altar and elbowed their way to the blood basin.

Again the earth dropped and rocked. Outside, masonry crashed; a caged lizard's heartbreaking song became a scream abruptly ended. Within, a dark man clutched the bars of the golden cage, pronouncing curses designed to bring the wrath of the goddess onto Cassia and Jarell, not him. He spat on the scarlet jewels buckling both their sandals; he shuffled away.

As silent thunderbolts crackled between the Dark One's flames, the moons beside it closed their silver grasp on the altar. Toward the altar, from the candlelit shadows, walked two gods. One was the goddess in her masculine role of Avenger, a young man in a white war tunic—the color for death. On one shoulder he slung a quiver of golden arrows and a golden bow. When he lifted a graceful hand to his mask and pushed at a coil of hair, Cassia recognized Anatta.

Beside Anatta ambled the lank figure of the goddess, also in a white robe and wearing the black-visaged mask of Sassurum in her aspect as Taker of Life. Anatta pushed the wearer of the goddess mask toward the cage. The wearer complained, "Oh, Anatta, do I have to? You're as bad as my mother. I don't know if I *want* to partner you any more." The goddess was Ibby.

"They dress like that for power so each gets the strength of the other half of the race," Jarell whispered as Cassia stared. But she did not stare from surprise. She stared because she remembered this ceremony—and more!

She remembered her closed palanquin carried by sweating priests from village to city to village again, stopping wherever a citizen offered coin for a vision or prophecy.

She remembered stumbling, drained, into yet another provincial temple. There she answered the questions of merchants, generals, and kings. All heaped coin at her feet: coin that she never saw again, coin that messenger priests scooped into chests and carted back to Oprekka.

She remembered resting in Sassurum's temple in Kaladussa, exhausted from her role as Mouth of the Goddess, played far more times than was healthy; recovering in the courtyard, tending the plants she loved.

She remembered befriending a child there, one as bewildered and frequently drugged as she, a boy punished or bribed with presents by his ambitious mother, teased, then neglected by his adored half sister; a boy called Ibby.

She remembered being routed out in the night by a furious Oprekka while priestesses whispered of an Unraveller of Secrets, sent by Cassia's mother to find her.

She remembered being drugged, sold into a slave coffle and trudging to the highlands.

Cassia's anger grew. What had been done to her was wrong by the laws of man and the goddess. She looked around the temple, knowing where the secret passages lay, and knowing where the speaking tubes were, with which the priestesses made the god masks talk. Cassia started to exclaim.

But Ibby said, "Oh, all *right*, Anatta!" and clanged open the golden cage door. He pulled Jarell to the altar and the blood basin. There, with the rest of the veiled clamoring women, the two very small Bearers of Children held up their blood vases.

Anatta reached in for Cassia. "I'm going to kill you," Anatta hissed.

As Cassia went with Anatta to the altar, Cassia thought of the knife in her sleeve. But knives were for butcher priests. The goddess had other weapons.

"Ibby's got a proxy for my manikin. I'll own him in spite of you." Anatta gripped Cassia harder and gestured toward a stocky blond man beside Jarell.

"But that's the leader of Ibby's team!" Cassia said. "He was his tutor, he's known him all his life."

"He was insolent," Anatta said. "And it's fair—Ibby killed *my* lead man."

Two butcher priests in their scarlet robes stepped from the crowd; they set lanterns on the altar beside the blood basin. Light bloomed in the white stone. Deep inside, its green veining seemed to pulse, asking to be fed. The crowd held its breath.

Behind Cassia and Anatta, Oprekka announced, "The Mating of the Gods has been completed. The goddess is satisfied. The Sacrifice will begin." The solemnity of Oprekka's phrases was only a little marred by the stifled yawn that ended them. Beside her, a heavy-eyed priestess leaned against a column.

Excitement rose in Cassia, fed by her anger. There had been no mating—her strange hunger had seen to that, and Tadge's sudden entrance. Oprekka and the witnesses knew it. The ceremony was a mockery. Sassurum did not permit mockery.

"Who Sacrifices the god?" the first of the butcher priests intoned.

No one answered. The crowd rustled.

Anatta let go of Cassia to nudge Ibby. "Speak, you fool!"

His great dark woman's mask turned. "Uh, I Sacrifice the god." From its visage, frozen in the silent scream of retribution, came Ibby's whispered addition: "But I don't want to. I like my lead man, Anatta. I'll kill this one!" Ibby swooped on Jarell. With a flutter of white garments he lifted Jarell to the altar.

"No, idiot! That one's mine. Take a member of the populace." Anatta dove for Jarell.

Just below him, Cassia heard heavy footsteps clump into the temple. "End this farce," a voice boomed. "Tonight is mine! *I* choose to sacrifice the god." A tall shape was framed in the open doors; the torchlight formed a nimbus around its stiff golden curls. The shape moved purposefully toward the altar.

On the altar, Jarell stopped swinging his heels. "Salimar!"

Salimar had resumed the black robes and scarlet surplice of a high priest of the Dark God. He put a hand on his chest. "Get in," he told Jarell. From his sleeve he drew a dagger.

Jarell's face blanked. Like a puppet he climbed into the long white basin and lay down, rainbows from his robe scintillating among the ceiling's black and scarlet arches.

Behind the altar, Oprekka began to chant, drowning Anatta's protests. The butcher priests and the priestesses joined in, though their contributions were irregular. Many of them leaned against the pillars; two elderly priestesses wrapped their arms around a column, pillowed their cheeks against a carved arch or flower, and shut their eyes. The incense in the sacred braziers flattened into layers.

The nobles and merchants nearest the altar called over the chanting, "Sacrilege! Eject Salimar's representative from the temple—from the city!" In front of them the Bearers of Children screamed agreement and pressed closer to the altar. Only with energetic jabs of elbow and sandal did the two littlest ones stay near Cassia.

But at the edge of the crowd, others muttered approval when a young man shouted, "The Dark God succeeds where the goddess did not. The Dark One rules the moons—he brings a Time of Changes. Down with the goddess and her reign of women! Give us the Dark God and the supremacy of men!"

Ignoring them all, Salimar ran his hands over Jarell. "The Stone!" he hissed. "Where is it?"

Over the top of the basin, Cassia saw black hair move as Jarell shook his head. Above him rainbows bounced.

The giant ground his teeth. "Who has taught you, manling? Where have you found the strength to defy me?" His pale eyes flickered with torchlight. He glanced at Cassia, and his mind hit hers. "I have no quarrel with you," he said aloud when she withstood him. "Release my servant—erase these thoughts of water that obscure his thoughts. And the child I saw—where is he? Or was he your invention? Help me and I will let you live."

Oprekka, still chanting, moved closer, yawned convulsively, and grabbed for Salimar's knife. "*I* command the Sacrifices here!" Jowels quivering, she swung toward Cassia. "This is your doing, isn't it? Just like your mother, all sweetness on the outside, while inside you've been plotting to destroy me and all I've worked for. Just remember, I know what that traitor and the Ensai plan. I can ruin her! I . . . Tell her . . ." Oprekka yawned until her jaws popped, then subsided into a shiny green and silver heap. From her mouth came a gentle snore.

Cassia smiled inside her mask; her wings stirred under their bindings. For the brazier before her, alone of all those in the temple, sent its incense thin and straight to the gods.

Gathering her anger to her, Cassia breathed in the smoke. Its haze formed patterns against the torchlight and shadows. They became the goddess's dark hair blowing across illimitable stars. Sassurum turned her head; her black eyes smiled at Cassia; unmistakably she winked. Then the vapors and the goddess dispersed and there was only darkness and the breathing of the crowd. But Cassia felt an inner sureness. Her chance would come.

"Cassia." Above her in the blood basin, Jarell's voice was a thread. "Remember the curses." Again he shook his head at Salimar.

This time the giant screamed with rage. Lifting his knife he began invoking the death gods.

At Cassia's back, Anatta snatched a golden arrow from her quiver. "Don't you harm my manikin. Take this one!" She pushed the stocky blond Kakano next to the altar and Cassia.

Salimar's chant continued. Cassia took a long breath.

". . . And now let the goddess speak her will." Salimar's ritual pause was infinitesimal.

"Go!" Jarell breathed.

Cassia stepped forward. "I speak for the goddess." The low timbre of her voice surprised her. From the silence, she thought they heard her throughout the room. A priestess clinging to a nearby pillar opened her eyes.

"You mock the goddess," Cassia accused. "You offer false sacrifice to a false god for actions which your own priestesses know have not taken place. They lie to Sassurum and to you! The God Signs bear me out." She pointed to the horizontal smokes above the sacred braziers.

By the altar, the two smallest Bearers of Children took out lanterns and lit them as if to see better. The flames briefly illuminated Ibby with his lead man, scratching the bars and stars of a game on the side of the wooden altar.

Cassia paid no attention. The goddess's anger seemed to augment her own. The words of the antique poets rhymed thoughts, not sounds in her mind. They flowed through her like yiann. "Oh, you hungry little people, I will show you Sacrifice, and it will be yours. You wish your fields to bear? Worship me thus falsely and I shall command the hot winds of perpetual summer to turn them to howling wastelands. You demand blood? I bring you blood! Your gray heads shall run with it, gore shall redden your beards. I will take your young men for my army and make them an infestation upon the hillsides. I will bathe in their blood, I will stack their bones for my footstools. There will be moaning and crying in the land as your sons and daughters sicken of the war plagues and die. For you are corrupt, siblings of the pallet of illness, companions of the pallet of disease."

Cassia paused to draw breath. The people moaned and swayed as if blown by a wind; shamefaced, and making signs of propitiation to the goddess, a few edged out the doors. From those who remained came fierce cries and terrified ones. "Sacrifice them! Satisfy the goddess!" Outside, the Fire Mountains roared, drowning the shouts; a grinding came from deep in the rock beneath the temple as an earthquake slid the floor downward, then sideways. The doubled bars of moonlight now illuminated the blood basin, outlining Jarell's figure within.

Cassia's gaze encompassed not this but the temple and the night beyond. Flown on the healer's golden drafts and her fear and rage, she had become the temple and the night and the stars. "I, Sassurum, have seen how you profit from despair. Do you sell your sons and daughters for coin so you may eat? Behold the inhumane who hear the cries of the broken in spirit and heed them not. I, Sassurum, shall avenge them. The high mountains shall weep for you, the peaks of the gods shall cry. Spent is the bread from your ovens, empty are your jars of yiann, gone is the oil from your cooking pots and your lamps. In mourning for your dead and enslaved children and your fields, homeless and without a city shall you roam until you are sated with weeping and you quaff tears like strong drink."

More of the congregation left. Many of those who remained sank to the floor, weeping and praying to the mother goddess for forgiveness. Others slunk away. A baby cried; Oprekka snorted in her sleep. The very short Bearers of Children crouched at the base of the altar feeding solid matter into their lamps, while at its side, Ibby and the lead man continued their game.

Salimar, apparently unmoved by the cursing, lifted Jarell from the blood basin. In the torchlight, rainbows shot from the gems sewn on his robe as Salimar shook Jarell, dagger in hand, demanding his Stone.

"I'm warning you! He's mine!" By Cassia, Anatta drew her bow; she aimed an arrow at Salimar.

Cassia wound up for the finish. "Oh, you who deny the teachings of the goddess and allow yourselves to be seduced into Choosing the Old Ways, your bones will be scattered and left for the carrion lizards to gnaw. Stilled are the harps of your fingers, silent the stones of your mouths. Empty, oh empty is your land like your hearts, oh sellers of children, defilers of the goddess.

For I, Sassurum, curse you and your children and your children's children until your seed is cleansed from the earth."

Murmurs rose from the stubborn worshipers who remained. "The Old Ways. Return to the Forbidden Powers. Rend her!"

By Cassia, the calm inhumanly beautiful mask of the avenging god turned from Salimar to her; the golden bow lowered. Beneath the mask, Anatta, its wearer, pointed at Cassia and screamed, "She lies to save herself! Kill the false goddess!"

With Anatta's attention drawn from him, Salimar trumpeted, "I'll teach you not to tell me!" He stabbed downward at Jarell.

Anatta whipped around, nocked and released her arrow. Salimar bellowed as it pinned his hand to the wooden altar. Inflamed by Anatta's words, the people groaned with a single voice and moved forward.

"Sunder her!" Anatta screeched. Leaving Ibby and the lead man behind, immersed in their game, Anatta hurried toward Salimar and Jarell, shrieking, "Eat her flesh without a knife, drink her blood without a cup!" In a lower voice she snapped at Salimar, "Give me my manikin. Then we'll both get out safe. Leave the Addiratu to the crowd."

The Bearers of Children closed in around Cassia, vases high, pushing the two smallest ones against her knees. The smallest ones still held their lanterns. Cassia turned her face from the lights' foul smell.

Beside her at the altar, Anatta grabbed Jarell from Salimar. Salimar tried to stop her; his pinned hand stopped him. The giant submitted to Anatta's breaking off the shaft and binding his knuckles with a cloth from her sleeve. Concentrating on her work, she let Jarell slip from her grasp. He ran. She screamed and started after him.

Salimar brushed at his eyes and laughed. "If I can't have the manling, neither can you!" Grabbing Anatta, he held her fast as Jarell escaped; cursing, Salimar dodged Anatta's clubbing hands and feet.

Cassia watched no more. The people closed in. They looked angry—and hungry. Her heart pumped with aching quickness.

Ibby's lead man glanced up, dropped their game, and pushed to Cassia's side. "Way! Way for the Addiratu!" With the clarion voice the lead man had once used to clear a road for his master, he opened a path through the Bearers of Children. The two smallest ones stayed close to her, swinging their lamps. The smell grew worse.

"Anatta! I'm all alone. Help me, Anatta." Ibby's plaintive voice cut through the rumble of the mob.

"In a moment I must go to my master. There are passages through there and there." The lead man pointed at the carved panelling of the walls.

"I know. I had forgotten, but I know!" In Cassia's veins, the healer's artificial joy and strength rose and bubbled.

As the stocky blond man ordered a seller of simples out of the way, Cassia asked, "Why?"

He forced the Bearers of Children to drop back. "Why do I help you?" The two smallest veiled cocoons darted around Cassia and hid behind her robe. "Because when you were here before as a seer, you were kind to my master."

"But . . ." Summoning Jarell's words of long ago, Cassia urged the lead man to escape Ibby's abuse and come with her.

He gave her a stern, shamed look and shook his head. "He needs me. And—gods help me—I now love what he does to me." Behind them Ibby's voice rose in panic. Indicating the nearest secret entrance, the stocky blond man merged with the crowd.

"There she is—tear her to pieces!" someone shouted.

"Cassia! Your mask!" Jarell called from behind her.

Of course—it marked her. She pulled it off and threw it. Jarell zig-zagged to her side.

"That way, Cassia!" Tadge's voice—but it came from the little pillar of veils running at her knee.

"We'll stop the crowd." The other small veiled figure had Talley's precise tones. Both children dropped back.

"There! In the scarlet and rainbow stones! Catch them!" Anatta cried behind them.

Salimar's deep growl accompanied her words.

A sea of heads seemed to bob between Cassia and safety. Despair burned like a hot stone in Cassia's belly. The crowd jostled her against an altar to the goddess as Bringer of Dreams.

"I can see her. She's down!" Salimar cried. "I've got her! Dark in here," he muttered.

With inspiration born of panic, Cassia remembered that she had brought dreams to Oprekka, and that she had other herbs. She stumbled to her feet. "Hold your breath!" she told Jarell, reached into her pocket for the coughroot she had almost forgotten, turned, and thrust it up toward Salimar's voice.

She glimpsed his pink and white face crumpling into a barrage of sneezes, his eyes streaming with tears. He knuckled them.

"Can't see." A look of surprise crossed his face; he clutched his belly. "Hurts."

"Where is she? Point! I'll get her," Anatta called behind Salimar.

Elated with her success, Cassia reached into her robe a second time. "Close your eyes and grab my skirt," she told Jarell. She threw a handful of the fire plant's stiff aromatic leaves on the Dreamers' altar.

Lightning blazed to the ceiling; smoke billowed after it. With the ease of practice, Cassia stepped into its obscurity. Towing Jarell, she followed the wall, feeling for the sequence of carvings that would tell her where to find a sliding panel so she could vanish.

She became aware of a vile smell, a compound of rotten tearroots and unscrubbed convenience holes, but with an acrid overlay all its own. With exclamations of disgust and an occasional retching noise, most of the crowd fell away. Cassia turned around.

Behind her the two little cocooned figures swung their lanterns, reached among their veils for more solid matter, threw it into the flames, and hurried toward her as she found the panel. She pressed it. And they were in the cool clear air of the corridor behind the kitchens.

The two little figures swept back their hoods, set down their stinking lanterns, and swung in a circle, pounding each other's backs, snorting with laughter. "This way, Cassia, follow us!" Tadge caroled. He and Talley sprinted down the hall.

They hurried through the kitchens and unlatched a timbered door leading to a storage room. They dodged around chopping blocks and tall baskets piled with green and yellow vegetables, winter fruit a little soft but plump with juice, and thick-skinned sand melons as big as a Rabu's head.

A door slammed far down the corridor. Voices—Anatta's and Salimar's—squabbled about directions. As Jarell cautiously pulled the door of the storage room closed, Cassia brushed against a basket of sand melons. It wobbled; fell. Melons hit the floor, bounced, and rolled in all directions. Jarell glanced back and grinned. With his help, more baskets toppled. The floor became a sea of bounding fruits and vegetables.

"Cassia, here!" Tadge called. "Talley, you better go before they catch you with us." Wordlessly the two clasped hands. Tadge scowled. "Kateeb, get going!" Talley went.

Cassia examined Tadge's escape route, a trap door in the storeroom floor. It looked very small. Smiling brightly she said, "Show us the way. Jump, Tadge."

The boy hung by his fingers, swung, and dropped. "Are you coming, Cassia? It's dark down here." His voice sounded hollow.

"Soon." Kneeling by the hatch, Cassia motioned for Jarell to go next.

He frowned. "That's tight. I should have checked. Try to get through. I'm not leaving you to face them. It's me they want."

"Then leave!"

"Take off your robe," he said suddenly.

"What?"

"Take it off, and bundle the skirt of the other one around your face."

"But . . ." *You'll see my legs*, she finished silently.

The deep Rabu voices that had vanished up the corridor interrupted her. They grew so loud she could hear individual words through the door. She found she didn't care what Jarell saw.

Slipping Jarell's knife into her inner robe's sleeve, she dragged the outer sacrificial robe over her head. It snagged on her wings' strapping, loosening it. She dropped the red robe through the hole. Pulling her flowered gown up to her waist, she sat on the edge of the trapdoor, face hot, refusing to look at Jarell. Her knees and thighs slid through; her hips stuck.

"Try the diagonal." Jarell's voice sounded choked.

She glanced at him suspiciously. His face, however, looked quite solemn. She turned and wriggled further. She stuck again.

With a snort, Jarell leaped behind her and shoved on her shoulders. "Pull on her, Tadge," he called.

Footsteps pelted below. Little arms and legs wrapped around Cassia's ankles; Tadge swung on her feet.

"Ohh!" she cried, slipped, fell, and landed with a bone-rattling thump.

Tadge rolled clear. Gulping down laughter, Jarell dropped beside her, pulling the the trapdoor closed behind him. In the last flash of light she saw him scoop up her robe that had broken both their falls. The tunnel was very dark.

"They won't know which door we used. May slow them up," Jarell explained. Cloth rustled. Cassia thought he tied her robe around his waist. "Let's go," he said.

"How?" she asked. "We left the lanterns behind."

"There are glow beetles ahead." Tadge's voice came from beside her knee. "Look. There's one."

Near Cassia' nose, a pink blot crawled across the blackness.

She looked more closely. Feelers waved over the stone wall; six tiny feet scrambled across its pitted surface. Above them wings like oval shells encased its back. When it stopped to eat, its light shed a minute pink radiance on the lichen covering an outcropping. As Tadge pulled Cassia farther down the tunnel, she saw more glow bugs munching on the lichen, all pink.

"They like to keep the same colors together. And their droppings all go in one place, too," Tadge added with a naughty chuckle. "Talley and I picked some up and burned them. That's where the smell came from."

As they ran along the dark stone corridor, the cloth tying Cassia's wings loosened further. The sluggish air was tinged with a familiar mossy fragrance. The lichen, perhaps.

Overhead, the door slammed against the wall; footsteps thudded. Bodies crashed to the floor. More hollow footsteps sounded, followed by additional thumps and curses. A shaft of light cut through the dark.

"Too small." Anatta's voice was decisive. "I know a different way. Come on. You too, Ibby."

"I'm tired of this, Anatta," Ibby complained. "I'll buy you another Kakano. Gods, I'll even give you one of mine."

"I want *that* Kakano," Anatta gritted. The trapdoor closed; its boom echoed down the tunnel, bringing with it the rich smell of crushed fruit and vegetables, and the harsh one of torches.

"Hurry!" Tadge said. "They'll cut us off. The tunnels meet ahead of us—they could use one of the cross-connections."

Cassia rubbed her back. Sweat stung it. Warmth pooled against her robe; the strapping was loose. She pulled on an end, rolled the length of cloth, and stuffed it into her sleeve. When they could see again she would ask Jarell to retie her wings—Wings? She had wings! She spread them inside her robe, loosening her collar thong to do so. It was an unusual sensation, but very satisfying. Perhaps, she thought, she would not retie them.

"Cassia?" Tadge said beside her. "We're almost there."

A pastel radiance dimly illuminated the chipped rock and moss. It grew stronger; they heard the sound of running water. "That's the stream that goes through the courtyard. Talley said so." Tadge was silent for a moment. "I miss Talley. But she had to go back if she's going to be head priestess someday and clear out Oprekka's corruption." Pride tinged the loneliness in his voice. "What are you going to do if they're waiting for us?" he asked. "I—I'm scared, Cassia."

Anger swelled in her. Something was wrong with a world that

made her nursling afraid. Her wings stirred against her back. "Fight," she said. One hand on Jarell's knife, she strode forward, her mind filling with a battle song of Sassurum, mother goddess, avenger of children. *How dare Salimar*, she thought, and again she was Sassurum. *The Dark God is only a minor deity, one of my many unruly offsring. He will be punished for his impertinence.* When they came to the stream she said to her nursling and Jarell, "Wait here, where Salimar can't use mindtouch on you."

Jarell stared up at Cassia. Ah, gods, he was so weary. And she had lost blood, walked half the night in procession—where did she get this manic energy, this idea that she must protect him?

"Cassia, you're being ridiculous. Do you know anything at all about hand-to-hand combat? I've fought in the battle circles, and—"

Her silver eyes flashed with torchlight as she stared down at him. "Wait here!" she repeated. The neck of her robe widened; the points of her wings pushed above her head. They moved restlessly. Blood streaked them. The fear crept down Jarell's spine that had shocked him in the temple's green, semicircular room: fear of something alien, unknowable. He stepped back beside the wide-eyed Tadge.

As Cassia splashed across the stream, Jarell scanned the vaulted chamber for battle advantage. The chipped stone floor was level; the glow beetles' light failed at the mouths of six passages opening into the room, none of which could be ignored; they might hide enemies. Beside each one were brackets for torches.

Jarell tensed. Yellow light moved on the crystals roughening the ceiling and walls by the opposite tunnel. Footsteps pelted downward.

Anatta leaped into the chamber, bow in one hand, torch held high in the other. Her black eyes gleamed in their bluish whites.

In front of Jarell, Cassia moved to meet her, golden sandals leaving wet prints on the stone, her crumpled gown bright with flowers and blood.

Plunging the torch into a holder, Anatta bared her teeth. "You! Where's my manikin?" She drew a golden arrow from her quiver.

From behind her came Ibby's nasal voice: "Anatta? Please bring back the light."

Anatta tossed her head as though a zitter whined by her ear, and watched Cassia. "No one takes what's mine!" Her eyes seemed to burn as she raised her bow.

"Please, Anatta?" In the passage, Ibby's tearful voice came closer. "You know how afraid I am, ever since we were little and you hit me to get my knife. I was lost in the dark for so long, I couldn't find you, not in any of my dreams."

With growing alarm Jarell watched Anatta circle and nock her golden arrow. Gods! Cassia didn't even turn sideways to present a smaller target. A presentiment of disaster seemed to build around the light.

Cassia touched her sleeve where she had put the knife. Jarell watched from his place behind the stream and drew a quick breath. *Now, while Anatta's closest and overconfident.* Instead, Cassia held up the knife, the pink and orange light liquid on its blade. "You are wrong; *wrong!*" Her voice held the resonance it had in the temple. Jarell's scalp crawled. "You would take lives not granted you, you would possess those not your own." She advanced on Anatta.

Cassia knows nothing of battle. Resolution firmed in Jarell. His blood ran cool and smooth in his veins as Anatta's eyes narrowed and she backed out of Cassia's reach.

"Why didn't you die?" the young noblewoman asked, distracting Cassia and circling so the torchlight glared in Cassia's eyes. "I gave you poisoned sweets. Your blood should have soaked the earth by now; your singer would be mine!"

Ah, gods, Jarell thought, *that too! Cassia's every trouble is through me! And she so loving, so transparent, come to me too late, too late. But I can free her.* The death god beckoned him like a boon companion, exhaling his honeyed breath that gave eternal ease, sleep from which one need never wake.

Cassia's eyes widened in shock, then in anger; she followed Anatta like the inexperienced child she was. Jarell groaned. But he would not move yet. She could have a lucky stroke; later she might need him.

"You should have sold me the Kakano," Anatta said. "I'd have given you the antidote—I'd have been a good friend to you."

"He was never mine to sell. He is his own." Straightening, Cassia faced Anatta and lifted the knife shoulder-high.

"Ah, gods, not that way, Cassia, you're leaving yourself wide open!" Jarell called as, with a feral smile, Anatta raised her bow. He crossed the stream.

"Anatta? I see the light. Wait!" Ibby's voice, accompanied by Salimar's growls, echoed through the room.

Jarell started across the floor, his hem slopping against his ankles. "Salutations, Lady." He stepped into the torchlight by

Cassia and greeted Anatta as an equal. As he expected, Anatta paused to stare down at him haughtily.

From the tunnel behind her came the sound of a fall. Salimar exclaimed, "To Mott with this weakness!" He stumbled nearer.

"Nice of you to stop by," Jarell told Anatta. "I'm not coming with you, you know."

The young noblewoman could not have looked more surprised if her arrow had spoken. She lowered her bow. "What did you say, Singer?"

"I'm not coming. I'd rather stay with her." He gestured toward Cassia.

"Her!" A growl came from deep inside Anatta. She aimed her arrow at Cassia, and let fly.

My cue, Jarell thought and moved forward.

"No!" Face pale and sweating, Salimar skidded into the chamber as, with the grace Jarell had learned in courtly presentations, he stepped in front of Cassia.

Cassia seemed to watch the arrow arc through the pink radiance forever, catching yellow fragments of torchlight and throwing them back at the crystals and walls. It thumped into Jarell's chest. In the silence of stone and rushing water, it squeaked past bone.

The impact shoved Jarell backward. His body glanced off Cassia's hip. Beside her, Salimar swayed forward and caught him.

After a moment Salimar rasped, "He's alive, but not for long. Dark in here." Leaning against the wall Salimar freed a hand and brushed at his eyes. To Anatta he said, "You fool—what good is he dead? He defied me with images of running water, but I would—I would have dug out his secret." He wiped his forehead with his bandaged hand. "Dizzy—dark. So cold. Don't know why..." Eyes widening, he stared at the sleeve cloth Anatta had tied. Slowly he looked toward her. "What was on that arrow?"

But her stillness had ended. She had flung away her bow and lowered her face to her knees in ritual grief. "No, no," she sobbed. "Bring the singer back."

Salimar's rumble turned to a roar. "Answer me!" He repeated his question.

Anatta looked at him through her tears. "Ah, gods! I forgot. The sacred arrows are poisoned. And I don't have the antidote. Its pouch clashed with my tunic and Oprekka wouldn't let me wear it. Now I've killed you too, and my singer twice over." She covered her face with her hands and sobbed.

Salimar groaned, dropped Jarell, and made for the tunnel.

Tears leaked through Anatta's fingers. "My beautiful little manikin. Ibby!" She groped behind her.

The young nobleman emerged from the opening, his blond lead man behind him. Squinting into the sudden light, Ibby took Anatta's square hand in both his long-fingered ones. "We can find you another singer." Ibby's voice was gentle with pity. "Come away. Would you like to take the body with us? You'd have that much, Anatta. I know a pair on a back street in Kaladussa who can tan it and stuff it until it looks so lifelike you'd swear it almost breathed."

Anatta sniffed and choked back a sob. "I never meant to hurt him, Ibby." Pleadingly she raised her wet face to her half brother's. "Just like I never meant to hurt you. You believe me, don't you?"

"Yes, Anatta. Shall we bring the manikin?"

She sniffed again and nodded.

As Ibby motioned for the lead man to pick up Jarell, Salimar choked from the passage, "No! He's mine!"

Anger burned away Cassia's paralyzing incredulity. She felt her wings struggling to rise; they pushed down the back of her robe and pulled free, opening with the sound of whips snapping. The lead man stopped and looked up. Cassia stood over Jarell. "He's none of yours! You're obscene, the lot of you. I'll take him." She lifted him. The arrow in his chest gleamed in the fitful light.

She heard a breath of a laugh. In her arms, Jarell tried to open his eyes; his mouth worked. "A perfect end." He stopped for air. "Fought over by three Rabu." He drew another painful breath. His scarlet robe was the color of blood. If she had not felt the hot wetness dripping through her fingers, Cassia would not have known he was hurt. His blood's sweet salt smell was strong. Her old desire twitched, but rage burned it away. Her wings clashed, splattering red over the gray stone and the watchers.

They stepped back. "Those wings. They're silver, but the blood— Look at her teeth," Ibby whispered. "And claws."

Jarell seemed not to hear or care. "What a difference from the way I planned it." He licked his lips. His voice strengthened. "I intended a heroic death. Scorched by a supernova while evacuating a planet, or at least hand-to-hand combat as I defended the helpless." His chest moved in a soundless laugh. "Thus do the

gods reward our arrogance." He coughed, struggling to rise.
Blood fountained from his mouth. The blood gushed, warm and
sticky, over Cassia's arm. His head fell back.

Hot fury leaped in Cassia at the waste, the callous dismissal of
a life. She made her wings burst wide and spread above her, the
talons at each scallop's end unsheathing. She clapped them together with the sound of swords on leather shields. She drew her
lips back from her teeth, she took a slow step forward. "Go! And
take the curse of the goddess with you." She turned her frenzy
into a murderous wall of hate and shoved it at Jarell's killers.

Ibby took Anatta's arm. "The Misbegotten," he whispered,
making the protective handsign. "No, Anatta, don't fight her.
She's got a demon or a god in her. She'd win."

Dully, Anatta resisted. She groped for her dagger.

Cassia spread her wings to either side of the corridor. Their
wind skewed the torch's flames. "You've killed enough!" she
screamed. "Go!"

Ibby pushed Anatta into the corridor and sent his lead man
with her, then grabbed the torch from its bracket. His worn face
was troubled. "We're going. I know you wouldn't—wouldn't
really— You were kind to me once. Ah, gods!" His green eyes
were bright with tears as he added, "She's really sorry, you
know." He retreated up the long passage.

Cassia settled her wings, folding them around her, and slowly
sheathed her talons; she watched until black snuffed his torch's
last glimmer.

After a while her eyes admitted a little pastel glow. She adjusted her burden and called to Tadge, "Which tunnel?" She tried
to ask the question as though it mattered.

Chapter Thirty-Seven

Choice lies at the heart of the goddess's mystery. Our reality is what we
perceive: we live in a thousand times a thousand overlapping worlds. For those who
Choose to see the goddess and whose mind's eyes are open, she will be seen, her
grant of unending awareness is real. For those who Choose not to believe in her
and whose mind's eyes are blind or closed, she does not exist, the life she gives

ends. Ours is the Choice of humanity, its risk, and its sorrow, which is the shadow of joy. And ours is the Choice of inhumanity, its safety, and its freedom from pain, which is the shadow of self-abnegation. Those Choosing the goddess and her life and the light, trust the side of knowledge that is intuition and feeling. Those Choosing a god and his death and the dark, trust the side of belief that ends with

their senses and the bounds of their rational minds. No Choices are wrong— all are halves of life's whole, as at the heart of each answer lies a question. Is that so?

Catechism of Mysteries, learned by apprentice priests of Sassurum in their second Thitamanit.

Tadge splashed across the faint glow of the cavern's stream; the light that the water shed upward made the boy's eyes look like hollows in a skull. He stared at Cassia's wings; he slowed. "Cassia? Is that you? Are you really— Are you all right?"

"Oh, Tadge! No, I'm not. Please, I'd never hurt you! But he's dead, they've killed him! He— Oh, Tadge!" Cassia's gulping sobs made it impossible for her to go on. She licked the cold tears streaming down her cheeks; she sniffed; they would not stop. In the end she stooped and let Tadge wipe them with her red robe that he pulled from around Jarell's waist. For she would not relinquish her burden.

"Cassia, you won't leave Jarell here, will you?"

"No!" She searched for the reason; his weight was an impediment, after all. And that was why. All his life he had been at the mercy of others' convenience. "He can at least go to the goddess with some ritual, some dignity!"

"He didn't believe in any of that. You do, though, don't you?"

Cassia stared bleakly over his head. In the glowing dark, she made out a tall shape and black tresses. The dark parted like vapors; the goddess's eyes looked through it to Cassia from the blackness of Sassurum's own eternity. Her eyes held neither compassion nor triumph. They were simply black and white and compelling. "Yes, I believe in the goddess," Cassia said dully. "I have to." She started forward; but she had nowhere to go. Yet something—a scent, an unheard song—drew her across the vaulted chamber to the openings where crystals flashed in the dim light.

Tadge followed. "I—I don't know where to go, Cassia. Talley and I were afraid to look any further. We followed Oprekka here; this is where she met the healer. He came up from one of those tunnels." The boy indicated the ones that drew her.

She scarcely hesitated. "Then let's take the healer's corridor. At least *it* shouldn't lead back to the temple."

As they followed the slope of the tunnel downward, the glow bugs increased in number, as did the light. The colors had shaded from pink to violet to blue and Cassia's arms were aching from bearing Jarell's weight when she noticed that Tadge had dropped back again, her red sacrificial robe bundled in one hand. "Tadge, what are you doing?

"I'm wiping up Jarell's blood. We're leaving a trail."

"He's bleeding? But then, his heart is still pumping!"

From below Cassia's chin came a thready whisper. "I fear my funeral oration was premature. I thought it best to leave our friends with the impression that it was not."

Cassia jumped. "You're alive!"

Jarell's head barely moved in a nod.

Cassia's eyes brimmed with scalding tears; they overflowed onto his robe and her hands. Clutching him to her, she looked down the corridor. If Tadge had seen one healer in it, might there be another? She walked faster. Her wings moved restlessly beneath her robe, leaving wet trails along her ribs.

The blue glow had faded, the last bright beetle had scuttled back to its lichen, when the tunnel smoothed underfoot. As it dropped down into blackness, it seemed more a causeway than a thing chipped by nature. The musky, tangy fragrance was strong.

Cassia was moved by a knowledge in her skin or her belly; she stopped and felt in front of her. She touched a wall. She followed it; she fetched up against the sides of the tunnel. It was a dead end. Dizziness born of despair surged over her. She leaned against the cool stone and sobbed.

"What is it, Cassia? Are we there? I'm so tired!" Tadge slid to the floor of the passage. Almost immediately his breathing grew slow and regular in sleep.

But Jarell will die, Cassia thought. *We should try the other tunnel!* She tried to rouse the boy but could not. At last, spent, she too sat, Jarell's body across her knees, and waited.

Peace moved within her, a trickle at first, then growing and pooling, until she seemed again to hear the song without words that had so entranced her in the walled garden outside Kaladussa. Eventually she heard the dry rustle of wings beside her. The hairs on her arms rose.

"We have been expecting you, Almost Beloved." The calm whisper was loud in the stone silence and dark.

"Please." Cassia's voice shook. "Are you a healer?"

"No. But I can take you to one."

"It's for my friend. Can you help him? He's lost so much blood!" Inside her was a cold lump of fear.

"What are you willing to pay?"

"I have nothing," she whispered.

"Robes," breathed Jarell.

"I have two robes sewn with rainbow stones." She groped for their scarlet Robes of Sacrifice. "And I can work!"

The passionless voice said, "Come."

With an oiled rumble the wall in front of Cassia slid aside. In the rectangular opening that replaced the dark, a pastel rainbow glowed.

"Oh!" Still holding her burden, Cassia got to her feet and walked toward the brightness.

She stood on a ledge gazing down into a vast cavern striped and lined with light—pink, yellow, soft green, lavender, blue. The colors pulsed, tier upon tier, in a chasm so broad their radiance obscured the other side, and so deep all she could discern was the shape of cliffs, hazed with thin shadows. And from everywhere came the gentle sound of the glow bugs' munching; the air was permeated by the mossy fragrance of their lichen feast.

Two tall black shapes edged toward Cassia, their wings opening and closing as they balanced on the narrow shelf. One held out his arms for Jarell.

Reluctant to part with him, her hunger rising in her now she had rested, she looked with suspicion at his black claws, and at the white teeth she glimpsed in the other's dark furred face.

His black eyes seemed to soften; she felt a tranquility of spirit and caught a wisp of song. She gave up her burden.

The tall being cradled Jarell in his arms, leaned out over space, spread his scalloped wings, and swooped down the air currents. He dwindled to a speck and vanished in the throbbing light.

On Cassia's other side, another body plummeted into the void, then spread its wings—above its shoulder she glimpsed red curls, closed eyes, and grimy fists clutching a scarlet robe. Tadge was cuddled between the creature's wing and pelted chest; he was still asleep.

"Will you fly?" the Misbegotten next to Cassia asked.

"I can't! I've never— Oh!" She gasped as he nudged her over the edge. She fell and fell into limitless light, with him beside her. She opened and shut her mouth in a vain attempt to breathe.

"Straighten," he said calmly as he dropped beside her. "Arch your back and open your wings."

Desperate, she flexed her shoulder. The neck of her robe widened; her wings snapped out and spread—and caught the drafts. She was soaring! Air and light were cushions and floor for her. She lay on them, she tumbled, she dived and rolled. Wind shushed past her ears, her hair lifted, she twisted into it, copper and gold swept past her face, it streamed behind her. The fine cloth of her gown rippled over her body. Its hem, heavy with flowers and blood, flapped around her sandals. The twittering and singing rose about her, vibrated in her.

Her guide indicated a ledge halfway down the precipice. She landed with a jar, her wings flopping around her. Overbalanced, she sat down hard. "Oh, that was lovely!"

Her companion braked expertly. He landed on his toes beside her, folded his wings into tidy peaks, grabbed the skin beneath his jaw, and pulled. His black, almost noseless face wrinkled; it stretched over his head. His dark visage dangled from his claw, a baggy, flexible mask.

"Welcome to Membliar, home of the Beloved who were the First Men, Companions to the Colonist Gods, and who now are Keepers of the Old Knowledge." The unmasked Misbegotten stripped off his clawed gloves. His hands were elongated and almost human, as was his pleasant face. It was very pale and dominated by his round black eyes. He smiled, exposing a mouthful of pointed teeth. "Forgive the deception. We do not wish the sun-dwelling ephemera to know that some of us may walk among them undetected."

Cassia tried to furl her wings as neatly as he had; their edges kept sliding out of place. Giving up on perfection, she left her wings in awkward bundles, and breathed in the cool dank air. She looked down into the radiance, then up to minute figures darting beneath the roof's crystals. "Is this really Membliar?"

Her guide nodded, balancing on his toes and refolding his wings. "This is the world beneath your world, forgotten by the short-lived ones of the surface, except in legends and fearful dreams. And now—your Choice."

He led her to a rocky chamber filled with light so bright it seemed to leap from the air. Against the cave's back wall, Tadge slumped against his flier, asleep, the other's wing across him.

In the room's center on a white bier lay Jarell. Anatta's arrow gleamed in his chest. The tall healer from the temple stood beside him, wings closed.

Cassia looked from the blood crusted on Jarell's mouth and chin, to the red network on his hand hanging above the cave floor. Coldness crept from the lump in her belly to her heart. "Can you save him?" she whispered.

"That is your Choice." The healer's voice was the deep insistent one from the Garden of the Beloved.

"Oh, then of course I Choose—"

"Wait." He lifted a slender black claw. "In the temple you were promised a cure. The Beloved honor their promises. We allowed the priestess to coerce us into deception, for when we followed your thread in the Tapestry of the Weavers of Destiny, that thread led here. Thus, we could do as both you and the priestess wished, and still keep open the passages to our city that she threatened to close."

"A cure!" *Hurry,* she thought. *Jarell's life is going.*

He nodded. "You may join the Beloved—we will assist you in completing your Change—wherein you gain virtual immortality. Or we will stop the growth of the Breeders of the Beloved now in your blood and lymph and cells, inoculate you against their return, and make you once more an ephemeral dweller of the surface. You will also lose your wings. Since the cost is less in the second case, we will give you this one's life, also." His black claw waved at Jarell.

"Choose well, Almost Beloved," he said when again Cassia tried to speak. "You, Almost Beloved, may have a flightless ephemeral's few short cycles under the killing rays of your sun, torn by the warring feelings and terrors of the surface dwellers who are doomed by their short terms to eternal childhood. As for him, for whom you also must Choose, his thread is almost done." The healer indicated Jarell. "Even cleansed of the Breeders of the Beloved and the arrow's poison, the Weavers allow him only a little time . . .

"Or you may become one of us. The Beloved of Membliar live long lives of study, meditation, and shared visions of great beauty. We keep the Old Knowledge alive, toward the day when we win all the Seed of the Gods back to our united beginnings. Our many strongholds encircle the globe. You may fly with us to them all. You have yearned for us; we have heard and answered you. Come to us—if you wish."

As he stood quietly, waiting for Cassia's answer, the Song of the Beloved seeped into her mind. It was stronger now, each note individual, but combining into a harmonious whole. She understood the joy of the vast melody underlying the simplest work, giving strength to the most difficult endeavor, sharing pleasures and thus intensifying them a thousandfold. To contribute as respected individuals, yet never to be alone; to learn unimpeded by illness, failing senses, or age.

Throat tight with regret, Cassia stared blindly into the chasm of light, its uneven circles teeming with lives she could now never know. For she had made her decision.

Behind her the healer rustled his wings and bent toward Jarell. "So be it, Almost Beloved. Your thread and his are woven elsewhere. Your Choice is made. Let the healing begin."

Once more Cassia flew, delighting in the power of her wings.

Leaving the healer to his most urgent patient, she watched the flier who held Tadge walk to the edge of the shelf, spread his wings, lie on the air a moment, then drop into the light. Even as her breath caught, the flier tilted his wings and floated upward. Cassia and her guide followed.

They tumbled past ledges glowing yellow, amber, green, blue . . . Cassia aimed her wings into the wind. They flattened and held. As she skimmed past shelves and outcroppings, she looked curiously at the Beloved hopping from boulder to boulder, their wings outspread for balance; flying, or sitting together at ease. Some hung upside down, combing their fur with thoughtful claws; others gazed at her, touched her with their minds, and brought her into their song.

She looked back, enchanted. The Beloved were not all black like the healer and the Keepers of the Entrance. Many were brown or amber, their fur lighter on their chests and bellies. Most had human faces—their eyes were large, their expressions tranquil. A few had white fur and faces as pink as those of the Snow People in the marketplace tales. Others were striped or mottled in red and yellow. They clung to walls or ceilings, twittering. Some slept, wrapped in their wings; others sucked globes of red fruit or took dainty bites from pale blue melons. A few passed a drinking jar studded with tubes, smelling of summer flowers. And everywhere was pastel light and the scent of moss and fruit and stone, woven with love into the song.

When they landed at last on a gritty ledge, tiredness washed over Cassia. Her mind was crowded with images—of the temple, of the passages and flight beneath the earth, and of Membliar—she saw only the pallet her guide indicated. She fell on it and slept.

* * *

When Cassia awoke, the air about her was warm and sweet,
the roof of the world quite near. She lay on her back staring up at
knobs on a ceiling jagged with crystals; the knobs seemed made
for climbing and exploring the niches and arches lit by scuttling
glow bugs. A pink radiance spread from the beetles, erasing the
shadows and the rock's harsh lines. In Cassia's head grew a
peaceful, healing song. Mind full of wonder and contentment, she
slept.

Someone lifted Cassia's head. A vial pressed against her lower
lip. Wet sweetness rolled into the corners of her mouth; she licked
it. It eased her throat. Grateful for the ministrations that turned
her and sponged her back that itched, and swept away the papery,
sticklike fragments she had lain on, she drank all that was offered
and lay back, ignoring the rustles and cheeping beside her, and
slept again.

When Cassia woke next, she felt alert enough to observe her
surroundings. She lay on a wide ledge. Large shadows blotched
its walls; the floor beneath her was smooth except for pebbles,
loose rocks, and an occasional boulder. She imagined Tadge
throwing them, skipping others, collecting a very few. She wondered where he was, if he was safe.

Pink light bathed all she saw. At the edge of her consciousness
a lullaby crooned. She squinted at the shadows on the walls—one
had seemed to flutter—and made out claws, wings, upside-down
faces, nictating membranes filming dreaming eyes.

The shadows were flyers! All were female, all had bellies
swollen with child. Cassia had once had a child . . .

Near her, several winged women leaned against the cliffside.
One bent to the floor and lifted a tray heaped with fruit. Passing
it, she glanced around, saw Cassia was awake, and came toward
her. The woman held her wings straight behind her as she set the
tray by Cassia's pallet, and squatted. "Will you eat, and tell us of
your life so it may become part of the song?" Her voice was light
as a summer breeze.

Cassia looked into the woman's fathomless eyes. Golden fur
billowed around her face and shoulders, shading to a rich brown
on the rest of her body. Her wings were brown, too, as were her
dainty claws that held out a greenglobe beaded with juice.

With the flier's help, Cassia sat up and took the fruit. Biting
into its tartness, she wiped her chin on her sleeve. Startled, she

looked down at her soft brown robe—new and clean, it was not the one she'd worn during her escape. And her hands! Jarell's blood did not crust them, they were clean.

Above her the woman smiled and made a chittering sound like laughter. "Do not look so surprised, Almost Beloved. You are safe here in our Place of Little Hopes. Of course we have cleaned and cared for you! Soon our babies will be born. As they learn to fly, you will strengthen, also. When they are independent and you are too, we will help you and your friends on your way."

"My friends?"

Again the chittering sound. "Look around."

Cassia rolled her head in time to see a sturdy child with red curls race through an archway to another chamber. "Tadge!" She looked more closely at the heap of blankets beside her. They were the color of winter leaves. At one end she glimpsed an angular cheek and a sweep of black hair. "Jarell." She swallowed and waited for the other strange hunger to rise in her. It did not. Elation tingled in her. The healer had done his work—she was cured! Then she saw how quietly Jarell lay.

"Is he—is he all right?"

"He is well, only very tired." The flier pressed Cassia's hand between her claws and warmed her with a wave of sympathy. "At intervals we feed him nectar and the healer's draughts, then let him sleep. Soon he may be well enough to sit up, even walk. Such movement speeds recovery, but we will be sorry when you both can do so, for then we must lose you. None but mothers, their children, and invalids may inhabit the Place of Little Hopes. Is it not so on the surface?" She tilted her head; her amber fur drifted across her cheek.

Cassia explained about families and work.

"Oh! The loneliness! You do not keep likes with like? No others share your joy in linking, then the travail of birth? Your babies are not even of the same age? Who can join in their up-bringing? I had heard the surface was cruel, but this!" With many rustles she retired to lean against the wall, filmy membranes covering her eyes as she gazed into a world invisible to Cassia.

"I'm sorry!" Cassia said, but privately she wondered what happened in a society where everyone did everything at the same time, if someone wished to stop and carve a green needle egg, or explore a new cavern, or go outside.

"Then he simply does it, oh Almost Beloved," an amused voice said by her head. Wings rustled; a flying woman whose dark fur was flecked with white stood by Cassia's pallet. "You find us unusual, I see. Yet most of our newly Beloved delight in us as we do in them. When one is too different to be happy here, we release that one to the outside world, though it is with grief that we let him go. For we know that his song will be shortened by the harsh light of the sun and by the star winds circling Naphar, his harmony forever lost to us. Such a one is your healer— my son."

"Your son!" Cassia's eyes rounded at the thought of the calm, dignified healer ever being a child like Tadge. Or did the Beloved have childhoods? Perhaps they simply stood in corners, wings folded, growing taller and taller...

The older flier burst out laughing. "Oh, Almost Beloved! Of course we are like you. All the peoples of Naphar are half brother and half sister, descended from the gods on one side and from the creatures of Naphar on the other. We, the Beloved, have taken care to remember when and how it was done—that is our only real difference from you who dwell on the surface. But come." Her tone changed. "I am Nest Mother here. The well-being of all who inhabit the Place of Little Hopes is in my care. My son wishes to assure himself of your comfort." Lifting Cassia, she held her against her furred body with her wing and helped her to the cliff's edge.

It was only when they were aloft that Cassia remembered that she too had once flown.

Cassia's weak tears of convalescence wrung more than the usual few words from the healer.

"You are not maimed, Almost Beloved. Your wings were only of the same stuff your nails are made of, and your hair. Our philters simply cut off the blood that fed them, and they withered and dropped away. And consider this, Almost Beloved: you and the one who travels with you need never again fear Night Demons. The tiny creatures that chased the Breeders of the Beloved from your cells and killed them, still swim in your blood. They will attack any of the Night Demons' poison and render it harmless."

Far from taking comfort from that fact, Cassia felt her face heat as she remembered in unwelcome detail how Jarell had become infected with the Night Demons' poison. How could she have behaved so in that green chamber! She had bitten him—attacked him! More images and words and touches came back to her; she wanted to burrow into the rock. She found she did not look forward to Jarell's waking.

* * *

Cassia blinked and yawned and stretched in her soft brown covers. The Place of Little Hopes had become familiar, home. This time, though, something was different. Through the twittering and the swelling cadences of the song, she heard speech, one voice high, the other a light tenor. She turned her head.

Tadge sat cross-legged by the brown package that was Jarell. "She's awake."

"Good. Move my covering, will you?" Jarell's voice was weak but his cut-crystal accents were unmistakable. "Tadge has been relating something of this extraordinary place." Jarell's angular face appeared as the boy turned back the blanket.

She could not look at Jarell. Cheeks hot, she spoke to Tadge. "Are they giving you enough to eat? Where do you sleep?"

"That's what I've been telling Jarell. I'm just around the corner from you. They're letting me stay with last cycle's crop of babies. Their wings are grown enough so they can glide a little and learn to fly. I wish I had wings! I sure have to run when we play tag. I've got to think of some kind of game I can win! And the food—have you noticed they don't eat meat, not even sausage? They all smell like fruit and grain! It's a good thing I like them—we sleep together in a heap at night, everybody's wings over everybody else." He stared past the ledge where a few small winged creatures wavered in short flights, escorted by larger fliers below and beside them. "I like it here, but it's awfully quiet."

"Don't you hear the singing?" Cassia asked. For her it threaded the days, along with the pastel light and the mossy scent of the air.

Tadge stared at his hands. "Oh, uh, sometimes. When I play that game Talley and I thought of." Prompted by Jarell he hurried to her side and put his arms around her neck. "I'm glad you're better. You were always asleep, everytime I came by!" When Cassia opened her mouth to ask more questions, he put his hand on his chest. A moment later he said, "Well, I got to go now. They're calling me!"

"I don't hear anything," Cassia said, but he was gone.

She lay still, scanning the ceiling, wondering if her face looked as red as it felt.

"Cassia." Jarell's voice was weak.

"Mm?" She tried to sound nonchalant.

"Are you regretting the night in your rooms' inner chamber before we were to be Sacrificed?"

She flung an arm over her eyes. "Yes," she said in a small voice.

"Don't."

She stole a glance at him. His face was pale; he looked all nose and sunken eyes. He was quiet so long, she wondered if he'd gone to sleep.

"I felt honored," he said at last. "And inadequate," he added with a faint smile.

She rolled over with her back to him and put both hands over her face. "Oh, don't! I've never, ever before—" Memories of a few nights with her mate came back to her. Honesty made her add, "Well, hardly ever."

At his breath of a chuckle she gasped and tried again. "It was wrong to force you! I knew how you felt about—kateeb, about all that. And in spite of what I knew, I— It wasn't just that I was brazen," she burst out. "I was going to kill you."

"Yes, well, I've known you might for some time. I've been quite willing to chance it. But those wings! Somehow I hadn't expected— As for your 'brazenness' . . ." During the pause that followed, Cassia thought he leafed through, then discarded a number of responses. His voice sounded a little strangled when at last he said, "I was deeply cognizant of the honor you implied, and furthermore—"

Rolling over, Cassia squinted through her fingers. The corners of his mouth twitched. He looked very much as if he was trying not to laugh.

He broke off. "Wrong answer?"

She nodded, hoping dumbly for his experience to come to her rescue.

"Let's see." He frowned in thought, looking quite unperturbed. "How about this? From time to time, we all make fools of ourselves. That night, it just happened to be your turn. I've noticed," he added as she squirmed, her face getting hotter, "that such episodes help to keep me mumble. And, as you may have noticed, I didn't need much persuading." He grinned; but his breath was coming in quick, shallow gasps, and his lashes fluttered closed.

Cassia watched, concerned. "That's fine, Jarell. But don't talk anymore. You need to rest."

He didn't open his eyes. "Just so we're friends again," he murmured, and went to sleep.

Chapter Thirty-Eight

For the Beloved there is a season—a season for joining, a season for flight, a season for thought, a season for renewal. These seasons are part of our cells and passions and minds. In early summer, the life-caches of the masculine Beloved fill, we find our mates and lie with them, rejoicing with our multitude of other selves in our completeness, our Tapestry, and our Song. In summer, as the feminine Beloved hold our seed within them, we fly to our many homes beyond the mountains and the tides: exploring, observing, learning, sharing with the other Beloved, our lost Beloved, and the ephemera what wisdom we may. In the fall we replenish our homes, we store our knowledge for those who must come after, when Naphar and all the goddess's children are at last united. In winter we retire to our Caverns of birth to study, to contemplate, to weave the skeins that bind our planet and those on it in their place, our feminine Beloved cherishing our quickening seed in their wombs. And in the spring, all at once, in pain and delight, our children come.

FATHERS' TEACHING CHANT FOR THE YOUNG BELOVED.

Twitterings and shrill chatter dragged Cassia from her sleep. Suppressed excitement quickened the song; tremolos of fear wove above long soothing notes that failed to quiet the frightened questions. The babies were coming! It could be nothing else.

Grief dropped over Cassia like night. With the vividness of a demon dream she remembered the smooth, unliving stiffness of her own babe's limbs, so cold, so cold, never to be warmed by sun, by love. Through her stormed rage at the Death Gods.

The song's anxious shrilling intensified.

Cassia looked around her. No longer did the mothers-to-be hang or lean in meditation. Instead, they lay in the air from spread wings hooked to wall and ceiling. The living hammocks writhed and hunched, sobbing and grunting in their travail.

Cassia suffered with them, her memory alive with her own grinding pain and its outcome: endless, changeless dark.

The song rose to a wail.

From the far side of the heated nursery shelf, a black silhouette hurried toward her, pausing only to lay a hand here, or administer a draft there. Beside her the Nest Mother said, "We had not realized the extent of your sorrow, oh Almost Beloved, or its freshness. Such constant awareness of death is foreign to us here. Your fellow traveler bears much in his mind, too, of endings and sadness; these things we acknowledge, but not now, not here, not in your way. My son offers you shelter until the Birthing of the Beloved is complete."

At Cassia's side, a tall shape enveloped Jarell. The healer's mother lifted Cassia, her wing caressed her; the song lapped over Cassia's loneliness. They plummeted down into the light.

Cassia stood alone in a cave. A faint radiance from its opening lit a pallet. She sank onto it, hiding her wet face in the pallet's scent of summer grasses. Lulled by a bittersweet thread in the Births' joyful theme, she drifted into sleep.

When Cassia opened her eyes she was back in the Place of Little Hopes. Everywhere were babies: some piled on the nursery floor, squeaking; others clung to the walls, fluttering their stubby wings; but most gripped their mothers with their strong legs, buried their faces in fur, and suckled, adding their tentative notes to the song of rejoicing sweeping upward from every corner of the cavern.

"Look, Cassia, their eyes are blue!" Tadge sat between Cassia's pallet and Jarell's.

The babies looked around with unfocused stares, bleating and chirping. They gave sudden toothless grins, flapped their wings, and waved their arms when their mothers held them close or crooned to them or set honeyed sucking cloths to their lips.

The unguarded trust between mother and child flooded Cassia, cracking her barrier of grief and suspicion.

The healer's mother stopped by Cassia's pallet. "Will you help with the babes, Almost Beloved?"

Cassia waited for her old knot to form of guilt and jealousy. Instead she found aching peace. She blinked away tears. "Yes," she said.

The mothers shyly presented their babes. And as Cassia touched smooth little cheeks and fuzzy heads, tenderness overwhelmed her for these children who were not hers.

The Nest Mother stopped by once more. "Perhaps, Almost Beloved, you have found our joy in the interweaving of life, all life, not just an owned one or two, and the Place of Little Hopes has become its other self, the Domicile of Realized Desires.

"If that is so, my son has plans for you, and gifts. We will be sorry to see you leave us, but soon your healing will be complete and we must present them."

Cassia had almost forgotten the outside world of sun, and palaces, and temples. Of course she must return to it.

And for the first time since she had fled down the tunnels beneath Kaladussa, she thought of all she had left so precipitately. She wondered what might have been happening there while she slept and woke and healed in this timeless world beneath her own.

Chapter Thirty-Nine

Oprekka Enna, temporarily retired as head priestess of Kaladussa, sat in her private apartments, fuming. It was too much that this meeting should be forced upon her by Anatta—a rude, undisciplined girl if ever there was one—and Ibby, who until now had been if not precisely a satisfactory son, at least a biddable one! Just because Oprekka had suffered a few reverses . . .

She winced at the memory of the giggles drowning out her naming ceremonies and her daily Welcoming of the Dawn. As she breathed harshly through her nose, remembering the valley-wide chuckles those giggles represented, her solid shoulders almost drooped. Kateeb, it was hard enough to lose Salimar and his coin, but to be laughed at too! Surely that awkward reaction of the peasants—yes, and of underbred nobles and merchants, she was sorry to say—must end soon.

"Put the cakes over there, stupid girl!" Oprekka sniffed at the appearance of her newest apprentice priestess. At least the child didn't waste temple provisions—she looked half-starved. Her long fair hair kept Oprekka from getting a good look at her; it swung across the girl's profile as she bent to set the tray on one of the many tables. She chose a pedestal of blue fire crystal within Oprekka's easy reach.

Oprekka had nibbled her second sweet—the tiniest morsel,

really, just to keep up her strength—when the door thumped as if pounded on with a sword hilt. Oprekka choked. *And it probably was*, she thought. *Whatever happened to old-fashioned courtesy? Young women simply are not as they used to be!*

After Oprekka finished her cough, her honeyed fruit, and her golden vase of yiann, she patted her lips, twitched her nose, and allowed the girl to open the painted and heavenstoned doors.

Anatta strode in, white tunic flaring. Fists on hips, she stared around her with the expression of resigned revulsion that so irritated Oprekka.

Ibby next came through the door, his newest gold fillet bouncing sunlight across the walls muraled and tapestried in pastel blue, turquoise, purple-blue, reddish blue . . .

"Took you long enough," Anatta said to Oprekka as the thin girl shut the door. At a sigh from Ibby, the girl left it unlatched. "Toping again, Oprekka? Careful it doesn't make you sleepy! Ha!" Anatta slapped her thigh.

"Dear Anatta, always so amusing." Oprekka waved toward a windslit nodding with deep blue tassel bells twined with lizard tongue vines. "Do please sit down. Over there should be comfortable, Anatta dear. And Ibby, darling, pray sit here by my side." She patted a shiny blue cushion among those piled around her, then signaled the new priestess to offer the sweets. "So pleasant to see you again, Anatta—and you are looking lovely today, so well after your illness; and so charming that you wanted only my Ibby by you at that time. Too kind of you, of course, while convalescing, to share my duties in the face of this unfortunate risibility on the part of the populace. I take it you have come at last for a tiny bit of motherly advice?"

"Dungballs to that, Oprekka. And Ibby sits by me. Ibby?" Anatta's glance up at her half brother was almost shy.

Ibby moved with new confidence, Oprekka was sorry to note, as he led Anatta to a heap of azure pillows midway between Oprekka and the windslit. "There. Safe from my mother here, Anatta." He gave his high-pitched laugh and snapped his fingers.

His lead man opened the door, the sunshine blazing on his fair hair and scarred, sturdy form. He carried a lizardskin traveling pouch half his size, and a scroll.

"Give the scroll to my mother, there." Ibby accepted yiann and spiced nuts from the child priestess. "And take a good look when you do—not many more chances!" He giggled again.

Oprekka's hands were suddenly cold as she broke the seal impressed with Sassurum's tree, star, and stone.

"Beloved Sister-in-the-Goddess . . . Outpost temples on Southern Continent . . . appeal for official presence, advice. Your unique talents . . ."

Scanning the antique picture writing of the request that amounted to an order, Oprekka let the parchment snap closed.

"You arranged this!" she accused Anatta. "You were always jealous! Screaming whenever your father left for my poor little house; with your two hands of slaves and tutors for company! Why, if I'd had a tittle of what you had when *I* was a babe!" Breathing hard, Oprekka forced herself to add in honeyed tones, "Though dear knows I tried to have your father include you, doting on children as I do, and you such a sweet child, dear Anatta."

In spite of Anatta's flared nostrils and narrowed gaze, Oprekka abandoned her cudgels. Her voice trailed off as the ramifications of her new assignment sank in. Why, in the South, even the stars were different. And how a woman of her age and stature could be expected to use breathing gourds in the mountain passes where the sky turned black and one's breath fell to the earth like snow. Worst, she had no acquaintance and no one owed her favors on that rich and partly subdued continent. She didn't know who had power, who only seemed to have it, who had coin . . . "I won't go!"

"I thought you'd fuss, Oprekka. That's why we gave this to you here instead of in public, before the altar. And you're right, I did work for your transfer." Anatta moved to the windslit and looked out at the streets radiating from the central temple, the head priestess's house, and the adjoining governor's palace. Anatta pulled a comb from her braid, which promptly fell to her shoulder, stuck the comb on the other side of her head, and glanced at Ibby. He nodded encouragingly.

"Here's our bargain, Oprekka," Anatta said. "Go south, and as soon as you've left I'll announce I'm partnering your son. Full consortship, equal titles, all privileges, everything."

"Oh! My dear, dear Anatta—dare I say, my daughter?—but of course I must stay for such a joyous occasion, and to help you and my darling Ibby, a mother's love and experience guiding you both through the flattery of courtiers, office-seekers—"

"No, Oprekka. Now only the laughing's a problem. But when that wilted soup leaf of a princess gets to Qaqqadum and tells how you tried to Sacrifice her and put Salimar in the goddess's place, calling your high priestess and the healers traitors, it could spark civil war. But so could my having you killed. And I won't have it! Civil War's bad for the people; besides, it upsets my troops' supply lines. So . . ." Anatta paced toward the window and again looked out. From below came the sound of voices. Ibby shot her a questioning look. She nodded, and continued.

"Oprekka, this is your second Thitamanit as head priestess. This winter, auditors from the mother temple won't be so easily fobbed off with stories of the sacred jewels gone for cleaning; altar candles of fish fat instead of whiteberry oil because of a mix-up, coin for this"—Anatta waved at the crowded room and Ibby's fillet—"coming from gifts and investments."

Outside, the voices grew louder. They were feminine and had a Western crispness foreign to Kaladussa.

"Dear Anatta, so full of fancies." Glaring at Ibby's head man and the child beside him, Oprekka clapped her hands. "Out! Or . . . stay."

Anatta gripped the sturdy man's shoulder. "You won't make them disappear, Oprekka; not because they heard me repeat gossip common in the fighting circles. Ibby needs this one"—she and the fair-haired man exchanged a guarded look of understanding —"and so do I. He brought us your scroll—and something more."

Beneath the windslit the clear voices conferred:

"Leave the accounts sheets."

"No, bring them. She may have an explanation."

"No warning. Tsk! Still, we agreed to obey the summons."

"Which ramp did they say ascends to her apartments?"

Oprekka's eyes opened wide. "The examiners! That comb was a signal. You've brought them here two seasons early!"

Hesitant footsteps started upward.

"That's right, Mother." Ibby's voice was unusually deep. He rose and stood beside Anatta. "We sent for them. I also told Huraya to pack you a journey pouch with robes and coin for a southern voyage. Behind your apartments a litter's waiting. It will take you to a ship in Qaqqadum's harbor, bound for the Southern Continent. Will you go, and quickly?"

"Or will you stay and take your oath of no wrongdoing—and be flayed by your temple if you've lied?" Anatta stared down at Oprekka. Her eyes were very black.

"I— Huraya! Send her to me. No, no time, she'll have to follow. Give me that pouch. I'll not forget you." Oprekka snatched the lizardskin bag; for a long instant she memorized her son's lead man. Stolidly the lead man returned her look.

"You're a fool, Oprekka, you could have stayed." Anatta moved toward the door, positioning Ibby and the others to block a view of the silk-curtained exit. "You had your own coin; honor; my father's gifts; but it wasn't enough. Did you think the people wouldn't notice how treasure stuck to your fingers? The bribes and payoffs may continue for a while, once you're gone. But someone will clean them up—I'll see to that. Maybe someone in your temple now. Who will it be, I wonder?"

Impudent chit! How dare she lecture me? As if she's ever been poor! She's never known the constant scheming, contriving, never being safe. Oprekka ground her teeth, blind to the level look the fair-haired child gave her from eyes the color of rain. As Oprekka hurried through the doorway, the girl bowed and closed the curtain, vanishing behind its blue shining folds as she did from her head priestess's memory.

On the ramp outside, Oprekka ran briskly on her little feet, pouch bumping her thigh. She reviewed what she knew of the Southern Continent: rich in silver and slaves; ripe, perhaps, for conversion to the goddess—so much nicer, really, than that nasty lizard-headed deity of theirs. No Homes of the Compassionate Goddess in that hemisphere! The old profitable order should last for a while, yet. And then, there was all that treasure. Which, if she found any, would be used for the greater glory of the goddess, of course.

Oprekka was feeling almost cheerful at the prospect of her abdication—after all, Kaladussa and the coast were small and cramped, compared to a whole continent. She dropped, puffing, into the waiting litter. And instructed the bearers hoisting it to their shoulders to hurry! She had a ship and a tide to catch!

Chapter Forty

The fortunes of those Cassia had known in Kaladussa were far from her mind as she lay in the Beloved's Place of Little Hopes, watching the growing babies. The high, warm nursery cave smelled of their clean newness, and of ripe fruit, and milk.

For the past sennights, day and night had blended as Cassia and Jarell slept, woke, exchanged meaningless pleasantries, and slept again. Tadge had visited with the half-grown Beloved, mysteriously appearing only when both Cassia and Jarell were awake. During this time the infants rolled, crawled, then tottered about, flapping their little bare wings for balance. As Tadge lost his fearful looks and tense walk, and contentment and well-being lightened the haunted shadows in Jarell's face, the babies' blue eyes turned black, gray, amber, or a rare deep blue.

Now Tadge and the half-grown Beloved sat piled, wing over wing, at one end of the nursery, talking and playing a game with stones. Around them, the babies suckled and napped, or tumbled on the stone floor of the Place of Little Hopes. A few mothers watched them; the rest of the women dozed, clinging to the walls with the talons on each segment of their wings, or hanging from the ceiling, their knees drawn up and neatly wrapped with their tails, their wings around them like great dry leaves, only their faces and black dreaming eyes giving them personality.

"Look, Cassia, a first flight." Jarell had returned from another session with the healer. He lay near Cassia on his belly, swaddled in brown coverlets. He looked toward a baby clambering onto a nearby projection. It poised, ready for a sail to the cave floor an armlength below.

Cassia's glance flicked to Jarell and clung. "Do you know how much younger you look?"

"It's the sleep, I expect. And the light's bad in here. Have you noticed how Tadge favors that very pretty little Beloved with the white fur and blue eyes?"

Together as they often were, Tadge and the little girl wrangled over who could heave a boulder farther. Tadge won; the Beloved carried most of their strength in their leg and wing muscles, not their arms. The children went back to their game. *Nothing to worry about there,* Cassia thought, not accepting Jarell's change of subject. "I think the healer's making the difference. At least, after a visit with him, *I* feel better. Because you look, I don't know—hopeful. And before, you didn't."

"Perhaps I have something to hope for. Cassia." Jarell reached across to her pallet; he carried her hand to his fever-roughened lips. "Have I thanked you for my life?"

Breathless, she pulled free. She stared at the floor. It lay in levels like water blown by the wind. She traced a ridge with her finger, still warm from his touch. "I didn't do anything. The healer saved you. I thought you were dead. Because of what I did."

He shrugged. "It's easy to risk something of small value."

She looked at him steadily. "Your life isn't of small value to me."

His smile reached his eyes; their wary look was gone. "I'm glad."

Delight warmed her to her toes. She wriggled them inside her blankets and smiled back, aware that her heart was in her eyes, and not even caring.

He rolled over and clasped his hands under his head. "Ask me something. Anything."

He wanted her to know him. Cassia hesitated, searching her mind for a question that would not destroy this new bridge. She thought of Huraya. "Do you remember, when you called for water from the Apsu, Huraya called you 'Adon'? Why did she give you a title? Are you nobly born?"

He shrugged. "The women in Ynianna's bower houses call everyone 'Adon.' Or perhaps she visited the court in Qaqqadum and heard it there. I doubt I'd remember her—with all their paint, the servants of Ynianna are nearly interchangeable and hence invisible."

"It's true? You are a lord?"

"Don't look so impressed. I told you long ago all that matters of my life. The title's a Kakano one from my mother—a bauble; meaningless. Anyway, I lost it the moment I became slave."

But Cassia scented a story, one from happier days. "Can you —will you tell me about it?"

Jarell looked up at the drowsing mothers and babies swinging as if blown by individual breezes. At the end of the cave the young Beloved leaned against each other, wing over wing, in meditative naps. Tadge and the white-furred child were still talking. "I can and I will. I expect you'd like my parents' story, the first part, at least." Without further prompting, he began:

"My mother was a Sea King's daughter. Though he had other children by his several wives, she was his favorite. He ruled the islands in the Western Sea just off the coast by Qaqqadum."

As Jarell had told Cassia before, his father was a fisherman from a village in one of the fjords that split the coast north of the capital. One day a storm came up; Jarell's father was shipwrecked. Like most sailors from Northern Naphar's coast, he had shown his pride in his seamanship by not learning to swim. But now, instead of drowning, he was lucky.

"Clinging to a ship's timbers, he washed onto the beach below my grandfather's palace. My mother and her handmaidens found him."

She visited him in his convalescence; he spun it out long enough for love to flower. In spite of her father's objections, she agreed to partner Jarell's father, "probably the most decisive thing she ever did." Jarell paused.

"And so, they lived in joy forever," Cassia said softly.

Jarell raised an eyebrow. "You have a great deal to learn about families, my dear." He watched a mother comb through her baby's haze of fur. An infant cooed and kicked beside her as another flying woman rubbed oil into its tender new wings. "My mother's defiance infuriated my grandfather and he cast her off. My father became the sole supplier of seven hungry mouths. He was often gone, following the catch. He and my mother fought. My grandfather relented in only one small way—he picked me for his heir."

Jarell spoke of the seasons he spent in his grandfather's islands, until Cassia saw wide white beaches rising to volcanic mountains topped with mist and perpetual clouds, and Jarell climbing through rainbows to scoop up ice for fruit drinks sipped later in the heat by the shore. He made vivid the garlands of scarlet obsession flowers and tiny white maidens' hopes worn for feasts; the fishing shared with his half brothers and sisters, climbing with them, their splashing him while he smilingly remained on shore, their talking in the sleeping rooms far into the night. "When I think of it now, I think of the sound of water. Surf outside the palace. Inside, a stream."

"A stream? Indoors?" Cassia glanced at Tadge. Hand on chest, he looked into the eyes of the white-furred girl. Other young Beloved joined their silent communion. Their stillness seemed unchildlike; the song coming from their direction grew muffled. Cassia shifted uneasily.

As Jarell described the floors of packed earth, the grass screens angled to catch the breeze, Cassia forgot the children. Through the series of long rooms ran a stream, Jarell said, widened into bathing pools, fish ponds, drinking basins, and ornamental pools. "Probably highly unsanitary. But I don't recall anyone ever being ill . . . or fighting, or being cold." Jarell's grin was wry. "I have a selective memory, you see."

"You were happy! That's how everyone remembers happiness." She caught her breath. "Jarell, that's the answer! You can go to your grandfather, you needn't leave Naphar."

He shook his head. When his father was lost at sea, Jarell's grandfather had offered to help only him, not the rest of his family. "So, being young, romantic, and a fool, I repudiated him. I stayed with my mother. Much good it did me. I was sold to the temple—the rest you know."

At the far end of the nursery, Tadge leaned against the wall, seemingly asleep, his friend's white-furred head on his shoulder. Cassia paid them no attention. "But—"

"No, Cassia. My grandfather's dead, the kingdom's gone. One of my first patrons thought himself in love with me. I . . . well, I knew less, then. In confidence, I told him of my grandfather. A confidence he did not keep. Jealous, his pallet companion imagined a slight—or perhaps it was real, I no longer recall. He revenged himself through me: he sent slavers to my grandfather's islands."

Cassia felt cold. Around her the song muted further.

"At first my master could not do enough for me," Jarell said as if, now he had started, he could not stop. "He ordered delicacies, costly gifts, all but the thing I desired so strongly I chewed it with my bread and slept with it by my pillow: my freedom. Then the reports started coming in. All had died—king, wives, concubines, children. By their own hands, rather than be dishonored and slave. Like me. The whispers began. My master grew questioning. Next—reluctantly—patronizing. In the end he sold me. Oh, for a profit. The story had been widely circulated and there was much competition for my favors."

"Such is love among the Rabu," Jarell whispered.

Cassia sat up. From the corner of her eye she glimpsed Tadge's extreme stillness. "Oh, but not all, Jarell! Surely not all. I would never do that."

He looked at her then and gave her a smile of great sweetness. "Ah, but you have been slave, too." He swept his lashes down, he sighed, and she thought he slept.

Cassia looked from his quiet face to Tadge's in the gray and pink shadows. The boy stared at nothing with half-open eyes. The little girl with white fur lay as still as he, her head on his shoulder. Or—not her head—her face lay on his shoulder, her mouth against his neck. As Cassia watched, the child fluttered her pink wings frosted with white, and licked a tiny rip in Tadge's throat. Her tongue was long and very red. A narrow line of blood trickled from the corner of her mouth. Tadge's blood.

"No." Cassia flung back her covers. "Tadge!" She staggered

toward her nursling and his friend, the Beloved children around
them hopping away. Only the girl and Cassia's nursling remained,
leaning against the cave wall. Tadge's eyes looked gray; blue
veins traced his eyelids and temples.

Cassia grabbed the girl, her hands sinking into white fur.

The girl's wings flapped, beating at Cassia's face as she
pulled. The child wrapped her strong legs around the boy, bleating and whimpering, her busy tongue lapping at the blood flowing
from his throat.

"Stop. You'll kill him!" Chills raced down Cassia's arms and
spine to lie like ice in her belly. Tadge was so very still. How
many other times had this happened while she slept, talked, or
otherwise neglected her nursling? She jerked again at the child.
The song became urgent and anguished, its discordant harmonies
cascading through the cavern.

Tall wings thrashed around Cassia—two, four, more. The
healer's mother set Cassia aside, spread her wings over the two
children. Behind the healer's mother, the healer himself stood tall
and separate. Mothers and babies woke, twittering from the ceiling and walls of the nursery.

A small woman fluttered onto the ledge. Her wings were
white, tears drowned her blue eyes.

The Beloved girl, separated now from Tadge, took his hands.
Leaning toward him, she pressed a blood-smeared kiss on his
forehead.

Tadge's palm was still flattened against his chest. He blinked
upward. "The giving was pleasure," he said with quaint formality.
"I'll see you again, later."

Shivering, Cassia gripped her own hands and wrung them,
wanting to push the white-winged child from her, snatch her
nursling, and take him far from these dangerous, alien beings,
where even the children . . . She shuddered.

The blue-eyed mother wept as if there were neither good nor
hope left in her world. Still weeping, she furled her white wings
and led her Misbegotten child away.

Cassia rubbed and rubbed Tadge's cold, heavy limbs. He
would not wake. Near her, Jarell too slept on. She heard a step, a
whisper of wings. Hunching her shoulders, she looked around.

The Beloved white-furred mother stood at her side, her white
lashes spiky with tears. Her voice was soft. "Please, Almost Beloved, my daughter did not understand. She is very young for this

Change. No one warned her of the harm she could do. We, the Beloved and I, are so very sorry." She gulped a sob.

Cassia did not answer. She could think only of Tadge. Tadge —her reason for life when her babe and her mate were dead and she too wished to die. Silent, unforgiving, she clutched Tadge closer, ignoring the voice in her mind whispering, *You would have done the same thing to Jarell. And you knew what you did.*

The little mother stood; her wings opened, furled; she drew a jerky breath. "She was my firstborn, and so good, so gentle. It will never happen again." When Cassia still did not respond, the woman paused a moment more, then crossed the Place of Little Hopes to the shelf where her daughter waited. She covered her daughter gently with her wings, led her to the edge, leaned out, and dropped, followed by the healer's mother, their scalloped silhouettes dark against the soft light.

Cassia pulled Tadge onto her lap. He still slept. She looked down at his copper lashes curling over the shadows beneath his eyes. *Live!* she thought. *Whatever I did to Jarell, you must live!* The song's discord thinned, dissonant notes winking out. The harmony began again but with an underlying tone of pain and loss.

Cassia became aware of the healer's mother crouched beside her, wings slowly moving the warm, milky air.

"The child who harmed yours is gone," the older woman said.

Cassia relaxed her grip on Tadge but she would not relinquish him though the Nest Mother indicated that she should. In Cassia's mind, thoughts like gentle fingers probed hers. Cassia grew stubborn. She would not let them in.

The Nest Mother was very still. Then, in a low voice, she spoke of the Beloved: "All species have their unfortunate inheritances. This is ours, a legacy of the first Beloved, before the colonist gods mixed their seed with the native fliers of this planet. The first Beloved lived on blood."

Cassia shuddered.

"The gods tried to remove this need; largely, they succeeded. But sometimes one is born who is called to the Old Ways. Then that one must live apart from us on the surface, stealing blood, finding companionship among creatures who die so quickly that over the cycles the exiled Beloved are like adults among greedy, passionate, frightened children."

Cassia felt a little pity seep through her fear. She further loosened her grip on Tadge.

"Do not look so distressed." The healer's mother smiled, her teeth sharp and white in the black fur of her face. "It has happened before, as have all tragedies, even yours, Almost Beloved. It will again. It is destiny, woven in the living tapestry among the stars. Each of us must follow our threads to the end. If you will release your nursling, we will see to him." The Nest Mother beckoned to the healer who had returned and waited in the shadows. "Would that we could see to that other child," she said as the healer came forward. "She has her own destiny, now. She may even be content in her way. But it will not be the way of the Beloved."

Helplessly, Cassia nodded and let go of Tadge; she stroked back his curls from his cold, moist forehead.

"It is time to move the last of our guests," the healer's mother said when her son stood beside her.

Cassia looked around. When had Jarell been taken? Even his blankets were gone.

"He awaits you." Lifting Tadge from Cassia's lap, the Nest Mother walked to the cliff edge, spread her wings, and drifted down, out of sight, leaving only a rustle and a rush of wind to mark her passage.

In his turn the healer took Cassia in his arms and looked down at her, his wings enfolding her in their stretched warmth. Silver rimmed his wide black eyes. "We will do our best to untangle your thread of destiny. Its snarling is due to my error; it is mine to return you to your place in the design. I misread your preference long ago by the Garden of the Beloved, perhaps because I wished to." His fur warmed Cassia; through it she felt the rumble of his voice and the bunch and stretch of his flying muscles as he unfurled his wings.

He clashed them wide—fell with Cassia and drifted and fell again through canyons of blue and gold, startling the beetles so they scuttled from their patches of lichen to dart, single spots of brightness, above the caves.

As wind combed through her hair and set it rippling behind them and flowing over the healer's powerful wings, Cassia stared from him to the ledges below, so many they were lost in a blur of light. It occurred to her that the healer, like the white-furred child, was a Drinker of Blood. *Where does he get his nightly supply?* she wondered suddenly. On the heels of that thought came another: *Where is he taking me, and why?*

Chapter Forty-One

This overpowering urge to life has led to amazing adaptations, as we have seen, in the world of animals. In the world of plants, we have the Chaian breadroot whose fleshy underground flower is pollinated by tunneling insects who regurgitate its nectar to feed their infant queens; Sol III's orchids and Naphar's cavern flowers—parasites that, with the aid of a mycorrhizal fungus, connect their roots to those of other plants from which they then draw nourishment.

Another phenomenon is the malleable gems said to grow beside these flowers. Living jewels are not unknown in the galaxy, but these are parasitic, move, and form an addictive tie with their host. If they exist, they may resemble viruses, being alive only when in contact with that host. Natives describe a dormant "seed" that seems to be attracted by body heat and pheromones. It is thought to secrete enzymes into the skin through hairlike projections; the enzymes then travel through the host's blood and lymph, stimulating its cortex to produce endorphins. Because of the host's resulting pleasure, the host lets the gem take the minute amount of proteins it needs to live.

> THE PREVALENCE OF LIFE IN OUR GALAXY:
> RELIGIO-SCIENCE HOLOS FOR YOUNG BEINGS.
> NEW LIFE-WORSHIP INSTITUTE.

The healer had Cassia wrapped in the innermost section of his wing as they plummeted through blue, then yellow radiance to a conflagration of orange. They banked toward the darkness of a cave mouth; the healer touched down on a shelf outside the opening. He nudged Cassia toward the entrance.

She smelled water, and when she passed through the jagged rock of the archway, she could hear it rushing. As her eyes adjusted to the shadows she saw at the room's end a silver cataract. It was flecked with the glow beetles' orange light, and cascaded into a wide pool. More glow beetles fluttered among the ruffled blossoms bordering the pool, and in the veil of scarlet creepers hanging from the ceiling. The vines' humid, sweet scent mixed with the dank one of wet stone.

"Flowers!" Cassia exclaimed, unaware until this moment of how much she had missed them.

Beside her, the healer adjusted his dark face into what Cassia had come to think of as a smile. "We want you to be tranquil here among so much that is strange to you. That is why we chose this place where the cave wall is thin and these blooms can reach through it for nourishment from the roots of trees stretching toward our water. This is your new home, Almost Beloved." The healer folded his wings and watched Cassia run to a small figure asleep on a pallet at the side of the room.

"Tadge," she whispered. She crouched beside him, afraid to disturb him, afraid that she could not. She touched his hand; it was warm. Behind her, wings rustled.

"If you will allow me?" the healer asked.

She made room for him. Extending a black claw, he peeled back the child's eyelid, studied it, then lifted Tadge's hand and examined his nails.

A splash from the pool made Cassia turn around.

In its center a man surfaced; water sheeted from his black hair and bare shoulders, bright with orange light. Jarell started out of the water, saw her, and stopped.

At the back of the cavern the shadows moved. The healer's mother opened her wings, folded them, bent, and gave Jarell a drying cloth and his robe.

"Why this change in living arrangements, Cassia?" Jarell asked when he reached her, still rubbing his hair with the cloth. "Has something happened to the boy?"

Cassia was well into her explanation when the healer bent over the child and set his mouth against Tadge's neck. Cassia started forward. With surprising strength, Jarell held her back. "Wait. He has never done us anything but good."

For what seemed to Cassia an agonizingly long time the tall creature rested his mouth beneath the boy's jaw. Then he reached under his wing and extracted a brass box that he set next to the child. The healer smeared something from it beside his mouth, and stood. Turning to Cassia he drew from his sleeve a crystal vial of purple fluid. "Give him this when he wakes. Already he has swallowed one such draft. It will help his blood to thicken when it meets the air; it will speed the closure of his wound and his recovery. I was sorry to frighten—or disgust—you just now," the healer added with difficulty. "I have given him the creatures that kill the Breeders of the Beloved swimming in his body. I treated the two of you thus, long ago; it is my deep regret that I overlooked the child's protection until almost too late. When he wakens, I will finish the precautions for all of your safety."

The healer's measured, dignified words faded for Cassia; behind them she seemed to see the great windy spaces of perpetual night filled with loneliness and guilt. For an instant she felt the desperation of one who to live must drink his fellows' blood; who fitted nowhere, not with the Beloved whom he deeply envied, nor with the ephemera of the surface whom he pitied and despised; and whose code made him cure the species that he hunted.

Shaken, Cassia reached toward his darkness. *Help him,* she thought. *Peace.*

For an instant the healer closed his eyes. When he opened them, the alien loneliness that had filled her vanished, as if a door closed. Again the healer was only a healer, silent, and aloof.

"Cassia? What is this place? Where's my friend?" Tadge's peevish questions recalled her to the cave.

She knelt beside him and gave him the healer's vial. The boy sniffed it, scowled, gulped it, and demanded water. When she brought it in her cupped hands she explained that his friend had gone.

"But she needs me!"

Cassia stifled the sharp reply she would have made if she had not glimpsed the healer's anguish. "I promise your friend is with others who can help her as you did." Cassia shivered. "And that she is cared for by those who understand her and her needs."

"All right. I believe you." Tadge sighed. "I thought if I went to the coast I'd make lots of new friends. And, I have. But it seems like I'm always losing them. The potmender boys and Talley; my—my kotellue." He looked up at her, his eyes huge in his wan face. "I miss them, Cassia. It's like having a thorn in my heart."

"Oh, Tadge, I know. But the goddess says not even endings are forever. Do you still have the kotellue's eggs?"

"Sure I do!" He rummaged in his pocket. She smiled at its contents: smooth, colored stones; a porous rock whose white spindle connected two pinkish knobs . . . He pulled out the eggs. "Look, you can see through them." Together they exclaimed over the black veinings just visible inside.

The healer rustled behind them. "It is time for the giving of the Jewels of the Beloved, our pledge to you."

* * *

Jarell stared into the pool, thinking of what he had just seen in the cavern's inner chamber. Apprehensively, he glanced around for Cassia. What would she say? And how did *he* feel about it—was he ready to risk even more with her? Gods. How had the simple taking of a beast from the highlands to the lowlands become so complicated?

He located her across the chamber where she stood with the healer; she bent over Tadge, who showed her something. As the boy put it back in his robe the healer looked up and beckoned. "It is time for the giving of the Jewels of the Beloved," he said.

"But I thought they were legends!" Jarell exclaimed as he skirted the pool. *One could be sold in Qaqqadum for any price,* he started to add, but thought better of it. Ahead of him, the healer lifted a curtain of the leafless flowers and vanished into the fissure they had hidden. Jarell followed with the others, still turning over in his mind how much to tell Cassia.

They edged deeper into the crevice. The air cooled, the glow beetles' orange light dimmed and failed, the Beloved's communion muted to a cradlesong. Soon there was only silence and the trickle of water down the walls. Then, in blackness, they stopped.

"Put out your hand," the healer said. "Find the cave's side; warm it. Deep in the rock your Jewel awaits you. As your heat seeps into its stone womb, the germ of the Jewel will awaken, send out threads, and come to you. Born in the dark, harvested in the cold, it seeks human warmth and the sun."

Jarell didn't move. *Impossible,* he thought. *No photosynthesis down here—it's a joke!* But he remembered the healer's unfailing strength and knowledge that had brought Jarell safely across the death god's lands; he thought of the healer's patient silences in which Jarell let out his rage and despair. Would one like that play a pointless trick? Jarell shook his head and with Cassia and the boy he stumbled to the cavern's wall. Feeling foolish, he set his palm against it.

The dark was endless. In it, time seemed to slow and stop and die.

"I'm tired of waiting!" Tadge complained. "My hand's cold."

"Oh!" Cassia gave a gasp of pleasure. In the black, a point of light formed; it spun to a thread shifting with color.

"Prime, Cassia," Tadge said. "Goddess great, look at mine!"

But Jarell did not look; he swallowed an exclamation of his own. For ahead of him, infinitely distant—or, wait, it was close, as close as his hand—an amber star lit the dark, elongating to a thread tinged with scarlet. Faintly shining on the rock, the light became a network of red and tarnished gold. A tendril found Jarell's thumb, twined around it. As more skeins slipped from the stone to loop about his hand and wrist, he felt a glow of comfort; it strengthened to the sureness of homecoming.

Endorphins, he thought wildly. *Parasites.*

He tried to feel endangered; he could not. He almost laughed; he had to restrain an impulse to pet his Jewel as beside him, Cassia and Tadge were talking and exclaiming over theirs.

The last thread slid from the rock; on his hand the filaments drew together. They nestled in the hollow of his wrist; they fused into a glowing scarlet and amber lozenge.

As he gazed down in wonder, Tadge cried, "Look, Cassia! It likes me." In their hands, too, the nets of iridescence pooled into living gems.

"The Giving of the Jewels is complete," the healer said in the blind black silence that smelled of stone. It was lit only by the jewels' faint radiance. "No Misbegotten or their servants who see these will take life or nourishment from you. Guard the Jewels well. Separated from you they will die; you too will suffer as from the withdrawal of a powerful drug. They creep toward the pulse spots of your body, searching always for heat and light. But if they should not be seen, then touch them, stroke them, guide them into hiding. They wish to please you. Already you must feel their love for you."

Slowly, incredulously, Jarell nodded. Spreading through him was a feeling of coziness, of hearth fires and safety, a part of his childhood he had all but forgotten. Near him, Cassia's sigh echoed his own. He heard a rustle, a dry wing grazed him; the healer signaled that it was time to leave this miraculous place.

And Jarell remembered what lay ahead of them. He found he had made his decision. He grinned to himself. He was going to enjoy this—he hoped.

When they were back in the cave, the healer departed.

Cassia felt warmed, happy. She looked around for Jarell to share her pleasure, but he had gone; she smiled down at her nursling, who seemed charged with energy.

"The healer says I can't let anybody see the Jewel, Cassia, but I can show my friends the eggs. And I got an idea for a game! I'd like to find *something* I can win." Tadge put his hand on a bulge in his chest pocket and gazed through the cave door to the orange light. A staccato call mixed with the song.

Wings thrashing, several half-grown Beloved wobbled onto the ledge. Putting their arms around a grinning Tadge, they wavered upward to the nursery level.

"I didn't know he could do that," Cassia remarked.

Jarell strolled from the back of the cavern, a peculiar expression on his face. "Before the boy returns I think you should see the sleeping arrangements, in case you'd like to change them."

Cassia followed him past the waterfall. Scarlet flowers beaded with moisture brushed her hair. Pollen showered onto the cave floor, adding its dusty pungence to the sweetness of the flowers.

Behind the cascade an archway led to a smaller chamber, lit with the glow beetles' bright bronze light. At its back, pale blossoms curtained a bathing pool. In front of the pool stood an enormous wooden box containing a sack patterned in gold that smelled of dry, sweet grasses.

"What's that?" Cassia asked.

Jarell's eyes glinted but his expression remained solemn. "I think it's a pallet."

She counted back. The small sleeping space in the outer chamber—one. This one—two. "Is there another room?"

He choked down a laugh. "No. I looked." He sauntered to the low-sided box and sat down. His glance held hers as he lay back, his hands clasped behind his head. "Well? They've made a natural mistake. Shall we disabuse them? Or leave things as they are?"

Cassia's knees felt suddenly weak. She took a step toward him. He held out his hand. "Do you want to?" she asked. "I couldn't bear to force you again—" Her throat closed as she remembered her maneuvers on the shiny green pallet in the temple in Kaladussa. But her heartbeat quickened.

His eyes crinkled at the corners. He gave a small nod and continued to hold out his hand.

She took another step. "I thought . . . you didn't want to be touched."

Something stirred in his eyes and he sat up. "Come here, Cassia, right here, beside me."

Afraid to presume too much, she did so, back straight, knees together, a careful handsbreadth between them. He smiled up at her and she saw herself reflected, tiny, in his eyes. Behind them rippled the stream that fed the pool.

Smile fading, he took her hands. "My dear, it is not that I do not wish to be touched. It is that I wish it too much." His warm grip tightened. "From the time I have been only a little older than your nursling, I have associated with some Rabu; daily, nightly. Do you understand me, Cassia?"

She consulted her own experience, her shamed speculations about him and his patrons, then her memories of the potmenders' scrolls and their explicit drawings.

He raised an eyebrow. "I see you do. Then I escaped." He looked away. "At first it was a relief. For a day or so. Then it was like being deprived of a strong drug. Exquisitely painful. You thought demon dreams drove me from our raft's shelter at night. So they did. But more often the dreams were of you."

His tone was apologetic but his eyes were not. "I thought you should know: I shan't be satisfied with a chaste arm about the waist and a quiet good night."

He lay back, only the quick rise and fall of his chest betraying his agitation. "Oh, yes," he said as if it were an afterthought. "I also love you. I failed to tell you so in the temple and what with one thing and another I haven't gotten to it until now. I've loved you for a very long time, my dear."

Cassia could not move from surprise. *He loves me!* she thought. Joy flooded her. Then, *But he's promised me nothing! Where are my safeguards? I could not bear the pain again that I felt before.* She tried to speak—she could not.

A flush darkened his throat, crept up his jaw. Smoothing his robe, he sat up. "Yes, well, we'll just forget about all that, shall we?"

In Cassia's mind she seemed to hear a whisper: *There is no safety, not for anyone. Only this moment . . . and trust.* The words rang through her like bells, like the truth of all she had met on her journey to Membliar. Scrapping her old frightened cautions, she cried, "Oh, my beautiful," put her arms around Jarell, and pulled him down onto the pallet.

Above her his face had paled. He touched her hair, her throat; he loosened her robe. "Gods. Don't ever do that to me again, Cassia. I think I died and came back while you looked at me with that great, blank, silver stare." He followed his hands with his lips to her mouth, her neck, her breast.

"Hush," she said, "hush," and shut her eyes. Only sensation existed for her, and Jarell, his scent, his kisses, his urgent body. And as she turned and moved and sighed with him the song rejoiced with her, swinging and caroling with passionate abandon.

Moistly entangled with him, feeling she had known him in this way for time out of mind, she whispered the names of love she had yearned to say when she walked and sailed and slept by him, when she dreamed— "It was you!"

He paused, blinked, and looked up. "It was?"

"When I dreamed! On the island, and later, after the flood. Oh, by the goddess. With Tadge and the kotellue right there! I thought— I thought—"

"Ah, so I did not leave you entirely unmoved! I'm relieved. For several days I feared I had lost my skills and that our interlude had simply slipped your mind."

"You didn't!"

He laughed but his eyes were wet. He hugged her, his damp hair cool against her cheek. "Ah, gods, the luck to find you! And you—can you care at all for me? Or is this only more of your compassion mixed with a little desire?"

Cassia was dizzy with the tides of feeling he had roused in her; she felt raw, almost wounded by the completeness with which she found she loved him. She wondered if she was a fool to say so, but she resolutely gathered her courage to do it anyway. "No, I—"

Booming crashes outside stopped her, and screams, her nursling's screams! "Tadge!" She lunged from Jarell's arms, grabbed her robe, and ran through the archway to the outer chamber. The yells and thunder continued. The light darkened and changed. Through the cave's opening, she glimpsed a small body hurtling down through the inconstant light.

"*Goddess, don't let it be Tadge!*" Not bothering with her robe's inner ties, she whipped its throat laces closed, stopped on the ledge, and looked down on a child, a Beloved child, falling. Boulders crashed and bounded below it, startling entire glow beetle colonies into flight. Screams made her glance up.

On the nursery level at the top of the cavern, below the roof studded with crystals, two small fliers plunged from a shelf, arms out to catch their friend. They collided, reeled, and dropped, shrilling despair as they plummeted down and down, the light around them flickering, congealing, failing, its colors transmuting and darkening as hordes of glow beetles whirred across the cavern or scuttled into its rock to hide.

Flier after flier swooped from the ledges to catch the young Beloved; all missed in the incoherent light.

From far beneath came a tiny splat, then two more.

In the ringing silence, Cassia felt unsupported, as if gravity itself had gone. She heard only children's hard sobbing. The song had stopped.

Steps scraped behind her—Jarell. She had forgotten him, his question.

From deep in the cavern a questing, grieving wisp of melody began. She turned to him.

Jarell's smile wry as he halted in the archway to shrug into his robe. "I have my answer. What you are willing to give is much. Hush," he said when she babbled awkward reassurances and watched some of the light return to his face. "Someone comes."

My feelings matter to him! Mine—a beast's, Cassia thought with incredulous joy. More strains of music joined the first, chanting anguish, resignation, and regret. Above her, several fliers spread their broad black wings and floated toward her.

The healer and his mother settled on the shelf with another flier; they brought a pale, subdued Tadge inside. Jarell and Cassia followed. Whole once more, the song pealed from every corner of the cavern but with new, shadowed harmonies.

Tadge awaited her by the waterfall. The healer and his mother stood beside him. For once, the Nest Mother echoed her son's stillness. She no longer opened and closed her wings, caressing with them, touching them to the walls for balance, or using them to scoop up an errant fledgling.

An opaque feeling emanated from her and her son. Cassia shrank from what must be anger. Reluctantly she reached out.

The Nest Mother stepped forward and extended her black claw. In its hollow lay four scarlet stones; carved, pierced.

"Those are buckles!" Cassia exclaimed. "From our Sacrificial sandals."

"They are yours to trade for your life's needs." Jarell held out his hand. The healer's mother gave them to him. As she moved forward her abrasive emotion flooded Cassia. It was not anger; it was sorrow. "You must leave us, my child. We had hoped to keep you until your spirits could be mended as are your bodies. The outside world may undo all my son has accomplished." She indicated the healer.

"Enough, Mother." He raised his black claw and touched the boy standing beside him, head drooping. "The Beloved have agreed we cannot keep you with us, for this one has made more mischief than he ever intended."

Tadge choked and ran to Cassia. The tears on his cheeks shone with bronze and silver light. She knelt to catch him; he buried his face in her neck. "I was only throwing rocks, Cassia! We wanted to see who could pitch them the farthest and make the loudest noise. I wanted so bad to win, just once! And then the glow beetles flew, and the light changed, and my friends fell—" He gave a gulping sob. "Now I'll never see them again. And I didn't even get to say good-bye. It's all my fault!"

Cassia rubbed his heaving back and looked over his curls to the healer. "Can you help them? I'll pay! You can have all the gems. And I can work!"

"Cassia. That's our passage off-planet," Jarell said behind her. *Ours.* Excitement, then fear, curled through Cassia's distress.

The healer shook his head, dark against the light of the entrance. "Their loss is great to their mothers and to the Beloved, but fledglings do sometimes collide and fall. It is a familiar grief. No, the Beloved fear your presence because the song stopped. This has not occurred in our lifetimes, nor in our furthest ancestors' lifetimes."

"Song?" Jarell looked puzzled.

"Haven't you heard it?" Cassia asked. "The song that keeps their community together?"

Jarell shook his head.

The healer explained: "It is more than that, Almost Beloved. The song is our part in the life tapestry that connects us to the other Beloved on Naphar, to the ones beyond us in the past, and those who weave our future. It spreads to the stars and the dance of the spheres, a part of the pattern of existence. Now its fabric is torn and we must reweave it, so that past and future and existence itself do not unravel. We cannot chance even one distraction." His wings fluttered in uncharacteristic anxiety. "That is why, much as you have become part of us, we must set you on your way, and soon."

Cassia nodded. But to leave again, just as she had begun to belong. The healer added that Jarell should stay to complete his healing; he could rejoin Cassia and Tadge at their friend the Dajo's camp near Qaqqadum.

The Dajo! Why, Cassia had almost forgotten him.

Beside her, Jarell stiffened. "We go together or not at all. I can't risk losing them."

Cassia smiled into his eyes.

In a low voice, the healer assured him, "Revenge is foreign to the Beloved, as I have told you. Take care that it does not cost what you hold most dear. Remember, the temples of Membliar are open to you. You bear the mark of the Beloved and mine. If you show it they will send for me and I will come.

"As for you, Almost Beloved," he said to Cassia, "you must gain strength. You must eat meat."

Cassia looked down, knowing her mouth was set in a stubborn line. She regretted it, but not enough to change. She thought the healer gave the breath of a sigh. In her head the Dajo's words repeated: *Ah, to be young and adventurous again and never, never to heed advice!*

Cassia felt a pang of yearning for the wily old man, for humanity itself, and for its setting—the change of seasons, the cool windy evenings and brilliant dawns, even if the sun's light did shorten her life. She had loved these strange, tranquil creatures of the night and she was grateful to them, but their ways were not her ways; it was time to go, time to complete their journey. And this time they could travel in moneyed comfort, without fear of Salimar. Salimar, whose raging loneliness could now never be eased.

"Come, Almost Beloved," the healer said.

He put his arms around her. His strong wings swung past the ledges of the Beloved. Followed by others carrying Jarell and Tadge, they shot through a jagged hole set with stars. They skimmed a mountain meadow alive with the scents and breezes of the night.

Joy thrummed through Cassia. Behind her, to the east, the waning sister moons and their dark companion peered between icy peaks. The first quakes and rockfalls rumbled through the dark. Flying safely above them with the boy and man she loved best and who loved her, she would soon be in a human city, their goal. The resulting happiness would be theirs to share. The goddess was right. The Spring of the Twin Moons was indeed a time of new beginnings.

Here ends the first half of "Spring of the Twin Moons," the chronicles of Cassia and Jarell. Watch for the stunning conclusion in *Burning Tears of Sassurum*, coming in the future from Avon Books!

SHARON BAKER received her bachelor's degree in history and government from Mills College. Upon graduation, however, she found to her surprise that historians are not much clamored for by industry. She earned her master's degree in library science from the University of Washington and worked at various jobs—from aviation librarian to piano teacher to physician's assistant—before retiring to raise a family.

Ms. Baker currently lives in Seattle, where she writes fiction in order to have something interesting to think about while driving her children to four different schools. Between trips she researches, interviewing professionals in astrophysics and acrobatics, medicine and the military, as well as such less-admitted-to specialties as killing, drug dealing, and hustling.

At the moment, much of her time is taken up with writing *Burning Tears of Sassurum*, the sequel to *Journey to Membliar*, which will complete the adventures of Cassia and Jarell.